KISMET

Kismet

.

Published by New Generation Publishing in 2012

Copyright © Anisha 2012

First Edition

www.newgeneration-publishing.com

 **New Generation Publishing**

Anisha

<u>Chapter 1</u>

The prison was a massive building that was several storeys' high, had barred windows and was surrounded by barbed wire. The barbed wire was a constant reminder to Anisha that it not only isolated its inmates from the life of London, but also that in the middle of life and beauty was evil and ugliness that festered like cancer beneath the smooth skin of society.

The women's prison not only consisted of endless rules and regulations, but was also an emotional cauldron that exuded feelings of frustration and anger.

Anisha had believed that its system would constitute and establish justice created not only from and around the beliefs and respect for human rights, but also in finding a right 'balance' between justice and security. A place where only those rules would be implemented that would safeguard the standards required to preserve a prisoner's dignity.

However, she soon discovered that the prison was a fortress where justice was applied only as a kind of cosmetic designed to soothe public conscience. It mirrored externally and institutionally what most prisoners had experienced in their past, for it had the same sort of surface gloss and care that covered an underlying indifference.

Anisha was a pretty girl with a dimple that danced on her face every-time she smiled. Her eyes were large and almond shaped and her thickly fringed eyelashes hid the sadness and disappointment in them.

As she saw, through the bars of her cell window, the moon faintly sweeping its ghostly radiance over the prison walls, Anisha reflected that perhaps its' faint rays were trying to protect her by shadowing her secrets?

The moon disappeared behind a cloud and the iciness of the night numbed her heart and spirit, and, as she saw the great hollow vastness in the sky, felt lost in the vacuum of its darkness.

This artificial gloss and care of the prison system reminded Anisha of her sister, for although both the sisters looked alike, petite with dark hair, their temperament was very different.

Azaria's nature was dark, secretive and jealous, whilst Anisha's disposition was one of gentleness and innocence. Anisha felt that the most accomplished form of justice had been Azaria's, for she had appeared to be affectionate and loving whilst she twisted Anisha's virtues into sins and her accomplishments into failings.

After her marriage to Akram, when Anisha had turned to her for support, Azaria had ignored her with a carefully masked gratitude that somehow Fate had passed her by and selected someone else as its victim, even if it was her sister!

She had come to visit Anisha once in prison, but only to revel in the truth about what had really occurred on the fatal day of Akram's accident that had led to his death.

With the realisation of the extent of her betrayal, Anisha realised sadly that not only had the thought of a loving sister died, but that at the same time a little of her had died too. Consequently, the beauty of Azaria's sisterly concern became a warm memory – like that of the heat of a summer sun on a winter's day.

Her husband Akram had deceived Anisha also, for his charisma had only concealed his ruthlessness and selfishness.

Anisha often wondered if she had spoken to Akram about his past she might have been able to exorcise his private demon's, and that by keeping quite she had somehow magnified them?

However, although she was caged like an animal, she somehow felt free from the deep dark emotional chain that had bound her in the past.

As she wiped the tears from her face and pushed her hair from her forehead, Anisha looked desolately round her.

'And if it had not been for them, I would not be in this predicament! The only positive thing is that here there won't be anyone to betray me!' Anisha put her hands over her ears and gritted her teeth as an inmate screamed.

In the four months that she had been at the remand centre, Anisha had discovered that she was not only locked in her cells for most of the day, strip-searched, and humiliated, but had to adapt to the atmosphere of gloom and foreboding in the prison. This feeling of depression and despair was magnified when she could not inquire about her legal representations for fear of being labelled troublesome, the punishment for which was time in the punishment block and withdrawal of privileges, all of which would have a bearing on her release date.

As Anisha looked across at Carma, an emotion stirred within her that was one of kinship and one that people have towards each other in the face of cruelty and injustice.

She wanted to confide in her, psychologically and emotionally she wanted to throw up all that mess of hurt, anger, bitterness and betrayal that she had not been able to control in her life. She knew that this is what Carma would want too as both wanted to break free emotionally, dissect the conflict in them about the past whilst voicing their concerns and questions about the present and future. However, Anisha knew that Carma was not ready for that, so decided to first enlighten Carma about the system and women prisoners.

"Carma, no doubt there is evil in the prison, but did you know that only a small percentage of the inmates are imprisoned for serious offences? For any woman whose appearance or behaviour differs not only from the male view of womanhood, but also against the social norms is likely to be heavily penalised by the courts. To me it seems that their sentence far outweighs their crime anyway, for isn't it punishment enough when your child is dragged screaming from you? And as the prison service focuses its concern on minor offences, and away from much more serious forms of social harm, harm that result in corruption, there is a sense of injustice amongst the women!"

Carma sat quietly on the edge of the bunk bed, her chin on her hand and looked at Anisha with enigmatic and sad eyes. She was an attractive woman with brown hair and eyes, but although the expression on her face was mild, it hid great force of character.

Her body tensed as she listened first to Anisha then to the sounds of the prison, which she felt, had a music and rythem of its own. The noise of the clanging of bells, shuffling of feet, crash of trays at meal times, slamming of the steel doors, crackle of the prison officers' radio conversations, screaming and shouting of the inmates during the day, and at night their singing and wailing.

Suddenly she got up and began walking around the cell.

"Anisha, I have only been here for a short while, but I get the feeling that I am surrounded not only by loneliness but also by hate!"

"The reason for the hate, Carma, is because of the discipline of the prison. I have heard allegations of physical mistreatment and brutality of the prison officers and there is resentment amongst the women at what they feel is the unfairness of any internal disciplinary system. They are always under pressure for the failure to obey the prison officers' is first accompanied by warnings and threats, then they are put on report, even if it is for something trivial. It is this pettiness and brutality, together with their personal frustrations and physical discomfort that leads to hostility and bitterness. You'll get used to it, believe me."

"I don't think so. It is so…so…"Carma shuddered.

"I felt like that too but now I find that whilst Time is just a flowing stream that has swept my past and the future away, it holds me tightly in its present! It took some time to adapt to prison discipline, believe you me, but now I cling to it, for it makes the long days go faster whilst lending structure to my uneventful days. You know Carma, I still recall vividly the first day I came to prison, the day my past became a memory and prison life a harsh reality!" Anisha shivered.

<u>Chapter 2</u>

As the car drove through the prison gates, Anisha read the inscription at the front which read "All prisoners will be treated with humanity, will be given every opportunity to rehabilitate themselves, so that at release, they may be successfully integrated back into society."

As soon as they filed into the reception area, Anisha noticed the wooden benches and the rubbish on the stone floor. They were encountered by a stony-faced officer who first shouted out their name, then four digit numbers that had been allocated to each prisoner.

"Some of you are going to be here for a long time and there is only one way you are going to make it, and that is by forgetting that there is a world outside these prison walls! We have rules here and know how to maintain discipline!"

That was the only induction that Anisha received, and none of them were given any information as to their trial or rights. Later she was to learn that the prison officers purposely withheld information from the inmates so they could put them on report.

The women were processed through the reception area, and everybody was strip searched followed by a 'mugshot photo' after which they were counted, inspected and checked by a doctor, and then as if they were a herd of cattle, were steered back to the reception area by a prison officer.

The girl who Anisha was to later know as Sophie, cowered next to her, and in a low voice addressed the prison officer. "Excuse me, officer I am innocent, I want to speak to…"

The prison officer whirled around, her face red.

"Shut your f…..g mouth!" She roared. "You will speak when you are spoken to, understand? Every woman who comes here says she is innocent! Now, I want you to give me all your belongings!" She collected the money from a few inmates, put them in envelopes, and then turned to face them again. "Follow me, you are to take a bath, you dirty…!"

They were marched down a corridor to a large concrete room with open shower stalls.

"Deposit your clothes in the corner over there!" the prison officer shouted. "Then get into the showers, and wash every part of your body, including your hair!"

Anisha trembled when she heard the prison officer shouting, but realised that that was the staff's attitude was going to be – that as they considered the prisoners to be depraved an immoral, they, therefore, could not have anything reliable to say.

Later, as they were paraded down another corridor, Anisha saw faces peering at them from behind bars. Some women were shouting to each other from cell to cell, whilst others were screaming and banging on their cell doors in frustration. The expressions on their faces varied from hatred to indifference, and Anisha quailed in terror as she looked at them.

She felt like a pariah heading for her cage, a stranger in some nightmarish place, but a nightmare that became a harsh reality when she was shown her cell with a card in front with her number, age, religion and name. Anisha first looked at the cell then at the seat-less toilet in the far corner that exuded a vile stench, and gave a cry.

"I'm not going in there!" She turned around but was pushed back in the cell by the prison officer.

"Yes you are!" She roared as she locked the cell door.

Anisha stood transfixed, shocked by the sound of the cell door closing behind her and felt a dreadful finality as she put the plastic bag containing the few items allowed on the dirty stained mattress.

She looked around the cell and noticed that its walls had once been white but were now heavily stained with a shade of brown.

'Must be from he cups of tea that the inmates threw !' Anisha thought forlornly.

There were large areas in the wall that were scrawled with messages of pain and revenge, and on the far wall was a small dirty window. The toilet and sink looked as if they had not been cleaned, and there were two bunk beds and a little table with a cracked mirror.

In the corner of the cell she saw a grey, thin, hollow- eyed young girl staring at her.

" 'ello, me name is Lisa. Wat 'r' yu in for?" Lisa asked as she turned her face, but not before Anisha noticed the glassy and vacant look in her eyes.

Anisha did not reply but sat on the bunk bed and wiped the tear that was streaming down her cheek with the back of her hand. Throughout her life, she had been crippled psychologically – and she recognised, with a maturity beyond her years, that there were only a few women who were successful in moving beyond the limitation society imposed on them.

As evening fell and the sky changed from pink to violet, it came as a harsh, but pleasant reminder to Anisha, that whilst Fate only chose certain people as its victims, Nature gave all its beauty and colours cheaply and generously to all.

That first night in prison, Anisha had woken with a start, trembling with fear as she heard the eerie wailing of the prisoners. She sat up and looked around her in panic for her cell was in semi-darkness. At first she had no inkling where she was and thought she must be dead and in hell for the setting was in accordance with the destination of a lost soul.

However, as reality returned slowly and she took stock of her environment she sat like an iceberg, thinking that this is what the rest of her life was going to be – a bottomless pit of desperation.

The weather had changed and it started raining, and as the thunder boomed, the sky zigzagged with electrical bolts. Anisha heard the faraway chant of the prisoners that seemed to be made up of a multitude of voices echoing up and down the cellblock.

A burly prison officer came running down the corridor, screaming. She shook her fist and started shouting.

"Shut your mouths – you, you alley cats – or I'll give you something to cry about!"

Anisha spent the following day experiencing and imagining every kind of terror, but gradually as she adapted to prison life, she sensed that not only did imprisonment cause unhappiness to the families' of the inmates, it also impaired an inmates prospects of future employment whilst exposing them to the criminal mind.

However, she soon discovered that prison variety was not only the spice, but also the very bedrock of life. Prison vine, to her astonishment, was incredible, for the inmates knew everything first. The inmates who were allowed to clean the offices read the prison officers' mail, eavesdropped on phone calls and picked up discarded memos. They distributed the information to other inmates, for as human beings they needed the constant flow of thought, action, and emotion to keep their isolation within the ocean of reality.

As she was a affectionate girl by nature, she tried to make friends time would pass quicly and pleasantly, but found that to be impossible as there was rivalry amongst the inmates and there were groups and factions who bullied and persecuted the weak.

And to make matters worse, she did not like her roommate.

Lisa was not only an addict but also a drug dealer, and many times she heard an inmate request and plead for a fix. Lisa her self often suffered from 'clucking' a term used when in need of a fix, and Anisha was revolted to discover that although she sweated, she did not attempt a body wash and the body odour she emitted was awful.

She had been in prison for four months when Lisa was transferred, and just when Anisha looked forward to having the cell to herself, Ruth informed her that a girl by the name of Carma would be sharing her cell.

"I don't want to share my cell with anyone!" Anisha stamped her foot angrily.

"It was I who recommended she share with you, she too is indian and you too is in for the same offence. And it is easier to endure prison life when you are surrounded by someone you can relate to…why, whatever is the matter?"

"But I don't want to….Ruth, can't you help?" There was confusion reflected in Anisha's eyes.

"Anisha, don't worry, trust me, you two will get along fine"

After Ruth left, Anisha realised that what she said was precisely what she felt sometimes, for Anisha's feelings of loneliness and isolation always intensified when she saw other prisoners receive visitors and welcome new inmates to jail. For, even if they did not know them personally, they often came from the same background and sometimes even the same area.

However, Anisha had been alone for the last four months and allowed her thoughts to run so freely that she did not feel the need to convey them to another person, who she felt would only encroach on her much prized privacy.

<u>Chapter 3</u>

"…And that is the best thing that has happened to me in a long time!"

Anisha turned and smiled, then walked back from the window and sat on her bed with her head in her hands, yearning to be free of her memories, yet knowing that they would haunt her forever.

"You know, Carma, just the knowledge that I am going to stay here for the rest of my life is punishment enough, without the added pressures of having to cope with the wretchedness of prison conditions, the unnecessary discipline of its system and the hostility that exists between the inmates!"

"It must be our kismet, Anisha, that we are made to endure such…" Carma said, as she combed her hair.

"Yes, it must be that." Anisha whispered.

It seemed to her that her future was enveloped in a haze, their remoteness enhancing the sense of unreality for even though she had been told that her trial was due to begin in a few weeks, she had no information regarding her representations.

Racism was a major concern to her, for she noticed that many of the prison staff and lawyers were racist in their attitudes, the minority group thus suffering a double injustice, for even when they were represented; there was a chance that their defence would not be prepared accurately.

Representations were important for she had heard that in the advent of a trial for battered women, prosecution often turned that fact into a motive for premeditated murder.

There was a jangling of keys and Ruth, her prison officer, entered the cell.

"Hello Anisha, how are you?" Ruth smiled.

She liked Anisha, who she thought to be an unusual girl, a girl who was a mixture of innocence and deep feeling. But although Anisha was always smiling, sometimes Ruth noticed on her face repose and pathos that sorrow always leaves.

She hoped that Anisha would obtain the proper representations so that a minimum sentence would be administered by the courts– for in the short time Ruth had been in the prison service she had observed occasionally that power, not justice instituted the framework for the judicial system.

"Ruth, when is my lawyer coming to see me? My trial starts next week. ..." Although Anisha's smiled weakly, her brow was creased in perplexity. "Don't worry, Anisha, your case has now been put up to the governor for there was a delay because of changed legal aid rules. Is there no way that your relatives can get a private lawyer for your defence?"

"No" replied Anisha with a catch in her throat, and as she thought about Azaria's betrayal, her eyes clouded with tears. "No, Ruth, there is no-one."

"Oh…I thought…."But when she saw Anisha's face, bit her lips.

Ruth felt sorry for Anisha, who was so young yet looked so tortured and broken. As she took the bunch of keys from her skirt and started to open the cell door, she turned towards Carma.

"Carma, how have you settled in?" she asked kindly

"Very well, thank you, Ruth, Anisha has been kind enough to explain about the prison system so I am now familiar with it. Well nearly!" she added with a smile.

"I am glad you two are getting along, but if you have any problem, do not hesitate to let me know."

As Ruth opened the cell door, turned and locked it, she felt angry that fate could play such cruel tricks on Anisha and Carma, who appeared to her to be like two buds that were imprisoned by frost and fated not to blossom.

"That was very nice of her," Carma commented.

"Yes, we are lucky she is on our wing for some of the others….!"

"Tell me about it! I encountered them when I first came to the prison!" Carma exclaimed, her eyes flashing. "As soon as I entered the prison gates, I heard the thunder rolling and crashing overhead and lightning split the sky, crackling every few seconds, and it was then, Anisha, that I thought it might be the wrath of God?"

Chapter 4

Carma had once been a defiant and headstrong girl, but, like Anisha, tragic circumstances had suppressed her spontaneity.

She accepted that her blossoming dreams had faded and the knowledge had tamed the fire in her. But then happiness for her had always been elusive – like a hidden light on a few stars that were only identified by the light's reflection on them. However, even though Carma was dimly aware of their source, she had never succeeded in grasping it. Horror and remorse seized Carma again and again by what she had done.

She went through the prison reception in a daze, signing bits of paper and when she opened her mouth to ask a question, was deterred by the attitude of the officers.

Having finished filling in the forms at reception, Carma waited anxiously for she heard of the infamous strip search to which everyone, guilty and innocent alike, were subjected. As she contemplated her future, a prison officer came up to her.

"What are you waiting for?" she yelled. "Go behind the curtain and strip!"

Although that is what she had expected, Carma's body was suddenly shaken with sobs which increased into intense little cries. Her hands trembled and her heart thudded painfully as she moved slowly, as if a calculated and deliberate move would create havoc in her again.

However she controlled herself for she did not want to let the prison office bully her, but stood up proudly and looked at the prison officer with tear filled eyes at the thought of violation of her privacy.

"I don't want to be strip-searched!" Carma gave a little hiccup as she tried to draw a long breadth and looked at the prison officer haughtily.

"I did not ask you, madam! Do you want to me to put you on report?" The prison officer barked at her.

Carma trembled then silently obeyed, thinking that this was surely the most traumatic ordeal of the remand centre when every external inch of her body was inspected,.... even her feet were checked to see if anything was taped to the soles. However, to be fair, this system, she was to learn later, was despised and hated, even though rigorously carried out, by most prison officers.

"Now that the formalities of checking you in are over, you are to take a bath, wear this then wait outside." The prison officer ordered, handing her the prison garments. "I will then take you to your cell which you have to share with another girl. Now are you ready, madam?"

"Yes, I am." Carma answered in a small voice.

Carma still had blue patches below her swollen eyes and on her temple and her eyes looked like large pools that conveyed not only her distress but also her hopelessness. But despite her distress and vulnerability, there was an air of aloofness and arrogance about her as she followed the prison officer with her head held high and well poised on her shoulders.

"You will be sharing the cell with Anisha." The prison officer quickly opened the cell door, shoved her through it, and then quickly locked it, leaving Carma looking around the cramped cell. Finally she discerned the small figure of Anisha, who came forward shyly.

"Hi, my name is Anisha." Anisha smiled and a dimple danced briefly on her cheek.

As soon as Carma saw her smile, thought she come to like Anisha, for she seemed to be a girl with no artifice in her manner. Her frank and childlike nature, her warmth and affection soon penetrated her cool exterior.

Anisha too had been apprehensive about meeting Carma, but instantly liked and admired her proud and enigmatic person.

"Hi I am Carma, and I am so relieved Anisha, that I am sharing the cell with you and not some…." Carms shuddered.

"So am I, Carma but if only….!" Anisha put her head in her hands looking bewildered. She took several deep breadths, feeling tightness in her throat.

"Anisha, whatever is the matter"? Carma asked with genuine concern.

"It's my trial", replied Anisha "it was supposed to be in a couple of days – now, you heard Ruth, she told me it has been postponed…again. I have been here for months!" Her face was white and her hands were clasped together."Sorry I don't want to bother you on you first day here and…!

"Don't worry about me, but I thought you would be pleased about the delay?" Carma asked.

Her voice was soft and gentle and her brown eyes that would sometimes flash excitedly now smouldered with a suppressed emotion that was not easy to define.

She was still experiencing the shock of being in prison – the lack of privacy, primitive sanitation, long hours confined in a small space, poor food and frequent strip searches, all of which she considered humiliating and degrading.

"Pleased, how can I be pleased? I want to know what is going to happen to me! I feel like a fly that has been caught in a spider's web – helpless, absolutely helpless!" Anisha exclaimed in frustration, even though her general attitude was one of a woman of impatient silence who was prepared to accept disaster. "I am also concerned about legal representation because awareness and knowledge of our particular kind of offence is not very well understood in the English system, or in any sort of system, for that matter."

"I thought everyone is entitled to legal defence?"

"Yes, but according to Ruth, she is our prison officer by the way, there has been a slight delay because of some changes in legal aid rules".

"Look at it positively, Anisha, the delay will give your solicitor more time prepare your defence."

"I wish, Carma, I haven't even got a lawyer as yet! And even if I had, I am sure I would not have been able to communicate with him for, for in prison the process of communication has its own pace. And it is vital that I have good legal representation for the distinction between murder and manslaughter relies on them. But do you know, Carma, we prisoners are like a human tide that are washed on the coast on justice. But the justice that we depend on is never be the 'Truth' in the true sense of the word. But I know that when the courts find me guilty, I will be labelled downright at fault, no matter what the truth really was!"

"I thought that at least Ruth would be helpful in sorting out the problem?"

"She has tried, Carma, but I don't think it is within her power, for she has just joined the prison service. She is the best though, for the other prison officers treat us horribly, as if we are not important. And it is this withdrawal of emotional trust by the officers, their unconcern, and the different interpretation of unwritten rules that causes a lot of grievance amongst the prisoners."

"Anisha, I am afraid I will have to ask you to explain a bit more. I do not know anything at all about the law, and it seems you do."

"Yes, I was studying law before my parents decided to get me married, and yes of course I will explain to you all that I know and have experienced, for unless one knows the prison ropes, one is lucky to survive. The prison officers do not give us any information on the rules and regulations, then, have fun playing this game for the odds of their winning are stacked heavily in their favour, and they are quick to put us on report

24

for any trivial offence. Anyway, the fact that a woman has killed her partner, even in self-defence, is not acceptable. You know that society the world over is male-dominated, as are the laws in the judicial system. There are thousands of women affected by Domestic Violence, yet the problem is either distorted or minimised even though the law is, I think and hope, changing. But the women are still blamed, victimised, diagnosed as crazy or locked up."

"Oh dear, Anisha, that sounds…" Carma had been listening with her eyes wide open.

Anisha took a deep breath paused then started pacing the cell.

"A person until proven innocent is supposed to be innocent, but we are treated as guilty people. But you know what is surprising, Carma, some prisoners actually want to stay in remand!"

Chapter 5

"Why would anyone stay here out of choice?" Carma's eyes flew open in surprise.

"For not only can they take advantage of remand privileges for the maximum amount of time but also because for most people, time spent in remand is deducted from sentences. Remand prisoners are supposed to be treated different to sentenced prisoners, but since I have been in the remand centre, neither I or any other remand prisoner has received any privileges. I always thought that the presumption of innocence is a cornerstone of the English Legal System and am surprised to find that it is not translated into practice."

"So did I." Carma looked forlorn.

Anisha stopped pacing the cell and sat on the only chair in their cell.

"It is frightening to think what the result of my trial will be! The Barrister who is to present our case in court depends so much on the solicitor, who has so little contact with the defendant, yet the success of the case depends on him! Doesn't leave us with much hope, huh?" she smiled wanly. "But then, I am sure they mean well, they are so busy and..."

Anisha was a naïve woman, however being in prison had opened her eyes to another aspect of society. That it was people who held positions of influence, be it in govt, in the judicial system or otherwise, who had least knowledge of how to treat people. After she had voiced her doubts to Carma, she added.

"And the sad thing, Carma, is that there are many people in the judicial system who can, if they want, correct the sometimes heartless decisions of their colleagues with kindness and understanding."

"And what makes you say that, Anisha, why do you say heartless decision of the judge? Don't you think that most of the women deserve to be here?"

For the first time in her life, Carma thought she had found a true friend, for she sensed that Anisha, although young, was a kind and wise girl.

"Yes, I do mean heartless, Carma, for many prisoners do not deserve to be here, many remand prisoners still awaiting trial, and many who should have been given a lighter sentence. And it is in prison that women who have offended the first time are exposed to the criminal mind. You won't believe it, Carma, but in the short time that I have been here, I have learnt how to 'hoist and steal,' can tell you where to buy drugs and even how to make them! And the sad thing is that in most cases women start taking drugs, one thing leads to another and…anyway, women who are sentenced for non-violent crimes end up being violent, and others walk out of prison as drug addicts. For a prisoner to change and reform, they first need to change their lifestyle, but sadly, prison not only tolerates, but encourages gang ethos and bullies. Drugs are easily available in the infrastructure of prison life; consequently the effort to 'save' a prisoner is lost!"

Carma was outraged that a system that condemned drug related crimes did little to cure it.

"Though I cannot understand why the women turn to drugs anyway, for Lisa was telling me that taking drugs only made her feel good in the beginning. In the end, it got to be a sickness and she did not get any fun out of it, for when she was not stoned, she was worried as to how she was going to get her next fix!" Anisha said as she prepared to turn in for the night.

But after the lights were out Anisha was tossing and turning for, despite her brave front, she had not come to terms with the aftermath of her marriage to Akram.

It surprised her that she had been so naïve and innocent, for had thought Akram to be a kind and caring man. She had married him in the hope that her relationship with him would fill the emptiness in her life, but was saddened when she felt the vacuum left by his absent love. Her emotional world had once again become strewn with sadness as she repressed her own needs whilst being compelled to anticipate and respond to his.

Soon after their marriage he had shown his violent streak, but although her dignity and pride were continuously battered, Anisha had always tried to justify his moods and tantrums.

It seemed to her that he had two personalities, one loving and kind, the other angry and abusive, and the kindness he portrayed to others merely an act covering his meanness.

She wondered again she why she had not opposed the marriage her parents arranged – or at least got to know Akram better? But he was a charismatic, charming and elegantly dressed man, and had charmed everybody herself included.

However, later, Anisha came to fear his charm, his small and beady eyes that gave his face a disagreeable expression, and came to learn that despite his façade of a tiger, he was a weak cowardly man with an undisciplined temper and sulky moods.

Anisha thought of the day that was to change her life for she could still visualise the scene clearly, the colour of the drapes and carpets and each piece of furniture. Images of the momentous afternoon lingered with Anisha like a multi-coloured explosion in slow motion.

****

<u>Chapter 6</u>

Anisha and Akram were alone in the house and the windows were shut tight to keep out the fierce rain which was scratching at the glass.

Akram's face was glowering face at her fiercely and she knew he was in one of his tempers. She felt trapped in the room and in the ominous silence heard the clock ticking. She was frightened by his cold control and did not know if it was his control or his violent display that frightened her more.

Her eyes were wide with fear and she felt herself drowning and going under in that same old familiar pool of despair so nervously began to rearrange the vase of flowers as she tried to calm Akram.

Akram I was talking to Azaria and…" she smiled nervously and the dimple appeared briefly before fright took over her.

"What did you tell her about me? I told you not to talk to anybody!"

Akram strode purposefully to the door and drew it shut. He did an about turn and glared at Anisha from beneath his thick-hooded eyebrows as his arms folded in anger across his chest. His attitude looked threatening as he moved towards her, the powerful ridges of his muscles rippling beneath his beige taut skin. He grabbed her arm yanked it behind her back.

"Akram, please don't…!"

"A husband has a right to beat his wife anytime he thinks she needs a lesson, you know! I will tell everybody that I was only defending myself against a violently hysterical woman!"

Akram snarled as he hit her and the punch knocked her backwards.

Although he spoke softly, the violence in his eyes was all the more compelling in contrast to the absolute calm of his voice.

'I am not going to scream, cry, whine or act the role of a violated and abused wife, even though it seems it is a role Kismet wants to cast me in. Any show of hysteria is only going to make me lose dignity!" Anisha vowed to herself.

She compressed her lips and cowered against the wall silently. However all the bottled up loneliness and unhappiness of the past months exploded in her as she heard Akram's taunts. Her eyes held more temper than fear as her anger exploded.

She picked up the vase, and then sprang back as it smashed on Akram's head. When Anisha saw Akram's head covered in blood, she screamed.

Azaria and Saleem heard her scream and entered the room to see Akram lying in a pool of blood. Akram was lying still and there was disbelief on Azaria's face.

"Anisha, what have you done? He's dead! You've killed him!" Azaria shouted as she grabbed Anisha's arm.

"Azaria, he was trying to beat me to death, you know what he is like….!."

"I don't know what you are talking about Anisha! I think you have killed him! Saleem, what shall we do?" Azaria looked first at Saleem, then at her sister.

"I don't know, my God, Anisha, what have you done!!" Saleem exclaimed as he ran his hand through his hair

Saleem was Akram's brother and was married to Azaria, Anisha's sister. He was a slim man with dark hair that was parted on the left and fell on a wide brow. He had dark brows, light coloured eyes and a face that was sensitive reflecting his purity of heart. He was not the most handsome of men but he had an attractive face. He was quietly intelligent and had a boyishness charm coupled with a quite and thoughtful air that endeared him to everybody.

He quickly bent over his brother.

"Akram, say something! My god, Azaria, can you phone the ambulance, the police station is just around the corner and no, I think I will go myself and explain for it might be some time before they show up. I think he might still be alive and oh dear....." Saleem hurriedly left the room.

Anisha sat huddled in a corner whilst Azaria left the room, panic pervading her body. After some time she got up and looked out of the window.

When she saw the white car with the red light flashing on top heading towards the house, thought vaguely that Fate had struck at her yet once again cruelly and seized her in its clutch.

The following day at the prison, Anisha spoke to Carma about the accident with Akram. They were sitting in the association room in the afternoon, and were trying to talk above the noise of the voices of the women and the TV.

"I was arrested and taken to the police station where I was told I would be taken to prison on remand. But can you believe, it Carma, Azaria, my own sister, did not accompany me for neither she nor my in-laws realised what had occurred was only in self-defence. It hurt me so much, for Azaria knew what kind of person Akram was! When I had got married I had thought, naively, that I was only losing one family to gain another, which I know now was an illusion created from my fantasy".

Association was a time when the prisoners could watch or do whatever they liked, and was supposed to take place every two days, but very often, due to staff shortages, was cancelled.

"Anisha, I am so sorry! I know exactly how you must feel, anyway, let's change the subject...., some of the women are talking and not fighting, as usual, would you believe it! I thought all they ever did was fight!"

"You can't really blame them, Carma, for it is difficult to make friends, not only because of the nature of the prison regulations.Plus a strong sense of shame and stigma is that is felt by most women makes them unwilling to form long lasting relationships. Anyway, I think you spoke too soon."

You're a stingy cow!" Susan shouted.

"Who do you think you 'r'? Shiela screamed, and a full-scale verbal match ensued. Her voice was shrill and vibrated across the room. "Yu can't even look after yer child!"

"The same way that yu do yours? Yu fucking bitch, yu don't even care where yer children 'r', or 'ho ther fathers 'r'!"

Carma tried to ignore the screaming, which became so loud that it drowned the noise of the television.

"What are they fighting about?" she asked.

"Just being bithchy, in the only way they know how, for everybody's family life is disrupted, to say the least. Shiela was pregnant when she was arrested. She gave birth in prison, and that I can assure you is very traumatic, for she gave birth wearing handcuffs and... Anyway, the child was taken away after a couple of months, but because Sheila suffered from post-natal depression, she could not look after the child. And relationships are a subject that most women feel strongly about, for most women are like us, they enter prison with relationships already in pieces.

"Sheila mentioned Susan's child as well, are there problems there as well?"

"You are not going to like this, but Susan used to flog her seven year old son with a belt, burn him with cigarette butts, give him cold showers, and make him stand all night long in the dark and...!"

"N..nnoo, Oh no, Anisha,!' Carma's hand flew to her mouth.

"Yes, it is true, Carma, that is why the other prisoners do not like Susan."

"I agree with them! At the very least, she should be in for life, Anisha."

"I think it is the fault of Social Services for they should have been responsible for the child and its safety. And actually she is in prison for another crime she committed, drug related I think, but you know how some women will exploit the vulnerability of another inmate, as you have just seen."

"I would not call that being vulnerable, Anisha!"

"No, you are right, for she must have a heart of stone, that woman, and it is not surprising that she does not receive any visitors. Anyway, the conditions under which visitors are received, letters written and censored, the absolute and total invasion of privacy, makes survival of any outside relationship a triumph against odds."

"And I thought that the prison service was designed to nurture at least the personal relationships of the inmates."

"So it is supposed to, Carma, but there is always likely to be a gap between proper justice as in the books, and justice in practice. As far as I can see, this gap is increased in prison by a lot of factors."

An Italian soft-spoken girl, who had been sitting alone, came and sat next to them. Anisha recognised her to be the girl who had arrived with her to the prison.

"My name is Sophie." She introduced herself, and then tried to justify her presence in prison. "I got five years for the supply of heroin, but actually it was my husband who was involved in drugs. Instead, the police arrested me!"

"Didn't you explain to the police that it was not you but your husband...?" Carma asked incredulously.

"I tried, but my husband disappeared and the police insisted that I had been 'aware and helped him in his drug pushing.' I told the police that I was being framed and bullied because I am foreign. What is this system they call 'just and fair?" there was anger and bitterness in her voice as she abruptly turned and walked out of the room.

"Do you believe her, Anisha?" Carma asked, surprised at how candid Sophie had been about her offence.

"She might be right, you know Carma, for the police have to make a certain amount of arrests, statistically, which they base on the assessment of the person's character. Which in turn is based on 'cues', of body language, such as racism, dress, their demeanour etc. Sophie and I came together to the prison and she tried to tell the prison officer, but of course that only angered her! But you know, if she did not show the police sufficient respect, or if they felt she was not, maybe because of language etc, that could very well have contributed to her being given a negative assessment."

"And is she only one who has been falsly accuseds?"

"No, you see Joanne over there? The woman sitting quietly with her hands folded on her lap? Well, she was a companion to an old woman, well, companion cum housekeeper. Anyway, after her death, she found out that she was left some money from her employer, a kind of thank-you. However, the employer's children accused her of taking advantage of their mother's declining health."

"How awful!" Carma whispered. "She should not have accepted the money or given it back."

"She wanted to but her offer was rejected, and would you believe it, she was prosecuted, found guilty and sentenced to one year. I think prison is considered a social dumping ground, you know, remove women from society even when there is no real danger from them."

The trivialities and complexities of prison life had begun to overcome Carma's, and as Anisha concentrated on her impending trial, she became irritable and jumpy, for the months leading up to a court case were fraught with uncertainty and the stress that an inmate felt was strenuous.

"Carma, I am feeling quite afraid of the authority that my trial will hold, it has first refused to protect me and now is going to condemn me to life when I was forced to defend myself. It is really tragic, how life forces one to do things contrary to one's true character, anyway...." Anisha smiled and her dimple danced briefly on her cheek. " I am going for my weekly visit to court day after tomorrow, when is your court appearance?"

"The same day, and I am feeling a bit tense, for I do not know what that implies, but I suppose any deviation from prison routine would be welcome!."

They went back to their cell where Anisha first paced the cell, then stood under the barred window,.

"What is the matter, Anisha?"

"I feel, well I am on my own and I feel so lonely, Carma." Anisha wiped her eyes.

"Do you have any relations other than your sister?"

"My parents passed away, I have relations back in Pakistan, but how can I appeal to them for help? "Anisha shook her head as she replied. "They find it difficult to understand the subject of divorce and consider it taboo, how can they understand the reality of my imprisonment? To them, like most people, imprisonment has a stigma attached to it, however justifiable the circumstances." Anisha shuddered. "No, Carma, it is better to keep silent, for I will not able to tolerate their humiliation, which I am convinced would turn into pity. And indulgence is the last sentiment I need." She smiled wanly. "You know, I am desperately trying to rebuild my damaged pride and fragile ego!"

"Anisha, we have better get used to it for even after we are released, we will come across the disapproval of self appointed ethical people trail us like flies on a summer evening!"

"You're right, Carma, I should get used to it, but it is difficult all the same." Anisha murmured.

Never had Anisha felt so alone, yet at the same time dreading the end of loneliness. Scenes from the past floated up and her memory filled again with ghosts of the past.

Her imagination rustled among the leaves of memories, trying to relive some pleasant one's which might comfort her soul. These acts of recall were intensely real and nostalgic and Anisha was haunted by the spectre of the past and she relived every moment in slow motion.

The strength of her emotions left her drained and numb, and her present retreated into a shadow that withdrew before the sunlight of her memories. Anisha felt guilt and remorse at what she had done, but she had been so badly hurt that her soul had become like numb lacerated tissue!

****

Chapter 7

"Is anybody home?" Anisha cheerfully called as she opened the door and entered the room.

Her parents were having tea in the living room.

Ishraq, Anisha's father, was an established businessman. He camouflaged the secrets of his past with an authoritive manner.

Her mother, on the other hand, had an unobtrusive and gentle nature with extreme degrees of patience and forbearance and her pale face was reposeful and sensitive …. a reminder that the family could depend on her for sympathy.

"Anisha, come and join us," Shahnaz called.

"Sorry, Mum, I have loads of work to hand in by tomorrow." Anisha quickly ran up the stairs to her room.

"Shahnaz, I too am going up to rest for a while." Ishraq felt a tightening in his chest.

"Why? Are you feeling unwell, shall I get you something?" there was genuine concern in Shahnaz's voice.

"No, I am fine; all I need is a little rest."

Ishraq climbed wearily to his bedroom thinking that if it had not been for his time spent in the jail in Pakistan, where he was exposed to all kinds of illnesses, he would today be a well man. His traumatic experiences in Pakistan had taken their toll, and to ease his stress, he was hoping to get his daughters engaged and married. His relations from Pakistan had written to him about matches for his daughters.

However, although he had been relieved to hear that his relations had found what they considered to be suitable boys for Anisha and Azaria, sons of his childhood friend, Arpad, who had shared time with him in jail. However, he had not met him recently so was doubtful about the arrangement.

As if to reflect the feelings of doubt, the weather too was uncertain. In the morning, it had been warm and the sunshine had played and streamed through the clouds. Later great masses of dark clouds had stalked up and crowded the sky. It began to grow dusk and there was a comfortless light, which is neither night nor day.

Ishraq closed the curtains, slipped into his gown, plumped up the pillows, and stretched out on the bed. His mind went on the dreaded journey – up the in warding spiral staircase of thought and to his awful experience in the Pakistan prison. Sometimes he wished he had no memory, no place where his mind could tiptoe every time he tried to sleep.

He was born in Islamabad (Pakistan) and his memory of Islambad was of surrounding high green-blue hills. He would often recall nostalgically the broad, tree lined trees that grew in a neat row against the hills and valleys- the ravines and gurgling mountain streams - the gardens, with a variety of roses, dozens of jasmine, all in a blaze of colour.

However against the town's beauty, Ishraq had witnessed the ugliness of Pakistan, for when he was unjustly imprisoned, he was exposed to its petty squabbles, malice and jealous rumours that formed a part of the jails atmosphere. He, who once had faith in Pakistan's justice system was shocked by its unjust procedures and served two years in prison.

The momentous day was etched on his memory. Together with Arpad, he had joined a youth debating group that met in a secluded house when one day the door was flung open.

Chapter 8

"Put up your hand!" Ishraq was astonished to see police officers brandishing guns at them. "Break it up, this is an illegal meeting!"

Disregarding their pleas of innocence they were all bundled into a jeep crammed with policemen and taken to a small bare room that was the police lock up.

A policeman with a fleshy and plump and eyes thick with kajol was sitting with his feet on his desk and twirling a pencil in his hand. Ishraq noticed with disgust that he was spitting betal nut juice at the already soiled wall.

The policeman stood up as soon as he saw them and harnessing his baggy trousers and steadying his swaying fez started shouting at them.

"You students are good for nothing! You are always making trouble with your strikes and protest marches!"

He sat down and grabbed their hands for fingerprints whilst Ishraq and Arpad vainly tried to convince him of their innocence.

Although Arpad and Ishraq were taken to the same jail, they were put in different wings. Ishraq was appalled and disgusted when he was shown his cell.

"You can't expect me to sleep me in that....?!"he asked as he saw a bed that scooped worse than a hammock and heard the buzzing of mosquitoes.

"Where else do you think you are going to sleep? In a five-star hotel?!"

The prison officers grinned and pushed him in the cell, and as Ishraq sat on the sagging bed, cursed the day he had joined the debating society. By morning he had a splitting headache and could not stop scratching his inflamed mosquito bitten arms.

"Your breakfast!" A servant boy came to his cell with a cup of tea and a chunk of bread.

"I do not want any food, I am innocent – can I speak to somebody?"

"All prisoner thinks they are innocent! And you better eat and drink this for this is the only meal you are going to get till afternoon! And there is nobody you can speak to, you will have to wait for you trial!" The boy replied as he opened the cell door and put down the tray on the floor.

Ishraq was so angry he kicked the tea into the dirt and hurled the bread after it but the boy merely shrugged and picked up the mug.

****

As Anisha told Carma the horror of what her father had endured, she exclaimed.

"I still think that prison life is worse here, no, I don't know, at least we don't have the mosquitoes! But, remember I told you that you would get used to prison life, well, I have been here for four months, and although I think I have adapted, I have to be alert all the time not to upset hostile prisoners. Not only that, I have to keep abreast of the fact that new rules of behaviour have to be learnt according to different prison officers. I am trying desperately to obey and comply with the expectations of those in authority, at the same time be accepted by the prison inmates, but I don't think I am succeeding in either!"

Although Anisha had tears in her eyes, she smiled wanly, for she had a sense of humour which was like a scent to the rose and served as a restraint to depression.

Carma tried to change the subject.

"Tell me, when are they going to allow us out of our cell?" Carma asked in exasperation. "Surely there must be a time when they let us out? It is suffocating in here!"

"They are supposed to let us out for exercise everyday for one hour at least, which is one of our few entitlements." Anisha smiled affectionately.

By talking to her, Anisha felt she was sustaining an independence of spirit and keeping alive her identity that was essential to her in the unchanging world of the prison.

"You mentioned that prison is a social dumping ground for women? What did you mean by that?"

"Black women, unmarried women, women who have many lovers, who have left their husband, those with children in care, homeless women or those who are addicted to drugs are I think more likely to find themselves in prison. And you won't

45

believe it, but the diversity of sentences handed for the same crimes is astounding. This does not help the women to have faith in the system, Carma; anyway, most of the women are sentenced for trivial and non-violent crimes and…"

"Anisha! You call these women non-violent?"

"Yes, they are, well anyway most of them, it is just that they find imprisonment traumatic which leads to incidences of flare-ups and self-mutilation."

"Enough of prison culture, tell me more about your parents."

"My father did not talk to me much, but when he did, he would he tell me about the time he got married to mother, came to London and also about his first impressions of the city."

Anisha relived nostalgically the rare and cherished times when her father spoke to her about his experiences and the time he got married.

****

Chapter 9

.

"I have got a marriage proposal for you."

Ishraq's father announced on the day Ishraq was released from prison.

"Father, I am only glad to be free! Anyway, how can I get married when I have the stigma of prison?" Ishraq voiced his concern.

"Don't worry about that, Ishraq," His father replied. "I told all our acquaintances that you went abroad for a couple of years. And meet Shahnaz before you decide about her."

Finally Ishraq relented and they travelled to Peshawar, where Ishraq jumped at the opportunity to wander the streets freely and go sightseeing.

He found the bazaars booming with trade, for there were stalls of rich cloths, Afghan rugs, and silver and exotic bangles and necklaces. After his time in prison, Ishraq wanted to partake of all the foods of the side street eating places that were overlaid with tantalising aromas, for the food was heavily spiced and sizzling temptingly in open pans of fat whilst cakes of bread baked in clay ovens.

After they had finished their tour of Peshawar, they went to see Shahnaz.

"Shahnaz, bring our guests some refreshments. They must be tired after their journey." Shahnaz's father's voice rang deep and rich..

He was wearing baggy trousers topped with flowing cotton over shirt, and a formidable turban of dark cloth on his head topped his apparel.

Shahnaz entered with the tea. She was wearing the traditional garment that was a tent of heavy material with eye-slits at the top and a mask of gauze over the nose and mouth.

They had tea with them and stayed for an hour when Ishraq and his father left.

"Well, what did you think of her? She seems a nice girl and…"

"Okay, okay, father, I agree," Ishraq knew if he did not agree his father would not leave him in peace and Shahnaz seemed to be a pleasant girl.

Ishraq's father was delighted and as Shahnaz's father was in a hurry, they were married quickly. Ishraq and Shahnaz moved to Islamadad where within the space of two years, their daughters, Azaria and Anisha were born.

One day, Shahnaz was feeding Anisha when Ishraq entered the room and suddenly announced.

"I am leaving for London within the week."

Shahnaz looked up in surprise.

"That's a sudden decision you have made. Don't you think you should have consulted me first? What about me and the children?" I need time to pack and…?"

"One question at a time please, wife. Ever since I was a small boy I have wanted to go to London. I have met many people returning from there, all with glowing accounts and now I have a chance, at last! The decision has not been made, not like you think, at the spur of the moment, but it is my, no a young boy's dream that has grown over the years. And you and the girls can join me as soon as I am settled."

48

By now Shahnaz had come to know her husband well and knew that once he made up his mind there was no changing it.

Chapter 10

Ishraq arrived in England wishing to get rid of unpleasant memories of the past and had written to his nephew, who had offered to not only meet him at the airport, but offered to put him up at his lodgings.

His flight had arrived in the morning, but after waiting for his nephew for a couple of hours, was told to go Victoria station. In the vast cavern of the station he saw what he later knew as theatre goers scurrying hither and thither hastening to the Strand. He stood looking lost and lonely under the space beneath the lamps when an Indian gentleman came up to him.

"Can I help you?" he asked.

Ishraq heaved a sigh of relief and explained his predicament.

"I know of a place that would be able to help." He hailed a cab and they drove to the Pakistanis Students Hostel in Knightsbridge. As they drove past Ishraq saw people in umbrellas and Macs having scone cream teas. He could not get used to the cockney dialect of the cab driver although he found it vaguely familiar as it summoned up pictures form Ealing comedy film reels he had seen in Pakistan.

He was dropped of at the hostel, and before Ishraq had a chance to thank him, his benefactor drove off. Ishraq waved to the disappearing car before he walked into the hostel apprehensively.

"You cannot stay here for you are not a student, but I can give you the name of a family who could be of some assistance to you." The man at the reception told him.

Ishraq took the address gratefully and finally managed to locate the house, for it was a low dark building crouching behind a screen of dilapidated trees. As Ishraq rung the bell he noticed that the garden of the house was a tousled mess of faded chrysanthemums.

A plump man with friendly eyes that twinkled with merriment opened the door and Ishraq explained his dilemma.

"You must stay with us till you find your cousin. By the way my name is Faizal and this is my wife Ayesha."

Ishraq liked Faizal; moreover being alone in a new city was glad of his hospitality. Faizal helped him find his way around London, where Ishraq soon felt comfortable and confident.

He started to know all he could about London – where he could find rich spicy food, the Big Ben, Madame Tussards etc. He soon discovered that London was a capital that with a divided series of places, some he had heard of whilst others were unknown to him. However, to him the variety seemed extraordinary, and he wanted to see not only the major sights of London but also the simple things.

It was summer when he arrived and he walked aimlessly amidst the trees and grassland of Hyde Park and stood on Tower Bridge at dusk, watching the red glinting waters of the river Thames. Late in the evening he went to Shaftsbury Avenue and was fascinated when all the theatres lit up in amber, ruby and jade and the roads shimmered with slow moving black cabs and red double-decker buses.

"Would you like to see the trooping of the colour?" Faizal asked Ishraq one weekend.

"Of course he would." Ayesha piped up.

She was busy knitting and remembered how keen she had been to see London when she had first arrived after her marriage to Faizal. Unfortunately her husband believed in Purdah and thought a woman's place was at home, and Ayesha was only allowed to venture out as far as the shop around the corner.

"Right, so tomorrow that is where we go!" Faizal beamed.

"Thank you…." Ishraq felt he was indeed lucky to have come across such a decent and sincere couple.

The following day, as they travelled on the tube Ishraq was surprised at the cross-section and diversity of people - from the art student and the bowler hatted man to the Chinatown Storekeeper reading a Cantonese paper.

"Some will be going for boating trips in Hyde Park and others to the markets of Portobello, Camden or Carnally Street." Faizal pointed out noticing Ishraq's puzzlement, as it was a Sunday.

Ishraq and Faizal saw a squad of lifeguards enter the gates of Hyde Park, erect and glittering with silver, white and red. They watched fascinated as the muscles of their smooth white thighs responded to the movements of their horses, their cheeks and chins bent in haughty masculinity. The body of men in scarlet and silver paraded down the leafless avenue in an elegant yet disciplined group to the beat and rhythm of the band.

"That was excellent." Ishraq remarked as the last of the men disappeared down the avenue.

"Yes, it was." Faizal replied as they walked down Hyde Park corner.

Ishraq noticed a man speaking under a tree and persuaded Faizal to listen to him. Faizal agreed and they heard the man speaking angrily about the continual miseries of the poor.

"Living in the city is a struggle and never-ending battle for the poor people who are deprived of even the fundamental elements of life!"

"What rubbish!" Ishraq exclaimed.

"So you do not agree with him?" Faizal asked as they strolled across the lawn.

"Well not really for they not tally with my opinion of an affluent and democratic representation England!"

Nevertheless, he was quick to reverse his judgement when one evening walking under Waterloo Bridge Ishraq discovered homeless people sleeping in the open air. They looked like ruffled heaps lying on the roadside, with their heads towards a wall, feet lying on the pavement.

As Ishraq stood in astonishment at the unexpected sight, he could see sweeping on their sleeping faces the trailing lights of a passing car. Ishraq winced in the dark as he picked his way past the line of feet and shrank from the sight of thin and bony ankles of a girl and a bunched up woman.

He saw the pitiable sight of some men who only had newspapers to wrap their legs in an effort to keep warm, others who were standing on the edge of the pavement their eyes fixed on a distant hope. Ishraq was shocked to see on a seat nearby a woman sleeping whilst the water from the rain that was falling trickled and hung heavily at the ends of her strands of hair.

"I did not know there was so much poverty in London," he exclaimed later to Faizal.

"Yes, but there is another side to London as well," explained Faizal, who had lived in London for a long time. "Here there are also men who pilot what is called advancement, men from banks, city offices and Government offices. They are silk bowler hatted men who guide trade, and although they appear to be considerate and thoughtful, their eyes are cold and they are careless of the value of human feelings, even life."

Ishraq was surprised at the cynicism in Faizal's voice and tried to change the subject.

"The weather is not as bad as I thought." he remarked.

After what he was told, Ishraq had come to like the English weather not only because it was a talking point considering its unpredictability, but also because it was a neutral subject to break ice with. When he commented on the present pleasant weather he heard a howl of protestation from Faizal.

"Wait till winter arrives, for then you'll see dark clouds, hailstones and gusts of icy winds. And the mists that engulf the town, Ishraq, they are like ghosts meeting! The weather is so unpredictable that you will often see at a bus-stop an optimist dressed in shorts standing next to a pessimist with an overcoat and an umbrella!" Faizal's belly heaved with laughter. "Anyway more to the point, would you like to work where I do? There are vacancies there and I thought you might be interested."

"Of course I am! I was thinking of looking for some kind of work and a flat anyway for I don't think I should intrude on your hospitality any more." Ishraq replied quickly for pride and duty meant he find a place of his own as soon as possible.

****

"My father worked in different factories, but he always used to say that he was met everywhere with suspicion and hostility, and not being accustomed to the legendary British reserve he mistook it for coolness. His temperament, of a simple and trusting soul, received shock after shock of what he thought to be rejection, and combined with the social unwelcome, began to feel unappreciated in England, the place he had dreamt of since childhood." Anisha paced the cell. "He tried his hand at business with the help of his friend and bought a newsagent and as soon as he was settled, we joined him."

"So he was successful then in business?"

"Oh yes! Soon after he ventured in the hotel business, and when that was a success he opened a second and later a third cafe. By the time we were grown up, he used to tease us, saying that he was now in a position to provide his son-in-laws with a café of their own! He was a good father really, and was relieved when his family in Pakistan told him that they had arranged our wedding. Poor father, if only he knew what the future had in store for his daughter!"

Carma began to feel claustrophobic in the cell.

"Gosh, I wish they would unlock us for exercise! Since I have been here we have not been let out once! I am dying to stretch my legs and…"

"Hey, Carma, I think you expect the exercise yard to be large with green grass on which you can walk and run…well let me put your straight on that. The exercise yard is small; though one can at least inmates from other wings and exchange gossip. It comes alive though, when women lounge around, smoking and rolling cigarettes, either hugging their friends or hurling abuse at them! Anyway, shuffling round and round the yard can hardly be called exercise, but at least it gives us a chance to get fresh air, and if the weather allows, walk barefoot on whatever grass there is!"

"I am quite looking forward to it Anisha, for anything is better than being locked indoors!"

"Another thing, Carma, even when we are let out, weather and staff permitting, the whole time involved is only ten minutes outside because somehow, the entire exercise period is calculated from time of unlocking until the women are locked up again! And as the long distance of getting back and forth reduces the time out of doors, I try to capture and retain the sensations of the open air by concentrating on smells, sights and feeling. I too am fed up, to say the least!"

Carma tactfully tried to change the subject.

Anisha, I noticed an Indian girl the other day when we were in the Association room, who is she?"

"Who? I think you mean Radha." Anisha was only too glad to keep her mind from prison conditions.

"She looks so sad." remarked Carma remembering the thin woman with dark brown hair that reached her waist and a melancholy expression. "What is she in for?"

"She is serving a six-year sentence for smuggling drugs." Replied Anisha, who was only to glad to change the subject.

"Really? I find that very hard to believe, for she looks so gentle and kind."

"You're right; she is innocent for it was her husband who was the brains behind the smuggling operations. He thought that Radha, with her innocence and quiet charm would make the perfect courier to carry his packages. Unfortunately, she got caught and was arrested."

"Wasn't he arrested as well?"

"Men!" Anisha snorted. "He turned out to be really evil, for he told Radha that she would never see her son again if she did not take the blame. And now her in-laws think she is the one who is the drug-pusher and are taking out an injunction against her so that she will never be able to see her son again."

"What a horrible man! And after all that she has done for him! The least he could do is to visit her with news of her son. It must be terrible for not being able to…"

"Oh, he comes to visit her alright, thought I don't why, for he never brings the son with him. Personally, I think he is cruel and only comes to gloat for she is even more disheartened than ever after his visit. The depth of her depression worries everyone, for she is kind and gentle, and the sad thing is that although the authorities know she is innocent, she is treated as if she were guilty!"

"She does not deserve that I am sure!"

"No, it does not. It seems to me, Carma, that the fundamental principle of justice in prison is forgotten – mainly the presumption of innocence till proven guilty. She is a very brave woman though, and tried to get a job in the prison kitchen, but her application to work was refused, you know why? Just because Radha, one of the gentlest creatures I know, was reported to display anti-authoritian arrogance!"

But that is so unfair!"

"Yes, I know, but according to the prison service, by breaking the law, a prisoner hassss no rights at all!"

They heard the bell ringing and the crashing of trays that told them it was time for lunch. Together with the other prisoners, they found that time dragged in prison, and meal times served as an event at the end of it, however revolting the meal.

"Makes one think that maybe our circumstances are not all that bad, huh? Are your in-laws from London?" Carma asked, changing the subject.

"Yes, my father-in-law, Arpad lives in London, but originally came from Pakistan. He was a close friend of my father and I did not realise how close till I overheard him talking to my father on the phone about the after – effects of their time in the jail, and that was the first I knew about it !"

****

<u>Chapter 11</u>

"Look, Anisha, forget what you heard, for my family does not know about those two years. Your father and I decided that it was best to keep it from our families, for we were innocent and it was all a mistake anyway." Arpad had put the receiver back and turned to find Anisha staring at him. He looked flustered and nervous as he spoke to her.

"Were you there with father?" Anisha whispered her eyes wide with shock.

"Yes, well that is to say I had hoped we would be in the same jail, however, to my dismay, although he was in the same prison, he was in a different wing"

Arpad looked at her thoughtfully. He was as a tall man of about 55-60 years, a wheatesh complexion, thick moustache, hair that was dyed jet black and eyes that protruded like marbles.

"Oh I see, and what was…?"

"Anisha, I don't want to talk about it anymore. Just forget what you heard," Arpad went to his bedroom where he recalled the day he had been taken to prison.

<u>Chapter 12</u>

.

"Here, take this!" he was thrown a straw mat, shabby cotton blanket and jail clothes after which he was taken to his cell.

Arpad was disgusted to find ants and cockroaches crawling all over the cell walls, and there were lizards and rats everywhere. He was sitting with his hands in his head when he heard a clatter of a tray.

"Your food"! A voice said gruffly.

Arpad took the tray hungrily but was sick as soon as he saw the pebbles on the thin curry, which was crested with flies. He pushed the tray from him. "Ugh…they don't expect me to eat that?

Seeing the look of disgust on his face, one of the inmates from the adjoining cell remarked.

"You better eat that for that is all you will get! The authorities should do something about it for we suffer from what I am sure is a combination of dysentery, malaria and cholera. By the way, my name is Rafat."

"I am not going to stand for this kind of treatment! There has been no trail and I have not been found guilty!" Arpad yelled.

After a few days, Arpad persuaded Rafat and the other inmates to go on a hunger strike. However, the protest was short-lived and as punishment they were sent to the isolation unit where they were locked in total darkness and left in what seemed to Arpad to be a tomb. Their food, from being bad went to worse and they were rationed to one Rusk of bread and perhaps one chapatti with thin lentil soup. They saw nobody and the jailer dropped the food through the small hole in the cell door.

"Now maybe you know what will happen the next time you decide to rebel!" he shouted.

A couple of days later they were brought back to their cells and gradually Arpad got used to the prison routine, where daytime resounded with the cheerless drugged laughter of the convicts which to him sounded like a hyena's.

Night time was usually divided between the groans and the startled sleep of men across the yard, and Arpad still had nightmares of the warden's voice booming at night as he counted the inmates. The echo of grunts, scuffles and roars of angry convicts followed his shout as he thumped them on the head.

"They treat us like dogs! I am innocent for I have not committed any crime to deserve this kind of treatment! We have not been tried as yet!" Arpad exclaimed in exasperation the next morning to Rafat.

"Neither have I." Rafat replied. "But as you have seen with the hunger strike, our objections are going to be futile, and you better accept the fact that you will be in jail for some time, because the wheels of justice turn slowly and any legal process, especially in Pakistan cannot be hurried. And anyway, a trial is usually a sham anyway."

Arpad and Rafat were finally taken for their trial, and as they entered the forbidding building saw lawyers running around the building corridors.

Rafat looked at them and remarked. "I am not confident we will be treated fairly by them. we do not know court procedures, have no contacts, no representations and are poor!"

"Rafat, I have faith in the system…."

"There is no fair system. Most of the lawyers do not like to represent innocent people like us." Rafat whispered as they waited in the corridor of the courts flanked by two policemen. "They only take on cases like family feuds and property/land, because those are the cases that make money, name and fortune by fighting costly court battles over succession certificates to titles and property."

"You have a very low opinion about them …any particular reason?" Arpad asked.

"That is because it is because of them that I am in this wretched prison!" Rafat's voice shook with suppressed emotion.

"What do you mean?" Ishraq asked aghast."I thought they were here to help us!"

"Not at all! I come from a rich family and my father left me a lot of money in his will. Unfortunately, after his death, my brother contested the will. It was all there in black and white and my lawyer could have won my case. But my brother paid him a lot of money to frame me for forging my father's will!" Rafat's voice trembled and Arpad could sense the pain in his voice.

Arpad grimly looked at the lawyers hurrying down the corridors.

"Rafat, don't you think the lawyers look like birds of premonitions with their black coats flying around them?"

Rafat nodded silently and sadly as they were taken back to the prison without a trial.

"Hey, what is happening…" Arpad stuttered as they were led to the lorry.

"I told you,…."Rafat said as he climbed into the van.

Rafat was right for they could not get a lawyer to defend them, with the result that they spent two years in prison.

It had been summer when they were arrested and in the daytime, Arpad saw the summer dust gather along the ground rising and whirling, hanging around the prison like a curtain, reflecting his disposition. Finally, after a month of dust storms, when the clouds looked black and sheets of water inundated the yard Arpad gradually began to lose his zest for life.

****

"Once my father-law knew that I knew about his time in Pakistan, he used to talk to me often about the conditions of the jail in Pakistan and the food they gave. This I suppose, in comparison is luxury!"

"Anisha, food for me has never been important, and I don't really care what kind of meal I get. There are other more important things to worry about."

"Maybe, but I look forward to mealtimes! However revolting and dull the meal, I prefer to inactivity."

Having taken their lunch tray, Anisha and Carma returned to their cells and were sitting on the bunk bed, trying to balance their trays on their laps. Carma's expression was one of indifference.

They tried to divert their minds from the revolting food by listening to the inmates talking and shouting to each other.

"Ave yer wrote to Dorothy?"

"Nah, but I will, but what is she goin' to tell me that I don't know?"

"Who is Dorothy, Anisha?" Carma grimaced as she sipped her tea.

"She is one of the psychics that the inmate writes to." Anisha replied as she looked at Carma's surprised face. "It is not an uncommon occurrence here, you know. There are various superstitions in prison and many women write to psychics and palm readers. I can get you her address if you are interested?" she smiled mischievously.

"I don't think so, Anisha, for I consider superstition to be half knowledge and half wishes put together, with anxiety fear and hope to be the main ingredients!"

"You're absolutely right; I too feel that it is built not on reason but on legends that are not surrounded with intellect, but it keeps alive a person's hope." Anisha looked whimsical.

"Under the circumstances, I suppose, it could be a good thing to cling on to hope when…you know, Anisha, I think nothing justifies this this…."

"You mean being in prison? I agree, I think the only thing it does is to reassure the public that crime is being dealt with. Emphasis is given to minor offences, whereas crimes of magnitude are ignored because the men who commit them are of influence. Because it is such a social issue, there should be something like social crime prevention."

"You mean by promoting change in attitude and personal attitude? But how is that possible?"

"Maybe via personal and social education programmes in school? Oh I don't know, but at least that might prove an attempt is being made to really get at the root of the problem, not just the surface care and gloss so that the public is satisfied that something is being done to tackle the issue."

"Hmm, maybe." Carma was not interested in the prison. "Were your in-laws married in London?"

"No, my mother-in-law is English; however, I did hear that my father-in-law was married before in Pakistan." Anisha looked down at her meal tray with a grimace.

"You don't say!" Carma tilted her head, surprise evident on her face.

"To tell the truth, my father-in-law is an obnoxious man, I didn't like him at all. He treats his present wife abominably and was no role model for my husband either! No wonder his first wife Sultana left him."

****

Chapter 13

"Arpad, don't tell me what to do all the time!" Sultana screamed.

"Why do you always insist on rearranging my clothes and papers? I have my own way of doing things and don't want you to meddle!" Arpad shouted angrily.

He grabbed Sultana's arm and slapped her across the face. His eyes burned with rage and when he saw a flicker of fear in Sultana's eye's, felt the first stirrings of mastery. He held on to her arm and waited for Sultana's expression to turn from fear to docility.

"What the…! Let me go!" Sultana put her hand to her burning cheek. She recovered from her fear and managed to shake off his grip, glaring back at him with eyes that were fiery and unyielding.

However, Arpad's violence had awakened unpleasant memories. She remembered her father who had invoked the same fear in her and the memory brought with it a pang of loss of her dead mother, who was continually beaten by her father. She remembered her mother suffering silently, unable to break free of her husband.

Reality returned and she heard Arpad apologising.

"I am so sorry, Sultana, I did not mean to….".

Nevertheless, to Sultana his apology sounded meaningless and automatic. She did not want to suffer her whole life like her mother and decided to leave Arpad.

"Arpad, I am going to stay with my brother!"
She announced the next day.

"Women! Why can't you realise that your
obligation and duty is towards your husband?"
Arpad asked in exasperation.

However, to his astonishment and surprise
Sultana left him.

His father had died soon after and Arpad had
come to London, bringing with him memories of
broken relationships. However, soon after his
arrival, he had met and married Nadia.

****

"Yes, he is an awful man. Sultana was a brave
woman, for she had the courage to leave him.
Akram used to tell me that he used to beat his
mother too!"

"No wonder Akram behaved the way he did,
you know what they say, that the child usually
takes after the parents and all that."

"But I think that theory is just an excuse, for
what about Saleem, his brother? He is the gentlest
creature ever, no wonder Azaria wants to hold on
to him, whatever the cost!"

"Yes, I suppose you are right, Anisha, but what
did you mean by your comment about your
sister?"

"N..Nothing nothing at all." Anisha hurriedly
tried to cover up her slip.

"Anisha, it seems you are not telling me everything, anyway, in your own time. But getting back to the present, tell me I notice that the general information regarding prison is not provided to us. I need to know about my rights, principles, procedures etc. and if it was not for you…"

"There is a prison information pack but that is rarely given to the prisoners." Anisha replied. "As you will find out, there is an almost tyrannical exercise of power and control in the prison, though personally I think a more humane approach by them would be more productive."

"Even the prison officers, I have noticed, have different attitudes towards the prisoners?"

"You're right again Carma, there is no consistency in their treatment and the prisoners rights often depend upon the 'so called goodwill' of the prison officers in either bending the unwritten rules of prison or by creating pointless rules! Although some of them are kind, to be fair, the majority like John are bullies. Most of the time they provoke tension among the inmates by continually reminding them they are from a lower rank in society, or by assaulting them!"

"I know, for I can feel the tension, Anisha, and even though the physical conditions are appalling, I find the daily discipline more damaging to the ego!. I hate being shouted at and feel so confused and helpless at not being able to do anything, however trivial without first asking permission. Anyway, you have told me about you in laws but not about your husband. What was he like?"

Carma wiped the back of her hand across her brow.

For Anisha, the reassurance of finding herself able to talk and help someone in a similar situation, when she herself needed help, boosted her confidence and she felt she could now face the conflict that had been raging within her.

"There were only two of them Saleem and Akram and were born and brought up in London. Because of the western influence, they did the fact that their marriage was being arranged by people they did not even know! Akram often teased Azaria about it, for apparently it was colourful, the way it all happened!"

****

Chapter 14

"Gandhi, where are you?" shouted Akram. Saleem had been nicknamed by his family 'Gandhi' because of his gentle nature.

Saleem resented Akram's teasing hin 'Gandhi'and his brow creased in a frown. He felt angry and frustrated because he had just learnt that his father had arranged their marriage, and was chafed because his disposition forbade him voicing his opinion. Although he was sensitive he was no fool and was and capable of passing quiet judgement on events and people that would have surprised the articulate. However, that was something he never did, leaving all the communication to Akram.

An arranged marriage was a common occurrence in their culture for many marriages were organised without prior knowledge of the children. Saleem had tried to talk to his father but although his father loved his children, he expected complete obedience from them.

Saleem had ried to talk to his mother.

" I am sorry, Saleem, it's been fixed and is very difficult for him to go back on his family's promise, as it would reflect badly on them" Seeing her son's downcast face, she added "But I will try and talk to him"

.

The quiver on Saleem's lips hardened into a little smile, even though it was against his nature to harbour any ill feelings.

Seeing his brother's worried face, Akram teased him.

"Hey, Gandhi, what's the matter? Are there no fasts to be kept, no speeches to be made?"

"Akram, will you be serious? I want to talk to you". Saleem glanced at Akram in annoyance.

"There is always a solution to a problem......" Akram said sitting on the bed. "Right, fire away and tell me all about it."

s"I'll try", replied Saleem, pausing to find the right words. "It's dad"; he finally blurted in a rush. "He's arranged our marriages and..."

"Whoa, hold on", replied Akram, "what are you talking about? Calm down and tell me slowly" he had just barely heard the words 'marriage' and 'arranged'. "What has father done now? Has his family arranged a third wife for him?" He chuckled at the thought of his father marrying again, and his mother's reaction. "There will definitely be fireworks in the house!" he remarked, still grinning.

"Akram, you've got it all wrong. It is our marriage he has arranged! I have tried to talk to him, but you know how stubborn he is and..."

Akram looked at him in amazement, his eyes darkened and his mouth tightened.

"I will not let Father to ruin my life and....... I'll, I'll talk to him and tell him he can forget his silly ideas". Akram shouted and was sputtering in anger as he rushed out of the room.

Nadia met him outside the room and saw the expression on his face.

"Akram, don't say anything to your father that would make him angry...Akram!" Nadia looked in dismay after Akram's retreating figure.

Nadia's whole life had been spent in foster homes, but eventually, as soon as she was old enough, she got a job and bedsit in Battersea.

One day she was with a group of her friends when one of them challenged her.

"Bet you cannot steal without being caught....all of us have

"You're on, though I have never stolen before. Cannot be much to it though...not if you lot have not been caught!"

However, although she had thought it would be easy, she was caught shop-lifting and sentenced to six months in jail.

She was not really a criminal at heart but was too embarrassed to tell Arpad of the six months she spent in prison. However, even though she had been in prison for a few months only, it had left its imprint on her.

Having lost all outside contact, she lost her confidence, and if it had not been for Laverne, her fellow inmate, she felt she would not have been able to finish her sentence. She had no self esteem when she married Arpad, and his constant criticisms made sure that she did not regain it.

Consequently she was willing to tolerate his violence, even though he later always managed to persuade her that it would not happen again it did till she finally accept the fact that he would never change.

****

"They showed a united front, Arpad and Nadia, but I could sense that underneath the show of unity there was unhappiness," Anisha breathed out deeply as she explained about Nadia's discontentment and her voice was quietly reminiscent.

"She was not too fond of Akram, Carma; I think his temper was too much like her husband's"

Lunchtime was as usual, a revolting meal. Balancing their trays and clutching their mugs of tea, they sat in their cell, looking at their plates in dismay. The meat, or whatever it was, looked inedible and tough and Carma could barely cut it with her plastic knife. The meal came with two great scoops of very unappetising potato and a vegetable, usually over-cooked cabbage.

"It sounds pathetic, Carma, but it seems like all we have to look forward to is visits, letters, and mealtimes. For us the first two are out, but at least you, being a non-veg, can eat something of the horrible food, but I can only eat desserts and puddings, one because I don't eat meat and secondly because I find the desserts are more appetising than the meal itself! You know it has been months since I had a proper meal! I actually think that hunger is a monster of many heads and arms, which can attack any vulnerability of mine –

loneliness or any physical weakness. Anyway, I do not understand why the prisons do not give up using meat and try Soya instead, though I have heard it is done in some prisons. To the non-vegetarians I think even Soya would be edible."

"Anisha, I don't want to talk about food. It is bad enough we have to eat it!" Carma shoved her tray aside. "Anyway, did Akram speak to his mother about getting out of the marriage?"

"Yes, although he, like Saleem, knew that it was futile to do so. He spoke to his father though…hey come on..it is time for fresh air, thank God!"

As they walked down to the exercise yard, Carma noticed a woman waving her arms frantically and shouting.

"Why is that woman shouting?" she asked

"That is the Psychiatric Unit and that is Emma, one of the patients. Apparently, I have heard that conditions there are worse than they are in the prison wings. The patients keep banging their heads, wanting to be let out, all screaming they want to go home. "Some of the patients do not belong there, whilst others on prison wings should actually receive proper psychiatric care. I overheard one of the inmates, Susan, I think, saying that one woman in the unit gouged her eye out so that she could be let out, and another who slashed her breast for the same reason!"

They were walking down the concrete path when one of the inmates walked past and purposefully pushed Anisha to the floor.

"So sorry, hope you are not 'urt, deerie!" She sniggered and started walking away.

"Hey, how dare you…" Carma looked angrily at the woman. "Anisha, did you see that? She did that on purpose!"

Carma tried to get the attention of one of the prison officers who had posted themselves along the path, but they ignored her. Suddenly, Carma was grabbed from behind and pushed.

"Don't ever let me catch you so much as looking at a screw! If you do, I will cut you so f.….g bad that…' The woman walked away with what seemed to Carma a cruel warning.

Anisha had got up and was calmly brushing her sleeve.

"Anisha, did you hear that? How dare she threaten me! Who does she think she is? The prison officers are supposed to assist us but they are ignoring us. Is there a complaint procedure here? Oh, sorry, Anisha, are you hurt?"

"Carma, calm yourself, this is something else you will have to get used to. Now you have been introduced to Mandy, who is a self-appointed bully. She leads a group of women who terrorise the other inmates… and don't worry Carma, I am fine. One thing I forgot to mention was that a prisoner is not meant to show anything but the utmost contempt toward a prison officer. The women feel that as the officers do not take their feelings into account, why should they heed authority?"

Carma, who was walking slowly, suddenly stopped.

"You mean there is no way a complaint can be made?"

"There is a grievance procedure, but I, like the other inmates, have no confidence that it will and can right an injustice. In our case, especially, I think it would be no use, for some of the prison officers are racists. I don't think their attitude is deliberately discriminating, it is there because of unconscious prejudice and stereotyping."

"I don't know how you can be so understanding, Anisha, Mandy deserves to be put on remission, for she did that purposefully! Why do you let her get away with it?"

"I don't think the woman meant any harm. As you stay here you will know there are factions and groups here, because of which there is always rivalry and bullying. You know that lady with the scar, guess show she got it? Doris was bullied daily when she first came, so one day she complained to the prison officer. Not only was she put on remission, but also one day three women from Mandy's gang went into her cell. Two women pinned her to the floor whilst one took a jagged tin lid and with the edge and slashed Doris's face from forehead to chin. No, it is better to keep quite."

"It appears to me that only the weak are bullied, Anisha!" Carma said in exasperation.

Anisha smiled in her fetching way. "Carma, drop the subject, I cannot stand up to them, now I was telling you about the psychiatric hospital."

"Anisha! Oh alright…alright, is the psychiatric treatment better than the medical one?"

"Oh no! It does not have any facilities for specialist treatment."

"Oh....but why is Emma in Prison?"

"Arson and she attempted suicide once – apparently her neck is badly disfigured with the scars of the razor she used."

"Poor thing!" Carma whispered, and as soon as they were locked in their cell, Carma continued in a quiet voice.

"Anisha, don't tell me about the inmates anymore, just tell me about yourself for then I feel that my present retreats into a shadow. And anyway, I am fascinated by your life story. Your husband could not persuade his father that he did not want to get married?"

"Na ah, although he tried to talk to his dad to change his mind, but of course, it had no affect. How I wish somebody had listened to him!" Anisha's eyes filled with bitterness.

****

Chapter 15

The bedroom door opened and Arpad walked in.

"Nadia tells me you want to talk to me", he bellowed "your mother said it was important. I hope it is – I am busy. Nadia, I would like tea. I am with the Akram and Saleem in their room." he ordered sticking his head out of the door.

"Now, what's the matter? Do you require some money to buy new clothes?" Arpad took his wallet from his pocket and his moustaches shook as he smirked slyly. "Sorry, boys. It will have to wait till this evening. I am going to the bank later in the afternoon."

"We don't want money dad, we only wanted to tell you that we will not consent to the marriage you have arranged!" Akram looked angrily at his father.

"How dare you....!!!" Arpad spluttered then turned his head and looked at Akram, his face ashen with anger. "Are you trying to tell me that I, no, we are wrong? My family has fixed the match with only your best interest at heart. Not only that, but Ishraq is a good and old friend of mine".

"I'm sure he is, but you talk of your family – you're parents are dead". Exclaimed Akram exasperatedly.

He began to feel a helpless rage, a feeling as violent as a passion that took hold of his father from time to time and turned him into an unreasonable tyrant.

"Yes, but there is such a thing as extended family." replied Arpad impatiently "and that includes grandparents relations etc."

"And anyway", Akram persisted stubbornly, trying to keep his temper in control "have you met the girls?"

"There is no question of my doubting my family! They have assured me that Ishraq's daughters are passive, docile and submissive, all the qualities of a good wife! If I can accept their word, so can you! I expect complete obedience from my sons!"

"Akram, Saleem, I don't want any kind of objections from you, the decision has been made!"

Arpad was unaware of the incompatibility of Asian and western culture and how difficult it was for the younger generation that was caught up in between.

Outside, the wet grey wind was howling and shaking the half - naked trees. The leaves on them were dripping with drops of rain that shone sullenly, and the trunks of the trees became black and trickled with rain.

"Nadia, can you talk some sense into your sons?" Arpad exclaimed as his wife entered the room with a tea tray.

Nadia flinched when she saw her husband's red face. She had worked hard for things to remain within the boundaries laid down by her husband whilst at the same time trying to protect her children.

'"Now I would never have questioned my father's decision." Arpad retorted as he poured a cup of tea.

"But Father, you were not happy with your first wife, the one your father chose for you?" Akram enquired shrewdly.

"How dare you talk to me like that!" Arpad exclaimed, amazed at his son's insolence.

He had been brought up in a strict Muslim background and one of the major offences in Islam was the disobeying of parents. However Akram was right, he had not been happy with Sultana, for she had been too headstrong. Arpad had a set image of what a woman should be, and Sultana had not fitted that image.

He stood up,massaging his knee.

"Akram, don't argue with me! Ishraq is coming tomorrow, Nadia, see that they are at home!" he said angrily, slamming the door after him. .

"But what your tea…? Akram, Saleem, I think you had better agree otherwise you know your father's temper…" Nadia looked desperately at her sons.

Akram knew his mother was right, for their father would make their life hell. And Kanan was getting too difficult for him to handle. He was too tired to think rationally and felt a strange kind of resentment towards Anisha – a girl he had never met, yet who was already causing him so much grief.

****

"Although he spoke to his father, it was of no use, for he was adamant, I believe he even tried to talk to his aunt." Anisha brushed her hand across her brow.. "I need fresh air Carma."

"I hate being locked up too!" Carma cried in exasperation." I know we had our exercise yesterday but...."

"They cannot let us out because there is not enough staff to supervise out-of-cell activities. And because of staff shortage, sometimes even visits to prisons have to be cancelled or restricted."

They could hear a steady flow of talking from the cell next to theirs and a girl in the cell above was ranting and raving.

"Anisha, why is that woman screaming?" Carma asked putting her hands on her ears.

"Most probably for no reason, well they have to let their aggression somehow." Anisha replied. "Anyway, it is not relevant to the woman screaming but there was the case of this woman – I forget her name, Judy told me about her." Anisha's brows creased in an effort of remember. "Ah, yes, Sharon, her name was Sharon and she was imprisoned for murder. Sharon was a woman nobody liked, and was a "Nonce" which in prison terms means a person whose offence has made them unpopular with the other inmates."

"I would have thought that all crimes are awful, for what can be worse than murder? You were telling me about Susan and..."

"Yes, 'nonce's' are much worse, for the term covers Granny bashing and crimes against children…"

"Do you mean she..?" Carma asked in a small voice then remembered her son. "No, don't tell me Anisha, I don't want to know! Anyway, you were telling me about how your husband tried to talk to his aunt."

"Yes, yes I have, well; she is not his aunt really, but a very good friend and neighbour of theirs. She was a very lonely woman, Laverne was. I liked her for we had something in common, Carma, we both did not like my father-in-law!"

****

Chapter 16

Laverne sat by the window, a cigarette in her hand, a cup of coffee in the table. It was her favourite seat from where she could observe the activity of the outside world.

However, occasionally, hearing the 'sounds' of life outside, she longed to be amid the storm of life and like a magnet was drawn to the door. However, feminine caution kept her from stepping over the threshold and the only real friend she had was Nadia.

When Leverne saw how Nadia was being bullied she had befriended her and tried to protect her from the bullies. Prison life was an experience she too had found excruciating to the extreme and had been grateful of Nadia's company.

However, she adapted to prison life by resigning to it and had encouraged Nadia to do the same, little realising that that very attitude would make life on the outside world difficult so that when they were free, found life did not offer the eagerly expected freedom they craved and dreamt about. Difficulties they faced in prison were multiplied by the time of release, for both lacked the essential confidence needed to regain control of their life.

This was made even more difficult, when in her first week of freedom Laverne remembered the threats from her husband. Although her husband was in prison for stabbing her; she dreaded the day he would be released for his last words were etched on her mind.

"I'll get you, don't think you have escaped. Next time I'll kill you!"

She sighed as she crushed her cigarette into the ashtray, which was already full with cigarette butts. She was by nature of a nervous temperament and needed some kind of activity, for her nerves were constantly on edge since the day her husband had viciously attacked her. Even whilst he had been in prison, Laverne was terrified. He was always bragging that he could kill her anytime for he had a lot of contacts who were willing to return a favour.

That was over twenty years ago, Laverne thought as she flicked the cigarette ash, but she was still unreasonably nervous. Her husband was killed soon after his release, but it took Laverne more than a year to get over her fear of being stalked, in fact there were times when she still felt the shadow of her husband.

Nadia and she had taken a bed-sit on their release and a few weeks later Nadia had introduced Arpad to Laverne, who had taken an instant dislike to for he reminded her of her husband. When she tentatively suggested as much, Nadia had laughed.

"Leverne, you've become a cynic! Not all men are like your husband!"

After a month, to Laverne's dismay Nadia announced they were getting married and moved out.

However, their friendship was strong, and whenever there was a problem, Nadia was sure to confide in Laverne. Akram and Saleem too had become fond of her and had approached her asking for her help when the question of their marriage was brought up.

"Akram, much as I would like to help, you know I cannot for your father does not like me and as for talking to your mother, you know as well as I do that she is completely brainwashed by your dad."

Nonetheless, when had tried to talk to Nadia, but as soon as she broached the subject, was told to leave well alone.

"Laverne, I know you mean well, but you don't know Arpad as well as I do. There is nothing anyone can say or do that will change his mind."

****

"Poor Laverne, she never did have much of a life." Anisha murmured as she started to pace the cell and bumped into Carma "Carma what are you doing?"

"I can hear a lot of noise I wonder what is happening?" Carma walked to the cell door and peered out through the hole and saw an inmate being led down the corridor..

"I wonder how the families of the inmates cope." Carma mused aloud as she walked back.

"The women come into prison with their relationships fragmented anyway, and imprisonment further damages, rather than maintain any kind of outside relationship."

"Anisha, you were telling me about Sharon." When Anisha's looked vague, she explained. "Judy was telling you about her and I believe she was a 'nonce'. What did Sharon do that was so bad, Anisha? You said she hurt a child."

"Oh, I remember now, she battered it; hit it, the poor vulnerable thing."

"Was it her own…"Carma asked in a shocked voice.

"Yes, she has two children. The younger child had been crying all night long, when according to her, everything went black. She shook her child, and then flung her on the cot. Except her aim was not good, and the baby's head hit the floor and the poor baby fractured his skull and broke his leg."

"What a horrible woman! Did the baby survive the injuries? And anyway, I thought the women who would do this kind of thing were kept in a separate unit?"

"No, the baby survived, but has got long-term brain damage. And yes, they are usually kept separate for their own protection, but as time passes they somehow get filtered in the system, and as you have seen, are persecuted by the other prisoners."

"But how do the prisoners know about what she did?"

"Would you believe it, the Prison officers tell them, for they do not like 'nonce's' either. It's an indirect way of giving a go-ahead to the inmates for they usually plunge the 'nonce'---by either stabbing or something. I even heard in one case a woman was 'plunged' with a bucket of boiling water with sugar thrown in, so that her skin was ripped open and…"

Carma put her hands over her ears. "Anisha, stop! I don't want to hear any more!"

"Sorry! Tell me about your parents, were they satisfied about your husbands families background etc?"

"I have often wondered about that, Carma," Anisha answered, wiping her glistening eyes. "I think father was not very impressed with them if only he had been more cautious I would not be here today!"

****

Chapter 17

Ishraq Ali drove slowly to Arpad's house in East London and found the small house lying desolate among the semi-detachecd houses.

He parked his car and walked up the small stone and pebble driveway. He noticed the hedge was overgrown, unkempt and untidy and the garden plot was strewn with fallen leaves. The wind blew and the trees moaned as Ishraq saw a crow close his wings and clutch the topmost bough of a tree.

A black mat of leaves were lying wet and sodden and Ishraq could see occasionally one of the leaves from the trees zig zag down to the ground as if it were staggering in a dance of death. As he crunched his way through the gravel, Ishraq heard the rustle of the discarded leaves as he trod on them.

Even though they had been close friends at one time, Ishraq had not met Arpad for some time. However, Shakil, and his relations in Pakistan informed him that Arpad was a successful businessman and his sons in good professions.

He pressed the button and heard the bell purring softly in the house. As there was no answer, he pressed again until he heard the soft footsteps climbing down the staircase and Arpad opened the door with an anxious smile.

Ishraq looked at Arpad with surprise for he had changed. The confident and assured man had turned into a man with a hesitating manner, a face with faded eyes and a weak mouth. His tempo had slowed down over the years, as luck had not been as favourable to him as it had to Ishraq.

"Glad to see you, come in Ishraq." Arpad embraced his friend and led him in the house.

"It is nice to see you too." Ishraq smiled bewildered, as they walked into the house.

Ishraq looked distastefully around the room that was much smaller than their lounge. He had been told that Arpad was a successful businessman, but the furniture in the house was old and the wallpaper torn. However he consoled himself with the thought that Saleem and Akram would live with them. Arpad introduced him to his sons who were standing beside the tattered sofa.

"Ishraq, this is my eldest son Akram and my younger son Saleem."

"Glad to meet you, my sons", said Ishraq sitting reluctantly on the chair.

Nadia entered the room with a tea tray and some sweetmeats.

"And this is my wife, Nadia", said Arpad introducing his wife.

Arpad ignored Nadia and concentrated on Arpad.Once more he observed how he had changed over the years. Ishraq remembered him as being a young handsome man with a sense of humour and a keen intellect underlying his volatile temperament. However, it seemed over the years instead of enhancing these qualities; time had faded the very qualities he once admired in Arpad.

"So tell me", he said addressing himself to Akram. "What do you do?"

A disagreeable look came over Akram's face for he did not like to be questioned, However, when he saw Ishraq looking at him oddly, he smiled a cold wry smile, a smile that for one moment left a layer of ice Ishraq's heart.

However, he noticed that Saleem, had not uttered one sentence since his arrival. He seemed a man of deep silences, a man who distrusted words, as though they were a trap rather than a form of communication. But there was something even in his silence and it seemed to Ishraq that he was the kind of man who could handle silence the way other men used speech and thought him to be suitable for Azaria who also was of a quiet temperament.

"Both boys run my business with me." Arpad said quickly, noticing the look on Ishraq's face as he offered him a plate. "Come, let us have some sweetmeats to settle the arrangement!"

****

"My father did not know hat the only reason Arpad was in a hurry to settle the engagement was because he did not want Ishraq to learn about Akram's reputation" Anisha commented.

"He sounds like an awful man!" Carma was pacing the cell, for she an active and self-willed woman. "I don't know how the inmates can sleep all the time; I just want to get out in the fresh air!" Carma's eyes flashed as she looked around her.

"Take it easy, Carma, but no, not all the inmates sleep and idle their time away, there are others, like Irene, who survive prison life by fighting and rebelling all through their sentence."

"I am sure that is not possible, Anisha. I mean the prison officers are so strict." Carma looked puzzled.

"Oh yes it is, Carma, for some challenge the decisions of the authorities even though they know the result of their behaviour is punishable. They are denied privileges, kept in solitary confinement in cells stripped of furniture, do you know why? All because they feel that by rebelling they maintain an independence of spirit, an identity essential in this...."this pri...no, demoralising world of the prison!" Anisha declared.

"And they are right, Anisha. I wish I could think of something to do too. A couple of years ago, I would have, but now I think I have endured so much so quietly, that I wouldn't even know how to begin! What about the woman in the cell above ours, Anisha, she is always screaming and sounds suicidal! What is she in for?"

"Committed arson and attempted suicide, I believe, and she is supposed to be monitored by the staff. Poor thing, she is actually not a criminal, like us, but comes from a good background."

"What made her so unhappy that she first committed arson then attempted suicide?"

"Her parents were divorced when she was young but she is so sensitive that she never got over it. Even when she grew up, she had problems with relationships and did not know how to cope with life. And that goes for the majority of women here, they have either been brought up in children's homes, like Nadia, or feel rejected and misunderstood. For them the quickest way to earn money and independence is steal handbags, forge cheques or rob. Single mothers who believe that material results of crime are quicker than working within the law! Am I making sense?"

"Yes, I think I know what you mean. That whatever they do is mostly out of desperation with the direction their life is taking?

Anisha nodded her head.

"Enough of these, these….people, Anisha, you were telling me about your father. You mean he suspected your husband's mean streaks?"

"Like me, he too trusted his friend, and Akram's father made sure he did not come to know about any indiscretions of his son before the wedding! Although Akram was a frivolous and vulgar character, he was so charming! My father did not know that he was a cheat, without any notion of honesty and was deceived into believing him. Though in his own way, he did try to stall for time. Maybe he suspected? But now I have accepted the fact that whatever happened to me has always occurred to set the pattern of my life. Not a good one, I know but how I wish…" Anisha voice was muffled as she broke into tears.

****

Chapter 18

Ishraq tried to justify the delay in finalising the engagement.

"I have just recently received a letter from Pakistan. You remember my brother Shakil, you two are also good friends, well, unfortunately he has had an accident, nothing serious, but we want to postpone any festivities for the moment". Ishraq hoped this explanation would suffice.

"I am sorry, nothing serious I hope?" Arpad wondered if it was an excuse, for he too noticed how Ishraq had changed. He remembered him as being very modest and humble, but it seemed his affluence had changed him. Was it only his imagination when he saw Ishraq looking distastefully around him as he entered the house?

"No nothing serious, but Shakil was quite keen that I let you know as soon as possible. My aunt wrote the letter, in case you are wondering why he wrote to me but he has requested that you reply a.s.a.p!" Ishraq requested as he rose and said his goodbye to Akram and Saleem.

"Yes, I'll do that", replied Arpad, walking with Ishraq. He opened the door and a gust of wind rushed in, bringing rain, fierce and heavy. "Will you be alright?"

"I'll be fine," replied Ishraq unfurling his umbrella and running towards his car.

Arpad came back into the room wiping his hands.

"That went well! Nadia, can you make me another cup of tea?"

"But I thought Ishraq didn't look very pleased," Nadia remarked meekly handing Arpad a fresh cup of tea.

Arpad did not comment but finished his tea and left the room. "I'm going to close the shop", he said over his shoulder.

Saleem and Akram breathed a sigh of relief. "Gandhi", whispered Akram "It seems we have escaped, at least for the moment. Have you been praying?"

****

"My father-in law was not pleased at all with the delay!" Anisha grinned wickedly, and then brushed her hand across her brow. "Gosh, I am getting these terrible headaches and..."

"Why didn't you tell me before, shall I call Ruth?" Carma looked at her with concern.

"No, don't fuss please, , I am alright really. "

"Alright, but what are the medical conditions like in prison?" and tried to change the subject.

Suddenly, without the customary warning of keys jangling, their cell door was thrown open and the two most feared guards of the wing came charging in.

"Stand against the wall!" one of them shouted.

"If you have anything you should not have, tell us now or...!" John, the second prisoner officer said ominously. He was a bald man who regularly boasted how he had been suspended three times because of brutality towards the prisoners.

"Anisha, what is happening?" Carma looked in alarm at the officer who were standing outside, truncheons in hand.

"There is nothing to be afraid of, Carma, we have nothing to hide." Although Anisha did not feel confident but tried to reassure Carma.

"Take them away!" Anisha and Carma were taken outside and lined against the wall.

"No talking and keep your eyes to the front!" yelled the officer as he watched Anisha and Carma like a hawk.

When they were finally allowed back into their cell, they found that beds had been overturned, mattress split open and the sheets lay in a pile on the dirty cell floor. The cupboards had been opened, and what few things that were allowed to them were strewn on the floor.

"What were they looking for?" Carma asked as she began to tidy the mess.

"Nothing specific, on the other hand, because I shared the cell at one time with Lisa, they might think that I have started to deal in drugs. Anyway, why were you asking about the doctor, are you feeling alright?" Anisha forgot her anger and looked worried.

"I am fine, Anisha, I just thought if there was an emergency…"

"Yes, there is a doctor who advises on food, hygiene, working conditions, suitability of prisoners for certain types of work and asses their fitness to receive punishment. Anyway, as I was saying my father finally agreed to get Azaria and myself married as soon as possible." Anisha put her chin in her hand and stared ahead.

She was now finding it easy to express herself even though she had at one time thought they would seem ridiculous. Now it was as if she, who had kept silent for long, could not wait to unburden herself.

****

Chapter 19

Azaria was listening to music when her mother walked in.

"Azaria, where is Anisha? Hasn't she returned from her college?" She asked angrily as she entered the room.

Shahnaz came from a rural district n South Pakistan and felt that obligations, values, traditions etc were a reflection of home culture and the upkeep of these norms and values were important to her. Although she felt she was tied as a slave to society – its impulses and expectations, she was wise enough to observe the changes in the current moral and social values, so different from Pakistan. Although she knew they were beyond her control, like her husband she wanted to shield her daughters from them. The sooner they got married …!

Azaria was thinking of a suitable reply when the doorbell rang.

"Ah, I think she mentioned she might be a little late, ah, there she is now", she said jumping up and running downstairs.

"Where have you been?" she whispered as she opened the door. "Mum's angry and you better have a good reason – she is upstairs in our room waiting for you!"

Anisha entered with a sheepish grin on her face, whilst Azaria looked at her impatiently.

"I'll tell you everything later, I have to go see Dad first". Before Azaria could tell her that he was not feeling well and most probably fast asleep, Anisha vanished.

Anisha knocked on her father's door and when she heard a feeble 'come in' entered the room.

"Anisha, where have you been? Azaria came to tell me that you were late and…." Ishraq looked angrily at his daughter.

"Sorry, Dad,", Anisha replied meekly, "I'm afraid our class was delayed as we had to stay back to complete an assignment."

Ishraq felt he was not strict enough with his daughters and lived with the constant fear that any unconventional behaviour on their part would almost certainly precipitate a great deal of critical comment from his community. Most people in his community were not liberal – for the villages they came from were still the focal point of reference.

"Have you seen your mother?" he asked , running his fingers through his receding hair.

"I'll go to her at once... Good-night Father." Anisha replied noticing how haggard her father looked..

"Mum, why does Father look so worried?" Anisha asked anxiously, entering her room.

"Don't worry about your father, why are you late?" Shahnaz exclaimed sharply glancing at her daughter.

Anisha looked sheepish yet defiant. She was 20 years old and could not understand why her parents did not allow her to go out on her own, yet was expected to take a prominent part in social and religious gatherings of the community!

She wanted to state firmly she wanted to go out when she liked, take part in activities and wear fashionable clothes. She longed for the freedom her friends in college enjoyed. True, they were not of her community but... Consequently she was beginning to challenge what she saw as repressiveness of her parents.

"You know I'm always home on time", she replied defiantly. "To-day we had to stay late and anyway I'm old enough. All my other friends can stay late." she murmured under her breadth.

"What did you say?!"

Her daughters never answered back and the lack of understanding of why Anisha did so today was evident in the tightening of Shahnaz's lips. She raised her voice slightly and Anisha and Azaria could sense the underlying anger in her voice.

"Nothing", Anisha muttered timidly.

"We have set rules in this house, Anisha, and we expect you to follow them!" Shahnaz said, adjusting the dupatta on her head, "There better not be a next time or else..!" On that ominous tone she left the room.

****

"It really is a shame when parents do not understand their children." Carma remarked as her forehead creased in perplexity.

She put her hands over her ears as an inmate screamed. She heard running of feet and the jangling of keys. As Carma went to the cell door and looked out she saw a prison officer escorting an inmate out of her cell.

" OMG ! Where are they taking Irene?"

"Most probably to the punishment block called a strip cell." When she saw Carma's puzzled face she continued. "A cell that is dirty, smelly, with no furniture, a mattress on the floor with nothing, absolutely nothing to do."

"Doesn't sound very different to our cells...." Carma remarked belligerently.

"At least we are let out for exercise and fresh air!" Anisha's laughter rippled in the air. "Granted it is not for long or as often as we are entitled to, but at least it is something to look forward to."

"Why is she being taken there?" Carma asked, once again experiencing again the inhumane aspects of prison life.

"She must have broken some rule, though I personally would prefer it if the officers put me on remission."

"Anisha, I am afraid I am being very tiresome, but what is remission?"

"When the release date is postponed by 7/14 days, and is usually the result of breach of prison discipline. It is usually for trivial offences like disobeying the prison officer etc."

"Hmm........doesn't sound too bad to me."

"Believe me when you have been locked for a long time, each day towards release in counted."

"No way can one make it up? Like good behaviour or something?"

"Apparently one can apply to the board of visitors to get the time 'back' and if the inmate has not been in trouble for six months, I think. I am not sure."

"Anisha, tell me about your conversation with Azaria." Carma was uncomfortable talking about prison for a length of time.

****

Chapter 20

Anisha took out the pins from her bun and her dark hair tumbled on her shoulders in layered curls

"Whew, that was close. But why were you late anyway? I have a lot to tell you".

."Now, what do you have to tell me?" Azaria asked sitting on the bed.

Anisha had changed into her pink pyjamas suit, and with her thick short dark curls, looked pretty as she made herself comfortable on the bed.

"You know Father went to meet Uncle Arpad today?"

"Did he now?" asked Azaria, putting a pillow behind her head, "So what about it?"

"Don't you remember?" Anisha exclaimed in exasperation "He is fixing our marriages to his sons. Anyway, he told them that nothing could take place at the moment because Uncle Shakil is ill or something like that! Anyway, the marriage is on hold, so to speak."

"Not if mother has anything to do with it"! Azaria muttered." Anyway we are not that close to Uncle Shakil, so what....!?"

"Father has explained the joint system to us so many times that I am quite fed up! Time and time he has tried to explain although we live in London, there are different types of joint families - one branch being even though we do not pool our incomes, all major decisions relating to finance, ceremony performance and marriages etc are supposed to be taken jointly!"

"One can't but hear him, Anisha, but I always thought he was just trying to instil some 'traditional values' in us?" Azaria looked thoughtful.

Anisha was gazing out of the window, for they had not drawn the curtains, and saw a fly crawling up the pane. Gazing out into the colourless black night, under a sky that appeared drained of all warmth Anisha felt miserable and life seemed bleak. The sky looked vast and deep, making her feel small and insignificant. It was so big and distant, yet so close that its eerie beauty filled her with a strange sense of foreboding.

The air seemed specially confining and tyrannical in the bedroom, like a mantle of despair, and Anisha wondered where her destiny was taking her. She felt as if she was waiting, marking time on the brink of a future – yet on the other side, there was so much unknown that Anisha thought it preferable to wait rather than the discovery. She heard a plane growling high above in the heavens and thought about Badal.

"I am fed up of the whole charade!" exclaimed Anisha, "Our parents have beliefs and values that do not stem from religion, as they claim, but are only just a matter of conventions which have little meaning outside the village they come from!"

"And I believe Arpad uncle believes in the joint family system too. That means we will be suffocated for the rest of our lives!"

"You are right, Azaria, because I have learnt that within joint family, especially for a woman, mind you, roles are defined. Granted that there is something to be said for common goals, and whatever the system, no importance would be placed on developing the personal identity of a woman!" Anisha's face lost its usual constraint and her eyes shone with passion.

"I don't know, Anisha, maybe we should agree, mainly because I have heard that the reason arranged marriages are less likely to fail is because they are based on sounder foundations than love marriages. Anyway, I think we better go to sleep now," said Azaria, fluffing up the pillow and yawning "Can you switch off the light please?"

Anisha switched of the light and climbed back into bed.

"Good-night, Azaria." Anisha murmured as she turned on side.

As she could not sleep, her thoughts turned to the women of her community and how they depended wholly on their husband till their identity finally became a shadow of his personality. And her last thought, as she finally drifted off to sleep was that she did not want to become one of them.

****

"But that is exactly what happened, Carma! Although both Azaria and myself were apprehensive about the family we were going into, the only reason I wanted to speak to Azaria was because I needed to talk to her about this friend of mine who…" Anisha looked thoughtfully around her.

They had finally been let out for exercise yard, and after shuffling around for some time Carma and Anisha decided to sit on the bench whilst the prison officers stood nearby smirking and looking pompous.

A scruffy looking girl came up to Anisha.

"My name is Margaret and I'm in for burglary!" she announced proudly as she puffed her cigarette. "I 'ad a collection of guns, you know." She winked at Anisha.   "Bitch!' she shouted at an inmate passing them. "I 'ate 'er!" she said scathingly to Carma before she went to another group of women.

"Nobody likes Margaret for she is sullen, snappy and rude to everyone." Anisha explained. "Whenever she is in the room, the atmosphere becomes unbearably strained, and she is usually greeted by an onslaught of insults."

"Do yu wantta buy some crack, luv?" A woman from another wing came up to Carma, who quickly shook her head Anisha had told her about inmates who tried to force drugs on innocent women to convert them as drug users.

"Whew! That was close." Anisha said as the woman walked away with a 'please yerself'.

As soon as they were back in the cell, Anisha walked back to the cell door and glimpsed the blank corridor with locked doors. She could not see any prison officers, for as the inmates were isolated in their cell, so the staff on the wing was isolated.

"You wanted your sister's advice about this friend of yours? Did you finally manage to talk to her?"

"Yes, though I wish I had not for it just precipitated matters." Anisha gulped. "You know, I was terribly worried about Father's health, but it was Azaria who managed slyly to increase his wrath. I did not sleep well that night, and Morning came slowly, for the sun did not leap with a laugh with the first kiss of dawn, but slowly and quietly, as if afraid, took its time to show itself!"

"I did not know yu were a poet too!" Carma chuckled

****

<u>Chapter 21</u>

Anisha woke in the morning to find Azaria lying with her hands under her head, staring dreamily at the ceiling. As soon as she saw that she was awake, propped up on her elbow, for she had wanted to tell her last evening about Badal, but Azaria seemed so excited.

Badal was a boy in her college whom she had known for a year. They met regularly for either a coffee or, as they both liked Pizza, would often saunter down the pizza shop. Anisha liked him for he was a handsome man and they both shared a similar liking for music and humour.

But yesterday Badal had taken her by surprise. She was about to bite into a steaming hot, melting with cheese Pizza when Badal had looked deep into her eyes, held her hand and proposed to her.

"Badal, what do you mean…"?Anisha looked at Badal with confusion and tears in her eyes.

A little winsome but wistful smile hovered on her lips, for she was mesmerised by her romance, but suddenly reality and hard cold facts subdued her and destroyed her rose-coloured world.

She had not told Badal about her arranged marriage for, not only had she thought that Badal was not serious, but also because she was content to live in the present. Anisha looked sadly at Badal, then had a fleeting thought that maybe they could mould their destiny.

'Maybe if Badal is strong enough to face all the obstacles that two people of diverse backgrounds face, there could be a happy outcome to all this?'

But although she hoped of a happy outcome for herself, she was also wise enough to realise that whilst the concept of tolerance was universal the practice of it was not.

In the beginning, she had tried to distant herself from Badal, tried to protect herself for fear of rejection and loss, but Badal always somehow managed to charm her. Now, when she thought her heart was ready to break, she wished she was strong, for whilst her emotional self believed in the reality of love, her clear intelligent self knew this was idealism.

Little did she know that Badal had only proposed to her in defiance, for his father too was arranging to get him married to his friend's daughter from the same caste. Badal did not like to be forced and had talked bravely to his father against caste discrimination and arranged marriages.

"Don't answer now, but promise you will think about it? If you want I will talk to your father." Badal said half-heartedly as he left the restaurant.

Anisha had been left dazed and bewildered. She needed to talk to Azaria, for the present she wanted to hope, wanted Azaria to give her the hope and encouragement in whatever was destined – for she was not strong. Yesterday, she had felt confused again, for her parent's had thrown cultural and tradition at her.

"Azaria", Anisha raised her voice tentatively, "there is something on which I want your advice on".

Azaria was in the bathroom when she stuck her head out of the door. "What! Anisha, you mean you actually want my advice? Since when have you listened to me?"" she smiles as she walked back into the room. She smiled but became serious when she saw her sister's grim face.

"Will it take long?" Azaria asked for she wanted to go shopping.

"I think so, Azaria, and it would make a lot of difference to me." Anisha replied.

"In that case, why don't you come with me to town and we can talk over a cup of coffee? As you are so fond of coffee I want you to try the try the coffee at this café I recently discovered. It is absolutely heavenly!"

Anisha agreed and they decided to go into town together after breakfast and left Shahnaz sewing and Ishraq Ali dozing over his newspaper.

It had ceased to rain and there was a pale yellow shimmer of sunlight brightening up some tree leaves nearby, which Anisha thought looked like small ripe lemons ready for plucking. They drove silently to the café.

"Don't talk to me until I have had coffee, Anisha, I am absolutely parched!" Azaria's tongue darted out to moisten her lips.

"But I want to...." Anisha remarked impatiently.

As soon as they had ordered and the waiter had bought the coffee, Azaria took a sip then looked at Anisha.

"Sorry, Anisha…. now you can tell me what is bothering you." said Azaria, holding the steaming hot cup in her hands.

"Azaria, now I don't know where to begin!" answered Anisha replied in a confused voice...

Her fingers curled around the cup, meeting so her nails pressed into her flesh, and she flinched with pain. She tried to think of reasons to be silent; at the same time feeling she needed to talk, for she wanted Azaria to dictate her obligations and duties to her.

Yet, on the other hand, she started to consider the fact that maybe she should be silent, for there could never be any future for Badal and her, it was hopeless and Azaria would not understand, maybe she would understand…. maybe…. But when Anisha looked at her sister, her eyes filled with an honesty and courage that had taken her a month to find.

"What mischief have you got yourself into?" Azaria looked at her sister with irritation, an expression that Anisha, in her naivety neglected to see. "As usual I am sure it is nothing of importance anyway", she muttered quietly, but not before Anisha heard her remark.

"I have not got myself into any mischief, and it is important!" Anisha replied indignantly.

Her face lost the petulant look and a streak of rebelliousness showed on her face for a moment, as she marvelled yet again why it was that nobody took her seriously.

She felt even the sky was jesting at her as dark clouds passed swiftly overhead, leaving the sky clear again. But after a short while the clouds reappeared again, spreading their darkness and gloom around her.

"Well, I have been going out for lunch, but not alone".

"That's understandable," replied Azaria looking impatiently at her watch. "Anisha, trust you to make a mountain out of a molehill! I hate eating alone too, and anyway, that's what friends are for...to go out for a nice meal! Nothing like it, I assure you!"

"Yes Badal is a good friend. We have been seeing each other for nearly a year and..."

After Anisha finished her coffee she felt she had nothing to do; her hand now had nowhere to go. They fell ineffectually into her lap, onto and around the empty cup, to her hair and then back to her lap.

<u>Chapter 22</u>

Azaria looked at her in astonishment, then said sarcastically " Maybe you should have left it a bit later, till maybe the day of your wedding that father is arranging? However, if he is a nice boy from a nice family and from our caste, father would have no objection. But tell me more about him."

"He is not from our caste, Azaria, his name is Badal and he is in my college also studying law. We have only been meeting for a year, it was not serious, but yesterday he asked me to marry him and …Do you know who I mean?" asked Anisha.

Anisha did not realise that her confession, however mild only served to ease her conscience. However, she felt emotionally empty, did not have a thudding heart, the dryness in her throat was gone and a heavy calm settled over her.

"Yes, I have seen him," Azaria said dryly as she signalled to the waiter for more coffee.

"Badal always told me that his parents were also arranging a match for him. You see, before yesterday, I had no not hope he would actually ask me to marry me and dared not cling to a dream that I could not put into affect …! But now..!" ?"

Anisha thought that her life, before she had met Badal, had been grey without any rainbows to brighten her days, and hers had been a lonely life, filled mostly with books, music and dreams. She looked wistful and dreamy.

"Anyway, I believe in love the same way that I believe only in goodness for the sake of rightness, which is beautiful, you know, like a perfect flower, a starry night, or something like that!"

And in spite of the evidence of her impending fate with Akram, she began to think of a happier outcome for herself and hope and fear changed places in her mind.

Azaria looked perplexed and worried as she saw the waiter approaching with a fresh pot of coffee. "This is all very confusing; Anisha..." was the only thing she could think of to say. "But if his parents are looking for a match for him why is he suggesting marriage?"

Anisha waited till the waiter had gone, but avoided answering Azaria's question "Anyway, the arrangement with Arpad Uncle's sons might never materialise and his wife is English so..."

"Anisha, don't be silly! She has converted to his religion, and is more religious than, I'm sure Badal is." Azaria said quietly, but seeing Anisha's downcast face quickly added. "Have you asked if he would be willing to change to our religion? And if he really loves you he will do so. And you still have not told me how he proposed to you when his parents want him to get married to somebody of their choice."

"I know, I know", cried Anisha impatiently, "but tell me, for that is an arranged marriage, like ours, could it be that he really loves me?"

Anisha wondered what she wanted Azaria to say... was it encouragement, hope or that she should remind her of her duties and obligations which would imprison her?

When she saw her mother relationship with her father, Anisha thought everybody was in some sort of prison and that only by by accepting one's imprisonment could one ever hope to become the caretaker in one's own home?

"How would I know if he loves you?" Azaria snapped. "But I think you love Badal, don't you?"

Azari had seen Badal in college and thought him to be a good-looking man, and resented the fact that Anisha was a friend of his. Lately she had started having an increasing animosity towards Anisha, however, her guilt over this emotion, when it hit her, was so fierce that Azaria trembled and always had to envelop her arms around her to keep her frosty conscience from overwhelming her

"Of course I do! Or at least I think I do!" Anisha exclaimed reluctantly, as if the defenceless emotion she showed left her more vulnerable than she liked. "Azaria, I know exactly where I stand, I just needed somebody to talk to, you don't know what torture it has been for me. Our marriage is being arranged with a stranger, and I feel I am being suppressed under a stupid custom and law which is shaping an event for me, one which I do not like and that which I have no hand in! It's not fair!"

"I know...but there is nothing we can do about it..."

Azaria looked impatiantly at her watch – had it really been two hours since they had been talking?

"Why can't social conducts be based on consultation and co-operation instead on being imposed on one? I wish I could..." Anisha said in a frustrated tone of voice.

"I think we better leave, Anisha, for I am feeling quite sick with al the cups of coffee I have had. I don't think I want to see another cup of coffee again!"

"Maybe we should...Azaria thanks for talking to me."

Anisha followed quietly, knowing that even if she tried, it would not be an easy thing for a girl in her position to step outside the boundaries laid down by society and culture.

****

"Yes, it had been nice to talk to Azaria, at least at that time I felt I was not alone, but as to your question, no, she did not give me any advice, for we left soon after."

They could hear a murmur of voices from the cell next to theirs. Carma looked at Anisha, who looked frail and pale. Carma's heart clenched with compassion for this small and young girl who was beginning to stand tall in her eyes.

"It seems that Sue is having a parole report read. I hope they have recommended her for release." Anisha replied in a small voice.

"What is parole?" Carma looked confused.

"Parole is when some prisoners are released under supervision of probation officers before their normal release date. They are assessed during, mind you Carma, I am not absolutely sure, but I think during the first three years of the sentence. Does that make sense? Sorry, Carma, am I boring you?"

"Not at all, Anisha. You mean I can hope that I will be able to meet my son?" Carma smiled softly.

As she spoke of her son Anisha saw a living woman take shape from a dead one, for Carma's face had become alive and her eyes had grown bright.

"Yes, but mind you the decision for parole is influenced by not only the gravity of the original crime, prison record, and conduct in prison but also whether the inmate has a place to go to. Though I think the prison service does help one in finding a place, hostel or something. Anyway, I am sure it is good news for you, but not for me, for I have nowhere to go, and of course no one to turn to".

"Anisha, there must be someone out there for you?" there was pity in Carma's eyes as she looked at her friend.

For a moment Anisha thought tenderly of Badal and wished he would wait for her, however, she also realised that waqs impossible.

"For me that does not sound bad at all, for I had given up hope of ever being free again! That'll show…!" Carma's eyes flashed with suppressed anger.

"I don't know about you, Carma, but how would you like to spend the rest of your life looking over your shoulder? For the licence can be revoked and an inmate can be recalled at any time, not only if the ex-inmate committed another offence, but even if her general behaviour caused concern She would then have to work her way through release all over again!"

"No, not very pleasant, I think, after all. I am tired Anisha, and am going to sleep. Well that is to say, I will try, for I don't think I can sleep in all noise."

"Good-night, Carma, I think I have been boring you and..." Anisha saw Carma lying still and decided to go to sleep but instead lay awake thinking about Badal.

She wished now she had listened to her heart, but although she had wanted to believe desperately in the truth of Badal's love, she realised in her heart he had not really loved her. However, for the present she needed to pretend that she could go back to him in the future. She began to blame Azaria, and thought everything would have been alright if only Azaria had been...had not been...if only...but then thought that it was maybe herself who had not been so, so.....naïve?

****

Chapter 23

Azaria parked her car in the driveway and they walked back across the balding grass and the concrete path towards their home.

They found Shahnaz still darning and their father his Saturday nap, and seeing them looking peaceful ..

"Ah, there you are!" Shahnaz looked up from her sewing. "Where have you been all this time?"

"Mother, we just went into town, why do you worry so much? It is not good for health!" Anisha's laughter rippled in the air as she hugged her mother. "Was there anything you required? Sorry, we kind of rushed off!"

"No, thanks for asking, but your Arpad uncle called. They wanted to visit.". Shannaz said curtly.

"I didn't know they were coming today. I'm sure we would have been here had we know, isn't it, Anisha?" Azaria smiled at Anisha, who looked confused at Azaria's behaviour.

"However, your father has invited them, with family, for tea next week, your father will speak to you about it later" continued Shahnaz.

Anisha noticed how her mother blind obedience made her personality into a shadow of her husband's. She was wise enough to admire it, but did not want to draw strength from it as her defiant nature thought such compliance to be contemptible.

'I will never be like that!' she vowed again as her lips tightened.

Shanaz saw the thoughtful look on her eldest daughter's face. "Lunch is ready; your father is waiting for you at the table."

Anisha and Azaria seated themselves on the table and poured hot cups of tea their mother had prepared for them and helped themselves to hot stuffed chapattis that were on the table.

"Yum"m said Anisha, biting into her chapatti that had been fried on a hotplate with margarine and added some hot chilli pickle on her plate. Both of them loved these stuffed and fried rotis, which could also be filled with mince, mashed potato or cauliflower.

"Absolutely delicious", agreed Azaria "Mum you are the best cook. I wish I could cook like this." she added wistfully.

Shahnaz smiled, looking pleased, and although she thought her daughters rebellious, knew they were basically kind and upright girls. However, she worried more about Anisha, who she felt had an affectionate and unrestrained disposition that should be controlled.

"Mum", Anisha said, handing her a plate. "Why aren't you eating? Aren't you hungry?"

"No…Of course, thank you, Anisha",

Shahnaz was not hungry, but as she did not want to worry her daughter, made an attempt to eat. She usually got up early in the morning, and by the time said her prayer and prepared the breakfast, was already tired – that reminded her - she must keep that appointment with the doctor.

"Father," said Azaria, finishing her breakfast. "Can I talk to you? It won't take long and…."

Anisha was puzzled by her sister's attitude and hoped she would not tell her father about Badal – then shook her head for she believed and trusted Azaria would respect her wishes.

****

"You know, Carma, I really trusted my sister, and when I confided in her, thought she would respect them, but she made them so…so…cheap!" Anisha shuddered and put her head across her brow, for she felt one of those excruciating headaches coming.

Not only was Anisha enduring her headaches silently, but also was also suffering increasingly from nightmares that kept her awake.

She felt the prison was like a hospital, where there was always some kind of movement of people walking and talking. There were the footsteps of the prison officers, their coughing and talking, for they did not bother to keep their voices down, as if they did not care whether the prisoner slept or not. But it was not only the officers and Staff that were loud, for the worst offenders against the silence of night-time were the inmates themselves.

Although it was not allowed, girls would call to each other through the window or cell doors and hold conversations of unbelievable trivialities, which carried on through the night.

However, these noises Anisha felt to be quite compared to the noises of the morning, when there was the ceaseless traffic of police cars, the occasional ambulance and people, officers, the governor, solicitors, social workers, psychiatrists and doctors and of course the appointed time visitors.

It was a sultry and stormy night, and after some time, Anisha got up and went under the window . There was no rain, but lightening was playing across the sky.

Unfortunately for her, it was John who was on duty that night and when he shone a torch in the cell, noticed Anisha standing by the window.

"Hey you! What are you doing out of bed? Get back at once!" he yelled.

"I can't sleep here, there is too much noise!" Anisha snapped irritably, but regretted it, for she knew that the incidence would be recorded on her fileso quickly added,. "Maybe you are right, I will try to sleep."

As Anisha tossed and turned, she noticed a number of small black shapes and suddenly sat up. From the light outside, she could see black shapes swarming in the cell and her spine crawled as she saw the cockroaches.

"Carma, help!" Anisha screamed as several of the cockroaches darted at her bed, she quickly picked up her slipper and hurled it at them.

"Anisha, are you alright?" Carma was wide-awake but also gave a scream when she saw the insects crawling around the cell. "Ugh! What the…"

"What's fuckin wrong with yer? I wanna sleep." Mandy yelled.

"We have got cockroaches in our cell and…"

"So bloody what? We 'ave 'em in our cell too. Just bloody keep quite, they 'r' just fuckin cockroaches, they 'r' not gonna eat yu."

"I am sorry to wake you, Carma, Mandy is right; it is just that I am frightened of creepy crawlies and…anyway, goodnight."

"I am too, Anisha, I hope they go away….Yukkk…" Carma shivered.

"I hope so too." Anisha fidgeted for her skin was still crawling.

As the night progressed, some of the inmates became more and more volatile screaming occasional obscenities at the prison officers.

As Anisha tried to sleep in the sordid surroundings, her mind like always, lingered dangerously in the dark recesses of guilt and remorse. She wished again that she had objected forcibly to her father regarding her wedding to Akram, had not confided in Azaria…..

****

Chapter 24

Ishraq was reading the newspaper when Azaria entered and sat on the chair beside him, her eyes darting around the room whilst she bit her nails.

"Azaria, you know we are trying to arrange a marriage a match for you and your sister?"

"Yes, I am aware of it, for Anisha told me".

"How come Anisha knows, for we have not mentioned it to her."

"Dad, she is not the sweet innocent child that you all think. " Azaria said deviously." Anyway, I think before you go ahead and finalise arrangements, you should know something about Anisha".

"What has she done now?" Ishrak smiled tolerantly.

Azaria explained the situation between Anisha and Badal then watched her father warily waiting for the expected explosion.

However, her devious mission accomplished, she wanted to leave the room, but did not dare because she was convinced her knees would buckle. Making an exit with dignity would look like a wobbly display of weakness and that would be showing her to be like Anisha, a perfect victim – trusting, loyal and forgiving!

"And that rascal thinks he is going to marry my daughter?" spluttered Ishraq. "Anisha, come here at once!"

Anisha had been standing nearby and entered the room meekly. As soon as she saw the furrows on her father's face, his tight concentrated frown and tight lips, she knew that Azaria had told him about Badal. Althgouh, he looked in control of his temper, howver Anisha knew that it would not be long before it exploded…..

"Er, I will leave you two to sort out…."

With an effort Azaria arose and left the room leaving Anisha seething with anger and frustration. "What disgrace are you bringing on my family?" Ishraq thundered and there was an ugly vehemence behind his words. His face became red and his neck cords stood out "I'd rather see you dead than…!"

In anger Ishraq was a fearsome sight and Anisha's frightened large eyes peeped at him from under her thick lashes. Her face looked as if it had been coloured thickly with smudges of red from a palette of fear and anger as she felt her father's cold presence. However, she was not as frightened of her father's wrath as disappointed and angry with Azaria.

"Father, please, I can explain, it is not what you think…! He's asked me to marry him and…." pleaded Anisha.

"Anisha, I am disappointed in you!" Ishraq roared.

Ishraq's clenched fists were held firmly against his thighs whilst his eyes burnt like glowing hot coals as the anger behind them blazed.

"I do not want to hear any of your excuses! From today you are not to leave the house and if you do, you will be accompanied by your sister or

Mother. Meanwhile, I'll telephone Arpad and persuade him to hasten the wedding!"

He walked out of the door, slamming the door behind him. Anisha followed him miserably – her father was going to keep her a prisoner in her own home!

Azaria had been waiting eagerly outside the door and went up to Anisha.

"I'm sorry, Anisha, I did not mean to tell him it …….. One minute we were talking of our wedding and the next….!" Azaria sounded contrite.

"What's the point of saying sorry now? He has only brought our wedding date forward and till then threatened that I do not leave the house, except with you or Mother! Azaria, why did you have to tell him? Nothing was going to come of it anyway. I only told you because I needed someone to talk to and you belittled our friendship …!"

"I am sorry, but the problems might not be as awful as you think, you know." Azaria put her arms around Anisha. "I am sure you will get used to your new life with Akram, and maybe even like it, for you know time heals all wounds."

"I doubt it," Anisha replied, wondering why it was that no one understood her.

Badal had seemed to be the only one who understood her and now even this relationship was being misunderstood! For a second she was tempted to run away from home and was filled with conflicting emotions – to follow her heart or relinquish her head? But it seemed she had not been given a choice, but an ultimatum.

"Mother said Akram and Saleem will be coming for tea soon, and oh, I forgot to tell you that Badal phoned and wants to see you urgently."

Badal had told her that he had no desire to meet Anisha, but only wanted Azaria to tell her that his proposal was made in error. However, Azaria had somehow persuaded him to meet Anisha personally to explain, her only objective being to witness Anisha's humiliation.

"You'll have to come anyway" replied Anisha bitterly. "Remember, I can't go out of the house alone!"

However, she had faith in Badal, and was confident that he would find a solution to her dilemma.

****

"I did not know it at that time, but there was always an ulterior motive to Azaria's suggestions." Anisha said bitterly.

"Anisha, all this talking about Azaria is not good for you. Tell me why is Mandy so depressed and irritable these days?" Carma asked folding her blanket to the prison requirement.

"Apparently her mother is suffering from cancer, otherwise she wouldn't have shouted at us last night."

"Oh that is sad! But thank God the cockroaches have gone, Anisha, I was afraid to put my feet on the floor in the morning!"

"Only to come back, Carma, for they are quite common. Anyway, Carma, I like talking to you, lightens my burden, you know last night I could not sleep and that is when it hit me! I knew what the problem with my marriage had been. I wanted a stable relationship, and that made Akram wary and suspicious, for he did not want any kind of relationship!"

"I somehow can't believe that, Anisha, you are such an affectionate girl. But what makes you think that he felt like that?"

"Azaria told me; She knew how I felt, and told Saleem, who in turn told Akram, who in turn taunted me with it!" Anisha's eyes were bright with tears.

A piercing bell began ringing; there was the sound of jangling of keys and a rushing of feet, for the bell was used to summon the prison officers to the scene of the offence.

Carma rushed to look through the latch to see a flashing light and water leaking out of the Irene's cell, which was opposite to theirs. Irene had purposely left the tap open and water was overflowing and seeping its way into the passage, for. Irene's cell door was flung open, and she was dragged out.

"Anisha, I think Irene has flooded her cell. But you know something; I admire her for even whilst she is being attacked by the officers, she manages to look arrogant and proud. I don't know why she does it though."

"She feels she is rebelling and has disrupted the prison regime." Anisha said quietly

"What's going to happen to her?"

"She will be taken to the 'strip cell', the punishment block that I told you about."

Although Anisha was confiding in Carma, she did not reveal details about Badal except for the fact that he was 'a special boy in her college.'

She was disappointed by his betrayal, but the good memories with him were all that she had, and those Anisha wanted to treasure.

****

Chapter 25

Badal was sitting idly in the chair, and as he blew the two perfect smoke rings, thought that the smoke evaporating in the thin air was akin to his time with Anisha. He crushed the cigarette butt into the ashtray and looked at his watch impatiently, wondering how he had let himself be persuaded by Azaria to meet Anisha.

Badal was just going to leave when he saw Anisha with another girl.

"Hi, I am sorry we got held up in the traffic." Anisha smiled at Badal and her face became alive and her dark eyes shone. "Badal, I want you to meet my sister Azaria. And Azaria, Badal!" Even though she laughed gaily, her eyes were troubled.

"Hi Anisha, did you get my message?"

"Hello, and yes I got your message that is why I am here!"

"Hi." Azaria stealthily sat on the empty chair beside Badal.

She had forgotten how handsome he was, with his curly black hair and twinkling eyes. He was wearing a dazzling white shirt, burgundy tie and dark slacks that set of his looks and charming manner.

"I am starving, shall I order a Pizza?" Anisha enquired in her charming manner.

"Not for me", replied Badal "I have an important class I must attend, so I only have a short time to be with you but... Has Azaria explained to you?" he asked abruptly as his eyes glittered with indignation.

Anisha looked puzzled"What do you mean …?"

"Yes there was something we wanted to talk to you about. Anisha I explained about your conversation with father and……no.. I won't have a Pizza but I would like some coffee". Azaria replied, feeling embarrassed.

"You told him about father! Azaria how could you!"

Azaria called the the waiter and gave him the order, but saw that Badal was standing impatiently.

"Azaria, I presume you have told her?" Badal asked rudely, all pretence of politeness and an attempt to control his resentment cast aside.

"No, I thought you should tell her yourself." Azaria could not wait to see Anisha's reaction.

"Yesterday I asked you to marry me, but as I explained to you on the phone my father…!" Badal began.

"Sorry, you were saying..?" Anisha finished her Pizza and licked her fingers. "Yum…Yumy! The pizza is absolutely deliciously. Anyway, Badal, as to the marriage you're parents are arranging, I was hoping that would not materialise, and now…." She gazed at Badal through the haze of her eyelashes, trust shining in her eyes as she moved her head to one side and asked innocently, "Badal, will you talk to father and explain?"

Badal looked flabbergasted. "Anisha, didn't Azaria tell you that I proposed to you without thinking, and maybe you should listen to your parents and…"

"No she did not and it was only yesterday that you asked....? Azaria?"

Anisha's face dropped for this was the second time that Azaria had let her down. She would not have come to see Badal. Had she known....!

The weather outside had worsened considerably. There was a clapping of thunder and the wind pounded savagely against the restaurant windows, followed by flashes of lightening. The wailing drafts of wind somehow found their way in the restaurant, and Anisha felt they were ridiculing such a thing as human refuge, and she shivered, both with cold and from a sense of foreboding.

"I am sorry but I simply must attend this class and...Look, I am sorry, but I must go now. Goodbye, Anisha.it was nice knowing you and..."

Anisha watched Badal's receding figure in astonishment. To think that for him she had endured her father's wrath and been willing to give up everything, and he was not even bothered to spend an hour with her!

Azaria looked thoughtfully at her cup then shrewdly looked up "Anisha, I think you had better forget him."

"Azaria, I thought he really cared." Anisha said in a heart-rending voice,

Badal's departure had marked her like a scar and she burned hot then cold in astonishment and felt the accelerated beat of her pulse. However, she tried to justify Badal's behaviour.

Suddenly Anisha smiled like some nun refusing to admit that violence and cruelty really existed in the world that God had created. Her good nature was incapable of facing and admitting the existence of evil in others, especially people she loved. .

"No, I think he does still care, Azaria, I think that was all an act".

"Anisha, be reasonable. Don't you think that he would have stayed longer if he really cared? He comes from a wealthy family of a different caste and his parents are looking for a match for him. For God's sake, Anisha, grow up, his father has refused, he has not even told you once he loves you and…do you want me to go on?"

Anisha had tears in her eyes for she knew there was logic in what Azaria said, but truth always has a sting in it.

Although her face looked serene, only her hands, which had clenched into fists, betrayed her repressed emotion, as she pressed them in prayer fashion.

It appeared the past would remain just a past – not become a reality as she had hoped. However, the quiet defiance that had permitted Anisha to withstand rejection, the solid determination to make something of her life, her belief in herself that enabled her to be beaten yet shed no tears, slowly began to reassert itself. Her jaw stiffened and tilted stubbornly.

"Maybe his class was very important. It is the last year and ..." Anisha said pathetically.

"I think we better go home now." Azaria rose from the chair looking jubilant.

Anisha got up slowly and stood with both hands on the back of the chair, fingers gripping so hard that her knuckles were white.

She followed Azaria out of the restaurant; feeling hurt and realising this particular chapter in her life was already written and closed, making sad readings with its chapters of tragic incidents and resented the smothering rules of fate that were dictating her kismet..

But being a positive girl she thought when she married Akram she would have no psychological tangles to confuse her, no memories to shadow their association.

****

'How wrong I was in believing and trusting everybody!' Anisha remarked.

She was feeling miserable for a prison officer had just told them that their daily exercise was cancelled.

"Don't worry, Anisha, even I am guilty of that, but tell me are there many prison offences that I should be aware of?"

"There are only about twenty-two, I think."Anisha replied bitterly. "They range from being violent to an officer to using foul and abusive language."

"So how come all the women use foul language?"

"Only amongst themselves, anyway the vague wording of the offences listed is misinterpreted and covers almost everything that a prison officer does not like. And I once believed that he/they were…"

"Anisha, what are you talking about now?" Carma looked confused.

"Sorry, my mind went back to Azaria and it suddenly occurred to me how naïve I was!" completely overwhelmed, Anisha broke into tears, as she thought of Azaria, Badal and Sunetra. "Carma, I feel we, being women, are fought over like a piece of meat by men, subjected to intolerable pressure and….'

"….and this attitude of men is supported by society that ignores the true identity of woman, who as a result suffer voicelessly." Carma completed, reminded of her aunt.

"I wonder what the reason for that is." Anisha wondered aloud "I think maybe because normally media is silent, deforms or trivialises women's issues. Most women, like my mother, gosh why am I going so far, even myself and I think you too, Carma, are constantly trying to fit in the mode of the male fabrication of femininity. Men like Akram and your husband." Anisha said bitterly.

"Yes, women need to speak out more to make people aware of the issues surrounding the infrastructure of our society."

"That would be quite difficult, speaking for myself, for even after I discovered Akram's meanness, his dishonesties and deceits, and felt my soul shatter into a thousand pieces, I kept quite, not having the courage to leave him. Whereas the friend I had pinned my hopes on, why, I realised that to him our relationship had meant nothing at all!"

****

Chapter 26

Badal drove slowly in his car, for the rain was pouring down, splashing out in wings from the car and running like silver jewels along the rims of the windows. The windscreen wiper was wet and swinging like a pendulum.

He had decided to miss college and pulled into the driveway of their house just as his father was getting into his car. Dilip Mittle saw and waved to his son.

"Hi, dad", Badal smiled, unfurling his umbrella and walking over to his father's car. "Are you going to work?"

"And weren't you supposed to be at college?" Dilip Mittle smiled at his only son affectionately. "Badal", what are your plans for this afternoon?"

"Nothing", replied Badal "I had planned to watch the cricket on T.V"

"That sounds to me a bit boring for such a nice afternoon. Would you like to come with me?"

"Cricket is not boring!" Badal replied indignantly. "But since it is a lovely afternoon, I will accompany you. Are you sure that I will not be in the way of your work?"

"No, of course not, come get in, and I will explain." said Dilip, opening the door of his car.

Dilip reversed the car onto the road. "Actually, I am going to see my friend – the one I have been talking to you about". He turned his head to see his son's reaction.

"You mean your friend Mr. Malik?" Badal asked.

He recalled that Mr Malik was Sunetra's father. Although he was not prepared to get into any more entanglements at present, the thought of marrying the only daughter of a rich father crossed his mind for wealth to Badal was very important. "Is he the father of the girl that you ...Will she be at home?" he asked.

"No," answered his father, parking his car outside a bungalow. "They are not expecting you, but I am sure Yogi will be delighted to meet you."

"How come we have not met before?" said Badal, assuming that 'Yogi' was a short name for Yogindra, which he knew to be the first name of Mr Malik. "Especially as you are such good friends.

"He has been living out of London and has just recently moved here", replied his father, opening the car door.

The rain, which had been pouring steadily, was coming down in torrents and Yogindra's house looked a fort surrounded by a grey-churning moat.

Yogindra had seen their car and came out to meet them with an umbrella, smiling, a boisterous man of about Dilip's age with small beady eyes and white sparkling teeth. He was a small businessman with one jewellery shop, however, with the help of his future son-in-law, was looking to expand his business.

"Namaste, Yogi", Dilip smiled and greeted his friend with folded hands. "This is my son, Badal".

"Namaste, Uncleji," Badal folded his hands, noticing Yogindra's receding hairline and the nicotine stains on his fingers.

"Delighted to meet you, my son", Mr Malik bellowed clapping him on the shoulder, startling Badal "Come in, come in, Indu too will be delighted to meet you."

"Indu, Dilip is here with Badal", he shouted, and as they entered a woman came out of what Badal presumed to be the kitchen.

"Namaste, Dilip Bhai Sahib, Badal, Beta, welcome. "Indu was a meek and timid woman who had once been beautiful.

"Indu, we'll be the sitting room, bring us some tea, I think my friend is thirsty!" Yogi clapped Dilip on the shoulder as Indu turned and went back into the kitchen quietly.

"So Yogi, how business these days?" he asked, sitting on the sofa.

"You know how it is," replied Yogindra "I am looking to buy another shop, but Indu does not want me to expand. Women, they think we have nothing to do but stay at home with them!" However he looked unhappy. "According to her responsibilities will increase, as you know, staffs these days are not very reliable, Sunetra is busy at college, but I am hoping that with my son-in-law I will be able to expand my business." He laughed heartily and clapped Badal on the shoulder.

Indu entered with a tray of tea and a plate of sweetmeats.

"How is Samidha Bhabi?" she asked, placing the tray on the table."I was looking forward to meeting her."

Yogindra glared at her.

"She is well", Said Dilip, taking the cup from her. "You know how she is, she doesn't go anywhere with me. Anyway, I hope you have not forgotten we are expecting you for dinner next week with Sunetra? She won't by any chance be home now, will she?"

"As a matter of fact, she is. She came back early from college and will be delighted to meet you. Indu, can you call her, Indu?"

Badal in the meantime was engrossed in his thoughts for after breaking off with Anisha, he had a definite image of what he would like his future wife to be like.

Being a product of western education he felt he needed an enlightened woman, one who would be educated and attuned with the latest fashions, at the same time to the Hindu ways – yet whose role would be primarily in the home. For his entire liberated outlook, Badal expected his wife to be old fashioned and subordinate.

****

Carma distracted Anisha from her thoughts. "I think we have to go get our breakfast. Anisha, are you feeling alright?"

"I am feeling fine." Anisha wiped the tears from her eyes as she recalled Badal's engagement to Sunetra. "I was looking out of the window at the dreary courtyard, and saw the solitary tree in the middle. Carma, I was thinking that that tree is so much like me, so alone." Her voice choked.

"Hey, hey, Anisha, this is not like you. You are the one who is always giving me strength. Look, here is the trolley, let us get our breakfast. I am sure that today too, we will not be let out for exercise, and you can tell me a little more about yourself. The truth is I find your life fascinating! I don't know about you, but I always feel better after I have made somebody else cry!"

"I hope I never do that, Carma, I would never hurt you!" Anisha looked at Carma in alarm.

"I was only joking, Anisha, now I don't know about you, but I am hungry and want my breakfast!'

Anisha and Carma carried their tray, which consisted of two toasts each and one mug of tea back to the cell.

"The tea is awful, as usual. Well, it is just hot water, but I think I am going to enjoy it, for it has been a long night." Anisha took a sip from her mug and grimaced.

"'ve yer 'eard about Judy?" Anisha heard Mandy shouting. 'tell yer what, she's fucking hyperactive, that one!"

"What's she in for this time? Wit' 'er it's usually dope innit?"

"Nah, she ain't got no one on the outside, so when she feels it, she come 'ere for three meals a day!"

"'Ey Mandy, 'ows yer mother? Wen' yu goin 'ome?"

"I ain't goin', yu fuckin idiot! The screws say I can't go 'ome to see 'er. The fuckin bastards!"

The shouting continued and finally ended by Mandy shouting obscenities at everybody.

"Who's Judy? Anisha isn't she the girl you introduced to me at the exercise yard?"

"You remember her, Carma? I myself am not very good with faces, a very embarrassing habit, I must say."

"I have a bad memory too, Anisha, I only remember her because I noticed her pale cheeks were flushed and there was a frightened restlessness in her eyes. I gather from their conversation that it is not her first time here?"

"She has been to prison many times, but she told me the other day that each time is like the first."

"And is she in for drugs?"

Anisha nodded and looked at Carma in surprise. "How do you know, Carma?"

"Apart from the fact that the women have just relayed the fact around the prison, I saw her cheeks were flushed and her eyes were bright. But I meant to ask you, you were telling me about Lisa and how she was a dealer, I cannot understand how the drugs get into prison without the prison officers detecting them?"

"Lisa told me when she was sober, for she was stoned most of the time! Anyway, she told me that one method of getting drugs into prison was by swallowing them! She also told me its disadvantage, for if any of the staff hears or suspects an inmate of having swallowed drugs, the officer has the authority to segregate the woman in the hospital wing and wait until it came out the other end! Another foolproof method Lisa told me about was that as the staffs are not allowed to search the inmate internally without prior permission from the Home Office, it can be bought internally…you catch my drift? That is called 'crutching' and then there is also what is called 'joey' that is when the visitors bring it with them. Anyway, Carma, should you ever decide that you wish to take them…" Anisha chuckled and her eyes danced, for whilst Carma coloured her sorrow with silence, Anisha's temperament was of colouring it with laughter and light-heartedness.

"Anisha, shut up! I am just beginning to feel the influence of corrupting convicts, the easy availability of drugs and the sharing of criminal activities in a prison where one should be protected, and I don't like it at all!" there were tears in Carma's eyes.

"I am sorry, Carma, I thought I would cheer you up. Seriously, though, even some of the prison officers are tolerant towards prisoners using drugs, in fact they are even known to have passed it around for according to them smoking keeps the level of tension down."

"But I'll remember you're offer, Anisha, for I have just realised, I might need drugs to get me through prison life. I have only been here a few days and... Anyway, I heard you tossing and turning last night, were your memories haunting you, as usual, or was it your headache keeping you awake?" Carma asked with concern, for the two women had formed a bonding friendship and alliance.

'Both, no, three, not forgetting all the noise! But actually, I was thinking to the girl that my friend got eventually got engaged to. She was supposed to be beautiful."

****

<u>Chapter 27</u>

Badal looked up quickly as he heard a soft yet nervous voice, and looked into a pair of soft brown eyes that were big, almond shaped and heavy with thick lashes. Sunetra had thick brown hair, and in the pink suit that she wore, looked beautiful."

"Namaste, Uncleji",

"Dilip, this is my daughter Sunetra". Yogindra looked with pride at his daughter.

"Hello, Beti" Dilip beamed at her, rising from the divan to pat her on the head, looking delighted. "This is my son Badal".

Badal looked at Sunetra with surprise, started to speak then ran his fingers through his hair. "Hi", he managed at last, grinning.

Sunetra stared at Badal, willing her body to stop quivering for she liked Badal with his dark curly hair and twinkling eyes.

She sat down, palms itchy with nervous tension, and willed herself to keep her gaze steady, to regain her self-control and talk to Badal with self-confidence. She inhaled deeply and forced herself to smile.

However, after her first pleasant impression of Badal she had changed her opinion, for she was an extremely sensitive girl. Although Badal appeared charming and handsome, she sensed ruthlessness, and at the same time a weakness in his character. Moreover, she did not want to get married at present, for not only did she want to finish her studies, but was also involved with somebody else.

Nevertheless her father had been insistent and she realised that the only reason he wanted the marriage was so that his son-in-law would help further his business.

Yogindra noticed the look that passed between the Sunetra and Badal and decided to leave them alone.

"Dilip", he said turning to his friend and winking. "Can you come out with me to the greenhouse? I want your advice on some gardening."

"Gladly", Dilip replied, following Yogindra out to the garden, feeling cheerful.

It had stopped raining, but armies of clouds were still marching in ranks across the sky that was heavily laden. They sat in an uncomfortable silence for ten minutes before Badal had the courage to speak

"Your father tells me that you go to college?" he enquired.

"Yes, but this is my last year, thank God" Sunetra smiled faintly.

They sat in silence for a couple of minutes and Sunetra looked relieved when she saw her father and Dilip walk through the patio door.

"Thank you for the advice, it was invaluable! If it had not been for the rain, I would have liked to show you something I am experimenting on. " Yogindra's voice boomed across the room. He glanced at Sunetra and Badal with satisfaction.

"Maybe next time, but how do find the time? Anyway, I think we better leave, it is getting late and Samidha will be waiting."

The qualities Dilip looked for in a daughter-in-law were the opposite to his wife and Sunetra, he felt, was just the kind of daughter-in-law he had in mind.

She appeared chaste, dutiful and tended to be respectful to her parents, and Yogindra had told him that she had a strong sense of family. This though, applied to most Indian girls throughout the social spectrum, but, to Dilip, it was not only the grace of wife for his son, or the style of the wedding, but about the wider consequences of conformity by his daughter-in-law that was important

"Thank you again for the lovely tea". Dilip said folding his hands together.

"Sunetra, we will see you all next week, my wife is looking forward to meeting you and" he smiled and winked at Yogindra. "Yogi, come early!"

"We'd look forward to that." Yogindra grinned knowingly.

"And give our regards to your mother", he said to Badal as he climbed into the car.

As they drove off, Badal looked quietly out of the window and decided he would tell his father about Anisha even though there was no reason to.

Dilip drove his car thoughtfully, as Badal looked pre-occupied. He sensed his son's insecurity and wondered if it had anything to do with Sunetra.

"What did you think of Sunetra?" He asked concentrating on his driving. "I thought she was beautiful and soft-spoken."

"Yes...very" Badal answered absently.

They walked across the lawn towards their house, a lawn that was grassy and still clogged with decayed and wet leaves, both deep in their thoughts.

Dilip threw the keys on the table, knowing that Samidha as usual would be at one of her kitty parties. He had become accustomed to an empty house – a quiet house and no affectionate and warm woman to welcome him.

However, in the first months of marriage, he had thought he had crushed Samidha's ego and instilled in her the kind of obedience he demanded.

But Samidha was not the seemingly self-involved, selfish woman that she appeared, but rather than submit to his controlling behaviour and row in front of her son, she chose to stay out of Dilip's way, his constant nagging and criticisms. She did not want to be a self-sacrificing, suffering woman nor did she want her life to be dominated by the need to serve her husband's overbearing ego Samidha had even contemplated a divorce, but knew that Dilip would not agreee, for the values of tradition and male dominance were predominant in him and his family.

She had expected him to be kind and considerate, but, gradually accepted the fact that their relationship was headed for disappointment. There was a gap between what she wanted and what Dilip could offer, and so felt doomed to an insecure relationship, until finally she felt he only provided her with little more than a form and a name for her existence.

However, her marriage provided her with a certain amount of security, till finally she felt that she needed him only as a backdrop to her daily activities. She loved her son, but she could not be much of a mother to him because she was too wrapped up in the solution for her distress.

Consequently, the only person who really suffered was Badal, who grew up amid the icy warmth of a disillusioned and indifferent mother. Although Badal had become accustomed to his mother's absence, hurt, disappointment and a sense of abandonment punctuated his childhood experiences. He remembered the lonely birthdays of the past, the pain of growing up alone, with a procession of nannies for company, for his father had always been busy with his business.

As soon as they entered the kitchen, Dilip put the kettle to boil and took two mugs from the cabinet unit.

"Dad, can I talk to you? It is nothing important but..." Badal pulled up a chair and sat at the kitchen table.

"There is nothing better in life than spending quality time with my son over a cup of my special tea!" he brought the mugs of tea, hot and sweet over to the table and sat down. "Now what is bothering you? Has it anything to do with Sunetra?" he asked.

He handed the mug of tea to Badal, but although he was smiling, a look of seriousness furrowed Dilip's brow.

"Dad, there is this girl I know, Anisha and her father Ishraq who~"Badal explained about Anisha and her father.

He had just given Anisha's family details when suddenly Dilip got up in anger and placed both hands on the table.

He gripped the edge of the table hard, the skin spanned tightly over his knuckles and the veins in his temple pressed out against his skin as he worked his jaw.

"You mean to tell me that you had an affair then proposed to a girl is not from our caste?!" He bellowed.

He was a Brahmin and a firm believer in the caste system – a system that according to him established a man's destiny at birth by either being born to riches or being condemned to a hell on earth. Judgements had been handed down by destiny – and who was Badal to change them?

"Badal, you have just told me that you like Sunetra, and they are willing so why do you want to give up everything for this…this….I strongly advice you to forget everything about her." Dilip's voice rang loud and the fury in his eyes transfixed Badal into silence. "I understand, Badal, you are young, therefore eager to love and be loved, and to make life exciting and full before you are mature enough to accept emotional responsibilities".

"Dad, you did not let me finish. All I said was that there was a girl who I had been keen about, but I have already told her it is off and the proposal was a misunderstanding. You have nothing to worry about on that score. I only told you because I needed to talk and…"

"Badal, why didn't you say so in the beginning? "Dilip smiled suddenly and clapped Badal on the shoulder.

"You're right, father," Badal smiled as he answered, for his love for Anisaha was fast becoming a memory, a memory without any heat or emotion.

The thunder rolled and lightening cracked as the rain beat on the windows whilst lightening flashed every few seconds.

****

"You know, Carma, his had been indecisive loves, without strong commitment, like the frail fluttering of a moth's wing's beating at a candle flame" Anisha remarked as they were taken out for exercise. They were heading for the bench when Anisha saw Radha crying.

"Radha, are you feeling alright?" Anisha hurriedly went over to her.

"Y...yes..I...I'm fine." Radha floundered as she reached put her hand on her flushed cheek and then blurted. "No, Anisha, it is my husband, he…" Radha could not speak for she had started crying.

"Take your time, Radha, what has he done now?"

"He came to see me, and as usual was taunting me that he is going to send my son to his relatives in India!"

"And that is not what you want, Radha? Maybe that is for the best, from what I know of you husband, I don't think he could look after anybody but himself." Anisha retorted angrily. "At least he will not involve your son in the drug business."

"You're right, Anisha, but wherever my son is, he cannot escape that stigma of my being in prison sand…we all know that the speed of innocence is much slower than the suspicion of guilt." Radha gave a sob, got up from the bench and started walking around aimlessly whilst a group of women nearby jeered and taunted her.

"Poor thing!" Carma had tears in her eyes for she had been listening intently. "I wish she was in our wing, does she have a friend who she can talk to?"

"No, I think not, just makes me grateful that I have someone to talk to!"

"No, I don't believe she does, and that is why I am afraid for her, Carma, she is such a nice person. It is at times like these that I think there is no God, no just God that is to say. Anyway, did I tell you how glad I am that I am sharing the cell with you?" Anisha said shyly.

"Believe me, Anisha, so am I, I really do not know what I would have done if it had been somebody else" Carma smiled.

"Carma, not only am I glad, but you are also therapeutic for me!" Anisha laughed and Carma noticed how it transformed her face. "It is nice not to have to think of what the future holds, or the present for the matter! I don't know about you but when I am talking to you, I forget the prison and its atmosphere. But having said that, I hope I am not boring you with my life history?"

"Of course you're not, Anisha, it is surprising, though, how our lives are similar, well not exactly for I was born and brought up in India."

"You mean you too…?" Anisha looked at Carma with guilt. "And here I am only talking about myself."

"Please, Anisha, don't feel guilty. Listening to you takes my mind of my own problems, for I too, have had my fair share of deceits and betrayals. They are still fresh in my mind and it hurts to talk about them. The pain is beginning to subside though. Anyway, you were telling me about Azaria."

"Carma, I think I am fonder of you than I ever was of her!" Anisha smiled sweetly."Yes, I was, and after speaking to her, I accepted where my duty lay, not that I had a choice,my but she never missed a chance to remind me of what I could have had. You know, something like the prison officers do, dangle it in front of me like a carrot, than snatch it away, just so she could witness my hurt and revel in it."

****

Chapter 28

Anisha went to her room miserably and immediately switched on music. In music, she always felt she could lose herself to the real world and float somewhere on a cloud and be instantly transported to another world.

Azaria furtively followed her into the room, put on her night suit and sat on the bed. "I think we need to talk"

"No we don't, Azaria, so just let's drop it."

Anisha was in no mood to talk about Badal She was too young to have a protective shield so had no had no armour against the terrible loneliness that was beginning to engulf her.

However she could not be sad for long and soon her optimisim took over and she smiled.

"Okay, so lets talk except there is nothing to talk about! I have accepted the fact he does not love me, maybe never did. Now tell me what else is happening?" Anisha smiled, her buoyant personality sweeping away the shadows and intangible worries.

She had had something beautiful with Badal, however temporary, and she wanted to keep that special time like a flower that she could press into the pages of her memory even though she regretted the emotional chasm he left in her mind.

"I have been to see father and mother." Azaria glanced at Anisha.

"And? We do live in the same house, you know!" Anisha chuckled.

It was amazing how life went on, how one could live without knowing what was around the corner, find something to smile about, laugh about even though the mind was in a daze, a place that had become numb and distant – dying crying, yearning and full of sorrow. She had had a naïve trust in kismet, that it would deal her happiness.

"Anisha!" Azaria retorted in exasperation "when will you grow up? There is a time and place for everything, and humour at this time is not one of them! What I was saying was that Father is not well. You know the Doctor has told us that he should be careful and avoid any shocks or pressure?"

Anisha looked thoughtfully at her sister thinking ruefully that her concern for their father was a little superficial as it was she who told him about Badal.

Anisha, on the other hand, loved her parents with an unconditional love, the kind of love that did not have to be earned and one that was never eradicted. She would never do anything to hurt them, although there had been a moment when she wanted to run away from them. Now felt she could not live with herself knowing she had hurt or been the cause of their sorrow in any way.

"You are right, Azaria," she announced aloud "To-morrow I will tell father that I will marry Akram."

"Oh, right." Azaria looked at her in amazement, envious of her sister's courage..

****

"When you needed support, all you got was harassment and betrayal! Oh, I wish she would stop screaming!" Carma put her hands over her ears, and then ran quickly to peep out through the cell latch.

As the screaming continued, Carma looked worriedly at Anisha. "Why isn't anybody coming to see how she is? She sounds terrible; it is not fair she should be left alone!"

"It took me a long time to get used to it too." Anisha replied. "But I have come to understand that the prison officers know that there are only a few of the inmates with genuine psychotic tendencies. Even though Mary is genuinely in need of psychiatric care, the others, like Emma, only scream to disrupt the running of the prison, and as the prison officers do not want to give them the satisfaction of thinking that they have upset the prison routine, they always ignore them."

"But what if she genuinely is in need of help?"

"I doubt it, for it has become a habit with her, anyway, I hope not, Carma." Anisha smiled weakly, a smile that did nothing to betray her feelings of disappointment and frustration.

"But tell me, what did Akram feel? I know you said he did not want to get married to you but…"

"The marriage only came about because of he was trying to escape from one of his girlfriend's"

"Anisha, what do you mean, he was involved with somebody else? How do you know?"

"Azaria told me." Anisha replied bitterly. "She told me many times about Akram's so called 'Flings'!"

****

<u>Chapter 29</u>

Arpad was getting ready to go to his shop and Nadia was bound for the kitchen when Saleem entered the house.

"Saleem, would you like a cup of tea?"

"No, thanks", he replied, as he sat on the sofa.

"Don't you have anything to do?" asked Arpad testily.

Akram came into the room and brushed the sofa with his hand before sitting beside Saleem on a sofa covered with a coarse fabric.

"Gandhi, I hope you remember that we are going to see a film today?"

The only reason Akram wanted to get out of the house was so that he could meet Kanan, his ex-girlfriend, for she had texted him saying she wanted to meet him urgently. He was hoping she was going to tell him that she finally accepted the fact that their relationship, such as it was, was over.

"You're not going anywhere, Akram!" Arpad thundered "your mother wants you to go the shop with her!"

"Dad...we've have wanted to see this movie since long and..."

Akram rubbed his forehead in perplexity. Frustration darkened his eyes and a raging temper started to engage a war inside him.

Arpad rose to leave.

"I don't want to hear any excuses....now don't forget we are going to your uncle Ishraq tomorrow" he shouted over his shoulder.

He pulled open the front door and slammed it so hard behind him the dishes on the kitchen shelves started rattling.

"Gandhi, it seems we will have to leave the film for the moment."

Saleem had been tapping his fingertips on the chair restlessly before he stood up abrubtly and went to the window. He looked out thoughtfully, then stood listening to the rain that beat a frantic tattoo on the window glass which, he felt matched the rhythm of his heart. Rivulets of water that must had sluiced down the roof tops was running down the windows

"Gandhi, don't worry, everything will turn out just fine, you look so….." Akram looked at his brother with affection.

His eyes, that could be cold and hard, warmed and deepened with affection unexpectedly. His mouth, which was a firm line and could straighten like ice, now curved with charm. He made a sound and the muscles near his thin lips moved spasmodically hovering between a smirk, laugh and a groan.

"Akram, you don't understand," Saleem wished his brother would stop calling him Gandhi. He did not feel particularly great and did not feel that he did the name any justice."

"Are you ready?" Nadia entered the room patting her hair.

"We do not have a choice, do we?" Akram grumbled getting up from the chair. "Come on Gandhi let's go!"

"And don't speak to me like that!" Nadia said sharply. "You're not doing me a favour. If you're not happy helping your family then…., Oh all right, go on, I'll manage."

Akram smiled at her receding figure. "Come on, Saleem, let's go, we'll be late". He said impatiently then decided to tell Saleem about Kanan.

"And what am I supposed to do in the meanwhile?" Saleem asked. "I was quite looking forward to the film".

"There's no reason why you should not go" Akram replied "It's just that we will be outside in the café outside the cinema hall, where we agreed to meet. Apparently she wants to talk to me about something. But just so that Dad or Mum ask, I was there with you at the cinema!"

As they walked out of the room, locking the door behind them Saleem wondered if Kanan was the girl Akram had been violent towards.

****

Anisha thought again about Kanan and tried to sweep the cobwebs of the present into oblivion. She was fast becoming trapped in a time warp where her present predicament was fading into insignificance compared to the reconstruction of the past.

She had always confronted her problems lightly and with laughter, but at night, shut in the cell, there was nothing to stop thinking until sleep came, but even the she had nightmares, which were often worse than the thoughts that preceded them.

At 6.30 in the morning the electric bell was rung to wake all the inmates, but Anisha had learnt to ignore the consistent ringing of the bell. She lay in bed, listened to the ocean of life in prison surging around her, sensing the wrought woes of deprivation, trembling drums of calamity and the ceaseless strand of sorrow and despair. By 7 they had been checked twice, once by the night officer going off duty and once by the officer coming in; presumably to make sure everyone were still alive on the premises.

As soon as the cell doors were unlocked, all the prisoners made a rush for the washrooms. After breakfast they were locked in their cells again in order to make their beds, scrub the floor and clean their cells.

Carma stripped her bed, neatly folded her blanket according to requirement, and then sat quietly, biting her nails, her expression moody and melancholy.

She was not used to any kind of work, even though she had discovered that she was willing of doing jobs that would have at one time revolted her.

"Do you mean that the …the prison officers actually expect us to scrub the cell floor?" she asked, her eyes smouldering with anger.

"These floors are clean, Carma." Anisha said sullenly, "they don't need a scrubbing brush. I think they only tell make us clean to make us feel our rank; anyway, we are in remand. I think it is used not only as a form of punishment, but gives the prison officers another area of control and an excuse for implementing discipline."

"You know, Anisha, I don't think scrubbing the floor is a kind of remedy, anyway, I cannot though for the life of me understand how 'scrubbing the floor' provides relief from boredom and respite from tense relationships with staff and other prisoners. And what I don't understand is how the cockroaches got in our cell; I think our cell is the cleanest!"

Carma looked around her and her eyes smouldered with anger. "I think you are right, all they want is to be under their control!"

"However hard we try, basically this is a dirty and sordid prison and there is a complete absence of cleanliness and order. The landings are filthy with stale mouldy food littering the floor. And when we go for exercise I have noticed the dustbins overflowing with rubbish and the windows! The windows are something else for they are so dirty one cannot see through them! Some of the prisoners even mentioned that the cockroaches were put in by the prison officers themselves!" Anisha's gaze wandered around the cell.

"Maybe we should ask for a transfer, Anisha."

"Carma, you forget there is no such thing as what we want. I have seen a large number of inmates being transferred at a moment's notice either to a new wing or to another prison. Friendships that have been built over months are instantly terminated. Prisoners are transferred without being given a reason, and this transfer is called 'ghosting' and rather than go through the pain of losing friends, most women chose not to be close to anyone. Anyway, I don't know if that would apply to remand prisoners."

"Enough of the prisons, Anisha, tell me you are such a nice and sweet girl, was your husband violent towards you from the beginning? Surely the first few months must have been happy?" Carma asked folding her blanket.

"Not even then, for Azaria told me early on thaat apart from his flings, there had been another girl involved in his life, well more serious than the others at least. Her name was Kanan."

Carma looked at Anisha in alarm. "And pray how did Azaria know?"

"Apparently Saleem told her, and she in turn told me. I confronted Akram with it, and instead of denying it, he said if it had not been for her, he would not married me at all!" Anisha exclaimed .

"But most men are involved at one stage of their life with some woman, Anisha, why did you take it so much to heart?"

"Carma, you don't understand, I actually sympathise with the Kanan, the woman he had the affair with. My husband was a monster, for Azaria told me what he had done, actually she revelled in telling me, time and again. How could he be so cruel" Anisha looked so trusting and naïve that Carma felt that it must indeed have been an evil man to hurt someone so sweet and innocent.

****

Chapter 30

"Kanan, what did you want to see me about?" Akram asked Kanan as soon they were in the restaurant.

"Let us order first", Kanan"s smile was small and weary as she walked to a table and pulled out a chair, looking pale and unhappy.

Akram impatiently ordered and as soon as the coffee arrived, inquired curtly. "Now what was so urgent, I thought we had decided not to meet again?"

Although he smiled warmly, his cold eyes and harsh face diffused the warmth.

Kanan, who was sipping her coffee, looked at him and shuddered. However she had always been fascinated by Akram's ability to speak cruelly with the same ease as he offered tenderness. As she looked into his eyes she thought that even the cold wind coming from a frozen lake would have more warmth and wondered why she was bothering to ask him for help.

"Akram, it's about my brothers, they have found out about us and…"

"What! You had assured me that they would never find out!" Akram was frightened, for he and the whole neighbourhood feared Kanan's elder brothers, who were involved in many illegal activities. However, they were also very religious and protective about their younger sister.

"Anyway we are not going out now, so I do not know what their problem is."

.Akram's looked at her callously as his hands clamped down on Kanan's wrist. An icy cold chill ran down Kanan's spine and her flesh crawled as Akram's fingers touched her skin.

"That is what I tried to explain to them, but they still feel that you should marry me and…"Kanan looked at Akram beseechingly.

"You know I do not want to marry you!" Akram spoke sharply and furiously. The savagery in his voice frightened Kanan, who knew that Akram was capable of untold violence.

"They say they will force you to marry me. Actually, Akram, the reason they are insisting is because they have found out that I am pregnant!" Kanan blurted as her eyes, which had grown enormous, dilated with shame and fear.

Akram looked horrified and sat motionless, except for his thoughts, which were spinning around, rebelling at what he thought was the unfairness of the situation. All he had wanted was a good time – he did not want to marry Kanan – and a baby? Christ.

Nevertheless, he was afraid of her brothers and what they were capable of. He had heard of honour killings in Pakistan, where he knew these customs were still prevalent, but in London? Why couldn't Kanan have gone to a doctor like other women and sorted out the problem? After all, it was just as much her fault!

Meanwhile, as Kanan saw the flitting expressions of disgust and fear on Akram's face, the colour drained from her face, leaving it paler than ever and an anguished sick fear rose in her.

She looked white and sat frozen, for she had been hoping Akram would help her, even though in her heart, this was the reaction Kanan expected. She put her head in her hands so that Akram could not see that she was crying.

Kanan had had a lonely childhood, her only companions, were of daydreams, for she had been allowed no liberties, no friends, whilst her brothers could do whatever they liked. She had longed for intimacy and closeness with her parents, but was hurt when she was constantly rebuffed.

Although Kanan was a dutiful girl, she was servile only because she thought it to be the only way she could guard herself against hurt. For any kind of rebellion against her parents would have brought not only physical abuse but the kind that lasted longer and went deeper, the anguish of feeling her parent's injustice, so she had the only thing under the circumstance.....she had withdrawn emotionally.

She had been happy when she met Akram for he had been the only person who had shown her affection, even though it had been for selfish reasons and only for a short time, and in the end even he had rejected her! But Akram was not the only person who abused her trust, and Kanan always thought it strange that even though she had tolerated injustice for so long, when she did have a choice, she should not have fallen prey to injustice yet again.

So caught up was she in the memories of fear her family invoked in her, that she was oblivious of the strange expression on Akram's face – an expression of such loathing that his skin was flushed. His teeth were clenched so hard that a muscle had begun to twitch in his jaw.

As Kanan looked at his scowling face she realised she did not want to marry him anymore than he did.

"Akram, I don't want to marry you either." Kanan echoed, quietly, for she was aware of Akram's false ego. "However, I think will have to run away from home, for I am afraid my brothers will kill me!"

"Kanan! Don't be silly, I am sure your paents will come around!"

Akram had no intention of interfering with what he considered to be a domestic quarrel and felt under no obligation to help. He dismissed Kanan's relationship with a shrug and attempted a smile, but underneath the smile, Kanan could detect his single-minded ruthlessness.

"I have tried to talk to father, but he will do whatever they say. As for my mother..." She sighed wearily.

Akram looked impatiently at his watch, and as Kanan looked at his face her pale face flickered like a weak candle against the strong wind of Akram's indifference, yet she jerked her head up with a proud and defiant gesture.

She pushed her chair and stood up, her eyes no longer clouded with the uncertainty or fear.."Never mind! I'll find a solution somehow!" Kanan said bitterly." I do not know how, but I will try!"

Despite her brave words, Kanan was petrified of her brothers. "I am sorry to have bothered you." she said quietly and vanished.

Akram looked after her in surprise, his expression changing from disbelief to puzzlement then to anger. He had expected Kanan to beg and grovel, but she had gone with dignity.

At the same time Saleem entered and approached Akram, a frown on his face.

"What's wrong with Kanan? I just saw her leave with tears streaming down her cheeks."

"She had to leave, some problem at home," Akram stated. "Sit down, Saleem, I don't know about you, but I would like another cup of coffee."

There were lines etched on Akram's face as he tried to figure out an answer to his problem, for he realised that Kanan's brothers were like loaded guns with a broken safety catch. Maybe the only solution to his dilemma was that he wed Anisha as soon as possible?

"And so have we", Saleem finished his coffee. "Don't forget we are going to see those two dreadful girls tomorrow."

"I was thinking maybe we should take our time and think about the arrangement." Akram remarked paying the waiter.

"You have changed your attitude! Was it Kanan who changed your mind?" asked a speechless Saleem.

"It's nothing to do with her." Akram was still shaking and instead of making an effort to put on gloves, tucked his hands into his pocket for they felt cold. "How was the movie?"

"Oh... anyway, the movie was good, I will tell you all about it as we walk home."

Saleem narrated the general outline of the film and they walked in a thoughtful silence behind a gang of youths who were slouching along, idly occupied with nothing, often silent, talking now and then in boisterous tones on subject of brief interest.

Akram and Saleem walked the rest of the way silently each speculating what the morrow would bring.

****

"Poor Kanan!" Carma had tears in her eyes. "Whatever happened to her?"

"I don't think you would want to know!" Anisha replied bitterly. It was visiting time in the prison and the inmates were led out for visits.

Both Anisha and Carma looked wistful as they heard the jangling of key rings and the banging of cell doors which were opened to let the inmates outside. Even though both knew that the other did not get visitors, they avoided mentioning the fact, although Ruth had asked them if they would like to have a volunteer visit them.

"All things taken into account, the prison service does try and look after an inmate's needs!" Anisha added. "Gosh, I would like a cup of tea."

"The trolley should be here soon, but Anisha, you were telling me that your husband only married you to escape from his girl-friend's brothers? He told you himself?" Carma asked in astonishment.

"Oh yes! He even told Azaria and they both, in their own different way, taunted me with it." Anisha replied sadly. "They came to see us the following day, the tragic day when his problem was solved and mine began! But then, Carma, I don't think his problem was really solved, for what he dreaded did eventually happen to him, only it was me and not Kanan's brothers' that killed him."

"Anisha, don't blame yourself. It was an accident, and from what you have told me, I think he deserved it."

"No man deserves to die, Carma, I still remember the first time I saw him, I was quite impressed, you know."

Anisha wiped her burning eyes then lifted her head as if trying to breathe in pure air, not the polluted air of the prison.

****

Chapter 31

The following day, daybreak came reluctantly with a shiver and Saleem saw great masses of grey rounded clouds sailing in a stately fashion in the sky. At times he could detect the sun, who he thought was playing hide and seek as it would sometimes push its way out of the clouds, and then as if it was sulking, hide behind another cloud.

"Saleem! Hurry up!" shouted Akram "We're late."

"Coming, coming," replied Saleem breathlessly.

As he entered the lounge he was tucking his shirt into his trousers and combing his hair.

Saleem was dreading visiting Ishraq Ali's house, but was amazed at the transformation in Akram's attitude, for he had virtually agreed to the wedding. As Saleem sat silently in the car, he felt Akram seemed tense, however, he was always high-strung, and Saleem had always attributed his psychological tension as a result of a clash between their domestic, cultural traditions and those of western society.

Once more the sun had buried itself somewhere behind grey laden clouds that were being pushed by the wind. However, this time the sun remained behind the clouds, and when the grey sky finally opened up, there was a torrent of rain, which began beating in a steady beat against the windscreen like tiny drums gone mad.

Ishraq was waiting outside their door when Arpad and his family drove up.

"Arpad!" he beamed at them, walking over to the car and unfurling an umbrella. "It's nice to finally meet your sons! Saleem Akram, how are you?"

They went into the lounge where Shahnaz was waiting with tea and sweetmeats.

"Shahnaz, I suggest that you leave the room as soon as you have served tea." Ishraq had told her earlier.

"No, I will not!" She had replied vehemently, for felt her sons needed her at this juncture of their life.

Shahnaz had tolerated been treated like a servant by her husband for the sake of her children. She did not realise that the only reason she did that was because then she would no longer be responsible for self – for being servile was easy, but to be accountable for the self was frightening for it could mean failing and rejection.

So, like a nun, Shahnaz put a veil over her face, which symbolised a sign that she no longer existed for self, but was a slave.

Arpad and Ishraq sat in the corner of the room reminiscing about the old days, whilst Akram and Saleem looked around the room.

After fifteen minutes Anisha and Azaria entered the room and Ishraq rose to introduce his daughters.

"Ah, Anisha, Azaria, let me introduce you to your Uncle Arpad, Akram and Saleem" Ishraq made the introductions then left both girls with

Akram and Saleem whilst he continued his conversation with Arpad.

Anisha sighed as she looked at Akram, and thought him to be handsome with his dark hair and dark-eyes, maybe not as handsome as Badal but…

Akram, however was pleasantly surprised, he found her to be attractive, with her hair in a bun at the nape of her neck, the smile of sad sweetness and eyes that reflected innocence whilst at the same time conveying sadness. The pensive expression made her look older than her years, and he thought her to be a perfect girl to get him out of his dilemma, a girl who was gentle and meek.

He looked at Anisha with cold calculating eyes, and a small smile flitted across his face like a shadow.

As Anisha felt Akram's gaze on her, her face flamed red and felt she might go up in smoke.

"Hello", Akram's eyes moved to clash with Anisha's, and his voice sounded like a faint wind rustling unpleasantly among dead leaves.

Meanwhile, Shahnaz and Nadia sat quietly sipping their tea whilst Arpad and Ishraq exhausted reminiscing about the past.

They had been talking for about half an hour when Arpad rose from the sofa.

"I think we better be going" he announced. "It is getting late and if we leave any later we will encounter a lot of traffic."

Ishraq heaved a sigh of relief when he saw his daughters relaxed and at ease for Azaria's account of Anisha's friendship had frightened him.

"The children seem to be getting along fine, I think we can go ahead and finalise the arrangement, don't you think?" Arpad beamed at him.

"You're right; I think we can," Ishraq returned the smile. "I would like to get them married as soon as possible, for you know; daughters are always a burden till they are married!"

Arpad smiled in agreement and got into the car

"Well?" Arpad asked impatiently, reversing his car from the driveway into the road. "What did you think of the girls? I thought they were nice."

There were no cars on the windswept road and the street was deserted except for the a few pedestrians.

"Anisha seemed nice; in fact I don't think I have met anyone like her." Akram answered.

In the short time he spent with her, he found Anisha's temperament to be a contradiction of gentleness and assertiveness and gradually he forgot about Kanan and the threat of her brothers.

****

"Akram thought his problem with Kanan was resolved; little did he know that they had just begun!" Anisha wiped her hand across her brow.

She heard the opening and shutting of cell doors as visiting time was over and the inmates were returning to their cell, the same time that the tea trolley arrived.

"Come on, hurry up and get your tea!' the prison officer opened their cell door.

Anisha and Carma went to collect their tea, which as usual, consisted of bread and butter, one cooked item and a tinned tomato. As they waited in the queue, some of the inmates started teasing Margaret.

'ere yu, Diana,'ve yer got fags fr' us?'

"Wot about getin som biccies for me, then,..?"

"'ey Diana, I'll tell guv about the clothes yer borrowed from Mandy an' about the drugs in yer 'andbag!"

"'ow do yer know, yu fucking….!"

The inmates started laughing and nudging Diana.

"We found 'em in yer 'andbag!"

"Yer lying scum! Bugger orf…!"

As Carma drank her tea back in the cell, she remarked. "You know, Anisha, I always thought prison had a big dining room where all the inmates ate together.'

"There are prisons and there are prisons. Each prison has different rules and regulations, and of course it also depends on whether it is a high security prison.

Carma munched her toast thoughtfully. "So Akram turned out to be a monster, did you find out what happened to Kanan?"

"Yes, I did, except I wish I didn't! It was awful! Again it was Azaria who told me, she was always gloating about the fact that she had married a good man while I married a monster who had pretended to love an innocent girl, taken her love and used it

175

against her. Carma, Akram made it seem that it was Kanan who was loose, depraved and immoral, and that it was he who had been seduced!"

"That is a horrible thing to do..." Carma had tears in her eyes.

"Actually I blame Akram, for had it not been because of him that Kanan's parents condemned what they thought was her immorality and depravity! Because they were afraid of the stigma of their community they had tried to keep her affair suppressed. But when they had found out about her pregnancy, their anger at what they saw as their daughter's betrayal seemed stronger than their love for her, so took the law into their own hands and dealt vengeance on their only daughter with a ruthlessness that was terrifying!"

"Why, what did they do?" Carma asked breathlessly.

"To me it seems that Kanan's only fault was that she was born a woman in a culture that was cruel and she finally realised the extent of her family's injustice when her brothers killed her, Carma!" Anisha looked at her hands first, then at Carma tearfully." And from that day what little regard I had for Akram died."

"Gosh, poor Kanan! It horrifies my own nerves to think that her own parents... her own family!" Carma exclaimed. "Did Akram know what had happened to her?"

"Yes, I think he did, he also knew he could have done something to stop it and that is what makes it worse. Kanan was a helpless victim in a ruthless world full of ruthless people, and the cruelty and contempt bestowed on her, the revenge taken on her by her own parents was awful, no terrifying!"

Anisha was breathless, her eyes grew enormous and her fingers became icy. She smiled weakly at Carma, but her weary eyes looked haunted as she recalled Akram's ruthlessness.

****

<u>Chapter 32</u>

Akram was happy when his mother informed him his marriage had been fixed and was to take place in three weeks. He also felt relieved for since his conversation with Kanan, he had been nervous, and every-time the phone rang, or he left the house, were times that had been full of terror for him.

He switched on the radio to hear the news and heard "they have found the pieces of a body of a girl who has been identified as a Kanan…"

"What!" exclaimed Saleem "Isn't that the name of your friend? The one you met the other day?"

"No, No, it can't be," Akram replied trying hastily to switch off the radio, but was not quick enough for Saleem had turned the volume higher.

"The suspects in the case are named to be her brothers and her father, who allegedly discovered that she was having an affair and was pregnant."

"Switch the radio off," Akram snapped angrily.

"So it was the same girl," exclaimed Saleem aghast. "Why did she want to meet you so urgently, Akram, what did she want?"

"Oh, alright, it was the same girl," admitted Akram sulkily. "She came to tell me that her family had found out about us. Only, by that time there was no 'us'"

"And, of course you must have tried to help…" urged Saleem in a soft voice.

Saleem looked at his brother's cold and inscrutable face for an indication that he was going to unravel his mysterious affair with Kanan.

He felt dreadfully sorry for Kanan, and thought it must be a callous God to have done such a thing to an innocent human person. However, he felt sure that had Akram known about her plight, he would have helped. According to Saleem anything that came his way was ready labelled and had to be either good or bad, and he could not imagine anything other than what it appeared to be.

"And nothing…!" Akram was not going to admit to his brother that he was indirectly responsible for Kanan's death.

For it was only because she had been going out with him, his refusal to marry her…it was he who she had turned to for help, which he had so callously, refused. Briefly, guilt pervaded him and he knew with certainty that Kanan's death was going to change him later, but for the present it worked through him like a knife, cutting through his heart. He wondered why, for he never really liked Kanan, and he tried to ease his pain by blaming her.

He recalled how she would follow him with large eyes, full of wishful yearning, pledging silently with him to love her again. First he began to hate Kanan, then began to love the way he hated her, and then was angry with her. However, Akram's guilt lasted for a short time, and his face finally showed no remorse or shame.

"And so it was because of you…?" Saleem asked incredously.

"I don't think so, Saleem. When we met she told me that she was finished with me and was seeing somebody else. That's the kind of girl she was!"

Akram's lips pressed and hardened into a thin line and his eyebrows pulled down towards his eyes. As this was always an indication that he was about to go into one of his rages, Saleem hurriedly changed the subject.

"I am glad ourt marriages has been finalised, for I too liked the girls, didn't you? Have they decided on the date?"

"No, but they have decided it is going to be soon." Akram answered with a smile.

Suddenly he realised that as Kanan's problem was solved, he would not have to marry Anisha after all, quickly followed by the thought that her family might still want their vengeance on him.

"Look, I have to go out for a while. Can you do me a favour and not mention to anybody that I was seeing Kanan?" asked Akram.

"I won't," replied Saleem quietly, as Akram shut the door behind him.

****

"And did you think about him? Obviously, you did not at that time know about Kanan, but did you feel Akram was right for you?"

"Oh, I never thought he was right for me, but what other choice did I have? Everybody was letting me down, and at least by marrying Akram, I felt I would be near my sister. How was I to know that she would also let me down? We had talked the whole night and...."

****

Chapter 33

Anisha and Azaria strolled into the dining room the following morning.

"And what do we owe the pleasure of your company?" He did not want to talk about Akram or Saleem but was unable to contain himself.

"I saw you were getting along well with Akram and Saleem!" he chuckled.

Yet he noticed sadly there was no excitement in Anisha's face, for it seemed to be overshadowed by a stronger emotion that Ishraq could not put his finger on – was it sadness, regret? However, he was pleased to see that Azaria blushed.

"Should I go ahead and fix the date for the wedding?" Ishraq asked as he sipped his tea.

Anisha was silent for she was indifferent to what was happening. For her, marriage to Akram represented a jagged fence, which would keep her forever trapped as a prisoner of... happiness or grief?

Azaria poured herself some tea and took the mug to sofa. She sat cross-legged and addressed her father.

"Yes, father, we have both agreed and.... Dad, please do not look so surprised!" she added with a smile.

However, although she noted the delighted on her parent's face, when she glanced at Anisha, saw that she was blinking back the tears that had sprung in her eyes.

The expression on Shahnaz's face was one of happiness as she got up from the sofa to embrace her daughters. She wished so much for her daughters – she wanted them to experience love that would grow from day to day, a love that would make them vulnerable to everything beautiful, and to see beauty even where there might be ugliness.

She wanted their feelings to be reflected in the ones they loved by sharing hopes and desires. That was Shahnaz's blessing and she had an unshakeable faith that all that happened in the lives of her daughters would be for the best.

"But that is wonderful, Azaria and Anisha, wonderful! You have made a wise decision, one that I am sure you will not regret."

Ishraq was grinning. "It most certainly is and Arpad will be delighted too. I'll call him immediately. Shahnaz, I know that Arpad is anxious to get them married, so we do not have much time as we have so many arrangements to make. Shahnaz, you look after their shopping, I'll take care of the catering and the hall and…"

"Hold on, father, you know you have not been well and mother also…"Anisha exclaimed, for she knew her mother was unwell, a consideration Ishraq conveniently forgot.

"I'm fine," Ishraq said ecstatically. "In fact, I have never felt better in my life!"

Anisha got up from the sofa. "Excuse me everybody, I have to go into town for… I think Azaria needs something too. Is there anything you would like, mum?" asked Anisha.

"Where are you going, young lady?" Ishraq asked angrily.

He took a paper and pencil and placed it in front of Anisha and Azaria. "I would like you to make a list of all the people we should be inviting. And it should be done 'pronto."

"And after you have made that list, I would like you to make a list of the things you need to buy". Shahnaz couldn't but smile at the look on her daughters' faces. "You haven't spoken to Arpad as yet!" She reminded her husband.

"I know he will be just as keen, and Ana, if you do go into town, make sure that you are accompanied by Azaria – I have told you that you are not to leave the house alone – and that order still stands!" he snapped as he turned and strode out of the room.

"Mother," Anisha looked at her watch and then at her mother. "We will make the list as soon as we get back".

Ishraq suddenly put his head through the door, looking apologetic.

"Anisha, forget what I said earlier, you can to town on your own".

Azaria slid the paper back in front of her. "I'll do what I can and Anisha can do the rest as soon as she comes back"

Anisha slammed the door loudly, and Shahnaz put her hands over her ears. "Why can't she be quiet?" She had one of her headaches and rubbed her head.

"One would think father is trying to get rid of us!" Azaria muttered under her breadth. "I don't know what the hurry is!"

"Now, now" chided her mother "you know that is not true."

Azaria's head jerked up in surprise for she had not thought her mother had heard.

"It is because of his health," Shahnaz tried to reassure her daughter. "Ever since his heart attack, he feels he is sitting on a time bomb. He wants to see his daughters settled and happy before he…"Suddenly she had tears in her eyes, for the emotions of the day had been too much for her.

"Mother, please don't cry, father will be alright. People in his condition can and do and live a long life." Azaria said with a catch in her throat as she saw the tears in her mother's eyes. She put her arms around her, but seeing her mother cry bought the tears in her eyes also.

Shahnaz wiped her eyes with her scarf feeling that guilty she was over-shadowing the moment of happiness with gloom and foreboding.

But the fact that she was getting both her daughters married and gone at the same time brought a sense of loneliness. She would miss their laughter, their pranks they're… After Anisha and Azaria were married she would be out of sorts, cut off from her roots and support systems.

She pulled herself up with a start feeling, that if she did not control herself she would start crying again.

"Carry on with your list, I'm fine," she said in a brusque voice.

"That's settled that," Ishraq said as he entered the room smiling and sat on the sofa grinning.

"I presume you have spoken to Arpad. When are you meeting to set the date of the wedding?"

"He says that he wants the marriage to take place within three weeks. That will give us ample time to get organised."

"No, it won't," it was Shahnaz's turn to get flustered.

"We'll have to manage, Shahnaz, Arpad wanted the weddings in two weeks, but I have somehow convinced him we need three weeks".

Azaria looked at her parents in bewilderment as she took the notebook and went to her room leaving her parents excitedly making arrangements for the forthcoming wedding.

****

Carma and Anisha were in the association room.

"I am beginning to think that I am quite lucky really! You have such a horrible life,, and when I look around me...! Anyway, Anisha, it seems to me all the women do is sleep around here?" Carma looked disdainfully at the inmates who were lounging in the Association room.

"What else can they do in such desolate and cheerless surrounding, Carma? However, each woman reacts to it differently, some accept it by sleeping, and others, like Irene, only endure prison life by resisting and challenging rules even if they have to spend weeks, sometimes, months, in the punishment block! But whichever way I look at it, I am coming to the conclusion, Carma that maybe this is where I really belong?" Anisha opened her eyes wide and looked questioningly and innocently at Carma.

"Anisha, what are you talking about? Forget about it,"

"How can I forget? How can I forget that I married a man who was responsible for another's death? But then how can I blame him for I too am responsible for another person's death! "Anisha choked then gave a weak smile." Anyway, Carma, remember, tomorrow is our weekly court appearance, your first court appearance."

"Gosh, I had forgotten, but I don't understand the difference between a trial and a court appearance?"

"The courts are not concerned about guilt or innocence at this stage, only what has to be done with us for the next week. If our circumstances have changed and to give us a chance, theoretically, mind you, to complain about our treatment and assure them that the prisoner is well and alive. And anyway, court appearances are a break in the routine, a voyage outside the gates of the prison, so to speak."

"That does not sound too bad to me, Ana."

Anisha gave a start and choked back her tears for Badal had teasingly called her Ana sometimes.

"Oh no, my friend, I don't think you will say that after you have been through it. Only then will you understand that the worst experience in life

186

has to stand in the dock having to hear the charge read out, yet being unable to express your side of it."

"How long do the court appearances last?"

"Until we are committed for trial at the crown court. After that we can stay in the remand centre for months and months when I am sure nobody would care if we were alive! I know of people who have spent a year in custody waiting for their case to be heard. I suppose it not a bad thing really, knowing we won't be forgotten in the system. Oh, you mean...only a few minutes, but it takes the whole day, well more really, for the wind-up to the court appearance starts the day before."

"Why the long delays before being committed to trial?"

"I don't know and not knowing is the worst! Week after week, it is inhumane in the extreme. The system is cruelly long-winded, Carma, added to that is the fact that most of us are unprepared and ignorant of what a trial entails. I have heard it is easier to plead 'guilty' to something you have done to speed things up, rather than plead 'not guilty', survive the trial and then end up being convicted anyway!"

"Has your lawyer been to see you about your representations?"

"No he has not, and that is another worrying matter, for I need to obtain and consult information on all aspects of my case, including plea, choice of venue, and a host of other matters, which I think are my right. Carma, I am worried that if my indictment is murder, as it no doubt will be unlawful homicide without aforethought needs to be established."

"Anisha, don't go all legal on me!" Carma put her hands on her ears as Anisha chuckled.

After Association time was over they were escorted back to the cell. They had only been in their cell for a little when a prison officer looked through their hatch, opened the cell door and stood with her hand on her hip whilst she called their name in a curt voice.

"Give me the clothes that you are going to wear to your court appearance!" she yelled.

She took their clothes, underclothes and sandals, and put in plastic bags.

"You can have these back tomorrow, after we have checked them!" she said brusquely, locking the cell door.

Carma looked after her in amazement at the prison rules.

"What about your friend that you were telling me about, you did not meet him again?"

"Only briefly." Anisha's eyes lit up, although a wave of sadness flooded her body as she thought of the last time she went to see him. She had left her parents happily organising the wedding.

****

Chapter 34

Although after their last meeting, she had no illusions about Badal and his feelings for her Anisha felt she needed to see him.

Consequently, she told her parents she was going to town but drove her car to the place where Badal usually spent his afternoons. She waited for over two hours and her eyes lit up and her heart leapt when she saw him walking towards the car. He bent his dark hair down to the window.

"Anisha, I don't know what you expect from me, but the past that I shared with you is forgotten, and the best thing is for us to move on."

Before she could answer, Badal turned abruptly and disappeared. Anisha sat huddled in the car, feeling cold as she recalled Baldal's words, which had been expressed with such callous indifference. She sat in the car for an hour before she finally turned her car and drove home, wiping her eyes occasionally.

Anisha entered the sitting room to find her parents enthusiastically talking.

"Ah, Anisha did you manage to finish your work?" Ishraq looked worriedly at his daughter's pale face.

"Er, yes, in a way," Anisha replied vaguely. "What is going on and where is Azaria?"

"She has gone upstairs to finish the list for the date of your wedding has been fixed. You'll be married within three weeks...Ana, whatever is the matter?" Shahnaz exclaimed

"Nothing, nothing at all," replied Anisha "She swallowed and ran upstairs to her room.

"Azaria!" she cried, flinging the door open. "Even though I knew that I was to get married in three weeks, it seems too sudden. My God! Things are moving too fast!" she sat down on the bed with her head in her hands.

"Yes they do seem to moving fast. Now let me see, you tried to see...?" She put her notebook aside.

"Yes, But I don't think there is any use for he...!" Anisha started sobbing and Azaria put her arms around her, trying to calm her.

"Have you had anything to eat?" she asked, for Anisha had left just after breakfast it was almost teatime.

"No," Anisha sobbed "I, I w w-wanted to t-to be with Badal, o-one last t-time but...!"

Her head turned towards the window to look at the brilliance of autumn, the falling leaves that were like her tears, and heard the wind whistling howls of anguish. As she looked at the birds flying through the mist of tears, to her each one of them seemed to be saying the same thing – that never again will there be happiness for her, nor would there be anyone to make her feel as special as Badal had.

"I'll get you a sandwich and a hot cup of tea. Things will look better after you have had something to eat!" suggested Azaria.

It had been an emotional and decisive day that was having its effect on Anisha's nerves, a day that was a turning point in their life, reflected

Azaria, as she went downstairs. But although she was enjoying her sister's distress, she was surprised to find Anisha crying.

"There you are, eat!" Azaria ordered placing the tray in front of Anisha." I guarantee you will feel better once you have eaten, and have had a hot cup of tea, made by my very own hands!" she said with a smile and an attempt at humour.

Anisha took the sandwich and tea gratefully and returned the smile weakly whilst Azaria went back to her notebook, leaving Anisha to finish her tea.

"You were right!" remarked Anisha, finishing the last of the sandwich and pouring herself another cup of tea.

"What was I right about?" Azaria turned her head.

"That all I needed was food and that I would feel better after it." retorted Anisha "I'm already feeling better."

However, Azaria was not deceived by Anisha's light-hearted voice and once again something in her resented Anisha's capacity, her inborn ability to cope with difficult situations.

"You now accept we are to get married in three weeks? Furthermore, you will not be seeing Badal again?" asked Azaria anxiously.

"Of course I do. I am sorry about my outburst though. Don't worry, Azaria, I am ready to forget the past!" affirmed Anisha and she grinned impishly even though there was sadness still reflected in her eyes.

Azaria got up to give a hug to Anisha. "I am so glad! More than just glad – I am happy – happy that we at least will be together." she declared cheerfully.

"I am happy about that too, now I believe we have things to do?" Anisha returned the hug.

"We do, I have done a little, but I think you will be better at it than I was." Azaria gave the notebook to her sister.

"Trying to make excuses, are you?" Anisha retorted jokingly, but nevertheless taking the paper and pencil from her. She did not understand what the hurry was – it was only this morning that...

****

Carma heard the rattling of trays as the supper trolley came to the corridor.

Anisha, come, you can tell me the rest after supper."

"I am not hungry! I don't want to eat anything."

"Anisha, please, if you don't eat...I know it is not much, but the food will do you good, even if is on an indescribable nature and a hot cup tea will do you good! The proportion of the food is small anyway and,.."

"Oh, all right, Carma," Anisha rose from the bed and as they walked down the corridor, thought how unlike Azaria Carma was. "But you know there has to be proportion control, for it means that theoretically at least there is equal distribution amongst the prisoners, but jealousy is common amongst the starving prisoners, and you must have noticed how the women examine the amount on everybody's plate! This is what I mean!" She whispered as she gestured towards Mandy who was looking at Margaret's tray.

"'Ey Diana, give us a bit of your sausage?"

"Fuck off!" Diana clutched the tray in her hand.

"Don't tell me to fuck off, yer lucky...yer 'ave more food than me. Because you are always talking to the screws, yu so..." Mandy prodded Diana.

"Mandy, don't touch me!"

"'an yu don't tell me what to do, you bitch!" Mandy's fist flashed out and grabbed Diana's tray whilst she kicked her in the knees. Diana went down with a cry.

Anisha was still shocked at the violence of the pisoners and looked at the prison officers hoping they would intervene, but they only stood idly, smugly ignoring the trouble that was brewing. Soon pandemonium broke, and only then did they blow a whistle was blown, and about six officers arrived on the scene. Some threw themselves into the fight, whilst others screamed "get behind your door!" to the other prisoners, a command that left no room for any misunderstanding.

They were sitting in their cell, trays on their laps, when Anisha moved to the door and looked through the small peephole, squinting with one eye closed so she that she could have a view of the commotion. But all Anisha could see was a wall of uniforms, which after a moment separated and she saw Mandy. Her right arm was behind her back in an arm lock, and the officer had her neck in a hold as Mandy twisted her head to one side. The officers had truncheons in their hands and Mandy was led away screaming in pain.

Anisha rubbed her forehead as she walked back to the cell.

"Poor Mandy, I don't blame her, she must be in a lot of strain for her mother is terminally ill but she can't even phone and find out how she is."

"Why?" Carma asked in surprise. "I thought all prisoners are entitled to phone calls?"

"They are but the prison officers like to humiliate the prisoners by withholding information. Mandy recently came from another prison, which had a different set of rules. The phone card that she had did not have to be signed at the back there, whereas it does here. And of course when she tried, she was threatened she would be put on report." Anisha rubbed her forehead again.

"Are you feeling alright?" Carma asked with concern.

"I have a headache, it is all this talking, Carma, I am not used to it!" Anisha gave a watery smile as she sipped her tea.

As they sat in the cell, Anisha told Carma about her wedding and the days preceding it.

"The following weeks just flew by, Carma. Our friends and relatives were informed, as was customary – and we prepared our house for the ones that would be arriving a week before the wedding. I rarely saw my parents during this time though. Mother said that she would like to do the

catering but was opposed vehemently by us and
Father!" Anisha smiled tenderly.

****

Chapter 35

"Why do you want to take on added responsibility when I have said I will look after the catering? It's not as if there is no other work to be done!" Ishraq cried indignantly. It was one of the rare occasions when they were all together in the room.

"Father's right you know, mother." piped up Azaria, who was busily sewing.

"I know, I know", said Shahnaz in an aggrieved tone of voice. "But it is something that I would like to do myself. It's not interfering with anybody, is it?" she asked scathingly.

"There is no point in talking to her!" Ishraq said testily.

He got up and left the room, feeling Shahnaz was, as usual, being unreasonable. Then again, he was sensitive to the fact that she was only suggesting doing the extra work because he had been grumbling about the cost of the wedding.

"And you are already looking tired and pale," added Anisha who was sitting cross-legged on the sofa.

Shahnaz had been humming before she went about the business of reproaching her daughter sternly.

"Why are you sitting idly, doing nothing? Don't you know that your wardrobe needs to be completed? Is everything ready?"

"Yes, it is," Anisha smiled roguishly at her mother.

"I doubt it," Shahnaz contradicted her. "I know you, to get out of sewing; you will include incomplete clothes in your dowry. And now that you are getting married, you should learn to be a bit more responsible. I am glad Azaria will be there to look after you."

"Anyone would think I was a child!" Anisha muttered as she got up and left the room.

"You behave like one," Shahnaz retorted after her" Go and have a look, for your aunts are arriving tomorrow and you will not have any time all after that."

"If there are any clothes that need stitching, bring them down, and I will do them for you," Azaria looked up from her sewing.

Anisha saw Shahnaz glaring at her. "Okay, Okay", she whispered in an undertone and sulked out of the room.

"You spoil her, Azaria," Shahnaz admonished Azaria. "There is not much of an age difference between you two yet… Anyway, all I can say is that I am worried about her childish and impulsive behaviour. After she is married she needs to…"

Azaria saw the worried look on her mother's face. "Don't fret, Mother. I will be there to look after her. Akram seems like a nice person and nobody can but help love Anisha."

"I hope you are right," remarked her mother. "It's only that…"

"There is something troubling you," Azaria put her sewing aside. They were alone for Ishraq had left the house to buy the groceries.

"It might be nothing," disclosed Shahnaz. "But you are right, I must speak to someone, you know what your father is like, everything according to him is in my imagination."

"Whatever is worrying you, please tell me," Azaria sat down beside her mother. She felt she was constantly trying to reassure somebody or the other and was beginning to feel quite adept at her new found role of adviser and confidante.

"It is just that I feel, no in fact, with my experience, I know Akram has a bad temper,"

"How can you tell? You have only met him once."

"Yes, I know, it is a mother's instinct, and also I had been observing him closely all the time. I saw him clench his fists and press his lips."

"Mother!" Azaria retorted feeling exasperated at her mother, yet knew she was right.

"I know, I know. But what if he does, how will Anisha handle him?"

"There is a side of her you do not know. Mother, for she is wise and mature, even though she portrays otherwise." answered Azaria quietly

"What secrets are you confessing to?" Anisha breezed in the room with a handful of clothes over her arms and smiled mischievously at her mother and sister.

"Whatever do you mean?" Azaria quickly answered before returning to her sewing.

"And I see, young lady that you did manage to find some unfinished work after all!" Sgahnaz remarked scathingly, yet with a look of tenderness in her eyes.

"Er, yes," replied Anisha sheepishly, handing the clothes over to Azaria.

"No, you don't", Shahnaz interceded. "Azaria, you are not to do anything for her. She has to learn to do things herself."

She gave a small smile as she looked tenderly at her daughters, Azaria sewing busily, Anisha with a grimace on her face and a pile of clothes in front of her.

They settled into a comfortable rhythm of sorting through the clothes, commenting on each and discussing plans for the wedding. It was the kind of evening that Anisha was to remember later nostalgically, sitting at home alone with Azaria and her mother, doing all the things that a mother and daughter do when the wedding day is imminent. Many times Anisha had dreamt of this moment, buying her trousseau and making wedding plans, but the occasion was overshadowed by her pain..

****

"In the following days, Carma, the houseguests gradually arrived, and the house echoed with the sound of singing. Our female relatives, some of whom I had rarely met, all clapped along with our friends, singing the traditional wedding songs"

A prisoner officer opened their cell and started shouting.

"Hey, you lazy husband killers, show me how tidy you really are! If I find that your cupboards are not tidy, I am going to send you to the punishment block!"

She started opening the cupboards and throwing the few things that Anisha and Carma had bought from the canteen on the floor. "I knew it! Your cupboards are untidy!"

Carma's eyes flashed with anger. "Excuse me, officer, the cupboards were tidy, it is you who have untidied them!"

"Don't you dare talk back! Why don't you go back where you belong? This is not the end of the matter; I am going to put the incident on your report."

"Carma, you should have not said that." Anisha said as the prison officer stormed out of the cell, locking it behind her. "Like she said, she will put you on report and…."

"…and so what, Anisha? She will put be on report for something I have not done. Is there no justice here? I thought it was supposed to be the first virtue of any social or political institution, it is not even the last!"

"Most prison officers resent us Carma, for they feel that as London is a welfare state, which means a system of 'care', it already includes in it justice and that should be the end of our entitlements. It is a pity that they don't realise that justice is not just a matter of abiding by general principles. You know I have come to realise that justice and what is considered to be just are sometimes not compatible…. I mean is that it should concern itself more with circumstances of people and…..anyway."

"You sound like Amit, my brother, Anisha,"

Anisha chuckled. "You have not told me about your family, Carma, but I will take that as a compliment!" She turned and looked towards the window, thinking of the days leading to her wedding.

****

Chapter 36

The Mehndi (henna) ceremony was held two days before the wedding, and the grooms' along with their families and close friends were invited. Anisha and Azaria joined Saleem and Akram, who were sitting on a green cushion inlaid with mirrors. Both Azaria and Anisha dutifully kept their scarves over their face so the grooms would not catch a glimpse of them before the wedding.

Relatives and friends from both sides brought in plates heaped with henna which were decorated with burning candles and silver foil. One by one, they pressed a piece of foil with henna on it on the brides' palms, putting a sweetmeat in their mouth and waving money over their head to protect them from evil. The night before the wedding, a professional woman came to decorate Anisha and Azaria's hands and feet with Henna.

The day of the wedding finally dawned and after a sleepless night Anisha got up early. She stood by the window, savouring the last moments in her childhood house, her heart and mind in turmoil. It was going to be a sunny day and Anisha could feel the warmth of the sun flowing in through the morning's haze of coolness.

She breathed in the fragrance of summer – and likened it to a memory and at the same time a pledge – an aching and yet, she wondered if would hold the draught of happiness for her? Anisha's thoughts and feelings were like the chirping of spring birds that have not as yet shaped their song. She could hear the faint undertone of traffic in the distance, and the noise was forming a base for her misery on a day that should have been her happiest.

She heard a knock on the door and turned to face her mother. She tried to smile when she saw that her mother had the bridal clothes for Anisha and Azaria hanging over her arms – the traditional red knee length tunic that fastened up to the neck, and loose fitting red trousers that gathered at the ankles. There was a scarf to go with the ensemble, also in deep red.

Anisha and Azaria changed and were escorted to the next room where the women were assembled. Their holy book was held over their head and they were asked, in front of everybody, whether they agreed to the marriage, as their religion wanted to make sure that the woman understood and agreed freely to the wedding.

As Anisha shyly whispered her consent, she wondered miserably why nobody realised that by this stage, it was too late for a girl to refuse even if she wanted to.

After they consented three times, the marriage contract was signed. The priest then went to the room where the grooms and the men were assembled with the good news, and afterwards read the marriage prayers for the Akram and Saleem.

In the evening, Ishraq held a reception where he invited most of his friends and business colleagues.

Anisha and Azaria were sitting on the dais decorated with flowers that were spreading their perfume amongst the guests and their friends brought Akram and Saleem onto the dais. Their female cousins and the grooms' friends held a red silk shawl over the couples head whilst a mirror was placed between them.

Tradition was that the bride and groom would look at each other for the first time after marriage in the mirror. Besides the couples', candles burned in silver candelabras, indicating their lives should be filled with light, and married cousins ground sweets over the couples heads' so that their life would be sweet. The sound of music resounded in the atmosphere as celebrations began and the guests lined up to off their congratulations.

Azaria looked content, but Anisha was feeling numb, as if everything around her was unreal.

After the festivities were over, their friends and relatives escorted them to Arpad's car under a holy book.

As they were driven away, Anisha looked back and saw her mother sobbing uncontrollably. Tears rose in her eyes and swam on her lids. She thought of Badal, trying to shun the fading pageant of a by-gone year, at the same time trying vainly to ridicule a romance gone sour. The romance, she was trying to convince herself, was only in her imagination and was travelling further and further from her mind.

Suddenly Anisha's body was shaken with sobs and she had wept with a kind of violence that was at once a protest and a passion. She had kept her face averted from Akram, but later peeped at him with tear filled eyes that were weary yet brimming with hope.

However, Akram had only looked back at her with coldness in his eyes that showed his insensibility, and his expression had not only puzzled but frightened Anisha. She felt that in her heart there was a tumult and conflict of emotions for even though a spray of tears and a sense of loss was blinding her eyes, she was young and defenceless to the roaring passion of life.

"Don't cry, Anisha, everything will be all right." Akram said soothingly.

Yet his voice was chillingly soft, shattering the tense silence as a cunning smile hovered on his lips.

****

"The moment he spoke to me in that tone of voice, I should have realised the kind of man he was!"

Anisha turned back from the cell window and walked to the centre of the cell.

"Not you, Anisha, you think everybody is good and even if you had suspected would most probably have justified it. Anyway, I am surprised there are so many drug addicts in the system, Anisha. Doesn't the system control it?"

"Yes, it has things like urine tests to help control the problem, but there is a problem there for the residue of cannabis remains in the body for up to a month whilst heroin is only detectable for three days. Almost overnight, I have seen drug users' change to heroin in an attempt to avoid detection. The consequences are that it has created an epidemic of addicts who I think are the worst kind of criminals. Their mood relies and depends on hard drugs and their world revolves around when they can get the next fix!"

"Was Lisa one of them?"

"Yes, she was." Anisha replied indifferently for her emotions were still too chaotic as she had recalled the hostility that Akram had shown in the beginning. "Carma, I was really frightened when I looked at Akram's face, for it looked hostile and indifferent." Anisha trembled and there was a catch in her throat. "But even then, the worst I could think of was that he had a bad temper."

"When did you discover that he was violent?" Carma realised that Anisha wanted to unburden her emotions.

"It was only a couple of days after the wedding when he lost his temper and started throwing things at me. He started losing his temper more and more, always with no obvious reason, and always on trivial things. Then he started beating me in our bedroom, but only in the evening and only when we were alone. He would put his hands on my arms, leaving them black and blue, and I can still feel myself shrivel within me skin as I think of each squeeze of Akram's fingers, each brittle tone of his voice!" Anisha shivered.

"He seems to be very much like Aijaz!" Carma declared.

"Do you think so? I thought there could not be anybody worse! Anyway I became so withdrawn, Carma that I created a world of my own, a world full of dreams and fantasies where there was love and justice.Even a bird's world was a happy reality, whilst mine was but a shadow!"

"All though I am not one to preach, why did you stay with him, Anisha?"

"You see, Carma, soon after my wedding I came to know about Kanan. I thought Akram felt responsible for her death, and the only way he could endure his guilt was by lashing out at me!" Anisha shuddered and looked deeply affected by the emotions she had suppressed for so long.

"I don't know how you coped!" Carma remarked in admiration.

"I didn't, Carma. It was a difficult time for me and I became very lonely, which increased during the following months." Anisha sighed. "If only I had been of a religious nature, maybe that would have helped, for I believe that at least the religious can turn to a spiritual sanctuary in times of uncertainty and fear. But I had never been religious and believe that true spirituality is in living and not hurting anyone. Anyway, somehow I came to terms with Akram's violence and Azaria's new found self-confidence."

"And even after I had endured his violence, I did not want to believe the worst of Akram. I naively believed that life was like a garden and people were like seeds – to be nurtured by love and caring – and if enough time and care was spent on them, could bloom into flowers. I have many times seen an old and neglected plant unexpectedly burst into blossom and become one to be cherished. I sincerely believed that even though it might take time, eventually the flowering of love would come."

"Her family was aware of his behaviour towards you?" Carma frowned questioningly

"Oh no! Akram was careful never to show his temper in front of his family, even though I think his mother suspected, for she saw my bruised arms and found me crying. But she always thought I must have done something to provoke him, and whilst blaming me exonerated Akram. The rest of the family upheld these double standards, and I felt weighed down by the need to sustain a failing relationship. I had thought of calling the police, but knew that they did not interfere with what they called 'domestic cases' and anyway was too ashamed for I felt that Akram's violence somehow reflected my own shortcomings. Consequently, I withdrew into my world of lights and shadows."

"Anisha, you must never think that for although it seems to me that Akram had the upper hand and won, you were never really defeated because you had neither resisted nor given battle!" Carma smiled gently.

"Carma! Thank you for those words...they mean a lot to me! You know you are more of a sister than Azaria?" Anisha's voice choked with emotion and she quickly hugged Carma.

"And so are you, Anisha, but Azaria is your sister; after all, surely she must have been there for you, at some time?"

Anisha brushed the tears streaming down her cheeks "Oh no, I wish. I did try to talk to her, though, but everytime I brought up the subject of Akram's violence she would shuffle her feet, cough and act ill at ease, till finally I realised she was ignoring the problem and would not help!"

"Anisha, it seems you are not telling me everything. You don't have to tell me if you don't want to, but you didn't speak to your sister at all?" "Oh yes, Carma, although she was trying to ignore my plight, I naively believed that Azaria loved me. But after marriage, Azaria was too wrapped up in her happiness although she was aware how Akram treated me. I think, Carma that she felt guilty at being happy and the only way she could cope with her guilt was by distancing herself so that she could keep her happiness intact. She developed a confidence and enthusiasm that had not been there previously, an ardour that was fuelled by her husband and my mother-in-law, for Nadia loved her!"

****

Chapter 37

"Azaria, can I talk to you? It's about Akram."

Azaria was looking out of the window waiting for Saleem. "Yes, what is it?"

"Azaria, Akram, he beats me and…! Anisha started sobbing.

Azaria turned from the window, her eyes flashing.

"Anisha, as usual, you are making an issue over nothing, for I don't believe that kind of behaviour from Akram! You have always been a selfish girl who thinks that the world should run around her!"

Azaria looked at Anisha with contempt for she thought Anisha's relationships to be a failure, and failure Azaria considered being a contagious disease, one she did not want to be contaminated with.

The sharpness of Azaria's tone and her unexpected coldness was as effective as a slap in the face and Anisha swallowed as she felt a lump in her throat.

"But, Azaria, he…" but Azaria had quickly left the room before Anisha could finish the sentence.

Anisha had tried to talk to her sister again, but had always been met by either a stony silence or accusations that she was lying. However, Anisha held no grudge against Azaria's allegations, and learnt to treat most of Azaria's remarks with indifference.

She would often catch her whispering to Saleem about her with the same cruel humour as would have a stranger, till finally Anisha came to realise that what she thought to be a close bond with her sister had only been a fragile bond which had been held together only because of the fear of what their individual futures might hold.

****

"I am so sorry, Anisha," Carma had tears in her eyes. "That was terrible of Azaria, but I know that self-indulgence, and injustice even, is a habit that is very easy to acquire. Azaria realised, in her manipulative way, that her behaviour would only be considered unjust by you but be exemplified by everybody else. What about your parents, though, Anisha?   Surely   your   mother   must   have understood?"

"She would have if I had told her for she was a kind an understanding woman, but how could I say anything to her? She was so happy to see me married, and anyway I did not get the chance for she died soon after. Apparently she had been suffering from terminal cancer for the previous six months. I can sympathise with what Mandy is going through for I looked after my mother during her illness."

"Your mother had cancer?"

"Yes, but being a proud woman insisted she spend her last days at home, and I was not only with her for most of the time, but was present when she died."

"That must have been awful for you. Were Akram or your sister there to support you?"

"Would you believe it, no. Akram and my mother-in-law came only once to visit her and Azaria only when it suited her! Although mother did not say as much, I think, she suspected my unhappiness. When she died, everybody else, friend's relations and neighbours, were kind initially, but then left me alone with my grief. They all, I think, detected something was wrong, and behind their condolences, I could feel a horrid curiosity, an appetite for gossip that they only held in check with difficulty. However hard they tried, I did not miss the sidelong curious and accusing looks I was given, as if all my unhappiness was my fault."

"What about your father?"

"His already frail heart weakened and it hurt me to see his once erect body became bowed and sunken. After my mother's death, he spoke little, going about the routine of daily living, and whenever I went to visit, I would find him sitting in front of the television, but always with the sound turned low, as if the jokes and laughter would penetrate and break his heart. Carma, it was awful seeing him sit in his armchair in a stiff demanding posture whilst his eyes, which were once like bright glowing flames, dim like candles in the night. Every time I saw him I swear his eyes grew smaller and smaller as if they lost the energy that had once fuelled them, till eventually he too died and they closed. I'll never forget the day my father was buried." Anisha whispered feeling that by talking about them, she was with her parents.

She wiped the tears from her eyes and her voice was poignant. "That time is vivid in my mind, the funeral was on a rainy day, but Azaria and I, being women, were not allowed to go. The sky was grey, as if mirroring my life. I cried so much that my heart felt barren and dry as a desert, were nothing is allowed to grow. I felt his loss deeper than Azaria, for she was so happy that sorrow touched her only fleetingly, but sorrow had changed me. Now, more than ever, I needed a friend, someone like Akram and Azaria to give me strength – but knew I was absolutely alone in the world." Anisha was completely overwhelmed and broke into tears.

Carma quickly came and sat beside Anisha and held her hand, but Carma's kindness made Anisha cry even harder. Was it her Kismet that only a stranger could express warmth and affection to her?

For when she had cried at her father's death, Akram and Azaria, her close family, had met her anguish with coldness and indifference. Although she had wept all night long so that and in the morning her face was red and her tired eyes swollen, Anisha felt that the crying had done her good for it had helped anethize her hurt.

"That day I made a resolution, Carma, I decided that I was going to arm myself with my own in-built defence and not rely on anybody, least of Azaria. I resolved that I was never going to feel, show any emotion or let anybody know how hurt I feel, and here I am talking to you!" Anisha exclaimed as she brushed her hair from her forehead. " "But it was after that that I began my so called transformation into another world, a world filled only with echoes and memories of my parents. I recalled certain of their phrases, phrases which had etched themselves into my memory."

Carma smiled tenderly as she thought how she and Amit had made fun of Devesh's proverbs.

Anisha felt cold, and her face was still. Suddenly, life returned to it for a fleeting moment, before the present claimed her again for her unjust present was just as precarious. A look of uncertainty and fear returned to her face as she brushed her forehead with her hand.

They heard the medicine trolley and there was a rattling of keys as the cell doors were opened.

"Anisha, if you still have that headache, I suggest you take something for it, and also take something to make you sleep," Carma walked to the cell door, and was peering out of the latch "It is Ruth who is on duty tonight."

Ruth opened the cell door and noticed that Anisha's eyes were fervent and intense, eyes of a being that yearned to be at home and at peace. She gave her the medicine and was turning to leave when Anisha called her.

"Ruth, please, I need to know, what is happening about my representations? I have seen that the ethnic community is not particularly well served by lawyers and…."

"Anisha, I have explained to you that the matter is being looked into!" She answered sharply, as she strode out of the cell.

"What's the matter with her?" Carma looked her at the door angrily. "She needn't be so rude!"

"Maybe the prison service has got to her and she is becoming like the others!" Anisha chuckled. "But no, that is not funny, anyway, Carma, don't forget tomorrow is our court appearance."

"Oh ya ha.. I had forgotten, anyway, Anisha don't worry about your reps, I am sure there will be news tomorrow and…."

"You know there won't, Carma." Anisha took the tablet with a glass of water and made a grimace. "Ugh, I hate taking medicine, you know, I think I am right and Ruth has become like the others."

"Ah, Anisha, that is to be expected, for in the first place, there should be justice and fairness in the prison system for Ruth to perform her duties effectively and fairly, and so far I have not seen…Anisha, hello, are you sleeping?"

"No, I heard every word and you are right, just people cannot be effective unless there is collective action …it is a pity, though …" Anisha was muttering as she turned over on her side and went to sleep.

Carma, meanwhile, could not sleep. She was glad that she had Anisha as her friend, for some inmates had a strong sense of shame, stigma and fear of being transferred which made them unwilling to form lasting relationships.

Carma remembered what Anisha had said about their legal representations, and as she glanced at her cell thought it strange that where there should be justice was the very place that injustice was frequently forgotten.

She realised that here injustice was not an abstract idea/conception of hers but something that was actually happening to her and to other real people in a concrete situation, surrounded by the cold concrete walls. The realisation was sudden, leaving Carma's thought spinning and oscillating in a kaleidoscope manner, shuffling, and reshuffling till the mosaic of her memories settled into their original design.

The following morning, after breakfast, an officer came to their cell to escort them.

"Hey, yu two, get your gear and come with me!" The prison officer yelled

"What the…?" Carma looked confused.

"We have to undergo the infamous 'strip-search', before we go to court!" Anisha remarked bitterly.

"What, again?"

"Yes, again, though I cannot understand why such a search is considered necessary, as anyone who wants to get something in or out of the remand centre can get it through the obvious places, a fact that makes a mockery of the strip search, I think."

"I don't want to go through with it again and…!" Carma's eyes flashed angrily as she was filled with futile rebellion, bitterness and humiliation.

"We have no choice, Carma, for only then will our clothes be given to us." Anisha watched with a mixture of fear and awe at Carma's sudden flare of temper.

Anisha bit her lip as they were taken to the reception area where they waited with the other women in an overcrowded room whilst the officers in the reception area checked their property against their property cards and put them in plastic bags. The inmates were dealt with in the order of the courts they were attending as some had long distances to go, and some women had already left by 7.00 am to get to court by 10.am.

She never was sure whether it was worse to have people shouting, screaming and smoking in a room, or whether she liked to be left alone with nothing to do. She looked guiltily at Carma who had resumed her look of coldness and detachment.

Anisha had been so busy reliving her life, trying to assuage her inner conflicts that she forgot how Carma too must need someone to confide in. However, Anisha was of the impression that although Carma, like her, had faced betrayal and disillusionment she was finding it difficult to face up to the aftermath of her actions.

However, Anisha was sure that her betrayals could not have been worse than hers, for she had not as yet admitted to her that she was innocent and the only reason she was in prison was because of Azaria, but how could she tell Carma? Even Anisha had not known the true facts surrounding Akram's death till the day Azaria visited her at the prison. Her sister's cutting voice still rung in her ears.

Chapter 38

"Anisha, I have just come to tell you that whilst you spend time in prison, you needn't feel guilty that you killed Akram! When I knelt to feel his pulse, it was beating and whilst you were sitting crying in the corner, it was I who hit him again, and firmly but surely...anyway I thought you would like to know....."

Anisha did not notice that Azaria's eyes glittered with malice, but she looked at her with relief and hope.

"So I will be free at last! But I don't understand, why, Azaria, why did you kill Akram?"

"I killed him because we had an affair, and then when I told him it was over, he raped me, and then told me he was going to tell Saleem. And I am glad he is dead for now I can be happy with Saleem."

"Azaria, what are you talking about? You have an affair with Akram!" Anisha eyes opened wide in astonishment. "But I thought you were happily married and....?"

"Anisha, you were always so naïve! Things are not always what they appear to be! And Akram was handsome! But you don't think that I am going to confess to the authorities, do you? Why, I am not going to sacrifice my happiness for you!" Azaria said spitefully

"Azaria, why are you being so horrible? I know it must be because you are afraid of going to prison, but you need not worry, once you tell them the circumstances, of how Akram raped you, the courts will understand and….please, are you going to tell them the truth ….Azaria you are not going to leave me here like this are you?" Anisha pleaded, for Azaria had risen from her seat.

"He only raped me the last time! We had an affair and Saleem does not suspect, for he loved his brother. I am sorry, Anisha, if I admit to the truth, it will destroy any kind of happiness for me. This way nobody is hurt, and their memory of Akram as a loving son and husband is intact. And as for the courts understanding, why, how long have you been here and have you even got a lawyer to defend you? No! And if you decide to tell them what really happened, remember, it is your word against mine, and Saleem was there too and he will back me…."

Anisha had tried to justify her sister's behaviour and could not believe she had not sensed her sister's hatred of her earlier.

"But I will see that you are represented by a good lawyer and,…Azaria!"

But her sister had vanished, leaving Anisha with tears streaming down her eyes.

After she had gone Anisha placed her head in her arms, sobbing uncontrollably.

****

As she recalled her conversation with Azaria, Anisha had tears in her eyes, but decided that she would not tell disclose Azaria's confession. She wanted to, but what if Carma decided that she should tell the courts what she…..had not done…? Azaria would be in trouble so …No, she felt it would be better to keep silent. As usual, when she was unhappy, she resorted to banter.

"Carma, why don't you tell me to shut up? I have been doing the talking whilst you….! Anyway, sorry to be so boring but you might find this bit of advice useful, Carma. You do you realise that you have to confront your feelings here, don't you, for if you keep them suppressed, you will be history! Sorry to be so blunt but… anyway, I would like to know about you and the circumstances that led you from India to London and then to this horrible place, that is if you want to…." Anisha looked at Carma with her kind eyes.

"Of course, Anisha, I would love to share my experiences." Carma said, and then looked at Anisha in surprise. "You know, I never thought I would be lucky enough to find someone I could confide in, especially in prison!"

As the names were called out, Carma stood with arms clenched at sides, quivering from head to toe as she recalled the numerous times in her life that she had been betrayed.

"Anisha, I had hoped and wished that here at least there would be justice, but in the short time that I have been here, I have come to the conclusion that there was, is, no justice, no absolute right or wrong."

"Maybe not, Carma, but you have to admit that justice is a natural law, just as gravity is, and it is only right to expect that breaking it, whatever the circumstances, would produce reactions just as severe."

However, Anisha got the impression that Carma's demand for justice was a silent cry to remedy the inequalities that she had been forced to confront in the past and at present.

****

CARMA

Chapter 1

Finally it was their turn and Carma and Anisha went up to the prison officer to sign their property cards, after which they were permitted out of the room full of chattering women and smoke into the reception area, where they were again told to wait.

An officer stood by the door asking questions. "Who are you and where are you going?" she intoned, and the expected reply – inmates name and name of court was given together with the paper she held in her hand.

They got into a Black Maria which was to take them to court. The car's inside was divided into little cubicles with just room on the ledge seat provided. Carma brushed the seat before she sat; looking out of the little window as the door to the car was locked behind them.

The car started with a violent honk and Carma fell back on the ledge seat and clutched Anisha frantically. Although she had looked forward to the court appearances as a break in the lock-up regime, as soon as the iron gates shut behind her, Carma was suddenly frightened, for in the short time that she had been in prison, the remand centre had become a refuge.

As she sat in the car, she tried not to think of the tragic circumstances that led her here. Nevertheless, she felt self-blame and guilt that she was somehow responsible, either by provoking the fatal accident or somehow failing to avoid it.

Carma knew she had done neither yet it reflected the need everybody has to rationalise powerful and painful emotions.

The prison van drove them to the underground car park beneath the courts and the got out and were escorted down a flight of stairs. They passed some corridors and were handed over to the police wardens and placed in a cell, which was about the size of a standard room.

The cell was dark and covered in dust and there was a strong smell of urine, a place, Carma thought, where all attempts at camouflage crumbled and reality embraced the inmates firmly and strongly. The only occupants of the cell were Anisha and Carma in the cell but Carma had overheard the police officers mention that more prisoners were expected.

"This is usually the time when a solicitor comes come to see the prisoner!" Anisha remarked, covering her nose with her hand, "although till now I have not even seen or received any lawyer!"

However, Carma was pleasantly surprised when she saw Anisha's solicitor stop outside the cell, but to their disappointment, there were only hurried and nervous exchanges between them.

"Is your name Anisha, I am your lawyer, sorry but I don't have time now to......" The nervous lawyer in his suit looked flustered as he opened and closed his briefcase.

"What do you mean? You haven't come to sort out my defence and now you say....! Anyway, when can I see you to discuss my representations? Maybe if you came to the prison....?"

"Yes, yes, ring my secretary." The solicitor left hurriedly leaving Carma dazed as to why he had come in the first place!

Soon after a policewoman escort and a male colleague came and opened the cell door.

"Come with me!" she roughly caught hold of Carma's arm and she was led along a corridor, upstairs in a lift and then told gruffly to wait outside the court room. Carma sat perfectly still and silent on the bench, pressing fingertips together, but by this time, her senses were blocked and she could hardly see or hear anything.

Finally her name was called and the policewoman went into the dock first, followed by Carma and a male policeman brought up the rear.

Carma first looked with awe at the austere magistrate, and then her eyes passed on to a girl mopping her forehead stepping down from the dock.

She was a girl of about her own age, with good features and fair hair. From snippets of conversation between the police officers, Carma gathered she was accused of stealing from a newsagent, for a young tobacconist had testified he had seen the girl pass his shop twice or thrice although he had not witnessed her shop-lifting.

As a policeman escorted the sweating girl out of the courtroom, Carma noticed her melancholy eyes and wondered if the tobacconist had been wrong and all that she had been doing was waiting for her friend?

Whilst standing in the dock, Carma numbly noticed that the policeman guarding her first shuffled his feet then bent his knees. Her legs were trembling and she could barely stand, but the procedure was faster than she expected.

Before she was allowed to sit, she was asked her name, prison no etc.

Although she was dimly aware of voices asking her questions, the only thing Carma could remember was that she was to be remanded in custody again 'because of the nature of the crime' and Carma felt again that she was encountering an ignorance of her crime. She not only felt frustrated by the red tape surrounding the courts, but also victimised by their off-hand approach.

Anisha had gone through the same process and once they were back in the police cell, Carma wiped her brow for some more inmates had arrived and the cell had become crowded and felt oppressively hot.

"Whew! Thank God that's over and done with! But Anisha, I don't see any prison officers waiting to take us back. What will happen if we are late for you told me that the time the women have to be back by the London courts is 6.00 p.m., and for those coming from distant courts is 7. 00 p.m?."

"We would be taken to custody in police cells at one of the larger magistrate's courts in the London area and…"

Before she had a chance to finish the sentence, two policemen came and Carma and Anisha were led single file into the courtyard, where two prison officers stood outside white buses ready to take them to back to the remand centre.

As they were sitting in the van, Anisha whispered to Carma.

"These vans are known as 'sweat boxes!'

"Good heavens, why?"

"The compartment allotted to each person is like an upright coffin, don't you think?" Anisha chuckled and her dimple danced on her cheek.

"Anisha, aren't you ever serious?" Carma said in exasperation.

"I am, Carma, scouts honour." Anisha grinned and held up her hand.

It was nearing evening when they finally arrived, and as they drove past the prison gates into the prison Carma looked with disgust at the odd bits of food lying on the floor and the walls covered with grime.

Two prison officers escorted them to the reception procedure, where, at a leisurely pace, a prison officer got around to attending them. Their property was checked again against the card and the prison officer then put them in a 'horse box', which was a little cubicle, then taken to have a compulsory bath and hair wash.

"Why do we have to go through that again?" Carma asked exasperatedly.

"Because they think we might have picked up some germs in the police cells! I think there is a certain animosity between the police and the prison officers!"

Back in the wing they were locked in their cell again, where they fell on their beds in a state of total exhaustion.

"Whew, you didn't tell me how strenuous going to court would be!"

"You'll get used to it for don't forget we are not used to exercise. It was the same for me too." Anisha answered "I feel it to be a vicious circus, for the longer I am locked up, the more I feel the need to walk, but once I do get the chance I get so tired!"

Carma looked at the stained walls and dirty barred windows of the cell and realised gloomily that her future looked bleak.

By sharing a cell and realising that their lives had been similar, Carma and Anisha had become bound by same way of thinking, came to understand each other's views and learned the art of compromise.

Carma had become fond of Anisha's face that looked so extraordinarily alive and mobile, as if she was ready to laugh, smile or frown at any moment. She liked Anisha's sense of humour and her gentle and affectionate ways, but underneath Anisha's brave exterior, Carma sensed a frailty. And because of this vulnerability and sensitivity, she felt she was like a delicate flower on a stem that could be easily broken.

Carma was getting used to the routine of prison life and learnt to separate tthe babble of meaningless noises echoing through the corridors. Feet thundering down the corridor and the jangle of keys meant that the officers were either going to unlock a cell or the duty officer was checking the fire door. A door may be unlocked, but unless there was also the sound of the lock being fixed back, it meant nobody was coming out.

And as she grew familiar with the prison officers too, so she could tell which of them was approaching and why, for their walks were as distinctive as their voices.

The thud of heavy feet after trouble usually meant the punishment block for someone. Two pairs of footsteps and a voice in a low monotone meant that someone was having a report read to them. Thus she had ordered the once confusing and meaningless noises, and then classified them into an understanding of sounds that made for a typical prison day/night.

She drifted off to sleep feeling stripped of dignity and self-respect. Prison to her seemed full of the world's unreasoning misery where she began to feel deprived of the greatest boons of human existence – independence and a private life.

Chapter 2

The inmates had been waiting impatiently in their cells to be unlocked for breakfast. Some had started to shout and Carma feared that they would become abusive and harm someone for tempers were snapping and she could hear fist beating against the cell doors.

"Anisha, I sense a feeling of suppressed violence in the air, which is almost tangible, as in the increase of pressure before a thunderstorm." Carma remarked as she put her hands over her ears.

"That's something you will have to get used to for bitchiness, excuse my language, and bickering are the root of prison life and contagious as well, as you can see! I don't blame the women really for after a while, the desire to hit and lash out at someone becomes very hard. It starts off with a temptation than turns into a strong feeling, one which most women cannot restrain."

Carma looked at her in amazement.

"Carma, why are you so surprised? You know they end up being violent one way or another– either through self-mutilation, setting fire or fighting with other inmates. Oh and by the way, did I mention that we are subject to rigid inspections at any time? I think somebody was saying they were going to do the same today."

"Oh no! Not that again, and yes, Anisha, I remember we had one of those a couple of days ago…"

"The time they thought I was dealing in drugs!'
Anisha grinned impishly

"Oh, I think they also came to check the cleanliness, and how they untidied everything and put the blame on me.'

"I think they are coming for the same reason and please, Carma, for heavens sake, don't talk back to the prison officers like the last time. They don't like it and will only put you on report."

"I'll try...though I still think they are bullies." Carma muttered

Finally, it was time for breakfast and Carma waited quietly in the queue, looking around her calmly, listening to the regular cries of "who will trade my margarine for Cornflakes?" and "who will swap my cigarette for a toast?"

The two women who had been shouting obscenities and profanities earlier came face to face and the second woman dropped her breakfast and lunged at her opponent.

"I'll kill you!" She grabbed her opponent's hair and banged it again and again against the floor. Her nose split and there was blood everywhere whilst there was a cyclone of flapping arms and legs.

Carma was shocked to see that the prison officers on duty stand passively whilst the two women bit tore and scratched at each other, and only intervened when they saw blood.

"Stop it, you, you ...alley cats!"

The women were marched away, and Carma knew that at the very least they be put on remission.

They had their breakfast of murky tea, toast, margarine and marmalade, and just as Anisha had predicted, a prison officer opened their cell door and walked in.

"Open your cupboards at once, and if they are untidy…!." she ordered, eyeing Anisha and Carma frostily.

Carma trembled for she was one of the prison officers who was a bully and was always trying to incite the prisoners with nasty remarks, hoping to provoke them into being abusive or violent when she could punish them with either by putting them on remission or by sending them into isolation

Their cupboards were thrown open and the beds were checked to see that the blankets were neatly folded according to prison requirements. After the prison officer was satisfied, she locked the cell door behind her.

"Well, didn't seem to be too bad this time!"As Carma paced the cell she heard snippets of conversations from outside as the women shouted to each other across their cell.

'My husband's just been arrested!'

"Wassat?'

'I thought 'e was goin' to elope 'ith 'is girl, innit?'

Another voice joined in.

'D'ya hear what 'appened to …? She cut 'er wrists!'

'Fuckin' 'ell!"

"There was blood all over…"

"Did yer receive yer letter?"

"Na."

"Bad luck, luv, if 'e ain't even written, forget 'im!!

Carma started pacing the cell, feeling distraught and confused.

"Anisha, what can I do, for I feel that any action on me part is out of my control, it always has been! At the very least, I hope that there is a God who would deal with us with mercy and justice by making the law to suit the accused, rather than the punishment to fit the crime!" Carma said vehemently, her eyes flashing.

However, looking around her and hearing the prison officers' manner exuding authority, she trembled with a jumble of emotions, mostly consisting of horror and helplessness. Carma found that in prison there not only was no balance between guarding and caring, but also found that there was no justice either, for justice meant the maintainance of the proportion between an offence and punishment.

Carma recalled the piece of advice a policewoman had given whilst waiting in the police cells.

"One has to adapt in an institution. However, to do so first learn what one would need to know for survival, that is how to get food and water etc, who one could trust, who was kind and who was not. Then, and only then, set about learning the system and then to learn to manipulate how to produce better conditions for comfort."

That piece of advice Carma was finding useful

"Carma, I think I have been pretty selfish in talking about myself all the time, I would like to know about you, that is if you feel you can talk about it."

"Yes, I would like to very much, for all this guilt is becoming difficult for me to bear." Carma said softly as she nodded her head slightly.

Her brown hair flowed with the movement, her face underwent a change, and she dug her nails in the palms of her hands as she thought of her father, Badal and her son, Abhay.

Her forehead creased first in perplexity then in sadness, for it seemed that she was going to be deprived of the entitlement of a mother enjoying a long and luxurious infancy of her child then the satisfaction of seeing him mature. She thought sadly of the times in the future when she could have indulged herself by cuddling her son and of him being deprived of a mother's love.

She could not find the words to explain to Anisha what she had been through...,her first day in prison, how she had been kidnapped by Aijaz, parted from her son and told that the one person she had trusted had betrayed her?

****

Chapter 3

Aijaz, her ex-husband, had kidnapped her and held Carma hostage in exchange for her son, xswho he thought was his, but her time as hostage was short and precarious, a time when Carma had felt she was playing the role of a pawn in a game of nerves.

Carma had regained consciousness after what seemed to her an immense passage of time. She was lying on a bed; her head ached and was feeling dizzy and drowsy. A horrible attack of nausea seized her and she got up from the bed gingerly, feeling queer as she approached the window massaging her head.

The last thing she remembered was talking to Badal, but at present Carma felt helpless, for at one time she would have been confident Badal would help her, but at the moment the more she tried to conjure up a picture of a reassuring and dependable Badal in action, the more the image of him faded and become and kind of faceless abstraction. How right she had been!

Aijaz was standing looking down at her.

"Aijaz, how did you find me? Why can't you leave me alone?"

"Do you really want to know?" Aijaz was speaking in a silvery whisper of a viper that is about to strike a blow. "You won't like it! Badal, your precious husband arranged the whole thing because he wants to marry somebody called Sunetra. He was engaged to her, was he not and is your cousin? He only married you because Sunetra ran away with her boyfriend and your father promised him that he would help him in his business."

Carma looked at him in astonishment... "Aijaz, what are you talking about?!"

"I am talking about your precious husband! The one your brother thought was a good man! Huh! I wonder what he would think now, or maybe he does not care? And your parents, do they know how you are? Did you know that they are not in Delhi but have moved? And your aunt too is not there. Now you really don't think that I was a bad husband after all, do you?" His eyes glittered and shone maliciously.

Carma had been passively waiting resigned to her fate, but Aijaz's words brought her to life and she gagged and clutched her throat.

"N.Noo...Badal wouldn't.....You are making it up!" Carma felt no fear, only a consuming fury.

Her anger gave her strength beyond her normal physical powers and she ran for the door, but Aijaz caught her before she could open the door.

She hung on to the door with all her strength, even though she knew it was locked, however, it was futile. When Aijaz caught hold of her she twisted in his grasp and it was all he could do to hold her squirming body.

"Let me go, you...You are lying!" she screamed, scratching his eyes like a cat.

When Aijaz turned his head to one side, her hand raked down his cheek, her nails trailing fine wavering bloody furrows in the flesh of his face.

He roared in pain and slapped her hard and her head snapped to one side leaving her briefly stunned. He grabbed her wrists, twisted her around so that one arm was behind her back. She moaned in pain and he pushed her roughly on the bed cursing and swearing.

Carma's head was reeling, but as she would not let disappointment get the better of her intelligence, she searched the shadows of her mind to find the truth about her time with Badal and found the reality horrible.

She recalled tiny moments, minute phrases of Badal's that now slashed into her heart like the blows and left scars, and she finally recognised how often his promises had turned into lies.

Terror and hatred for Badal swept over her like a tidal wave, and she suddenly slithered down the wall, crumpled into a heap and started crying.

The cavalier attitude he had towards had in India had only covered his monumental selfishness, and she now realised the true meaning of the sentence that there is no one as blind as one whom refuses to see.

She had got the impression that the emotions he had displayed in India had bespoken of righteousness and been impressed by them.

Aijaz saw her distress and began yelling.

"Carma, I want my son!" Aijaz shouted, two cruel lines running from his nose to his thin lips.

"He is not your son!" Carma cringed against the wall.

Aijaz smiled cruelly, and began goding and taunting her, finally succeeding in breaking down her patience.

As she watched Aijaz's face, Carma saw on his face a mirror of her own feelings. Yet as rage, anger, bitterness, helplessness and hatred for him fought for dominance, one emotion showed itself stronger – rage – rage as Carma never felt before.

The alien emotion that she suddenly felt was responsible in giving her the strength to fight back, and she kicked Aijaz, scratched him and even tried to bite him. However, Aijaz was too strong and her resistance and aggression only fuelled Aijaz's anger.

"You brought my to son to London, away from me! And don't even think that you will be able to oppose me for I will get him! You know what happens to people who stand in my way! I will bring him up in the tradition of our family and….!"

Aijaz walked towards her and punched her on the face and Carma cringed against the table defiantly as she thought of the cruel 'tradition of Aijaz's family.' Her big dark eyes held more temper than fear as she thought of Abhay, and as she leant her hands behind the table, her fingers felt an object.

"Abhay is not your son,!" She repeated as she quickly picked it up and hit Aijaz with all her strength.

There was a look of surprise on Aijaz's face as he fell, his head bleeding profusely, but as she saw the blood spill on the carpet, Carma panicked. She looked at Aijaz's still figure in astonishement and terror then fled from the room as quickly.

She walked down the street, limping and barefoot, her blouse ripped and her hair flung wildly around her face. She was in shock when the police picked her up in the late evening wandering the streets lifelessly, shivering and sweating, muttering over and over again "I have killed him, Oh my God, I have killed him!"

There was blood on her sari and her lips were cut and bruised. Carma's one eye was swollen and partly closed, and she blinked as the strong beam of the police flashlight hit her in the face. She was immediately arrested for a few people had seen her running from the house with stained clothes.

She was taken to the police station where she confessed to killing Aijaz in a voice devoid of emotion. However, the style of police questioning had triggered fresh feelings of humiliation and helplessness in her so could not enlighten them further regarding the incident.

However, to support her confession, the police had found a body of a man fitting Aijaz's description in a house nearby and investigations had identified the dead man to be Aijaz. The post-mortem had revealed that death was due to severe blows to his head.

After having spent a day in the police cells, still shaken and in a trance, Carma was taken to the local prison, where she sat huddled, looking lost and forlorn. She felt disoriented, feeling as if some inner part of her had been erased,

"Hurry up, get your belongings and come with me!"

Carma looked at the prison officer in amazement, suddenly overwhelmed and alarmed by her surroundings and the prison officer's abrupt and rude voice. She smiled weakly, but her attempt at a smile looked frightening to the prison officer as it seemed so far removed from any feeling.

"I said hurry up! I don't have time you you…., do you think you are in a hotel and we are here only to serve you?! If you do you are mistaken, as you will soon find out!" The prison officers glared at her menacingly.

Carma gulped and wiped the tear that had begun to ooze out of the corner of her eye. She clasped the plastic bag that held the bare ecessities that were permitted with trembling hands and followed the prison officer.

Chapter 4

Carma was still thinking of that first day when it was time for their evening tea. There was the familiar jangling of keys, one by one the cell doors were flung open and everybody rushed quickly to grab a plate and stand in the queue. For once mealtime was a sombre affair, and Carma was glad that apart from the usual teasing and banter, there were no outbreaks of fights.

As soon as they were seated in the cell with the tea tray on their lap, Anisha pointed to her tray and smiled the dimple danced briefly on her cheek as she spoke

"Right, for our first course we have some rolls, for our main course there is some over burnt cabbage, but as a speciality of the prison service, I ordered some fleas in my food! I did not think that my order would be catered for but as you can see it is! As for drinks, there was so much variety that I could not decide, so I have just ordered hot water, again with fleas and insects and maybe an odd cockroach or so and for…." Anisha's eyes were twinkling.

Carma laughed hysterically then put her hands on her ears. "Anisha, stop!" she looked at the unappetising meal thinking that even lousy food was edible if you had someone to laugh with, and as soon as she could speak, asked a question that had been preying on her mind.

"I have noticed many young girls in prison, Anisha, it is so sad, I wonder what makes them commit crimes?" Carma sipped her tea thoughtfully.

"I think it has something to do with the fact that they have been abused in some form or another, and it is a natural instinct to inflict wrong and injury to avoid suffering from it. And I am not only taking our example but Lisa's also, you know the cell I shared with before you came. Anyway one day when she was sober, she told me how when she was very young, her mother had got involved with a bloke who turned out to be a pimp. Lisa did not get along with him and they often used to row. Matters escalated when one day Lisa walked in the kitchen, (she was only 13 at that time), only to find her mother screaming as her boyfriend slashed her face. Lisa thought he was going to kill her, so picked up a kitchen knife and stabbed him. She told me that she had nightmares to this day of the blood that was splashed on the walls! Anyway, she was taken to a young offender's camp, where she started hanging out with a gang who then introduced her to crime and drugs."

"Just convinces me that first offence prisoners, who actually want to abide by the prison rules, should be protected by the prison service, and not exposed to hardened criminals, who first victimise the 'first timers' then encourage them into a life of crime." Carma shuddered as she saw a cockroach crawling on the cell floor. "Hey, Anisha, are you enjoying your gourmet dinner!"

"Ha, Ha! Anyway, I agree with you, for with drugs available and prisoners telling you that 'bird is easy if yu 'r' doped up', it is hardly surprising that on their release many prisoners become drug addicts! The prison service does not realise that mixing the least bad with the worst in no solution. By the way, Ruth told me that you had no relations in London?" Anisha asked abruptly.

"Actually I do, but the reason I did not tell the authorities was because I do not want my husband to know what I had done and where I was. You see, Anisha, there was a time when I regarded him to be my emotional saviour, one that would be a source of comfort to me"

There was a wistful look on Carma's face.

"Actually, he was the one who manipulated events that led me here. Anyway, I have since discoverd that he was a weak man, one who would not only ignore my present emotions but also project his own negative reaction back on to me. And I cannot withstand the added emotional pressure, not at this time, for I need to be reassured that my reaction had been normal and only been guided by clear instinct. I cannot face his criticism or judgement, I think you will understand, Anisha, he is so much like Azaria. Also, I do not want Abhay to have the stigma of prison attached to his life." There was a grim expression on Carma's face as she folded her blanket.

"But by suppressing your feelings Carma, you are taking on a huge load of stress on your shoulders." Anisha remarked as she yawned.

It was strange that the intensity of their emotions was always distracted by their surroundings. Anisha took it in a positive manner for she knew instinctively that both could not have faced the intensity of the conflict that raged within.

"Gosh, even though I had a sleeping tablet last night, I could not sleep. I don't know about you, Carma, but I hate nightime in the remand centre, for with it comes the thinking and the suffering, for both the guilty and the innocent. And I have come to the conclusion that there are two kinds of innocence, firstly the actual truth that is only known to the person concerned and God, and the secondly, the legal decision, which is based the solicitor who prepares our representation. " She gave a weary smile.

Carma bit her under-sip thoughtfully as she stood quietly with her head held high proudly, then suddenly started pacing the cell. She stopped beside the minute window and looked out her cell into the dreary prison courtyard, reflecting that Anisha was an odd mixture of shyness and maturity.

"And in answer to your question, I am not from London, Anisha, I am originally from India. I got married and came soon after."

"Really? I myself have never been there, though I have heard a lot about it. Do you ever feel homesick?"

"Oh yes!" Carma replied, and her eyes lit up with joy as she thought about India. "I miss its tropical moonlight nights - the hot nights with a delicate fragrance of Jasmine amongst the cypress trees. India has a lot of colour, variety and strange bee like busyness, and you know strangely enough, I miss and can almost sense its power, vitality and grandeur. And that is only the positive side of India. But my time with Aijaz overshadow the pleasant memories, for you know, Aijaz was a terrible man, with a vicious temper!"

"I presume he was violent towards you?"

"Oh yes, amongst other things, but like you, for a long time I suffered silently and did not say a word to anybody."

Carma trembled as she experienced again a fear - a dread that Aijaz had instilled during her marriage to him. She experienced again the agony she had endured silently because of her faith in love and marriage, and what it had represented to her – an economical, social, cultural and emotional existence.

****

<u>Chapter 5</u>

The hot summer breeze fluttered against the tattered and cheap curtains and Carma saw the frail bodies of flies and insects beating vainly against the windowpane, trying to escape the strong sun.

Carma was engrossed in her thoughts and did not hear Aijaz enter the room, She was startled when a glass narrowly missed her and hit the wall behind her, shattering into tiny fragments.

"Carma, I have been calling you for the last five minutes!" Aijaz tilted his head back and a cunning smile came to his lips.

"Sorry, Aijaz...I..." Carma shuddered as she saw the expression on his face.

She hated and feared that smile for it meant that Aijaz's violence, which at the moment was directed at throwing glasses, would soon be aimed at her. However, on this occasion she was feeling rebellious and tried to think of ways she could defend herself.

"Aijaz, please, I don't know why you are angry", whimpered Carma, moving to one side as another glass was flung at her

"What are you crying for?" Aijaz moved towards her, his eyes bright, voice soft. "I haven't touched you as yet!" But his eyes were blazing as he raised his hand and walked threateningly towards her.

"Please, Aijaz", Please don't hit me, I haven't done anything and….." Carma sobbed and cowered against the wall.

The real Aijaz, the one that she had been deliberately blinding herself to, was visible and made an ugly distorted image of what she had once believed him to be.

"What have you done?" yelled Aijaz "you are asking me what have you have done?" he hit her with the back of his hand and sent her sprawling on the floor.

As Carma crumpled on the floor she began to weep in fear, but Aijaz's eyes were like steel and his voice shook with anger.

"You could help us - I need a job, I need money - and your parents are rich" He kicked her with his foot. "Get up!" he snarled.

His eyes were cold and a slow menacing smile curved his mouth.

"How can you blame me!" cried Carma, rose from the floor and wiped the tears from her face.

However, just when she thought she was safe, she saw Aijaz's fist heading towards her face. She quickly averted her face, but was not fast enough for his fist managed to land on her eye. Again and again his fist landed on her face and there was blood spurting from her nose and lips as Carma crawled towards the sofa.

There was an expression of disdain on his face and the snakelike hardness of his eyes showed disgust. His face twisted in rage as he clamped his hands under her arms, leaving them black and blue.

"Oh stop crying…..! I'm going to see my friends. You disgust me", he muttered as he strode out of the room "and I don't know what time I'll be back!" Aijaz looked over his shoulder to see Carma sitting on the sofa sobbing. "You're forever sobbing and I don't like crying women!"

The door slammed after him and Carma felt a rush of blood through her veins. She felt the drumming of her pulse and heart, and the ringing in her ears pounded all breadth out of her lungs. She gagged, clutched at her throat, and then fell down on the sofa sobbing uncontrollably.

After some time she got up and went into the bathroom to rinse her face with cold water and was shocked to see her face in the mirror - all bloody, black and bruised. She felt she was cracking under Aijaz's emotional and physical violence and decided she was not going to tolerate his violence anymore.

Her legs were trembling so hard she could barely walk to the telephone to phone her brother, Amit.

As she picked up the receiver and heard the dialling tone, she dreaded the thought of anyone else, especially her parents, answering, and breathed a silent prayer.

"Hello", Carma heaved a sigh of relief as she heard her brother, Amit's voice boom cheerfully over the phone.

"Hello, Amit Bhaiya", Carma's voice was quivering,

"Carma - is that you? What is the matter?"

"Amit, can you come at once please?" Carma was sobbing and quickly slammed the receiver back on its cradle before Amit could ask any more questions.

Carma went back to the lounge but started crying in heart-rending sobs and her fingers grabbed her hair as if to pull out her pain.

Gradually as her sobbing subsided, she closed her darkly shadowed eyes and her head dropped forward in tiredness and a wave of regret swept over her.

****

"My father warned me about Aijaz", Carma admitted grudgingly. "He had seen, with all his maturity that Aijaz had a false ego man and that for all his promises would not make me happy, I realise now how naive I was, but honestly, Aijaz simply swept me off my feet with his devilish good looks. Later, the only feelings I had for him was fear!" Carma trembled.

They could hear snippets of conversations from outside as the women shouted to each other across the cell.

"My husband's just been admitted to 'ospital!"

"Wassat?"

"I thought 'e was goin' to a loony bin, innit?"

Another voice joined in.

"D'ya hear what they done to Margaret? She smashed 'er 'ead 'gaisnt the wall!"

"Fuckin' 'ell!"

Carma listened to the conversatioand and shuddered. She was a refined and aloof woman and hated the invasion of her privacy and the sordid aspects of prison. She recognised the voices to be those of Sue and Irene. Both were in prison for drugs but whereas Irene was a heroin dealer and only pushed drugs to pay for herself, Sue was only a user and had never sold drugs but bought them for her use only.

"Now I wonder why Margaret did that?" Carma asked forgetting for a moment the fear that Aijaz had embedded in her.

"I don't really blame her, for she is always being teased by the other women. Must have all got a bit too much for her to handle."

"Is she badly hurt though?"

"No, just a mild concussion, I believe. You know how the women love to exaggerate anyway; most probably they loved the fact that Margaret is wounded, for they can be cruel." Anisha shuddered. "And as Margaret could not handle her own conflict that I suppose can be classified as 'individual injustice.'"

"In a nutshell, Anisha, I suppose that is what injustice is." Carma sat thoughtfully. "Festering in a group, I see it is rendering everyone incapable of common actions and deeds and is often the cause of mobs and quarrels. Actually, I have seen it in action in India too, of course in a different form."

"Is it this division of purpose you are speaking about, Carma, which sets Margaret at variance not only with herself, but with all the women?"

"Yes, I think so, Anisha, maybe she should try to 'blend in', so to speak." Carma paced the cell.

"She tried, Carma, remember the time she came up to us in the courtyard and bragged how she had all those guns? I even overheard her the other day telling a new girl from another wing that common burglary was out for her. Margaret was bragging how housebreaking was too dangerous because of alarms and all. The solution she was telling this girl was to break in during the day, 'tie up' the occupants, torture them till they tell where they have their money hidden, then beat them senseless and leave them. But,only after completing the robbery, of course!"

"How awful!" Carma shook her head in wonderment. "What a thing to brag about."

"Don't forget, she was only trying to fit in, maybe she did not do anything. Anyway, tell me, did you get married soon after you met you husband?"

"No, we went out a few times and he was so immaculately dressed at all times, that I thought him to be a bit a dandy really!"

Carma smiled as she recalled how impressed she had been with Aijaz's easy grace that had been set of by his good looks. There had been a lot of devilishness in him, stubbornness and a good deal of vanity.

"You too did not suspect that he had a temper?"

"Yes, I did, Anisha, no I mean gradually as we met more and more, I realised he had an explosive temper, however, in the beginning his volatile emotion was exciting. Although I was only completely happy in the first month, after that I realised I had mistaken his male chauvinism for arrogance, his forceful personality for determination, and that in reality he was only utterly selfish, spoilt, really."

"He seems to be like Akram!" Anisha retorted.

"Yes, I think he was, he could control me by coaxing, flattery or charm, bribe me with kindness, then threaten me with abandonement! When I began to feel that I was the one to blame, he manipulated me emotionally through my sense of guilt and shame. With him I was always confused and spent a great deal of time in trying to figure out why things had changed and why our relationship had become so stifling for him."

"And you know now that you are not to blame, Carma? That is very important for I too felt like that and realised in time that it was not my fault, anyway was he always controlling and demanding?" Anisha asked, her eyes brimming with affection and sympathy.

"No, There were times when he was kind, and then I loved him to distraction, Anisha, and these were moments of happiness that I tried to lock in a safe place to shield them protectively for I felt that any kind of exposure would kill them! And I was right for when Aijaz was violent; I became convinced that I had nothing but hatred for him. The flare-ups happened quickly, like flashes of lightening, one moment I

would feel something magnetic about his dark eyes, almost mystical and compelling, at other times he was a cold and distant stranger."

There was a faraway look in Carma's eyes.

"But my love for him was gradually being swept away by his humiliating me constantly. But silly me, I always came to the conclusion that my marriage was most important, consequently his wishes had to come before my own! My daily-married life became dull, for Aijaz was very possessive and I was not allowed out on my own, and I lacked, because of our financial situation, normal and small pleasures for then maybe I would have felt it easier to tolerate…..?"

"He sounds so much like Akram, what men we married, huh?""

"Tell me about it! However, like you, I too tried to ignore Aijaz's hatred, for I had learnt he was an insecure man who had developed a distorted ego. As a result, he was nervous and psychologically disturbed. But his charming personality concealed another man, one who was cunning, sly and shallow whose relationships could be built on nothing but sand! But I was struck by his sensational good looks and my heart still skips a beat when I remember the first time I saw Aijaz!"

****

Chapter 6

"What a handsome man." Carma commented to Anushka, her friend, as she saw Aijaz nonchalantly toss his cigarette butt to the ground and crush it with his foot.

With his brilliant white shirt, burgundy tie and dark grey slacks, shiny black hair freshly barbered and brushed sleekly back, Aijaz seemed a natural star who drew people towards him with his charm and good-looks.

"He is a friend of mine but I will introduce him to you some other time for I promised your brother I would drop you off home by 5."

"Can't you introduce me before you go, after all I might not get another chance and....?" Carma had asked shyly.

"Oh, allright...I know how shy you are and rarely get a chance to go out!"

Anushka introduced them and then when they immediately started chattering like old friends, opened her mouth to ask Carma if she wanted to be dropped home but Carma was oblivious to everyone but Aijaz.

"And what am I supposed to tell Amit the next time I see him?" Anushka asked the following day. "Was he very angry that I did not drop you home?" "No, he wasn't home, and don't worry, he doesn't know about Aijaz!" Carma's eyes sparkled and her cheeks were flushed.

"Carma, be careful, Aijaz is a ladies man and...."

"I can look after myself, thank you!" Carma replied angrily.

Anushka shrugged and walked away and Carma was relieved, for she did not want anyone to interfere in her happiness.

Aijaz had been so charming and they got on so well that they had gone out as much as possible during the preceding weeks, and a month later, Aijaz had took her hand in his.

"Carma, will you marry me?"

Carma was flabbergasted and delighted at the same time. She could not think of a life without Aijaz so quickly answered

"Yes, Oh yes,! But you know, my parents have met you only once and even that when you dropped me. I don't think they will agree so…"

"Does that mean you do not love me, Carma?" Aijaz lips pouted like a small boy.

"I do, Aijaz, it is just that…." Carma floundered for Aijaz was of a different religion and her parents were orthodox Hindus.

"If you really love me you will marry me. You know, as you are there only daughter, I am sure they won't be angry with you for long."

"Okay, Aijaz, maybe you are right, but give me one more chance to talk to them"   But when Carma tried to persuade her father, he had shouted at her.

"You mean the one who dropped you one evening? I did not like him, and no, you are not going to marry that, that man, Carma; I have not even met his family!" Devesh had shouted.

He was of a staunch Hindu background brought up with the belief that Indian marriages were not merely a union of two people, but a linking of families. He believed that parents had a responsibility to find a compatible and decent partner for their child within their social requirements. He had confidence in arranged marriages and thought that love was an emotion that developed in marriage.

"I will marry him! Dad, I love him." sobbed Carma.

She tossed her hair, thrust her hands in her jeans and her huge brown eyes, usually doe like and soft, had flashed rebelliously.

"That's what you think, young lady. Carma, I mean it," Devesh glared at her "if you go ahead with this silly notion, I will never see you again!"

"Mother?" Carma looked at her mother beseechingly, but seeing Sumitra's deferential and compliant expression had retreated to her room sobbing and crying.

"Sumitra," Devesh glowered at his wife with bloodshot eyes, bristling with anger. "On no account will she marry that, that…..man!"

"I agree", Sumitra replied meekly

"What she sees in him, I don't know!" Devesh fumed as he paced the room.

"Well, we don't really know hime." Sumitra replied vaguely "and he did seem charming, handsome, polite…" her voice trailed off.

"Yes, Yes," Devesh interrupted her "but there is something about him I did not like. I cannot pinpoint what it is but I think he is an emotionally dangerous man and will only make her unhappy".

"I know", Sumitra acknowledged quietly "but Carma is at an impressionable age and Youth has no doubts, the young, and no fear."

Sumitra sighed for she had bestowed Carma with her selfless love and did not want to see her unhappy.

"But she is also very mature and sensible for her age" remarked Devesh hopefully "we'll give her time to work things out. I am sure that given time she will admit and recognise that we are right."

"You forget she is very naïve and in many ways immature. And like you", Sumitra added, feeling bold, "she is also very stubborn. She will marry Aijaz once she has set her mind to it, regardless of what we have to say on the matter. I think it would be sensible for us to keep quiet".

"You mean you agree with her?" exclaimed Devesh and glared at Sumitra in disbelief.

"No, of course not", Sumitra snapped, and then quickly corrected herself in a self-effacing manner. "I too do not like him at all, and that is disregarding the fact that he is from a different religion. I too feel if she had to fall in love why could she not have chosen a nice boy from our caste?"

"I wonder where we went wrong?" muttered Devesh; seething with anger "we introduced her to the children of our acquaintances and gave her everything she wanted. How could she get involved with a man like to Aijaz?!"

"There is no point in blaming ourselves", Sumitra replied, surprised at the intense dislike both of them had formulated in a short meeting with Aijaz.

Sumitra sensed the situation had become delicate and did not want it to become worse. Words had been said that Devesh, she hoped, would regret later. But as Carma and Devesh were both stubborn, she did not expect that to happen, thus making any kind of compromise by either to be impossible.

Events moved rapidly after that, for Carma was adamand and they were married in a registry office.

****

"My father was right, I now realise," Carma said sadly, looking around her. Then as if her memories were too painful, she changed the subject. "By the way, Anisha, the soap and shampoo the prison supplied with has run out. What do I do?" Carma asked.

"You'll have to ask a prison officer who is responsible for them, but I must warn you that he will use his power to cause you maximum humiliation before he gives you any more supplies!"

"I think I am prepared for that, Anisha, for I have seen how a prison officer does not miss a chance to bully a prisoner. At least most of them that it is John, you know the bald prison officer who is always boasting about how he has been suspended from the service twice because he brutally assaulted some prisoners?"

"I know the one you mean, you mean to tell me that he was reinstated?"

"Just shows, eh, anyway, just be sure and say 'please' and call him 'guv'. He is a pompous so and so…!"

As soon as Carma saw him she went up to him with a sense of foreboding.

"What do you want!?" John glared at Carma.

"Eh, my soap and shampoo have finished and I need fresh supplies to…"

"Wash with water then or buy it from the tuck shop! Anyway, I don't think soap will make any difference!" John sneered.

Carma stood her ground defiantly. "Look, all I want is some soap, and I think that is my right. If you don't do anything, I would like to see the senior officer."

"Shut your fucking mouth! Now would you like to see the senior officer?" he shoved Carma against the wall and raised his hand threateningly.

John turned away with an expression of disdain on his face when an inmate came up to him.

Carma was still smarting from her friction with John but could not help overhearing the terse conversation.

"I would like to make a phone call."

"Show me your phone card."

The new arrival took out her phonecard and showed it to John.

"This card is not signed; you cannot make any phone call."

"But at the other prison, I did not have to sign it, Guv." The new arrival was flustered. "I need to phone urgently as my son is sick and…"

"I don't give a fuck about either the other prison or your son! In this prison you do what I tell you, and if I ever catch you trying to use the phone card again like this, I will either put you on report or you will end up in the block! Understand?" John warned the new arrival with a sickening grin.

Carma staggered back into her cell and recounted the incident to Anisha.

"When an inmate is subjected to extremes of either selfishness or anti social behaviour, the least the authorities can do is to act with appropriate firmness."

"I told you that is what would happen, Carma. And as for the authorities doing something, John himself is an example. They know what kind of officer he is but choose to ignore his behaviour, but I have no doubt that an innocent officer will be persecuted and dismissed. Carma, it is best we do not talk about the prison, it is too depressing……you were telling me that you married Aijaz regardless of your parents objections?"

"I agree, Anisha, we won't talk about prison life, it is too depressing, but then on the other hand so is my life! Anyway, yes, even though my parents did not give me their blessing, I remained adamant in my resolution and married Aijaz soon after."

"But what about your mother? I would have thought she would have supported you?"

"I wish…..on one hand she does what my father says and on the other, she is very staunch in her beliefs….. for to her caste is a kind of trademark, a kind of determining factor in our level in society which provided her with rituals and rules, one of them being that it is the parents who choose a companion for their child within their social circle. For me to marry outside our caste, why, whatever would her relations think!! It did not matter to her what made her daughter happy but… anyway, we went to the registry and got married."

"You must have missed having your parents present, though." Anisha said sympathetically.

"Oh, I did. But I soon realised that they were right, for even though Aijaz was a fascinating and handsome man, he was also clever, manipulative with an explosive temper and it was not long before my love turned sour. And I realised than that love alone is not enough to sustain a relationship."

"So right….do you think it was because you came from different backgrounds and religion?"

"I really do not know, Anisha, I suppose he never really loved me and also Aijaz started to find domesticity stifling. He started craving the life of a bachelor, and although he worked in various jobs, was always distracted by more pleasurable activities - hobbies like gambling, wondering which horse to back etc. He started going out with his friends and resumed his constant visits to his family. And when he was at home, he would sit around moodily, shadowing the small house with his dreary depression!"

"He sounds like an awful man, Carma. I am beginning to think he even outclasses Akram in degradation!"

Carma nodded. "But in the beginning of our marriage he was perfect, though, but when he started being violent! It started so casually, first by pushing me gently during a tantrum, then by shouting in a thunderous voice to abide by his useless and petty rules! By that time I began to accept my kismet, and recogonised the fact that if I defied him he would leave me, and for me that was inconceivable even after finding out about his true nature!"

She began pacing the cell.

"Also as I had nowhere to go, I swallowed my pride and endured my pain, managing somehow to busy myself with dreams of a pleasanter future, and you know who my only companion was during that time – it was hope."

Carma's face twitched as she looked around her at the walls of the cells, feeling like a captured animal caught in a trap. Her memories were too painful as she relived the time spent with Aijaz, so tried to change the subject.

"Anisha, I have not seen Judy for some time. Has she been discharge?"

"No, I believe she has been transferred to another prison." Anisha saw the tears in Carma's eyes.

"Is a prisoner transferred often?" Carma did could not think how she would survive if she were separated from Anisha.

"Yes, they are, I believe the term is called either 'dislocation' or 'ghosting'. I miss Judy, you know, for she would tell me about the entire courtroom formalities and procedures. But Carma, you have not told me about your father? Mine, though loveable, was very strict and unapproachable."

"My father was a cold, arrogant, self-centred man, and oh, not forgetting stubborn, whose slightest whim was fulfilled by mother. But he too, was quite loveable really. I loved the way he knew a proverb for almost anything in life! He thought that spiced up his speech, however Amit, mother and myself used to laugh because he inevitably got them all wrong anyway!" Carma smiled tenderly.

"Sorry, Carma, if it is too upsetting for you to talk…?"

"No, I'm fine; Amit my brother was very supportive, not my parents, and he was the one I turned to when I needed help when I was married to Aijaz." Carma clenched her hands, and looking down at them her face became distant and pensive. "Amit had always been very protective toward me and even in college, we were quite popular."

"I always missed having a brother.." Anisha said wistfully.

"He is a wonderful brother, always very protective towards me. There was only one year's difference between us but we were complete opposites in character. In fact everybody said that the only thing in common between the tall and broad shouldered Amit and his slim and small sister was their good looks! I am scratching my own back here, Anisha! But seriously, whereas Amit was bold and easy with strangers, good in sports, his obsession for games was equated by my dislike for any kind of sport. Whereas Amit avoided books, I spent all of my time with them! And it was this combination of sports and intellect that had made us popular in the University. Amit was so caring that I only called him once and he dropped everything to be at my side to give me support!"

****

Chapter 7

Amit could hear the rumbling of thunder and saw the dense masses of dark clouds that had started sweeping across the heavens and that were the first signs of the monsoon season.

Although he was worried about Carma, he drove fast but cautiously, for the other drivers seemed to be driving blindly, with no regard for the other's safety. To add to the confusion, there were cows strolling on the roads, impervious to traffic. Finally, after what seemed hours on the road, Amit finally reached Carma's house.

She was waiting at the gate and as soon as she saw Amit's car rushed at him, gripping his hand fiercely and glancing at him with eyes full of humiliation and terror. She hid her head on his shoulder and sobbed uncontrollably. Amit felt her trembling and the sound of her voice alarmed him and as he tenderly brushed the hair from her face he gave a gasp.

"Carma! What has happened to you? It must be Aijaz who has done this….. I'll kill him!"

Amit felt a feeling of protectiveness and responsibility surge through him as he saw Carma's bruised lips part beseechingly.

Carma slowly wiped her eyes and opened the door.

"Come in Amit Bhaiya. No, Aijaz is not at home," she said with a catch in her throat. She blinked and swallowed, but it seemed as if her heart stuck in her throat.

Amit walked in the room and was horrified to see the state of the room with the broken glass strewn across the floor.

"Before you tell me what happened, I will call a doctor", said Amit in a shocked voice.

"No, there is no need for that." replied Carma, her voice quivering with feeling for Amit's presence, his deep warm voice and concern, bestowed Carma with confidence and comfort.

"What do you mean you do not want to see a doctor?" exclaimed Amit, "Look at your face! God alone knows what he has done to you - how many bones he has broken!" He looked at her protectively and his soft brown eyes filled with understanding. "I am taking you out of this place and back home."

"No, that is not the solution, Amit bhaiya, anyway, I am used to it by now."

"What! You mean he has beaten you before? I don't know who is to blame here for if father had not made it so difficult for you to come to us….but then, you too, are as stubborn as a mule! There, there," he said, soothingly, as Carma started crying again at his reproach. "Sorry, I am being insensitive, as usual!" He remarked with a grin, trying to comfort Carma.

And it was the lilt of laughter in his voice, even in this situation, that dragged Carma from the depths of depression and self-pity.

"Amit", how can I come home?" asked Carma, suddenly remembered the threats Aijaz had made. "Aijaz threatens to kill me if I leave him and Father has said he never wants to see me again."

She looked at Amit with big soulful eyes that were brimming with tears. "And he was right - right about everything. Aijaz only wanted to marry me because he thinks I am rich. He is a gambler - and ever since Father disowned me - he has beaten me - as if everything is my fault", she sobbed.

"Don't worry", said Amit. There was warmth, gentleness and strength in his words. "I, or rather Mother, have tried to persuade father. I, we will look after you."

"Unbelievable, Mother having the guts to speak to him?"

Carma was astonished that her mother would have the courage to talk to her faher. However, being a proud and sensitive woman, she did not like the condescending and superior manner of her brother.

She stood up straight, her head turned and her eyes flashed with fire. Moreover, she realised that whereas it was a matter of phrasing with her brother, his intonation would be negligible compared to the patronising manner of her father. Her expression changed and became obscure. Her eyes no longer flashed but became dark dim pools.

"You obviously cannot stay with Aijaz, Carma; all we have to do is to decide how we are to get you out of here." Amit said confidently, unconscious that her sensitivity was due to an emotional torment inflicted not only by Aijaz, but her father as well.

Carma's expression changed and dimmed. "I know it is impossible for me to stay here, but I cannot go back home either, Amit."

Amit looked at Carma in dismay. She was very stubborn, and he knew that once she made up her mind, it was futile to argue with her.

****

"Although Amit tried to convince me that everything was alright back home, I could detect that he was actually not sure of father's reaction." Carma paced the cell.

A prison officer can and looked through the hatch of their cell.

"It's time to go to work!" she barked

"We will start work tomorrow, guv." Anisha told the prison officer as she was leaving.

Anisha saw the look on Carma's face and tried to explain.

"The Home Office allows prisoners to work for a minimum wage, but this is not compulsory for remand prisoners, so the choice is yours, but prisoners prefer to work to for it enables them to buy items such as shampoos, toothpaste and cigarettes. And to buy cigarettes even for those that do not smoke is useful for they serve as a barter commodity for the prisoners who smoke. As the women who smoke are often reduced to the humiliating practice of picking up butts from the rubbish bins, they are only to glad to be given the chance to smoke with dignity!"

"Whatever the benefits, Anisha, I don't think I like the idea of work!" Carma said in alarm.

"Believe you me, Carma, it is a good idea, for work will provide us with an opportunity to increase the amount of money that we spend in the canteen. Anyway, remember the time when you need soap and John would not supply any….? Well, you can buy from the canteen…anyway, you are always complaining that the shampoo is not enough!"

"Yes but…"

"Before you make up your mind, remember that work would also be an escape from the tedium of long hours locked up, we can meet other women from other wings and also catch up on prison gos!" Anisha chuckled. "It offers a break in the routine of the prison, but maybe since you have not been here long enough, you don't feel the need for a break in routine?"

"I don't think that is the reason, Anisha, anyway we get the chance to meet the women from other wings when out in the exercise yard, and as for prison gos, why, I can hear the inmates yelling to each other from across their cells! But at least the prison service does something to help the prisoners." Carma said with a grimace.

"Oh yes, they do, at least they try. The idea of the prison system started of as being as one of punishment and retribution, but at present is not based on the primitive idea of vengeance, thank God!"

"Surprise, surprise! Seeing the prisoners around me makes me think that it does bring out the primitive instincts! All the fighting and yelling!

And that reminds me, do they do anything regarding educating the prisoners?"

"Yes, but whilst classes for education are considered important, there are no specific hours allotted to them, and if there is a staff shortage, which is often, they are the first to suffer, no, the first is not letting us out for exercise!"

"Oh, because I would have liked join some kind of course ….to help me find work once outside! Anyway coming back to the subject of work in prison, I suppose it might be good for me to get used to the idea for I will have to once outside, for there is no one to support me and…."

Carma's heart thudded painfully as she paced the cell, and ,as though in a dream, she moved towards the broken dressing table of the cell and started to brush her hair. She looked at the reflection in the broken mirror, and seeing her brown eyes look like two broken windows, turned away with a cry.

Suddenly there was a rattling of keys and she heard cell doors opening and closing.

"It's alright, Carma, it is only one prison officers are going to another cell. They must be taking an inmate to the punishment or something. Poor women! What we have to suffer! Tell me, Carma, I have often wondered, is the situation bad in India for women?" Anisha remarked as she saw the confused, slightly dazed look on Carma's face.

"Yes, in fact it is much worse, Anisha, although there are some women, like my aunt Sajata, who are leading a fight against caste divisions, the religious superstitions that plague the poor communities and male domination. She is chairperson of an organisation that tackle women's issues by highlighting cases of dowry and sexual assaults." Carma saw that Anisha was looking confused.

"Mostly, her organisation arranges demonstrations that demand modifications to the law. However, though Sajata later admitted that because the injustices were too widespread and embedded to be changed overnight, justice would be denied to a lot of suffering women. She felt strongly, and even convinced Amit and myself and Mother, of course, that we were surrounded by a society that tainted women with self-images of weakness and impurity, that Indian society, custom, religion and even economic demands stress the importance of males. Girls, especially amongst the rural areas are seen as a burden and discriminated against since birth!"!"

Carma usually prized her silence selfishly, but by talking to Anisha, she felt the guilt that had been holding her down ease slightly.

"I am not surprised at the suppression....the women in my community suffer the same fate." Anisha said grimly.

"Really? I actually never really believed her till Sajata told tell me incidents in India that proved to me how suppressed a woman really was, how their accomplishments, both in quality and in quantity have been ignored. I was shocked to learn that in custody in India, women are first raped then blamed for having loose morals.... and if their husbands or relatives accuse the police of harassment they are beaten to death! The police are reluctant to listen and act upon crimes against women, but at the same time lenient to male criminals and of course, especially indifferent if the accused person is influential!"

"That is horrible! I have heard of I think it is called 'Sati?' Is that a custom that if a husband dies before his wife, she is burnt along with him?" Anisha asked.

She stood up aware of the ache in her back and neck and arched her back gingerly, trying to ease the tension

"Yes, although it is illegal, some villages do practice it for it is idealised by most villagers to be an act of romance, sacrifice and devotion. Amit too was not in favour of the many traditions of India, in fact there were times when my father and brother used to clash on the topic of the judicial system of India"

As Carma recalled the many discussion of Amit and her father, of Hansa, Ramu's niece, who had been made to renounce her life in the name of her husband, her voice quivered with emotion.

****

Chapter 8

Amit threw his keys on the sideboard, glad to be in the cool shade of the house, for the sun had been relentlessly blazing all day long in a cloudless sky.

"Ramu, where is everybody?" It was hot, humid and Amit was thirsty. He was sweating all over, his hands were sticky and his shirt was sticking to his back

"Sahib", Ramu, their manservant, replied "Memsahib has gone shopping and your father is in the sitting room."

"Ramu, get me a cold drink, please," Amit demanded, mopping his forehead with his handkerchief. "I'll have a lime juice with loads of ice. And bring it to the sitting room - I'll be with Father."

"Yes, Amit Sahib", Ramu said, scurrying off in the direction of the kitchen.

"Ah, there you are, Amit,"

Devesh, his father smiled and peered from behind a paper that he had skimmed over and thought would be put to better use as a fan. It was for too stifling to read thoroughly as it exposed the usual sleaze…. judicial injustice and the usual dowry deaths –

"Did you drop Badal?" he asked, fanning himself vigorously.

"Yes, father, I have." Amit threw himself onto a blue and red checked sofa whose cushions were making the room hotter, if it was possible. "Father, who exactly is he, I mean, is he a relation or something?"

Amit had a cragged handsome face that had character etched on it, and the telltale signs around his eyes bespoke of good humour. He was wearing grey flannel slacks and a pale cotton voile shirt.

"Well, sort of, he is engaged to Sunetra, my brother Yogindra's daughter. I was delighted when Yogi phoned from London asking if we could have Badal as a guest. Badal is here, as you know, on a business trip."

"Oh, I see," answered Amit non-commitedly. "Dad, is there anything of importance or even interesting in today's newspaper?"

He took the ice-cold lime water that Ramu had brought on a tray with one hand whilst with the other he grasped the newspaper that his father handed him.

"You can read it for yourself, but its full of the usual nonsense," Devesh replied indifferently, his face impassive. " Dowry burnings, infanctide etc, though I don't know how much is really true."

"It's all true, dad, there is evidence and statistics that prove that many girls end their lives because they can no longer tolerate the harassment of their in-laws. Do you know, Dad, just the fact that dowry and female infanticide exist proves how a woman's life is of little value?"

Amit had a compassionate temperament and a spasm of helpless anger smote him as he continued fervently.

"Even the legal and democratic system of India fails its people! There are a number of untried prisoners who are buried under the system, which is cracking under the strain of its numbers. Dad, you know that what I say is all true, I mean look what happened to uncle Nitin…"

"Stop it Amit! I hear enough of it from Sajata." Devesh remarked in a biting voice.

He put his hands over his ears then ran his fingers through his collar. The prickly heat was erupting behind his neck and body till he felt his flesh was prickling like a porcupine.

"Dad, I know you don't believe me but apparently there are thousands of people in jails awaiting trials. Aunt Sajata was telling me about one woman prisoner who was arrested when she was pregnant and kept in jail for nine years awaiting trial. She also told me how one woman was caught without a ticket, and then spent twenty years awaiting trial as the police lost her papers! They fed her and all that, but not once did anyone question or care to find out why she was in prison in the first place!"

"You sound like you aunt! I see she has kept you updated!" Devesh remarked in a cutting voice.

Amit who was usually calm always got annoyed when he thought about injustice in any form.

"And I am glad she does, dad! And when a woman becomes a widow, why that too stigmatises them, much like women who can't have children, and in many traditional families they are still regarded as people who cast a shadow - her presence being considered inauspicious at events likes marriages. And because of that stigma and attitude many widows think 'Sati' to be preferable!

****

"OOOh! That sounds terrible!" Anisha looked alarmed.

They were waiting in the queue to make a phone call for Anisha had finally decided to call her solicitor to make an appointment.

"But that mainly happens in the villages." Carma added.

They were waiting behind Catherine, the new arrival who Carma had seen being bullied by John because of her phone card.

It had taken Catherine visits to various officers before her phone card was finally signed, and there was a worried look on her face as she picked up the receiver for she still did not have any news about her sick son.

Suddenly Mandy barged in front of Carma and grabbed the receiver from Catherine's hand.

"'ey, I bn waiting 'ere – I is first!" Catherine said angrily.

Whether Mandy had heard, or she chose to ignore her, Carma did not know, for she had her back towards Catherine.

"'ey yu, I said I is first! I wanna phone my 'usband!"

"Whattya say! No one talks bck to me!"

In one move, Mandy turned and swung her fist. Catherine just managed to move her head to avoid the blow to her face, but Mandy's knuckles got the side of her face and she fell, blood spurting from her lip.

"Anisha, I want a transfer from here!" Carma cried in horror.

"That's not easy, Carma. Come, let's go back to the cell. You look pale and a glass of water is what you need!" They walked down the corridor. "You know Doris, the woman with the scar who was attacked and bullied? Well, she tried and failed. She was told to fill in an application form to see the senior officer. When she handed in her form, it was thrown at her face, saying it had nothing to do with the senior officer, but had to see the allocation officer instead. When she finally got to see him, after innumerable delays, of course, she was asked for her risk assessment. Of course she did not know, and when she said so, she was told to see the risk assessment officer!"

"Seem's that the prison officers were just stalling."

"You're right, for in the end, she gave up, which I think is what the intention of the prison officers was all along. And it is not as if 'transfers' do not happen, they do, but only at the say so of the officers! The authorities use transfers as a combination of segregation, reallocation and of course as their means of control"

"Well, I do not like this degree of control that the prison officers have over us, Anisha!" Carma's eyes flashed.

"We have no choice, Carma! Anyway, before we got interrupted, you were telling me about

'sati'. I did not think that in this day and age…"
Anisha looked surprised.

"Yes…well.." Carma said grudgingly, not wanting to acknowledge the prison officers' authority. "I did not think 'Sati' existed either, and would not have believed it if it had not happened to Ramu's our servant's niece."

****

Chapter 9

"Memsahib, please can you help?" Ramu pleaded in a voice that trembled with emotion.
"Whatever is the matter?" Carma asked.

"It's Hansa! my niece." Ramu's eyes were glistening.

"Why, what is the matter with her? Is she sick? Do you need money?"

"She is fine, health wise at least, but she got married a couple of months ago and…"Ramu wiped thetears that were trickling down his cheeks.

"Ramu, calm down. If she is married, is she not happy?"

"It's not that, sahib; her husband was a drunk and was killed in a brawl a couple of days ago."

"I am sorry, Ramu, do you need a few days off?"

"I don't know how that would help. Memsahib, her in-laws, they are saying that she should die with him!"

"What!" Carma's eyes flew open and she put her hand over her mouth.

"Memsahib, what can I do to save her? Hansa will do what her in-laws ask, for she knows that it would be preferable to having her head shaven, made to wear white and have her to be disgraced and cursed that she would bring bad luck on those that even looked at her! If not that Carma Memsahib, in our villages widows are forced into beggary and prostitution that are attached to brothels or temples."

"I am sorry, Ramu, but all we can do is give you a few days, and maybe bring Hansa back with you?"

"I will try, and thank you." He wiped his cheeks and hurried back into the kitchen.

A few days later, Ramu returned and as soon as Carma saw him asked about Hansa.

"How is your niece, Ramu? She has not come back with you?"

"No, Carma Memsahib" There were tears in Ramu's eyes." As I thought Hansa chose to commit Sati as her escape from her fate if she lived. Although I pleaded with her to come with me, she refused, but made me promise that I would stay till the end, so I saw her, looking beautiful in her bridal clothes, tears streaming from her eyes as she climbed onto her dead husband's funeral pyre. I don't know what kind of people there were in her village, for she was watched and cheered whilst Hansa was slowly consumed by ......oh....the funeral fire!"

Wiping his eyes he left the room and Carma went into the sitting room where Amit and Devesh were having an argument.

"Amit did you hear about Ramu's niece?"

"Yes, I believe her in-laws were harassing her, has she back with him? Is everything all right now?"

"No. I wish..." Carma quickly outlined what had occurred.

"See dad, you wouldn't believe me, Sati exists, and child marriages exist, girls are sold because....."

"I am sorry to hear about Ramu's niece." Devesh said in a gruff voice. "But do you mean to tell me that it is because of extreme poverty, the possibility of more income and the anticipation of a full stomach that persuades some parents to sell their daughters? Ha! And giving in to the dowry system is kind of selling your daughter, isn't it? And isn't Sati illegal anyway?"

Devesh's tone was mocking as he pierced Amit with a diamond hard glare from his scowling bloodshot eyes.

"Dad, although Sati is illegal it still existed in some villages, and that although it rarely occurrs there existes tradition and rituals in some villages. Unluckily, it appeared that Ramu's village was one of them!"

"Yes and dowry only flourishes because it somehow plays a major part in social and religious tradition, in family self-respect, and social pride. I can't understand it! To me it only shows the greed of people, is not only to humiliating for women, but the newspapers are full of dowry being the cause of violence and murder. Sometimes it is the in-laws who kill their daughter-in-law but sometimes husband are responsible for murdering their wives if their parents fail to continue dowry payments!"

"Dad, he is right, you know, and the common method for either one to commit the crime is by pouring kerosene over the woman, set her alight, and then claim to the authorities that it was suicide!" Carma added.

Amit raked his long strong fingers through his hair, leaving it rumpled. His kind and gentle nature could not envisage such cruelty. Day by day he was becoming cynical not only of his father, fellow Indians but also of the nation as a whole.

"And do you two really believe what the papers print?" Devesh asked contemptuously as he raised his eyebrows.

"It is not what the papers print only. Sajata has first hand tales of Sati, Dowry, Deaths, murder, infancticte...you name it! I only have to look around me to see that dowry for the wealthy has become a business. Not only can they meet the expense but I suspect they like it, for provides them with an opportunity to display their wealth. Carma, do you remember Megan's wedding and the lavish banquet in the marble palace hotel?"

Chapter 10

Carma nodded her head.

"Well, they are one of the richest families and like the rich, the wedding was a means to first attract and then display their wealth. They either do not know, or want to know that the poor have to borrow and take on debts that shadow their lives! That is why I always remind you to increase Ramu's wages."

As Amit thought of how hard Ramu worked so that he could give a reasonable dowry for his daughter his brown eyes filled with compassion.

"Yes, dad, their only solution is to go to moneylenders, who in turn force them to remain slaves forever! For these unfortunate poor people dowry becomes a prison! All because they are greedy and they think dowry is a means to control their woman." Carma spoke passionately.

"Carma, don't repeat everything your brother says! You don't know what you are talking about! This is India, and what you call control is only protection." Devesh remarked, his face inscrutable.

He was a typical Indian man, and believed a woman to be in a subservient position always.

"A young Indian girl, for your information, should be controlled by her father when she is young, by her husband when she is an adult, under the control of her husband, and when she was old, by her son! Although some women like your aunt are independent and modern, thank God, the majority still live homely lives."

"I personally admire and am proud of Aunt Sajata, for at least she is fighting to get women to out of their traditional role and reach some kind of independence.In fact I find it hard to believe that she is your sister" Amit, who was of a humane temperament found it hard to accept his father's caustic opinions on women.

"Your aunt, my dear boy, is an extreme fanatic! She should keep her fervent desire to protect the needs of the so called 'suffering woman', to herself and not preach to us at any and every opportunity. And if there is no opportunity to preach, you can be sure that she will create one! And to top it all, you have started to talk and preach like her! Why can't she leave my family alone?" Devesh's eyes took on a cold and imperturbable look.

"Dad, she is right." Carma remarked meekly.

"Ha! As for child marriage no parent could.....I don't think her work does any good, you know, even though she thinks she does." There was a sneer in Devesh's voice.

"Her cause if very useful and is more important than you believe, Dad, and as for the custom of child marriages, that still exists and parents do sell their daughters like slaves in a markct!" Carma had been reading the newspaper." Take this article for instance. Some relatives from a neighbouring village chose a young girl for marriage. I can just imagine ......the girl must have been so young that whenever there was a ceremony and the only thought in her mind would have been that it was a happy diversion. The only meaning it would hold was that it meant new bangles for her whilst for the men in her village it must have meant a day of drinking, as a tremendous responsibility would be off the father's head. And the mother would sigh with relief, as there would have to be no looking around for a suitable boy when the immature girl would be of a marriageable age."

"You have a lively imagination, Carma!" Devesh retorted.

"It is not her imagination, dad, but fact, a harsh reality that Ramu upholds. He has a niece who was married when she was a mere child"

"Ha" how many nieces does Ramu have?" Devesh snapped.

"Dad! You are as usual missing the point! He is the one who told me that, ordinarily, though not in his niece's case, the child bride stayed on in her parent's house and years later, when she was grown up, would be taken away in a palanquin to her new husband. And that is the fate of most women when girls are married as children and they who created her become her executioners. " Amit said sorrowfully.

It was with intelligence and determination Amit spoke of justice, for he did not like to be a part of a world that could be cruel to innocent and vulnerable human beings.

****

When Carma spoke of her brother, her eyes swam with tears and her chin trembled.

"That was only one of the arguments they had when I was at home. I know they had many more when I left for Amit would often tell me how fed up he was and how difficult it was becoming to tolerate father's attitude."

They were in the association room and Anisha saw a look of pain flit across Carma's face as one of the inmate's spoke about Diane's husband.

Diana had a reputation of being a grass because of the lies she told the prisoners and because of her friendliness with the prison officers, she was jostled, pushed and hackled wherever she went.

"So 'ow's yer 'usband, Diana? Wass 'is name, Michael?"

"'as he gone 'orf with the other girl, then?" Irene cackled cruelly.

"'Yer should tell 'im to drop dead, 'oney. 'ow did 'e tell yu? Did 'e tell yer 'e was goin' on 'oliday wiv 'er?"

There was a lot of tuch-tuching and clucking, and as Diane could not bear the taunts and teasing, she started crying.

"Why don't they leave her alone? And why is she in prison?" Carma asked, for everybody knew that Diana's husband had left her for a younger woman. Diana had big brown eyes which always looked sad.

"Would you believe it, Carma, she is in prison because of her husband for his heavy gambling resulted in the loss of virtually everything they owned. Her company could not give her a loan unless she had been working there for 20 years so, in desperation, she lied on the form. Even though she was successful in raising the money, unfortunately her company went bankrupt. As soon as they realised that she had lied, she was prosecuted before she had a chance to repay her debt."

"That does not seem such a major offence to me, Anisha, there are many inmates who are in for major offences and are even violent!" Carma commented dryly.

"I agree, although she was lucky for later her company wanted to drop the charges, but her husband insisted that it was a habit with her so the police had to pursue the case. Her only other crime, if you call it that, is being friendly with the prison officers, for the other women think she 'tells' on them!" Anisha thought of Azaria and Carma's brother. "You know, Carma, you are lucky to have a brother like Amit. Not only that, he seems to be a compassionate and humane man, not at all like your father. I can't believe it, though, that the dowry system is still prevalent in India.

"Unfortunately, yes, for both Amit and myself found it distressing, and at every opportunity, Amit would try to highlight it as such."

Carma sat quietly, letting her mind travel as it chose, roaming and darting floating between thoughts of her parents and Amit.

****

Chapter 11

Amit wanted to inform his aunt about the situation surrounding Ramu's niece and Megan, for she was always looking for true stories on which their group could run their campaign around.

Devesh looked at his son with a frown.

"Is something worrying you, son?"

"No, nothing is the matter, Papa," answered Amit. "Ramu, before you go, can you switch on the fan? I think the electric power supply is back on".

Ramu tried the switch and the overhead fan started whirring with a quiet insistent hum.

"Thank God for the fan" remarked Devesh, swatting a mosquito that was buzzing nearby. "But I know something is bothering you, for ever since you were a child you have only called me 'Papa' when you are worried. Tell me what is bothering you, Amit. You know the saying 'sorrow shared is sorrow halved.........'"

"Yes, yes", replied Amit hastily for he knew that as usual he would get the proverb wrong.

He had recently heard that his friend's sister, Megan, who married recently, committed suicide because her in-laws had harassed her continually.

Hemant had been distraught when he told Amit how Megan had patiently endured their taunts and abuse…only because like all women, she was blinded by the notion of privacy on family affairs for her parents would have thought it disgraceful if she returned home.

Consequently, because of the the pressure of choosing to remain in a volatile relations, and the thought that life outside her husband's house was a wretched and frightening prospect, she had chosen suicide rather than divorce as a way out.

"So what did you do to-day?" asked Devesh.

"Oh, I showed Badal the rest of Delhi and.... Ramu!"

"Is that all? Did you not have any 'Chaat' the spicy snacks that we are famous for?" asked Devesh

"Yes, Sahib", Ramu entered the room "you called, sahib?"

"I'd like some more of that splendid lime drink - with more ice this time." Amit wiped the sweat from his brow.

Amit could see the haze of rays of the sun was making mirage lakes of quicksilver that shimmered in the afternoon heat.

"Yes, sahib," Ramu left the room with the empty tray and glass.

"Now, you were saying?" Devesh inquired.

Amit decided to tell his father that he had been to see Carma.

"Dad, we did have chaat but ...." Amit said slowly, aware and in awe of his father's volatile and erratic temper.

"Which restaurant did you take him to?" pressed his father, starting to fan himself vigorously again for the fan-air was not cool enough. He suddenly had a craving for pani-puri with ice-cold spicy water! "Was it the Taj Mahal? They do very good Chaat and ......"

"No, Dad. We did not go to a restaurant." he replied calmly. 'There he goes again", thought Amit "the mention of food and there is no stopping him!'

"Not go to a restaurant? Why...!" spluttered Devesh. "You didn't take him to any road-side shop, did you? He has just come from London, and would not be immune to germs as we are. Yogindra has asked us to take special care of him".

"Dad, Dad, don't worry, we did not go to any road-side restaurant - but we went to see Carma". Amit looked anxiously at his father for he had turned pale at the mention of Carma's name.

****

"And as usual, my dad's reaction was the same!" Carma remarked bitterly.

There were frequent interruptions during the course of the afternoon lock-up period. This was sometimes the time of day when letters would be brought round and the inmates who received letters regularly looked forward to receiving them – for others, like Anisha and Carma, it was a harsh reminder that they had no family or friends.

"Carma, how come Amit does not write, you two were so close, I am sure he would be worried sick if he knew about your plight! Carma?"

"Huh? Oh, that is what I cannot understand, Anisha! I only hope he is well for I only got two letters from him after I came to London. In the first he said he was very happy for he had finally got his visa for America, and not only that, but that he was getting married."

"What about your mother? Surely you wrote to her?"

"Uh,huh," Catrma nodded. "But somehow father must have intercepted the letters for they always came back unopened!"

Anisha did not think that Carma, who such a kind and gently girl, warranted such cruel behaviour from her parents, and could not help voicing her opinion.

"Carma, I know you love your parents, but doesn't it hurt to know that they have an emotional duty, that is other than just feeding and clothing them. They have a duty to love and support their child, especially in trouble."

"Tell me about it!" Carma exclaimed wearily. "Everytime I see the other inmates receive visitors, I miss them, Amit especially. I even miss my father, for all his indifference, I love him, eccentricities and all!"

They were talking behind a background of conversation between the inmates.

"'er Catherine, ain't yu got no visitors?"

"Na, my son is sick so 'usband is in 'ospital"

"Did yu speak to 'im?"

"Yes, what 's wrong with Mandy? She is a fighter that 'ne"

"You know, Carma, women are victimised in different forms in India, but here too there is abuse, though not to that extent." Anisha got up to stretch her legs and began pacing the cell. "I overheard Catherine mention to another inmate how she was beaten up by regularly by both her parents. As they were alcoholics, she had literally to bring up her sisters and brothers on her own." Anisha remarked.

"How horrible! She seemed such a loner it nice to know that she has made some friends at least." Carma thought of the incident with Mandy. "Say, I haven't seen Radha for some time. Is she alright?"

"She received a letter from her nephew, yesterday afternoon some bad news. She is even more depressed than before!"

"More bad news?"

Anisha nodded as she looked at the prison officers delivering letter to the inmates. This routine of delivering and receiving letters in the afternoons changed as the censoring officer changed. The prisoners were allowed to write one letter a week, or sometimes maybe two extra letters, however, one of the remand privileges was that they could write as many letters and have as many visits. However, these privileges were often overlooked for in the juggling to place new arrival and/or returning prisoners, the rights of an individual inmate almost always assumed secondary importance.

The letter had to be written on prison paper, be of a regulation size and was censored. The knowledge that their letter was read by the prison staff inhibited the inmates to freely express themselves, leading to misunderstandings and tensions between their families and friends, thereby jeopardising their links with the outside world.

"Carma, did Amit contact you after that?And what about your husband?"

Questions she wanted to ask were clanging and clamouring in Anisah's head as she had listened to her friend. She only hoped that that Carma would not construe her friendliness as interference.

"Only once…..in the second letter he informed me that he had got married and was moving to America. He sent me the photographs of his beautiful bride and the wedding and said he would send me his address in America in the following letter. I did not receive any other letter though." Carma bit her under lip and her face began to twitch. "I am going to sleep." Carma said abruptly as she brushed the tears from her cheeks.

Ever since she had come to the remand centre, Carma had been awake most of the nights, listening to the shuffling of footsteps as prison officers made their rounds, the coughing and the wailing, in which she sensed the intense anguish, sorrow, frustration and anger of the women.

At night as she lay in bed, she thought about her mother and how she had tried to help her by persuading her father to change his way of thinking.

****

<u>Chapter 12</u>

"How many times have I told you that I do not want to talk about your sister!" snapped Devesh, as he glared at Amit indignantly. "I don't want you to mention her name in front of me!"

"Sahib, you wanted another lime drink", Ramu quietly entered the room with the cool refreshment in a large glass topped with ice.

"Leave it on the table", Amit replied absent-mindedly as he looked at his father's pale, severe and harsh face. "Dad, she's not very…."

"And if you insist on talking about her, I won't speak to you either!" Devesh remarked angrily and his features tightened to granite.

Amit knew it was futile to continue the conversationand thought he would talk to his mother for Sumitra was sometimes adept at handling Devesh by boosting his ego.

"I'm home", he heard his mother's voice "Ramu, where is everybody?"

"They're in the lounge, memsahib", Amit could hear Ramu's reply. "Shall I get you a drink?"

"Yes, Ramu" Sumitra replied breathlessly as she placed her bags on the floor. She was followed by Sajata.

"No, its alright, I'll take them in a minute", she remarked, as Ramu stooped to pick them up.

"Whew, it's hot!" she remarked entering the room with her sister in law, sensing the tension in the room.

She placed her shopping on the floor and flopped thankfully into a chair, vigorously fanning herself with a newspaper.

Sumitra was an attractive soft spoken woman with sharp features and a fair complexion and the sky blue sari that she wore set of her dark hair tinged with grey that was coiled in a bun at the nape of her neck.

"Do you know what time it is? Where have you been, Sumitra?" Devesh asked in a gruff voice. "Eh, hello Sajata."

"Devesh, Sumitra does not have to report her every activity to you!" Sajata retorted indignantly.

"'Sajata, Devesh's sister, was an attractive woman with eyes that were curiously elongated, almost but not quite almond shaped and her beauty was intriguing and different. What people usually noticed about her were her hands that were slender and white, with tapering fingers and long perfect nails.

Devesh glared at his sister.

"It's alright, Sumitra, I am used to your brother. Devesh, I went shopping with Sajata. And from there I went with her to her group meeting. Whew! I must say I was impressed!"

She wiped her brow, glad to be in the shade of her home and away from the blistering heat. However, her usual poise had been ruffled but the attitude of the over-zealous women who had tried to persuade her to join their group.

"We hold rallies and demonstrations and would like you to join our group."

"Er, I don't think so." Sumitra found the situation difficult.

"No? You mean you will allow injustice rather than help us?" Some of the women had looked at her arrogantly.

She thought that some women were hyprocrital and were not all the justice-loving generous souls they portrayed.

"Hello, Amit …whew, it is hot!" Sumitra looked at Amit with affection

She threw the newspaper back on the table and picked up a thick magazine, hoping it would produce more air.

"Devesh", Sumitra addressed her husband with quivering voice. "I have been meaning to talk to you about the air-conditioning".

"What's the matter with it now?" Devesh replied in annoyance.

"Haven't you noticed how hot it is in the house?" Sumitra said irritably, taking a glass of cold water from Ramu.

"Of course, now that you mention it" Devesh replied irritably "but I thought it was due to the temperature outside – you know, global warming and all that!"

"Men", Sumitra said, wiping her face, hoping her make-up was not running. "You never notice anything. Amit beta, at least you must have noticed and done something about it?"

"Yes, Mum" Amit replied. "I had noticed but nothing working is an everyday occurrence in India and I have been so busy with Badal, I have not had any time to check it out. We've been out daily."

Sumitra noticed the preoccupied look on her husband's face. The worried and faraway expression on Devesh's face and his set jaw meant he was in one of his stubborn and obstinate moods.

"Amit, I know how busy you are with Badal, but can you ring up the engineers today and sort out the air-conditioning?" Sumitra smoothed her hair.

"Yes, Mother", he replied, rising from the chair. "Ramu!"

"Amit, stop calling Ramu for every little thing. I thought you were self-reliant, being a 90's man! , Sajata had been sitting silently, but could not resist teasing her nephew affectionately.

"So I am", Amit grinned cheekily at his aunt and left the room. "I just need to know when the laundry-man is delivering my clean shirts!"

****

Carma chuckled fondly as she thought about Amit and his obsession for freshly laundered shirts.

"You know, Anisha, there was a time that I too was very fussy about my clothes and would only wear clothes that were crisply washed, starched and ironed. Now all that is a luxery and even the thought of washed and ironed clothes is a distant memory, for we are only allowed to do our laundry once a week! My clothes stink of the stale smell of smoke and food!"

"And so do mine, Carma, and talking of laundery, I think today might be laundry day for I hear Catherine's name being called."

"I was wondering what her offence was, Anisha, do you know? Is it something serious?"

"Apparently not, Carma, well that is to say, nobody knows, for her record from the previous prison has not as yet arrived here. But I did overhear, I think this is becoming a bad habit! Anyway, I heard her enquiring about drugs, she seems very emotional, and I have found that drug addicts are very volatile and their moods are high and low. Anyway, enough of the prison and its inmates, tell me, did your brother tell your aunt about Megan? I mean, imagine driving a woman to suicide because of greed! How cruel!"

"I think so….anyway it is not only Megan who suffered because of dowry and greed, for Ramu had a daughter who suffered a similar fate. But what happened to Megan was unforgivable for her in-laws were wealthy from so called good family background. One would have thought they did not need to…." Her voice trailed away as she recalled Ramu's unhappiness.

Carma, like Amit, was a sensitive girl and felt deeply sorry for Megan and Ramu's daughter. She lay sleepless, tossing and turning, listening to the noises of prison.

But amongst the fanfare of the cries of the women, she thought she heard the voice of Megan's and Ramu's daughter, united, crying for justice.

****

Chapter 13

Sumitra commented smiling feebly "Devesh, I think we need another servant as Ramu is not as young as he was. It is getting difficult for him to do everything".

"Why? Is he not well? Oh, hello Sajata." He nodded his head to his sister.

"He is alright but…."

"Sumitra! I don't want to know anything about household matters! I think he is coping well, and anyway, you should take care of the matter." Devesh snapped, forgetting that he had given strict instructions to his wife he was to be informed of all domestic matters.

"Well, actually that is not the only reason. He spoke to me yesterday and mentioned he needs to go to his village to see his daughter" .

"I thought he went last month. Didn't his daughter just recently get married?" Devesh raised his voice.

"Dad, all mother is trying to say is that his daughter's in-laws are asking for more dowry and as her husband is a drunk, Ramu is frightened for her." Carma intervened for her mother looked scared as soon as Devesh rose his voice.

"I think she must have done something to drive him to drink!" Devesh exclaimed furiously.

"Devesh, how can you say that?" Sajata's eyes flashed angrily."It is men like you who….."

"Aunty, there is something else you should know about….."Carma began when Amit entered the room.

"That reminds me, aunty dear, I think you should know about Megan. Mother, you remember her?"

"I was just going to tell them, Amit." Carma brushed her hair back from her forehead with her hand.

"That sweet girl, Megan, she is the sister of your friend?" Sumitra vaguely remembered a shy and timid girl. "She got married recently, didn't she?"

"Yes", Amit replied "but apparently she was unhappy as her husband turned out to be an alcoholic and used to beat her. She could not tolerate anymore and killed herself."

"Oh no, how dreadful!"

Sumitra and Sajata both looked startled for even though were used by now to hearing similar stories, it was nevertheless shocking when it happened to someone close. All they could think of was that sweet-natured girl who like many others had thought that suicide was the only way out.

"But you know, Amit, it is a common occurrence, and happens daily. And even though Dowry is illegally, it still flourishes but very difficult to prove as an offence!" Sajata's eyes blazed and her hands gesticulated wildly as she continued. "One would think that the woman would walk out of situation like that. But by then she is so dependant on her husband for survival that not will most women stay, but also defend him if anyone finds out that he drinks or beats her!"

"Maybe they are not to blame for society does make it difficult for her to return to her parent's home after she has been married. I can imagine that for an uneducated woman, with few or no friends, a woman who been conditioned to a life of security, life outside would seem daunting." Carma added.

"Carma, what makes you an authority? For I can understand Sajata knows about these things, anyway, dear sister, how come nothing is changing, for aren't you responsible for alleviating these problems?" Devesh asked sarcastically."Anyway, I think you have a tendency to over-dramatise a situation. And what you have to understand, Carma, is that emotions are imprecise and untidy – they are a waste of energy that cannot even move a grain of sand, whereas logic and reason can!"

"Devesh, there is no need to speak to Carma in that tone of voice! Everybody is entitled to an opinion. She, like other among young educated women, is aware of the issues surrounding women." Sajata ignored her brother, her eyes fiery as she pushed her hair from her forehead with her slender hand.

Devesh grinned at his younger sister's enthusiasm and decided to take it lightly.

"Shall I procure a stage for you?" he asked teasingly.

He was always surprised at the zeal his sister showed for the downtrodden woman, since they had a background of coming from one of Delhi's most rich and powerful families.

"Now, about the subject of Ramu...I agree he should go to his village and sort matters, but I am sure that matters could not be as bad as he says."

He rose from his chair. "I'm going to take a nap, Sumitra", he said abruptly "It's too bloody hot!"

"Shall I get you anything?" Sumitra asked, "Shall I get Ramu to bring you a cold drink?"

"No, thanks," Devesh went out of the door shaking his head.

****

"How cruel...." Anisha whispered as she heard about Carma's father's reaction to the fate of Megan.

"Yes, it brings our problems into perspective, doesn't it?"

"Well, I don't know about that, Carma, we are innocent too."

"Are we, Anisha? We have taken a human life, whatever the circumstances. Megan and Ramu's daughter did not; they just endured what they had to. Maybe that is what I should have done!" Carma whispered.

"It was not your fault, Carma; I am more at fault than you are. You were at least trying to protect your son, but me? I only lost my temper! And we only have to look around us to see how even the innocent are suffering.

They were in the exercise yard when a woman came up to them.

"Ey yu got a fag for me?"

Carma and Anisha shook their head and the woman sauntered away swooping to pick up any cigarette butts she could find.

Carma saw Radha sitting on the bench, crying.

"Let's go and talk to her." Carma said impulsively.

"Why are you crying, Radha?" Anisha felt foolish asking the question.

"I have just received a letter from my sister saying that my brother, a most gentle creature, is in prison too, for grievous bodily harm, she says!"

Radha hiccupped and looked at Anisha with tear filled eyes. She had no friends in her wing and often wished she was in the same wing as Anisha and Carma.

"What happened, Radha?" Carma raised her delicate eyebrows.

"My brother is a sportsman, well, anyway, he loves cricket and was driving home with his children from a cricket match when a van pulled up beside his car at the traffic lights and the young boys in it started shouting abuse at him. First he ignored them, but when their car actually hit his, and he had to stop, two men with spades got out of the car. My brother's mistake was that he got out of the car, I think he was trying to protect his children, anyway, he took out the cricket bat from the boot and confronted the two men."

"It looks like it was racially motivated." Carma looked compassionately at Radha. "I would have thought the courts would have understood."

"Of course they did not." Radha had tears in her eyes. "Even though he was badly hurt , he managed to hit one boy but only my brother was prosecuted. The others, who had previous convictions for assault and burglary got away Scott free for those facts could not be brought out in court!"

Radha started crying and walked away, muttering to herself, leaving Carma wondering why the justice system did not serve the ethnic minority more effectively; for it appeared that it was not concerned in delivering justice but only in ignoring victims who had suffered gross injustice.

"You know, Anisha, I am worried about Radha. I don't think there is anybody to talk to and it is getting all too much for her, what with her son and husband…we'll ask Ruth to keep an eye on her."

"Carma, I don't think that would be any use, for you are forgetting that now that Ruth has been here for some time, she has changed."

"That is so disappointing for I quite liked her. But it is strange how fate controls our life by making one act in a manner contrary to our true nature…after all, it is not that we had planned to kill our husbands. If we were in India and rich, we would have been able to bribe out way out of this!"

"Carma, you make it sound so….."Anisha shuddered.

For a moment she was tempted to reveal her secret, that it was not she who had killed Akram, but Azaria. That it was her own sister who had framed her. But as Azaria had pointed out, there was no proof that it was she who had struck the fatal blow. Consequently, she bit her lips and decided to keep quite.

"Anyway, on the subject of corruption, is it true that there is corruption in India?'

"Oh yes, Anisha." Carma's eyes lit up and she smiled, for she loved to talk about India. "Although corruption is embedded in society and is frustrating, the good thing about it is that it gives employment to many. Anisha, don't look confused, I'll give you an example. Instead of everything being done by one person, in India, it takes one man to sell, another to wrap, another to take money, another to give change and receipt and if you are at a post office, another to put the stamp at the end of the process!"

"Seems that corruption is not only a way of life in India, but also a national problem." Anisha remarked.

"It is, Anisha, even though there are people in India, like my brother for example, who are searching for the root of bribery and corruption. And many a time I have heard him talking to his friends and the discussion was usually full of shame, anger and helplessness. That led me to the conclusion that talking about the problem not only tainted Indian lifestyle but also fuelled the issue! Most people, though, unfortunately, do not feel this sense of shame for corruption has not only been a framework of the public, but the poor have come to depend on these meagre economic handouts by the rich! It is prevalent in Indian society, and sometimes I think in Indian temperament too! Amit found it very frusterating too and corruption was another one the topics of contention between my father and him!" She smiled tenderly.

****

Chapter 14

"Did you speak to the engineers?" Sumitra asked hopefully.

"Yes, but only after being transferred to god knows how many different departments and having spoken to a dozen different people", replied Amit in exasperation.

"I hope they said they would come soon to fix the problem? I for one cannot tolerate this heat any longer!" Sumitra fanned herself with the corner of her sari.

"After giving me the usual crap of how busy they were, and how he'd have to make some cancellations to fit us in, one guy finally said he would send somebody the day after tomorrow!"

"What!" exclaimed Sumitra in dismay "you mean we have to tolerate this heat till then? Amit, you should have mentioned to him that we would be willing to pay extra money."

"Mother! You mean bribe, don't you?" remonstrated Amit "you know I do not agree with that! There is enough bribery and corruption in the country without my adding to it.

"Talking about corruption, did you know that there is corruption even in our judicial system, where court clients, for a certain fee, can change the court lists and decisions to favour them!" Sajata remarked.

"Whilst on the other hand, the poor innocent people are framed and sent to prison for crimes they have not committed! I think it very sad, mother, that the people who have access to the law are not aware of how it should be operated…fairly that is." Amit added.

"Amit! You sound like your aunt! Given half a chance you start a lecture about injustice! All I wanted to know was when the engineers are coming." Sumitra retorted in exasperation. "Anyway, I don't agree with you, for we are not the only ones to pay money to get things done and it would make no difference if we stop! And I don't call it bribe anyway – we can afford to pay extra, as I prefer to call it, and the only reason there is corruption in India is because of poverty and low incomes. I agree it is sometimes done from greed, but it is mostly to achieve a decent standard of living."

"Mother, don't try and justify it." Amit remarked, surprised at how articulately and passionately she spoke when Devesh was not in the room "for the person offering the temptation is just as much to blame as the receiver."

"Actually, your mother is right. I don't condone it, but I suppose one is helping a poor person send their children to schools and with dowry etc. And Sumitra, what do you mean when you say that Amit takes after me? I think it is a good thing, don't you? After all, you don't want him to take after my brother, do you?" Sajata chuckled.

"Yes…no, I did not mean…..Sumitra liked her sister-in law and did not want to offend her.

Amit wanted to hange the subject for he was fed up of the corruption, superstitions and caste systems that seemed to be imbedded in Indian caste system and caused so many problems. He was so fed up of it all that he had applied for a visa to America, and was waiting to hear from them anyday.

"Mother about Father….".

"What is the matter with your father? He looked ghastly." Sajata asked anxiously.

"He's fine, be we had a sort of disagreement, well, not disagreement, more like a difference of opinion."

"Well, that's nothing new" retorted Sajata sarcastically. "I don't think I have ever known a man like my brother with such strong opinions, half of which I don't agree with…well more than half really. Anyway, with his opinions on women, I only hope you don't share them!"

"No, I don't, thank god. It is commendable to have strong views, but not if one is stubborn as well, then one tends to become bigoted. However, I am surprised you think that about Dad?" Amit asked in astonishement.

"There's a lot you don't know about me, Amit, and you know, sometimes you too are quite stubborn too."

"Mother, I think I am a man of very liberal and flexible views, unlike father!"

"Ha! But I don't want to go into that now. What exactly transpired between you and your father to upset him so?" Sumitra knew it was futile to argue with her son.

"I told him that I had been to see Carma and that she was unhappy and…"

"Ah, you met Carma? How is she? And what do you mean she is not happy?" Sumitra exclaimed in a voice full of emotion.

"That is to say, she is well, but not happy. I was trying to tell father that she seemed unhappy and we should not abandon her so, for she needs our support. But of course he wouldn't even hear me mention her name!"

"Forget your father for the moment, what do you mean when you say she is not happy."

"Mum," replied Amit with a grimace "you know Carma, she did not say much, and considering how stubborn she is, nor is she likely to".

"So how do you know?" Sumitra and Sajata asked in unision.

"Well", answered Amit "it was her manner. I know her well, and she is not the kind of person to break into tears easily. I know something serious is going on.

Amit did not want to alarm his mother by saying that Aijaz was violent with Carma.

****

"My parents never forgave me for marrying not only against their wishes, but also to someone out of our caste. You see, Anisha, Aijaz, anyway, he followed me to London." Although Carma was trying desperately to remain in control, her voice choked and her eyes were glistening.

They walked down to the bathroom with the other prisoners and Carma was quietly washing her face when Catherine screamed.

"Mandy is a stupid bitch and I am going to…!"

"Say it to my face then!" Mandy happened to be in the bathroom and had overheard her remark. She glared at her with an insolent and angry face.

There followed a tongue lashing argument and Carma and Anisha left the bathroom whilst the women gathered around the fighting pair.

Carma had discovered by now that the women's poor social background coupled with their low level of tolerance meant that the threshold of violence was easily and often crossed.

"Where are the prison officers? They should do something before serious is done to one of them, or both!"

"You can rest assured that today at least nothing major will happen, Both know that if they are caught, they will be sent to the prison block or lose privileges. Hah! As if by doing so the inmate will change her behaviour!" Anisha remarked. "But reform has to come from within the inmate and they should only concentrate on providing the inmates with conditions in which they can reach that 'something' in themselves. They aree oblivious to the fact that having been to the punishment block, the women come out even more depressed, bitter and hostile. The authorities should balance the benefits to prisoners in the system rather than segrating and isolating them."

"You know I feel as if I am walking on ice, here, Anisha. The only consolation I have at the moment is that at least I have parole to look forward to. By the way, Sue was having a parole report read to her, I wonder what happened?"

She has been recommended for release, but she is not very happy about it."

"How come? I thought she would be delighted for any woman would be glad to get out of here!"

"She has nothing on the outside…no family.!"

"She has children? I thought she was….."

"Oh, she has, she is married and has two children, but her husband is in prison and…"

"He too? And anyway now more then ever her kids will need her."

"Her children were not with him and won't be with her either, and before you ask me why they were not with the father, at least when he was out, it was because liked little children and….Do you get my drift?"…"

"Anisha, how disgusting! You mean he is a paedophile? That is even worse than battering children…no…I don't know. I did not know so much evil existed in the world! What about her parents or in laws?"

"Her family has rejected her, not only that, the children were taken into care. It is a vicious circle, she is such a nice person and does not want to offend, but finds the pressures too much. So she finds comfort in drugs and to sustain that habit, she is willingly to do anything."

"She was imprisoned for drug dealing?" Carma asked.

"No, well, yes, she assaulted and seriously hurt the person who used to supply her, and no doubt she will be in prison again, for he will be waiting outside, enough of the inmates, did your ex-husband know that you had married again?

"Yes ,he did." Carma replied wearily, and her voice sounded cold and distant, as if trying to ward of the memories of Aijaz." I thought my present husband to be nice. Amit too thought he was a compassionate man, a real gentleman, he said. And my father too liked him but I think only because by the fact that my husband was over-awed by India!".

****

Chapter 15

Badal looked at his watch. There were still two hours before the plane landed at New Delhi airport. This was the first time he was going to India and he was looking forward to it. Not only did he intend to clinch an important business deal, but also to meet Sunetra's, his fiancée's, relations

"The plane will be landing at New Delhi airport in precisely 60 minutes and the temperature there is...." The captain's voice boomed over the speaker.

Badal beckoned to the stewardess, who came forward with a smile, which Badal thought, looked artificial, as it did not extend to her eyes.

"Yes, sir", asked the stewardess "what can I get for you?"

"I'd like a coke please, with lots of ice, thank you."

"You're Coke, sir, and can I have your completed landing form?"

"Yes, of course," Badal said, handing her the form.

As soon as Badal had handed her the card, she turned and disappeared into her cabin in the middle of the plane.

Badal leant back and closed his eyes, for it had been a tiring journey. On the seat behind him was a family with two restless and excited young children. They did not want to sleep and had been talking and fighting throughout the flight, and beside him was a newly wed couple, too engrossed in each other.

The mother of the children had dropped off to sleep as soon as the plane took off, and had been snoring continually, whilst her husband talked to Amit all through the journey.

By the time they landed in Delhi, Badal was well versed in their family history, and knew that Kishore and his family were going to visit his sister whose seventeen-year-old daughter had committed suicide because she had had a miscarriage.

"Many women get over that", Badal replied, feeling ashamed at his earlier feeling of irritably.

"I dare say she would have", he had replied "if it had not been for the continual taunts and the jibes of her in-laws, who blamed her for it. Poor thing," he had tears in his eyes "she never had a chance to recover."

"I'm sorry to hear about it," Badal had mumbled, not knowing quite to say. Kishore had just met him, but he was opening his heart to him, a total stranger.

"Please fasten your seat belts"; he heard the stewardess voice on the speaker. "We will be arriving at Indira Gandhi airport in 15 minutes. Thank you."

As soon as the plane landed there was an onrush of passengers, all exhausted with being cooped up in the plane and every one wanting to be the first out.

Badal waited in his seat, letting the family behind him go first, then got up and walked towards the exit of the plane, wiping the sweat from his brow with his handkerchief, his jacket hanging over his shoulder, hoping that Indian customs would not be a prolonged affair.

The stewardess was standing at the doorway, her hands folded. "Hope you had a pleasant flight", she said with her affected smile "I hope you will travel with us again".

Badal took a deep breadth as he stepped out, glad to be out in the fresh air. It was afternoon, and he was grateful to feel the sun's rays, warm and mild gently caress the tension of travel out of his neck and shoulder with tender caressing fingers, when he suddenly felt the impact of a gust of hot air. He could not breathe as he felt the intense heat.

He walked into the airport building, where he was directed to the immigration control counters, and stopped suddenly, shocked. There were four counters, but all had a queue reaching the end of the building. He was hot and tired and the prospect of waiting in the queue did not appeal to him at all.

When Badal looked at the immigration officers, he observed with surprise that one of them was a woman who was very slowly going over the passports and then asking unnecessary and irrelevant questions.

"Have you come from London?" the immigration officer asked him when it was his turn. "How long will you stay in India?"

"Only about a month or so", replied Badal. He looked at the immigration officer with his usual steady glance.

"Why have you come to this country?" she eyed him with suspicion.

"I came for some business", Badal replied, taking out Visa and business papers "and also to meet my fiancée's relations".

"Oh?" remarked the immigration officer impatiently and pretentiously, for she wanted to finish her duty quickly.

"That will be all", she nodded her head, apparently satisfied with Badal's answers, and stamped his passport.

"Where do I go from here?" Badal was surprised that he was to be allowed entry without any further harassment.

"Next!" the immigration officer shouted, ignoring the question.

Badal was flustered and confused at not seeing any directions, and by the unhelpful attitude of the officer. To Badal, and to any tourist, the immigration officer was the first focal point of arrival in India, and he felt the officer should have represented India in a favourable light. But she seemed to Badal passive and full of apathy and prejudice.

Badal was looking around him helplessly when he heard an alluring and lovely voice.

"You seem lost, can I help you?"

Badal turned and saw a lady with a bright scarf wearing beads around her slender neck, and he remembered vaguely that he had had seen her on his flight.

"Can you please tell me where I'm supposed to go to collect my baggage?" he enquired anxiously, grateful for her assistance.

"Your luggage should be waiting for you, that is if it is not lost, no sorry, please, I did not mean to worry you." The woman replied with a smile and gave him the directions.

"Thank you." Badal gave a sigh of relief."

His luggage had not arrived and he was restlessly waiting for it when the woman joined him.

"There are a lot of flights that have arrived at the same time, maybe that is the reason of the delay." she said conversationally.

Badal, though grateful for her assistance, was feeling weary and hot and did not want to converse. He was normally of a friendly disposition but the ordeal of the flight, the intense heat and the unhelpful attitude of the Customs officer had rankled his friendly demeanour. Finally, after what seemed an interminable time, he saw his baggage. He quickly snatched it and ran out of the green light as he had nothing to declare. As he walked out of the airport, he was enveloped by waves of sticky air and pungent unfamiliar smells.

****

"Many times my husband told me of his first impression." Carma said tidying the bed.

They had been woken at 6.30 am, but after breakfast had been locked in again for staff shortages had resulted in the cancellation of work. "I myself have never been to India, but have been told of its splendours."

"I don't think that is what my husband meant, Anisha." Carma said dryly, folding the blanket.

"Anyway, Carma, have you decided to work?" Anisha asked. "Although the main reason for work is to keep the prisoner occupied, it ends up by being a means of control and exercise of discipline. Added to that is the fact that the work is not constructive and is dull and repetitive, not forgetting demeaning!"

"Doesn't sound like it, but what kind of work is it?

"Let me see, work is catagorised in two fields, one there is work that is related to domestic duties such as sewing and cooking, then there is work like cleaning and scrubbing. Like I said, it does have its benefits for not only is it a relief from boredom but offers a rest from extremely tense relationships with the staff and some of the inmates. And of course I must not forget to point out the financial side of it – the earning of a meagre wage!"

"I still cannot make up my mind though I think I will have to soon."

After lunch they were headed towards the Association room when four women rushed past Carma and Anisha.

"wo the fuckin 'ell does she think she is! She comes to my prison and borrows from me. From the goodness of me 'eart I give her what she needs. And she 'as not repaid me as yet!"

The women were shouting and in their hands they were brandishing sticks, but even though they looked and spoke threateningly, the prison officers standing nearby completely ignored them and started talking amongst themselves.

"Carma, it seems to me that someone is in debt, and they are going to settle their score." Anisha whispered.

"What do you mean 'in debt'?" Carma asked in alarm.

"If one of the women runs out of cigarettes, drugs or any personal item that they need urgently, they usually borrow from one of the women on the understanding they return it soon. It is not very easy to repay so it is not a good idea and ....Oh my God!"

Anisha put her hand over her mouth in alarm for as they had neared the Association room, she saw Irene with her arms over her head whilst chair legs were being rained down on her. Suddenly Irene went down in a foetal position on the floor whilst one of the women took out a jagged tin lid and ripped her face.

Finally, there was a whistle and the prison officers who had seen the attack came strolling over to Irene whose face was bleeding profusely. They ignored the four women who had perpetuated the attack, giving them time to disappear.

"That must have been Mandy's gang." Anisha whispered as the prison officers escorted Irene out of the room.

"Did you see that, Anisha, how awful the prison officers are? They saw the attack and did nothing, and not only that, they let Mandy get away with it! They are ignoring the fact that Irene is being persecuted, just like Doris was."

"My dear Carma, did you not know that is one of the functions of injustice... to produce hatred wherever possible, cause people to hate each other and fight. The prison officer's try they're hardest to render the inmates incapable of any joint action, I think that may be so there is no chance of rioting. And I am sure they only ignored the incident because Irene always tries to upset their discipline in any way she can."

All the prisoners had gathered and were whispering amongst themselves.

"That's enough, no Association today! Return to your cells!" John barked waving his truncheon.

As they returned to the cell, Anisha sighed as she sat on the bunk bed.

"Carma, you mentioned earlier that your husband was visiting India at the time he met you?"

"Yes, he was." Carma replied. "I don't think he was very impressed, for what with the heat and his treatment at the immigration counter, he met my aunt Sajata. They drove back together, and it gave her ample opportunity to point out to him the social issues concerning women! However, he was quite impressed at least that is what he told me!"

****

Chapter 16

"You must be Badal"; boomed a loud voice.

Badal turned and saw a squarely built man with deep-set eyes. He noted with disappointment that he was alone, for Sunetra had told him that her cousin Carma would meet him at the airport and he was looking forward to meeting her.

"Yes, that's right, and you must be…? replied Badal, looking around him in bewilderment.

"I am Devesh, Yogi's brother!"

Badal was engulfed in an embrace and for some time the conversation was incoherent and inconsequential. There were ejaculations, eager queries, incomplete answers; messages from Sunetra and Yogindra, and explanations as to the journey were all jumbled up together.

"Here let me", Devesh grabbed the suitcase from Badal. "You must be tired after your long flight. My wife and son are anxiously waiting to meet you. Why, hello Sajata", he cried in delight as Badal saw the woman wearing the scarf with beads. "I didn't know you were travelling? Are you going or coming?"

"I have come from a meeting in London." Sajata replied in her soft voice.

"You're usual….?" Devesh asked disparagingly, then remembered he had not introduced Badal "Sajata, this is Sunetra's fiancée; you know I had mentioned that he was coming to India? Badal, this is my younger sister, Sajata".

"We've met," both answered in unison.

"Yes, you would have, coming by the same flight and all that".

"No, we met at the airport," Badal replied. "She was kind enough to help me".

"That's my sister", said Devesh tauntingly "always the Samaritan!"

"Devesh, there's no need to be sarcastic!" Sajata said scathingly. She did not like her brother's behaviour and thought it to be lacking at the best of times.

As they approached their car a porter came up to them and started to grab the suitcase from Devesh's hand.

"Sahib", he cried, "let me take your luggage."

"No", Devesh replied. "We'll manage."

The porter's face became red with anger, his lip curled back in an ugly sneer and his right eyebrow raised in cynical contempt, and Badal was surprised at this intense emotion at a trivial refusal. They got into the car, the make of which was an ambassador. This model, Badal was to later learn, had once been the backbone of India's private industry for its strength and high chassis fitted it well for the rugged Indian conditions.

"I hope you had a pleasant journey", Devesh asked genially, driving carefully.

Yogindra, his brother, had not told him much about Badal other than that he was engaged to Sunetra and the son of his friend Dilip.

As they were driving to the house, Badal looked around him in amazement. Everywhere he looked there were coaches, auto-rickshaws, taxis and huge public carriers flying down the road. All had total disregard for not only their own, but the safety of others, and he saw many cars passing each other on the wrong side of the road.

There were horns blaring and cars were either weaving in and out of traffic or suddenly braking and stopping, for Indians, Badal was to later learn, did not park -they arrived and then stopped - oblivious to confusion and traffic jams!

On the road there was utter chaos as he saw rage, gesticulations and scratched bodywork on cars. With amazement he saw there were some bullocks and camels strolling on the streets whilst others stopped to stand and stare where and when they pleased.

"What's going on?" he asked shocked and distressed as he saw a young girl being beaten by a policeman with a stick whilst a crowd watched with satisfaction.

"Even though India is supposedly a land of mystic spirituality, here justice can be rough. I daresay the poor woman was unfortunate enough to be caught," Sajata said. "I don't think her crime must be any more than to have been caught in the act of stealing, only so she could feed her sick parents."

"Why don't they report her to the police?" asked Badal.

"People in India do not have faith in the working of justice," replied Devesh, his face impassive. "As they want to see results quickly, in villages sometimes even in the city, robbers are punished by the people themselves – they are beaten or hanged."

Devesh braked hard as a cow came in front of their car and even though Devesh hooted, the cow would not budge.

"Isn't there a traffic warden who can deal with the cow? " Badal asked in a surprised tone.

"No, so we will have to wait." Devesh replied irritably. "I will take this opportunity to explain that my sister here is a fighter of women's rights".

"I only identify their achievements and want others to recognise and appreciate the various roles a woman is responsible for." Sajata replied fervently, her eyes blazing   "Badal, you shall see in your stay here that it is the woman who not only does the work at home, but helps her husband with his work. But even though she does this for the convenience of male, in different roles – as daughter, wife, and mother - she always ends up as a victim!"

"I can see many women working in this heat. I don't know how they do it!" Badal remarked glancing out of the window.

He saw female coolies, women labourers wearing thin, saris that were torn and patched, some with tiny babies clinging to their hips, digging trenches, first breaking then carrying stones on their heads.. They were hauling bricks and working side by side with their men in at the construction site.

One woman came out of a line of skinny labourers carrying mounds of wet concrete in baskets on their heads. He saw her go to some children with matted hair playing in the dust and pick up a baby. She squatted in the sand nearby and drew the child to her breast. After she quickly fed him, she wiped his face and returned him to her children.

Badal watched amazed as she fixed a pad on her head, and, picking up her basket, went to the cement-mixer, to join the file of people that were climbing up a crude plank to dump the load. She then descended again via another ramp to fill her basket once again.

"They work hard, beside their husband relentlessly, even on a hot day," Sajata remarked sympathetically. "a woman almost always submerges her personality, only to find that she has become her husbands' dispensable possession!"

"They do seem to be working hard." Badal remarked thoughtfully.

He saw signs of suffering showing on the women's faces, which he was sure, could not stay young or pretty for long, as they worked under strenuous conditions with the sun blazing all day in a cloudless sky.

Listening to Sajata, Badal came to admire the strength of the Indian woman who, he observed, shouldered and balanced paid work as well as the burdens of housework uncomplainingly.

"They do all this silently against the restraint of traditional culture where male dominance still prevails." Sajata added compassionately. "Do you know one girl in a village was raped by three policemen, then accused of having a loose character? And to top it all, even the Supreme Court upheld the view?" Sajata's hands started gesticulating and her eyes were blazing as she tried to illustrate her point.

Devesh looked at her scathingly. "Sajata, this is not a stage but the harsh reality."

"You call it reality, but you are like all men, you are actually looking for a reason to justify your own egos. You know, "Sajata continued with a quizzical smile as she saw Badal looking at the construction site "Women work alongside their husbands, but they are not paid separately. Often a woman, who has worked hard alongside her husband, will come home to find there is no food and listen to her children cry helplessly for her husband will have spent the money on drink! One woman even threw herself and her children in a well because she could not feed them. Shocking, isn't it?"

Badal thought Sajata to be a sensitive woman, with strong views about the discrimination of women. Her voice, gestures and actions were all passionate and he speculated as to the underlying cause, for he felt her discourses were only for the benefit of her brother.

He yawned for he was not really interested in how oppressed most Indian woman were.

Devesh meanwhile knew it was futile to argue with his sister, so contented himself by giving her a nasty look and tried to change the subject.

"People are part of Delhi's throb…." remarked Devesh, starting the car as the cow had decided to move.

"You are right there, uncle!" Badal remarked for he was amazed at the multitude of faces he saw.

Not only were people sitting on bullocks but they were also on street houses. Even the two-wheeled Tonga carts, drawn by thin horses, were piled hight with swaying men and women carrying babies. Cycles carried more than two people and he saw that Scooters accommodated whole families.

Badal smiled to himself as he saw the pot-bellied men looking comical as they rode on motorcycles, and noticed that even lorries had more passengers in them.

"Badal, this area with its trees is one of India's most agreeable places, for they provide the city with blessed shade in the heat and add a sense of maturity to the city, I think." Devesh said as they drove past the tree-lined avenues. "Not only that, but the trees are useful too, for in the spring people camp under the silk cotton trees and collect the cotton like fibre which fall from them and sell it as stuffing for cushions. Or they sell it to be woven into silk, for they know that Silk is very important to the Indian tradition. The craft of making Silk usually involves the whole family – the wife degums the Silk, Grandma warped it, and one child would wind it and another assist the father at the loom."

"Really? So much work to produce it?" Badal said " I love the material and Silk, to everybody, I think, to men and women, it echoes luxury, elegance and mystery!"

There were a few men in white dhotis slumbering in patches of shade, whilst out in the sun a group of women in saris sat in a small circle talking and laughing. He saw girls in dresses and shiny black hair in thick plaits eating ice cream.

Chapter 17

"I hope you have come for a long holiday?Damn it!" Devesh asked.

He suddenly braked for another cow was crossing the road. The horn from the car behind them started blaring as the cow decided to stay where she was.

"Shut up, it's not my fault!" yelled Devesh, sticking his head out of the window "the cow is blocking the road! Women drivers," he muttered angrily.

"What did you say?" Sajata bristled, ready to seize upon his remark.

"Nothing", murmured Devesh, scared that Sajata would start one of her discourses again.

Badal had been looking around him incredulously." Don't they have any traffic regulations in India?"

"Not really", replied Devesh waiting for the cow to move "Discipline of the simplest laws and standards would cause disruption and anger for the travelling public. But don't let this shock you, Badal, for only a few cities in the world can match Delhi's traditions with its variety of monuments and treasures. I think that, no, I know that India is a city almost as rich as Rome in culture, and nearly as spectacular as Athens. But its history is shrouded in mists and legends and complicated with the profusion of dynasties. However there is also a lot of care and compassion in India." There was pride in Devesh's voice.

"Now shall I procure a stage for you?" Sajata teasingly remarked.

The afternoon breeze had whiffs of hot air and Badal was beginning to feel hot and tired. His eyes were becoming heavy with sleep and he was craving for a cup of tea and something substantial to eat. However more than anything he needed a long cold shower. He saw the cow standing motionless on the street and wished it would show some sign of activity.

"Paisa, Ek Anisha", Badal heard a soft voice and looked at the face of a child peering at him through the window.

His languor disappeared as he saw the face of a tiny girl whose nose was running with snot. She was wearing rags, had eyes that were wide with hunger, and her grimy hand was stretched out in a desperate plea for money. Her hair was lank and greasy and her body looked painfully thin and bony. Badal felt his heart constricting with pity when he saw the girl had only one arm and rummaged in his pocket for some money when Devesh suddenly started closing the car window.

"Shoo, go away", he shouted at the beggar girl "we don't have any money! Go away! These beggars, I don't know where they come from," he muttered "Why don't they work, like the rest of us?"

Badal was unnerved at the sight of the beggar girl and looked at Devesh incredulously for he had been talking of care and compassion a minute ago and was now...! How could he say that to a poor girl with only one arm? Badal was finding Indians, especially Devesh contradictory.

Devesh looked at Badal and saw the distress and horror on his face.

"Badal, please don't jump to any wrong conclusion. As you will no doubt see in your stay in this country, there are many beggars. And to how many people can we give money? At any rate, most of the beggars here are richer than us."

"I find that very hard to believe", replied Badal quietly, noticing with relief that the cow had finally decided to move.

"It's true, Badal, in India begging is done as a business," declared Devesh, driving slowly yet impatiently through the onrush of taxis, scooters and buses, all blaring their horns. ". Children are kidnapped from their homes by a so-called godfather, and then raised to be either a thief or a beggar. And to make them realistic, they sometimes have their arms or legs broken. And of course, the so called god-fathers take their commission!"

"He is right," confirmed Sajata sympathetically, her eyes alight with suppressed emotion. "Girls specially suffer. Occasionally, infanticide is still practised, when the parents kill the girl at birth because she is seen as a financial burden."

"Sajata! Don't you ever think about anything else?" Devesh retorted angrily. "Do you know even Amit has started lecturing me about all these injustices? One in the family is enough, but two is unbearable!"

Badal listened aghast and appalled at these inhuman and barbaric customs. "And the government doesn't do anything about it? Surely they must do something".

"They do" replied Devesh "and actually there is much less poverty and beggars now than there used to be. And India has progressed a lot…anyway, here we are!"

Badal heaved a sigh of relief, as not only was he tired of listening about India, but the banter between brother and sister was too much on his first day.

Devesh turned the car into the driveway of a huge bungalow and parked his car. "You must be tired", he remarked, opening the car door.

Badal got out of the car and gazed admiringly at the white bungalow with a huge lawn. There were flowers of all colours, and in the middle of the garden was a table with cane chairs. On the table were a silver tea tray, china cups and saucers and plates of savouries and a very elegant woman sitting beside them.

A gardener was sprinkling water nearby in the garden and the damp smell of the earth, mixed with the sweet smell of jasmines, floated across the garden.

****

And that was the first time my second husband met my mother," They had just finished their lunch and Carma was plaiting her hair.

Anisha's head was spinning for she was suffering increasingly from headaches. But she understood Carma's necessity to confide in her, for she too had been trapped by a combination of circumstances – her husband's increasing abuse and the failure of others to help her.

"How come they have not collected the lunch-tray? I know we are expected to give them but they usually come and check don't they?" Seeing the plates Carma was reminded of the revolting meal and felt sick. "I thought you said they always did the checking on time as they wanted to be 'off-duty' as soon as possible?"

"They usually do." Anisha replied "but sometimes they are delayed by a panic – for example if a spoon is lost it has to be found for the cutlery is counted before and after every meal."

"Do they suspect us of stealing their plastic cutlery?"

"No, I don't think that is the reason, but I think they have to make sure that no one possesses a dangerous weapon."

"It does not appear that plastic cups and mugs can be dangerous, Anisha. What is that noise?"

"I think it is Irene, she is rebelling with a vengeance, for she knew that the prison officers ignored to help her."

Irene screamed and they heard a prison officer unlock the opposite door and enter the cell.

"Give us your lunch plates!"

"No, I will not!"

"Then I am taking you to the punishment block!"

"No!"

"I am not asking you what you want, Irene, You will f.....g hell do what I say! If you do not come willingly, you know we will take you by force!"

Two more prison officers burst into her cell and Irene was pulled by the hair and dragged out into the corridor.

Suddenly Irene brandished a spoon and as soon as one of the prison officers came near her, she lashed out and stabbed her with it. The blood started dripping from the chin of the prison officers whilst the rest jumped and tried to restrain her. Irene managed to kick and wind another prison officer before they overpowered her into a restraining position. She lay writhing and screaming on the floor wildly.

Carma had been watching through the window in their cell door …and was horrified at the violence she was witnessing and covered her face with her hands.

The drama was relayed around the prison wings and Carma could hear the inmates yelling.

"'Ey, Sue, did yer 'ear what Irene done? The dragged 'er screaming and yelling…"

The incident had left a bitter taste in Carma's mouth.

"And now do you still think that cutlery is not dangerous?"

Carma did not reply, and even though she was still in shock, showed no emotion.

"Now, you can be sure that if ever there is a fork or spoon missing, even it is plastic, and we will all usually stay locked till it is found!"

"And rightly too." Carma replied. "I am sure some of the patients would use the so called weapon against somebody they did not like too. And that frightens me."

Carma, who had been staring out of their cell window, turned and saw Anisha's face. "Anisha, you look terribly pale! Shall I call Ruth?"

"No, Carma, it is nothing to worry about. I have my usual headache, that is all, and the stress and the uncertainty of the trial is adding to it, in fact might be due to it."

Anisha smiled weakly and lay down whilst Carma stood staring out into the courtyard through the small window recalling Badal's first day in India.

****

336

Chapter 18

"Welcome to India, Badal Beta", Sumitra's voice was soft and mild as she folded her hands and smiled.

She was about fifty, with her hair in a bun at the nape of her neck. She wore a pearl necklace with matching earrings and looked elegant with a pale blue sari and a matching blouse.

"This is my wife, Sumitra, and guess what? I met Sajata at the airport, so she has come along with us." He looked at the table with the empty cups and saucers. "Why isn't tea ready?" Devesh snapped angrily at her then kept quiet as he saw Sajata glaring at him.

"Namaste, auntiji, thank you it is good of you to have me stay as your guest." However, Badal was surprised and puzzled to see Sumitra tremble beneath Devesh's glare.

"I thought a fresh pot of tea when you came…"Sumitra's voice faltered.

"Yes, whatever," Devesh grumbled.

Sumitra greeted Sajata with a peck on her cheek. She was glad to see her sister-in-law as she was always trying to stand up for her.

"Would you like a cup of tea", Sumitra asked Badal sitting on the cane chair "or would you like something cold?"

"A hot cup of tea would be fine," replied Badal.

"Ramu", Sumitra called in a loud voice. "Ek Chai lao.. he'll bring you a fresh pot of tea"

Ramu, their domestic, was standing nearby and hurriedly collected the tea tray.

"Yes, memsahib"

"May I have a glass of cold water first?" Badal asked.

It was hot, he was feeling thirsty and he could not wait for tea.

"Yes, Sahib, at once." Ramu said as he bustled of into the house.

"How is Sunetra Beti and Yogindra Bhai?" Sumitra asked.

"They're fine", answered Badal, as Ramu promptly arrived with the cold glass of water, which he hastily gulped.

"Where is Amit?" asked Devesh in exasperation. "He knew we would be home by this time! He was looking forward to meeting you as Sunetra has told us so much about you. He must have got delayed. Ah, there he is now", he exclaimed joyfully.

Badal saw a debonair young man of about twenty-five with wavy black hair walking with long strides towards them. His hand was outstretched hand and his wide humorous mouth was smiling showing his white teeth. He was powerfully built with broad shoulders but unlike his father, his face showed sensitivity and understanding.

"I am sorry I am late", he announced, smiled disarmingly at Badal, as he shook hands with him then winked at his aunt.

"I am Amit, Hi, aunty. Whew, it is hot! I have lived here all my life but still can't get used to the hot weather. And it's supposed to be the monsoon season soon, which I think anyway, is worse than the summer!"

There was something charming and fresh in the way Amit spoke. He was wearing a white shirt which was open at the collar, showing his tan, jeans and trainer shoes.

"You might hate it, son but most people greet it with joy, and women and children welcome it by singing on the branches of trees." Devesh looked at him in annoyance.

"True, dad, but after a few days the enthusiasm usually goes as the town gutters get clogged and streets became flowing streams! I like it when the grass begins to grow and leafless trees turn green, but hate it when insects appear out of nowhere! Badal, you have to see it to believe it, for the earth becomes alive and clamouring with earthworms, ladybirds and tiny frogs! Ugh!"

"Sounds terrible, but at least night-time must be cooler?" Badal listened to Amit aghast.

"Sometimes I think that it is worse at night, when moth's first flutter around the electricity light inside the house, then drop in everybody's food and water, whilst the humming of the mosquitoes maddens almost everybody!"

"And that is why there is such a thing as insecticide!" Devesha glared at Amit.

"And what use are they? I have never found them to be helpful for even when I spray it, the floor became a layer of Wrigley bodies and wings, leaving me to believe that the insects are gone forever. But the following evening there is even more flapping and fluttering of moths around the lampshades, even though they finally burn themselves in the heat."

Badal was beginning to feel uncomfortable, for he thought that the disagreement would end with Devesh and his sister, but it seemed that it extended to his son! However, Badal liked Amit.

"It's much hotter than I expected. It's evening and it is still so hot and humid. It must be boiling in the morning!"

Just when Badal thought that everybody had forgotten about tea, Ramu came out carrying a tray. Badal had heard about the famous 'Indian Tea' and gratefully took the cup that Sumitra handed him.

"Oh yes", replied Devesh amiably. "This is just the 'tip of the iceberg'" he grinned at his adage, his bad temper abated after a cold glass of water.

"Badal, I am sorry I have been going on about the whether. Very selfish of me, tell me how was your trip? I hope the customs staff did not harass you? Is it too much to expect that they did not trouble you at all? They didn't ask you for any money before they let you in?" Amit asked with cynicism.

His countryman's code of ethics always confused him and he wanted to immigrate to America as soon as possible.

"Amit!" Devesh glowered at his son. "Can you be a little less cynical of India? And anyway, so what if by paying extra Badal could be free of harassment?"

"Dad, you know I am right." replied Amit sullenly. "But you have become so accustomed to corruption that instead of realising and reacting to it as being destructive to decency, you accept it as a recognised way of life. Anyway, enough of that, we mustn't bore our guest".

"No, not at all, but I am a bit tired", Badal replied hastily, hoping to avoid an argument on what he felt were two extreme points of views.

"I think Badal would like a bath and some rest before dinner, come, Badal, I'll show you to your room" Sumitra said with her unperturbed manner rising from her chair.

Badal followed quickly, leaving father and son still arguing, but looking forward to a cool bath.

Chapter 19

He came out of the shower, feeling fresh after his bath to hear knocking at the door.

"Come in!" Badal said, vigourously rubbing his wet hair.

Ramu entered carrying a tray and placed it on the table.

"Memsahib wants to know if you'll be down or dinner? "

"Yes, yes, of course, I will be down shortly

Badal lay on the bed beginning to feel the jet-lag. The air felt thick and heavy and the warm air made his eyes and head heavy with sleep.

He looked up at the ceiling and shuddered when he saw Lizards scouting the walls, wondering if summer was the wrong season for them to crawl down the walls and hoping one of them would not fall on him, as Sunetra had explained they sometimes did? Outside the window there were doves sitting, looking into each other's eyes.

After a while, he rubbed his eyes and rose, poured himself another cup of tea and stood looking out of the window that overlooked the garden planted with jasmine flowers.

'No doubt chosen for their delicate fragrance.' He mused, wrinkling his nose.

The afternoon had worn on and the sunlight was taking on a ruddy colour. He wrinkled his nose as he smelt a pungeant kind of smell, which, he realised, was one part of India's vast array of odours, the smell of jasmine and marigold being a major component. It seemed to him that nothing was more memorable than a fragrance, for although it was unexpected, momentary and fleeting, it recalled memories associated with it, in this instance of he was reminded of Anisha.

He wiped the sweat from his brow, thinking of her, their break-up and his subsequent engagement to Sunetra.

He had found her to be an attractive girl, and when Anisha informed him about her engagement to Akram it seemed natural for him to marry Sunetra, so he had spoken to his father.

"I told you Sunetra was the right wife for you! Anyway, shall I speak to Yogindra again to finalise matters? You know they are quite keen. And let me give you a piece of advice….., Badal, marriage is like a roller-coaster – in the trip one needs a strong companion, someone to cling to, as the descent begins and someone to laugh with when the car climbs up safely." Badal had been surprised at the analogy given by his father, but knew he spoke from experience.

Suddenly his whole life had been suddenly mutated and rearranged. His engagement had been announced a week later, and within a month he heard Anisha got married to Akram.

"I'm not marrying her on the rebound", he hastily explained to his friend Sunil when he announced his engagement to Sunetra.

"Oh?" Sunil replied nonchalantly, unimpressed by the effort Badal was making to convince him otherwise

'Anyway, here I am in India" Badal finished his tea and turned from the window, shaking himself out of his nostalgic reverie.

****

"I did not know it at that time, but my husband had recently broken of with a girl and got engaged to another, my cousin….and then married me!" Carma chuckled with dry humour. "Gosh I am hungry! When are they going to serve us our meal? Anisha, I keep thinking of food even though it is revolting, I wonder why?"

"It is supposed to be a psychological, substitution of some sort. I too feel hungry at the oddest of times, but then we are not the only ones with a preoccupation with food, it is a well-known symptom amongst the prisoners. Oh, by the way, did you hear about Catherine? I overheard some of the prisoner officers talking."

"Huh? What did you say?" Carma had been thinking how the prison meals contrasted to the meals in India.

"About Catherine? You know the new arrival? She is supposed to be a woman of exceptional intelligence and…"

"Anisha! Do you really believe that? If she is so intelligent what is she doing here?"

"Hear me out, Carma; intelligence does not necessarily mean good…but I know what you are getting at. She should have been able to get away with her crime! Anyway, I believe there must be a twist in her character that drives her to fraud and dishonesty, which is what she is in for. I pity her, you know for the first time she was convicted, she was pregnant. She had the baby in prison, handcuffed to the hospital bed! And as if that was not traumatic enough, the baby was taken away from her. She has been suffering from depression ever since…you know I have been here for some time and am still surprised at the huge range of personalities of the prisoners and their experiences. I am beginning to understand how difficult it must be for the prison service to provide to the needs of all of them by different programmes."

"Well, I think everybody here has a twisted character, all the same, I feel that just as society needs protecting, so does a prisoner on his release. For I can just imagine the difficulties I would have to go through – the stigma attached at being in prison etc. As for educating the prisoner, maybe it is the hearts and minds of the ordinary people that need changing, for they have an attitude of steadfast unforgiveness and rejection of the ex-prisoner!"

As Carma turned towards and looked outside the minute window in their cell, she felt homesick. Talking of food had made her realise how much she really missed the sumptuous meals prepared by Ramu. And she missed Amit, his wit, her aunt and mother.

****

Chapter 20

Devesh, Sumitra and Amit were already seated at the dining table when Badal joined them.

"Are you feeling refreshed after your bath, Badal?" Sumitra asked, and as a thoughtful hostess added "I asked Ramu to stay with you in case you needed anything"

"Come and sit down, yaar", Amit waved at him, pointing at the chair beside him.

"Yes thank you, auntiji." Badal replied.

They were all very hospitable, and even though they had only met him for the first time, made him feel welcome and part of the family. There was still no sign of Carma and Badal thought she must be away on holiday.

"Would you like rice or chapatti?" Sumitra asked handing him a plate.

"Thank you but I am not hungry." Although there were a variety of dishes on the table, Badal was not tempted.

"Sumitra!" Devesh bellowed, rudely interrupting Badal "The poor boy must be hungry, give him something to eat!"

"Do have something to eat." Sumitra said meekly wondering why her husband always found fault with her.

"I'm sorry to have kept you waiting, I am just starting to feel the jet-lag, besides which I have just realised I am not hungry!" Badal flushed with mortification as he felt he could have stayed in his room instead of keeping them waiting. "Amit, can you tell me what there is to see in Delhi, for I would like to do some sightseeing before I start my business meetings?"

"Of course, Badal, there is much to see so I think it would be best if Amit took you around," Devesh answered. "But Delhi is not what it used to be. Old Delhi especially has changed beyond recognition, not only in physical terms, but also in essence. The leisured way of life has disappeared!" He sighed remembering the old days.

Badal looked at him in surprise. "Really? I thought that rich Indians could not lead a lead a more leisurely lifestyle than what I have so far seen. In my short time here I have also seen the other side of the coin, so to speak, that is poor people toiling under the blazing sun!"

"You are right, Badal, and Dad, "Amit interrupted Devesh's nostalgia. "this is Badal's first time here, he won't know the difference!"

"Sorry", answered Devesh, "As I was saying, Badal, to-morrow I am sure Amit will be delighted to take you around."

"I'd like that," Badal yawned. "But if you'll excuse me I'll wish you good-night". He left the room and went upstairs to his bedroom.

The sun had gone down and the reddish-brown sky turned grey as the tint of twilight spread across the city. Shades of grey mixed with the glow of sunset as dusk and gave way to twilight, which was sinking wearily into darkness. As Badal looked out of the window the moon came up and even though it looked wearied and exhausted, managed to shower the city with its pale and silvery light.

An overhead fan whirred and whined and Badal could hear the buzzing of the mosquitoes in the silence.

Badal had barely closed his eyes when he heard a loud thump - the chowkidar, the night watchman, had arrived. All through the night, just when Badal dosed off, he would hear the thump of his bamboo stick on the gate and his whistle. Another watchman in the neighbourhood would hear and whistle in return. To add to the noise, Badal fought a losing battle against the fleas' mosquitoes and the noise and it was some time before he could sleep.

Chapter 21

The sun stretched its goldenn hands and ruthlessly peeled the darkness of the night, and Badal woke to the cool breeze of the morning With the sun's rays glaring in his eyes, Badal woke up to the yelling and screaming of peopl "Radi, Radi wallah!"

"Sabzi, Sabzi wallah!"

"Good-morning, Sahib", Ramu was hovering over his bedside with a cup of tea in his hand.

Badal sat up in bed and put his hands over his ears. "What is all that racket, Ramu?" he asked looking at his watch for it was barely 6.00 a.m., but from all the commotion, it seemed afternoon!

From what he could only understand vaguely was that one vendor was trying to sell vegetables and the other trash!?

Ramu's face was grim as he handed the tea-cup to Badal for his niece, Chaya, had arrived that morning.

He had been surprised to see how much Chaya had grown, for the last time he had seen her was when she was six years old, on her wedding day.

Badal took the cup gratefully from Ram and looked with amazement at his arms, for even though his body had been layered with mosquito repellent; his arms were swollen with mosquito bites.

"Tell me, Ramu", he asked, and "What does 'Radi' mean

"A gentleman comes to collect old newspapers and magazines, and in turn gives you a pot or dish."

"Gosh!" In London this was just plain recycling – with nothing in return!

"Will you need anything else, sahib?"

"No, thank you, Ramu, that will be all. I will shower and join the family downstairs as soon as possible".

"There is no hurry," replied Ramu "Amit Sahib wakes up at 10.00 a.m."

"And what about Devesh Sahib?"

"Oh, he is usually downstairs by 9.00 Am., but memsahib usually rises early".

"Oh", Badal's acknowledged absent-mindedly, his mind racing ahead to Mr Varma, who he was supposed to have contacted immediately on arrival.

As he dressed he thought of Sunetra's family. Badal was a little scared of Devesh but liked his Aunt and thought Devesh's treatment of her was humiliating. However, he liked Amit and Sajata, and wondered again about Carma, for none of them had mentioned her absence.

Sumitra was arranging fresh flowers on the table when Badal walked in the room, feeling refreshed after the cold bath and rest.

"Morning Badal Beta", Sumitra turned to greet him. She was once more wearing a blue sari, which rustled as she turned.

Sumitra, like the majority of Indian women wore a sari, the Indian traditional costume that was worn with a blouse. The Sari was always in fashion and was comfortable, and the only changes were mainly in colour and in pattern.

"Morning, Auntijee", Badal replied.

"Morning beta, Ramu!" Sumitra called "I think Badal would like a cup of tea, would you like your breakfast now?"

"No, just a cup of tea would be fine. I'll wait for Amit for breakfast.."

"You'll have to wait long, for he usually gets up late, though his father will be here soon."

Badal followed her into the dining room, wondering why she endured Devesh's treatment. He did not know that like most Indian women, she was culturally contrived and disciplined for in India a woman was regarded as a non-entity, and the only identity she had was bestowed on her either as someone's daughter, sister, wife or mother.

He was drinking tea when Devesh entered yawning into the room.

"Where's my tea?" he demanded for he was always grouchy and irritable in the mornings.

"Waiting for you", Sumitra replied meekly, handing him the cup.

"He's always like this in the mornings." Sumitra remarked.

"I'm starving", said Devesh sitting at the dining table.

Badal was surprised at the amount of various dishes on the table especially as it was only breakfast.

He was not hungry and had never laid importance on meals, and considering his mother spent all her time at parties, it was not surprising mealtimes in London were haphazard.

However, it seemed that people in India gave importance to food and mealtimes, for he had noticed on his way from the airport there were a lot of food stalls on the roadsides, with flies and mosquitoes buzzing around the food.

"Would you like a stuffed chapatti, or a scrambled eggs and toast?" Sumitra asked handing him a plate.

"Don't ask him!" Devesh snapped at her. "He'll have both!" he clapped Badal on the shoulder. "He's a growing boy, what?" he chuckled.

"No I ….." Badal was going to refuse when he smelt the aroma of freshly scrambled eggs and fresh toast and suddenly felt a pang of hunger

"I'll have some egg and toast, please, with some of the delicious tea."

Sumitra silently handed Badal a plate.

"Have you phoned Mr. Varma as yet - that is the name of your business associate, is it not?" Devesh inquired, helping himself to a stuffed chapatti.

"No, not as yet", Badal replied, delving into his breakfast and taking a sip of the freshly brewed tea. "Absolutely delicious! Eggs in London do not taste like this!"

"If I am not mistaken they are artificially…- maybe that is the reason for the difference of taste, for eggs in India are naturally matured!"

"Huh", Badal was not really interested in the technique of farming.

However Sunetra had told him that Devesh had an in-depth knowledge of agriculture/farming or anything to do with food, for his 'hobby' was food - raw and cooked.

"I was under the impression that everybody starts work late?"

"They do! But it would be better to phone him there and make an appointment for he might be away or at a meeting."

"Yes, yes, you're right! If you'll excuse me I'll go to make that phone call." Badal finished his breakfast and strode out of the room.

"I'll have another cup of tea," Devesh handed his wife his empty cup. "You know, Sumitra, I like Badal. I think Sunetra has done well for herself. Now why couldn't…" Devesh muttered under his breadth but the expression in his eyes was veiled.

"Kismet, that is what it is….Kismet." Sumitra whispered with tears in her eyes.

****

"Kismet, yes, I suppose my mother is right, my husband related the conversation to me. Anyway, how else would I be here?"

"I don't believe in fate, I believe we are responsible for our actions, in fact I would go so far as to say that we control our destiny!"

There was a jangling of keys and a prison officer started shouting.

"You fuckin no good…..you need exercise!"

"Whew, thank God!' Anisha breathed a sigh of relief.

In the courtyard Carma saw that whilst some women were walking, others were sitting on the bench, whilst others were kneeling. As Anisha saw Carma's bewildered expression, she explained.

"They are called 'swoopers', they pick up the cigarette butts from the floor, you know I was telling you about them earlier?."

"Oh yes, the smokers who…Yukk…Anisha, that looks like an unhygienic habit! Anyway, I don't see Joanne but isn't that Diana in her place? Has Joanne been transferred, I quite liked her for she had a lovely temperament and…."

"No she has not been transferred anywhere, there she is sitting on the bench, looking lost. A couple of days ago, a new prison officer took over the duty of supervising and looking after the workers. Unfortunately their personalities clashed and very soon Joanne found herself out of that job and as you see, it has been taken over by Diana who had her eye on that job."

"Isn't she the one who is friendly with the prison officers?"

"That's right, and now Diana is hated more than ever, for everybody is convinced the whole unfortunate incidents showing Joanne in an unfavourable light was planned."

"Poor Joanne! She loved gardening, now I know why she looks so bewildered and lost!" Carma commented as she saw Joanne sitting on the ground. "Hey, Anisha, there is Radha, looking more unhappy than ever."

"I forgot to tell you, Anisha, her son died and…"

"Oh no! Oh no Anisha, she loved that little boy. It was bad enough to have him snatched from her but…. How is she taking it?"

"As you can imagine, very badly, she even tried to commit suicide. Anyway, let's go and talk to her."

Radha was sitting muttering and wringing her hands. Her face was deathly pale and her eyes were bloodshot. Her body was slumped forward screaming defeat and as Carma noticed the two plaster cast on her wrists that covered her wounds, she was dismayed by Radha's helplessness.

As soon as Radha saw Anisha and Carma her bottom lip started trembling and she blurted. "I am going away to another prison"

"Which prison are you being transferred to, Radha?" Carma smiled sympathetically.

"They mentioned Broad moor…. the hospital unit." Radha's voice quavered. She rocked back and forth then started to cry.

Anisha stepped forward and hugged tenderly, but Radha looked at her with vacant eyes and pushed her away.

"My husband murdered my son, Anisha, because he did not want me to have him after I was released." She whispered, then abruptly got up and started walking around in circles, wringing her hands.

"Poor Radha!" Anisha wiped the tears from her eyes.

"I don't think she needs to go to Brood moor, Anisha!" Carma's eyes flashed "She is only depressed, and who wouldn't be after what she has been through? I am sure the authorities are just trying to get rid of her, proving yet again that to the prison service justice is only a matter of convenience!'

Anisha and Carma walked back to their cell in silence each engrossed in their thoughts.

"Carma, I was thinking, it must be nice to have had home help in India and…"

"Anisha! Amid all this injustice that is happening to all the people around us, how can you think of something trivial like that?" Carma cried in exasperation.

However she realised that to keep their emotional equilibrium, they had to talk of matters other than the harsh prison culture.

"Sorry, Anisha. I did not mean to be rude, and of course we did not mind, but Amit was of a different view. Even though he was brought up amid the luxury of domestic staff, Amit did not believe in the poor being, in his words, exploited for their own personal benefit." Carma smiled and tiredly brushed a stray curl from her ear. "You should have heard how my brother and dad argued on that subject! Even my mother used to join in sometime. Amit used to joke about those times to me."

"What was she like? Tell me more about her."

"Ah, my mother. I have not really thought of other than in the role of a mother…just shows, eh. But having said that I do know that she is of a temperament that is inflexible in her belief that her lot in life was what she had earned in the last existence. This kind of fatalist temperament, I think we have the same kind of temperament, Anisha, is what ties us to our men, silently enduring their abuse."

She turned and paced the room

"My mother believes in 'Karma', a strong belief that present troubles are the result of former lives sins, and that the future can be lessened by unselfish and dedicated actions. In other words, that our present actions affect future existence and the soul is eternal and goes through a cycle of births, deaths and rebirths. I personally find this religious belief hinders progress and stops people revolting against the deplorable conditions that are endured by most of them. What do you think?"

"No, I, we don't believe in 'Karma.' We believe that everything we deserve is given to us in our present life."

"How strange, for I have never met anyone who thinks like that. No, I am wrong; Aijaz was a Muslim too, but not a practising one. At least when he was not with his family, and when he was with his brother whom he idolised, why then he would be the most religious fanatic! Anyway coming back to mother, she, like most Indian women, also believes in 'dharma',"

"You have lost me there, Carma, what is 'Dharma', never heard of it before." Anisha asked a puzzled frown on her face.

"'Dharma' is the fulfilling of one's duty and should be dictated by conscience, social background and custom. But to me it seems that this belief is only a process of making a woman feel she is destined to be the weaker sex, an idea that is only encouraged by the self-proclaimed guardians of religion who happen to be men! I think that explains my father in a nutshell, but Amit, well, his way of thinking was different , more caring and compassionate, always thinking about the welfare of others."

****

Chapter 22

"I hope that Sunetra, at least will be happy! No doubt she will for she obeyed her parents!" Devesh said cruelly.

Sumitra tactfully ignored him. "I got a letter from Sunetra, and she has asked us to help him with his business knowing your influence."

"Yes, I know, Sumitra, you don't have to tell me! Did you manage to contact Mr Varma?" he asked as Badal entered the room.

"Apparently he has gone out of town, which suits me for I can finish my sightseeing in the meantime."

"Morning, everybody!" Amit voice boomed cheerfully across the room.

He entered the dining room wearing a silk dressing gown, his dark hair falling across his eyes.

"Morning, Beta", Sumitra looked tenderly at Amit. "We've just finished our breakfast – shall I ask Ramu to heat up everything or make you fresh toast?"

"Not as yet, Ma", Badal looked exasperatedly at his mother, "Don't worry, when I'm hungry, I'll ask him or better still I'll get my own breakfast.Mum you know I do not believe in the poor being taken advantage of just for our personal benefit. We have had this conversation many times!"

"We are giving them employment, or else they would starve on the streets. And we not only treat them as one of the family, they are paid too!"

"How much money do you pay them?" Amit asked.

"1000 rupees", his mother replied.

"1000 Rupees a week is fine". Amit had looked approvingly at his mother.

"No, 1000 rupees a month."

"What! Nobody can live on that amount of money!" Amit expostulated looking thunderstruck

"But Ramu for one has a family – parents and children – back in the village that are dependent on him".

"Yes, we know, and the money he earns he sends back to his home!"

"Good lord"! Do you know that he a daughter who he has to get married? How much profit does our business make?" Amit was stunned at how his father and mother were missing the point.

"Young man, I do not like your tone of voice. Do you think we are the kind of people who would exploit anybody for our personal use?" Devesh retorted as his fingers drummed the table impatiently

"That's right", Sumitra nodded her head. "That is the rate, set by their unions – for you know they too have their unions these days! And I am sure Ramu will come to us if he needs anything"

"He might be too proud to." Amit retorted.

Amit ended the discussion then as he and Badal had planned to go sightseeing. Anyway after his endless discussions on the subject he had actually stopped debating the issue, however his silence was misconstrued as concession and defeat.

"Gosh it is getting warm!" Badal replied.

Amit quickly finished his breakfast and they left the house.

Badal was beginning to like India for mostly everybody had home help, owned at least two cars and had a chauffeur. Added to which was the fact that nobody ever did any work, for the passivity of Indians and their belief in kismet was part of India's easygoing characteristic.

<u>Chapter 23</u>

Coming out of the house and into the blazing sunlight, the scent of the perfume of the flowers drifted from the garden to delight his nostrils and Badal admired their garden, bright with snapdragons, roses, Dahlias and daisies.

"It's beautifully maintained," remarked Badal, getting into the car as a chaffeaur in a crisp white uniform opened the door of the car.

"No thanks to me" answered Amit "we have a gardener - a mali who does wonders! Oh, by the way, I spoke to Carma and she has invited us for a late lunch!"

"But I thought Carma was on….?"

"It's a long story, Badal." Amit answered noncommittally.

Badal, looking around him in awe as they drove down the road, surprised at how right his father had been when he had told him to expect India to be stimulating, and daunting. He had been a bit confused by his father's description of India, and admitted as much to Amit.

Amit tried to clarify. "For all my cynicism about India and its drawbacks, it has its qualities, but don't tell my father I admitted as much! I will never hear the end of it! India is aiming to be independent, and although most people who come from abroad are disconcerted by its image of poverty and starvation, not all people live in thatched houses in villages that are only connected by dry tracks!"

He looked out of the window thoughtfully.

"But what really puts me off about India is the vast imbalance, Badal, for there is a wide gulf between the poor and the rich. For the wealthy, the sight and fear of poverty is an inducement to get richer anywise to strengthen the walls of wealth. Wealth that would keep them safe from poverty and they are taught from an early age to ignore the underprivileged and keep compassion on a tight reign. On the other hand half no, more than half of the population is seeped in extreme poverty."

"And the traffic here Amit….! Aren't there any traffic rules? "

Badal repeated the question he had asked Devesh on his arrival, for the roads looked turbulent. Neither the authorities nor the people seemed particularly interested, or even concerned about the regularity with which worn out and loaded cars were driven by what appeared were incompetent drivers.

"Nope and there can't be because the poor need and are dependant on bus services, even if they are dilapidated, poorly maintained, jammed and polluted. Because it is so easy to corrupt an official, bribes take care of matters like driving tests and licences. Therefore accidents are normal in India!"

They passed the secretariat buildings, which were impressive and imposing with a mixture of classical and Indian motifs, with carved stone screens, Sculpted elephants and fountains.   . . ..

The driver weaved the car in and around the traffic. Black and yellow taxis drove shoulder to shoulder aside a rickshaw and the cars lurched along like crocodiles in the traffic stream, drivers looking neither left nor right or behind, leaving his and his passenger's safety in the hands of God.

"Aren't the people scared to drive in this manner?" Badal asked in astonishment.

"Not really, Badal, they are all fatalists who believe in fate, and Cars, Lorries and rickshaws are painted with religious symbols. The postcard picture of their god taped to the dashboard they believe to be their insurance policy against accidents or any kind of misfortunes that might strike."

The taxi in front suddenly swerved into the pavement and parked with some of the taxis that were gathered in small herds under the shelter of the roadside trees.

"That is where the drivers set up their beds, light a fire and built a hut for a telephone." Amit explained as he saw Badal looking intently at them. "The drivers live in and around their taxis, tinkering and dozing waiting desperately for a phone call. Some of the encampments even have a bath where the drivers can bathe themselves. In winter, these taxi-drivers often sleep in the back seat, wrapped in blankets and one can often see them sitting at the wheel, hunched in a blanket, looking like some kind of bandit!"

They drove past a temple which was resounded with religious intonations of priests and the devotional prayers of the faithful. Badal gave a start as he heard the hollow boom and echo of massive drums and the ringing of bells.

"I have heard that religion is at the root of India's heartbeat?" Badal enquired as he saw the multitude of people flocking the temple gates.

"Yes, people are religious embraces the whole of Indian life both external and spiritual. On their way to and fro from work, stop to offer homage and on weekends take their families bearing tiny bowls of coconut, fruit, vegetables and incense. Many homes too have small temples and the rich usually had a room set aside for worship" Amit explained.

"The temple buildings are beautiful!." Badal remarked.

Amit, getting carried away in his role as a guide, proceeded to give an architectural background to the temples.

"Most of the small temples are carved, plastered, painted and decorated with dyed cloth hangings whilst the more important ones are decorated with precious metals and gems."

The sun was blazing away in a cloudless sky. Badal was hoping for some cool breeze, but even the air was warm.

"And the beggars, your dad was telling me that most are con people, not genuine at all? Can't the government put them in jail or something?"

"That would not be practical for the jails are overcrowded as it is, for not are there only convicts in there, but thousands of innocent people with no prospect of ever being tried. But enough of the depressing side of Delhi, there is a pleasant side to it as well. I am sure you must have heard of the Red Fort?"

****

"Yes, my husband often told me that he thought india was wonderful.......although extreme! Carma remarked." Is it time for a bath, Anisha? I need to rinse my mouth of those awful cakes!"

They had just eaten their supper, which as usual had consisted of a large jug of tea and a plate of cakes of an indescribable texture.

"Yes, I think it is, at least not for a bath but...."Anisha had barely finished her sentence when a prison officer unlocked the cell door to let them out.

Whilst a few prison officers lurked in the corridor, they walked down the corridor to the bathroom and passed two young girls from Nigeria wearing multi-coloured national costumes cheerfully talking.

"Surely they are not the ones we hear ranting and screaming?" Carma asked.

"I don't think so, they look much too cheerful to be screaming and shouting. They like many others are awaiting trial for importing drugs"

"They are so young; I wonder what made them turn to drugs?" Carma mused. "Do you think it has something to do with the social factors in the community, for I gather there are not many opportunities for employment?"

"Yes, that is part of the problem, and if crime levels have to be reduced, society attitudes should be addressed first. Having said that, the situation is made difficult for most people of ethnic background have a chip on their shoulder. And because of it, I dare say they look and misinterpret any sign of rejection which maybe causes them to turn to crime. Seems like a vicious circle to me. Anyway, there is so much bias at every stage of the criminal system that punishment of different classes is magnified. Most people, like Sophie, end up in prison again and again. Sad…."

They had nearly reached the bathroom when John, the prison officer, glowered at Carma. "I want both of you back in your cells…now!" he barked.

Carma looked startled. "But I, we haven't…."

"Do you want me to put you on report, or would you like the punishment block?!

Carma bit her lip and stood clenching her hands into fists. "But I, we.."

John looked Carma up and down very slowly, very insolently, then with lifted eyebrows he sneered.

"I am fuckin going to put you on report….you…why don't you go back from where you came from?"

Carma's eyes filled with tears when Anisha took her arm.

"Come on, Carma, let's go to!." Anisha led Carma away as the prison officer glared after them.

As Carma walked back she felt there had been no reason for him to be so cruel yet…was this incident a reflection of the racism they had been talking about earlier?

"You know, Anisha, I thinkh society feels safe by pretending that all evil and crime is locked in prison. But in reality wickedness exists in every living person and cannot be captured nor locked up. Oh, and by the way, did I mention that I am grateful to you for being so patient in explaining the system to me? You are a true friend, Anisha."

"Carma, yes you have, many times! Please, you don't need to thank me for you have been a friend and listened to me as well! Gosh! I can't wait for the medicine trolley for I am going out of my mind with pain; in fact I think I will ask for something stronger than the last painkiller!" Anisha brushed her hand across her forehead.

"And here I am selfishly talking about myself!"

"No, Carma, please your experiences are a distraction from my pain. Why was Sajata so cynical about life?"

Before Carma could answer the medicine trolley came and Anisha went to get her dose

As Anisha returned and sat on the bed, Carma looked at her in surprise.

"Aren't you going to have your tablet?"

"No, not as yet, later, it will help me to sleep. Anyway, you were telling me about your aunt?"

"Oh, yes, that was very astute of you, Anisha, for something did happen to make her so.Her husband was, would you believe it, lost by the Indian prison service!"

****

Chapter 24

"I feel I have to apologise form my behaviour yesterday, I did not mean to put you off, and I believe my aunt enlightened, or should I say, tried to brainwash you to her way of thinking? Even though I agree her on almost everything, she tends to be over-zealous." Amit ran his fingers through his hair.

"Not at all! I think what she does is admirable, but I was just wondering if something happened in her life to make her so bitter?"

"You are right….she fell in love and married a man against her parents wishes,"

They strolled along the streets admiring the variety of colours displayed.

"That was not exactly the problem, for they got married and were very happy. But apparently, my aunt was surprised when one day the police knocked on her door and arrested him.

"Good Lord! He was a criminal?" remarked an astonished Badal.

"No, no," Amit replied hurriedly. "Like many other people, he was locked up not because he was a criminal, but because he was witness to something incriminating, and the authorities wanted to make certain that he attend the trial of the accused."

"That's alright then he should be out soon." Badal heaved a sigh of relief for he quite liked Amit's zealous aunt.

"Yes, so we were all hoping, but we forgot the indifference of our judicial system for he seems to have got lost in the system. And after his disappearance, aunt Sajata lost the zest for life, added to which her mother-in-law taunted and blamed her for it, as if it was all her fault."

Badal could not picture an innocent and vulnerable Sajata and when he said as much, Amit's reply was.

"Oh, she was, Badal, it's only since the last couple of years since she broke away from her mother-in-law that she found an objective in her life…ones she understand and relates to.."

"Bet your father was infuriated, could he not have bribed...?

Amit was silent and did not answer.

"I think we better take a scooter rickshaw, now." Amit raised his hand to an empty rickshaw as the chauffeaur had parked the car at the Red fort car park whilst Badal and Amit toured the area.

They got into the scooter, a contraption that spluttered and made a noise that was kidney rattling.

After a nerve-racking drive they arrived at the mosque's main approach and after they had looked around went to the Jama Masjid.

Badal looked around him and sensed vitality and resilience that he was sure could not be found elsewhere, combined with a pride, which was even more difficult to ignore.

The afternoon was wearing along as they walked back to the car along the main road, which had been converted into a street bazaar. .

They drove through the streets of Old Delhi, Badal could smell the pungent spicy smells as there were stalls of food, sugar cane crushed on a barrow, and cold juice with ice.

"And Carma....? I thought we were going to her place for tea?

"No, she rang and asked if we could make it tomorrow? I accepted...since we will be sightseeing tomorrow as well so we can stop there as arranged."

After seeing some time, Amit stifled a yawn. "I don't know about you, Badal but I am knackered! Shall we call it a day and leave the rest for tomorrow?

Badal nodded his head. "Yes, I am feeling tired too! And Amit,I am very grateful to all of you for being so kind and hospitable."

The sky, which had turned dusky, showed orange. The orange turned into copper and then into brilliant bronze.

Badal watched fascinated at the alternating variations in the sky and at the scarlet tongues of flame that were leaping across the sky. There was a soft breeze, cool and refreshing, yet sensuous and pleasant, and it comforted and caressed Badal's burning skin.

As they walked back to the house he notices the soft amber of the setting sun softening the white of the veranda and a moon, looking like a finely sculpted finger, was slowly appearing in the sky. The stars had begun to show themselves and the ones that were visible started twinkling in the dark night as if on black velvet.

They arrived in time for dinner and it seemed to Badal that again Sumitra had gone to a great deal of trouble, for there were a variety of dishes.

Sajata, had been invited and she was sitting on the sofa, a sad and wistful look in her elongated eyes. She was wearing a light pink sari that set of her dark hair that was nestled against the nape of her neck.

"Ah, there you are" Devesh had risen from the dining table. "And how did you like our Delhi?"

"We have seen Delhi, but not all of it, gosh I don't know about you, Badal, but I am starved!" Amit sat on the table and stretched his hand for a bowl of rice.

"Don't you think you should wait for our guest?" Sumitra tapped his hand lightly.

"No, it is alright, Amit please carry on." Badal said as he sat next to Devesh.

"So Badal, don't you agree that our monuments are a museum of architectural splendour? That includes the Taj Mahal in Agra - a massive white structure which glitters like a priceless jewel in the moonlight and is a monument to love! Remarkable! Truly remarkable!

"I agree, uncle, I am sure it is." Badal replied though he secretly felt that the social injustices far surpassed the splendour.

"In fact, you have seen 'the tip of the iceberg, so to speak." Devesh chuckled at what he thought was his witticism. "Have you rung Mr Varma for an appointment?"

"Actually I thought I would just drop by his office tomorrow first thing in the morning."

"There are a few things about India you must know" Devesh remarked "And one of them is that is no such thing as 'early morning office work! Most people, especially business people do not arrive in office till at least 11.30 a.m – then they go for a long lunch! They work but at their own leisurely pace, that is why it is advisable to phone and make an appointment".

Sajata, who had been sitting quietly, recoiled as she recalled how it was an appointment her husband had kept for his office that sealed his kismet. For the following day the police were at their house.

<u>Chapter 25</u>

"Put your hands behind your back and come with us!" They roughly seized Nitin and started dragging him when he resisted

"Let him go! Please let him go! He is not a criminal!" Sajata had begged and pleaded with the police.

"We will let him go as soon as he has testified against the man he had an appointment with yesterday."

"Who are you talking about? I only met a client...."

"Shut up! You can talk all you want at the police station! One of the officers slapped Nitin in the face and started handcuffing him.

"Wait, where are you taking him? I will phone my lawyer to......."Sajata had pleaded as they dragged Nitin to the jeep.

"You can bring your lawyer to your police station, and as soon as your husband testifies, he will be allowed home."

"I don't believe you!" Sajata screamed.

She, like many Indian people did not have faith in the workings of its justice. She regarded the police as being a corrupt and oppressive law enforcement who continuously failed to gain the confidence of the people. They were hated and condemned by all as a brutal force, for it was a noted fact that prisoners were tortured.

"I want to see my husband." Sajata had gone to her local police station the following day.

"What is his name and what was he arrested for?"

As soon as Sajata blurted out the required details, a policeman lazily went through some papers on his desk.

"I am sorry but I cannot find anyone of that name on my files. I suggest you try the police station at a nearby area. Maybe he was taken there."

Sajata had gone to various police stations, and the answer was always the same.

"We do not know who you are talking about; we do not have anybody of that name on our files. I suggest you go to …police station, and if you have already been there, I suggest you go to …prison."

Sajata had finally gone to a prison that had been recommended to her by a police officer, but there she was told that Nitin had been transferred to another prison. She had been directed to various prisons and the answer had always been the same…..they did not know of a prisoner by that name and since Nitin's arrest two years ago, Sajata neither had heard from her husband or from the police.

There were tears in Sajata's eyes, as she thought that she could have found the loss of death bearable, for a grave or cremation, however unpleasant, was at least tangible. However, not knowing where her husband was or even if was still alive, were questions that remained unanswered and tormented her.

Amit saw his aunt's eyes glistening, he was angry at not only his father's thoughtlessness, but also at the lack of official control that made it lose one of its prisoners in its system, thereby failing to gain the people's sense of security.

Sajata got up and hurriedly left the room.

"What is the matter with her now?" Devesh asked with a frown

"You are not the least bit sensitive, dad, she thought of Uncle Nitin when you mentioned appointment."

"Oh dear..."Devesh looked perplexed. "I did not mean to ....but we cannot tiptoe around her!, it has been a long time and she must get used to it!"

****

"You're poor Aunt!" Anisha's eyes glistened as Carma recounted her aunt's tragedy.

They were sitting in the Assocoation room and the air was so thick with cigarette smoke, the loud constant talking and screaming was drowning the noise of the television and radio.

"Anisha, no wonder our clothes smell of stale smoke!" Carma wrinkled her nose. "Hey, what is going on?"

"You're a selfish cow!" Susan yelled as she turned to switch the channel to the programme she wanted.

"Who do you think you are, you bitch?" Sheila screamed as she got up from her chair and a full-scale slinging match ensued. Her voice was shrill and her voice vibrated across the room.

This went on for ten minutes before there was an ominous hush when Sheila lunged forward and slapped Susan, who tried to fight her off, but Sheila clung desperately to her hair.

"You don't know anything, you evil woman, let go of my hair!"

Two prison officers came hurriedly to disentangle them and, Susan was lead screaming out of the room.

"What was all that about? Carma asked.

"Being locked up, inmates argue a lot as they have a lot of pent up aggression. They tend to make mountains out of molehills, so to speak! But in this case, I think Sheila is justified for she was expecting a visit from her family, but because the prison is located so far from her home, they couldn't visit. So, of course, she took out her aggression on Susan! And anyway, most of the women here have low levels of self esteem, which makes it difficult for them to relate to each other, and the prison atmosphere does not help!"

"Maybe if they have a disciplinary system whereby a prisoner can complain if they are being harassed? I have seen that some prisoners need protecting from other prisoners."

"You mean to protect women like Doris and Joanne, I think. Even though they do have a disciplinary procedure, it too operates in an unjust manner. Because it can only either increase the time limit of the captivity or worsen the conditions, the inmates do not make use of it.."

"That is not only awful, Anisha, but it scares me to, for I have seen the women who come in for petty crimes being bullied by the women who are in for most serious offences. I have come to the conclusion that by the end of my sentence, I will either be stabbed or become a drug addict!"

"Er, maybe not, Carma, I have survived so far!" Anisha grinned impishly.

After Association they strolled back to their cell, and Anisha looked at its brown walls and the black shapes scurrying across the floor with a shudder.

"So what happened to your aunt after she left in a hurry? Have they located Nitin? And in this depressing place, tell me more about the exotic beauty of India."

"No, well that is it I don't know, for Amit had mentioned in his letter that there might be a chance her husband could be located. As for the beauty of India, my husband, thought that the injustices far outweighed the beauty. And his feelings were justified when he heard first about Ramu's daughter then his neice, Chaya. Chaya had been married when she was six to a much older man, whose family was greedy and selfish and.....

"Carma, you mean she was a victim of child marriage? That is still prevelant in India?" Anisha asked in astonishment.

"Yes, unfortunately, the tradition of child marriages is still followed in most villages."

****

Chapter 26

Unlike the previous day, Badal woke to a grey morning and a cool breeze. A faint rumble drew him to the window and he could see rolls and bulges of dark clouds covering the sky. As he rubbed his eyes and yawned he could see lightening followed by another peal of thunder.

Badal thought that the monsoon season had arrived, as predicted by Amit, and hoped for some respite from the previous day's heat. A gust of cool, damp breeze blew across the room as he heard raindrops falling in gentle patter.

However, regardless of the weather, there was still the morning activity of India. There was the early morning paperboy and then came the postman followed usually by the gardener. Last but not least there followed a procession of fruit and vegetable sellers, each with a distinctive yodel.

Surprisingly, when he went downstairs, Amit was awake and having a cup of tea with Devesh and Sumitra, and greeted him with a cheerful "good-morning, How are you, ready for more sightseeing?"

Badal took the cup of tea handed to him by a girl who he had never seen before.

" Fine, and yes I am actually."

"Badal, you managed to contact Mr Varma?"

"Yes, surprisingly, I did, and I have to meet him this afternoon. I will be free in the morning though; can I have your promised snacks? I am quite looking forward to it."

"What is this I hear? You will have food outside?" Sumitra looked at Amit disapprovingly.

"Yes, yesterday we passed some food stall which looked delicious and we thought…"

Sumitra and Devesh both looked aghast and appalled.

"Look here, like I mentioned Badal is not used to our climate and the food outside is swarming with flies!"

"I noticed that, but that is not what Amit had in mind, I think".

"Rather than going out for a meal, I have a better idea." Sumitra glanced at her son. We'll get Chaya to make the snacks for lunch. Chaya, yaha aoun. Come here!"

"Wait a sec, who is Chaya?" Amit asked in bewilderment

"Amit!" Sumitra exclaimed in dismay. "Chaya is the girl who served us a minute ago. She is Ramu's niece, before he left for his village, he told me she would cover for him. She has a problem of sorts. Anyway, I think we should encourage in her quest for independence."

"You cannot let Ramu go to his village every time he has a problem, Sumitra!" Devesh glowered at his wife. "Even if Ramu manages to appease their greed, the quantity and quality of whatever he gives would be made as an excuse for further harassment!"

"Maybe you are right; Devesh, but we do have a certain moral responsibility too. From what Ramu told me, he was afraid for his daughter because he had heard of cases where in-laws murder their daughter in law because of dowry".

Sumitra thought her husband's attitude to be cruel, as he knew the in-laws would send Ramu's daughter back home at the slightest pretext of inadequate dowry.

"Anyway, is Chaya as nice and helpful as Ramu?" Amit asked, looking slightly embarrassed.

"She is but you can see for yourself", Sumitra replied just as Chaya entered the room.

She was a young girl of about twenty and was wearing a ghagra – village dress that was a full pleated skirt consisting of a blouse and scarf that was like a stole.

Chapter 27

When Chaya was just a child her parent married her to Vasudev, a much older man. Even though the girl usually stayed on in her parents house till she was grown up, her in-laws had come to take her to their house soon after.

"She can't go with you! She is too young!" Her parents had protested.

Her parent's protests were in vain, for Vasudev was adamant.

"If you do not send her with me immediately, the marriage will be cancelled and I will find another wife!"

Her parents reluctantly agreed, for it would have been dishonourable if they had not. So it was not long before Chaya left for her husband's home, clutching a small bundle of clothes while her parents stood and wept, helpless.

However, once they had arrived at her husband's home, she was treated like an animal and a slave.

"You have to help Vasudev in the land as well do the housework!" Her mother-in-law shouted at her as soon as she arrived.

From 5.am.onwards, Chaya did all the household duties before she joined Vasudev in the fields whilst her mother-in-law gossiped and her father in law smoked hookah.

Ramu's brother heard about her maltreatment and went to collect her but was openly insulted.

"You have not paid us enough dowry! Do you know your daughter is no-good and how much we have to put up with?"

They threatened that unless he gives them more dowry money; they would send Chaya back home.

Chaya watched powerless as her father wept and pleaded with them, trying to explain he had no money, at the same time thinking he could not have a married daughter at home, as that would bring disgrace on her and his family.

However, they were adamant and Chaya came back to her father's house, where she lived for a year.

"I don't think you should stay with your parents. Maybe your husband will take you back now? I will talk to my husband and see what he can do. Is that okay with you?"

Kasturi had come to stay with her cousin, Chaya, and they were washing the dishes after feeding the rest of the family.

Chaya nodded her head wearily, for things were not the same as before.

It seemed she was always in the kitchen, for she spent most of her time in doing tedious tasks for the food preparation in advance as well. The only fuel for lighting the hearth was either cow-dung or wood, and she spent a lot of time in trying to light the fire, and often envied the better class who had kerosene stoves

It was finally arranged between Kasturi and her parents that she should go back to her husband.

However, when she arrived at her in-laws, she found her husband married again.

Yuri, his second wife, swooned and shouted, screaming Chaya be sent back, not realising that Chaya was the first wife, and therefore the legal one. When she realised that nobody was listening to her Yuri finally showed Chaya a tiny room at the back of the house.

"Take that, you…!" a ripped quilt was thrown at her. "And from tomorrow you get up at 3am in the morning!" Yuri shouted and swore at Chaya.

"You have got to be joking !" Chaya exclaimed.

"No, I am not, as you will see!" Yuri smirked.

Chaya was woken up at 3 in the morning, given a large bucket and pail and ordered to get the water from the well.

Yuri regularly threw tantrums, shrieking and yelling

"I will kill myself unless Chaya be sent back to her parents house! She is useless!"

Vasudev finally was not able to withstand her outbursts and left Chaya again at her father's house. And this time Chaya felt her humiliation to be complete, but although what she had suffered and endured angered her, she showed no outward signs of animosity.

Back in the village, her father told her to stay with her brother, where Chaya cooked and the rest of the time worked. She spent the mornings mixing cow dung and straw, with which she repaired broken patches in the walls of their hut and with cow dung and water, re-plastered the floors of the hut.

However, Chaya took on a part-time job in the fields to earn extra money to prove she was not a burden, for matters were becoming difficult for her in the village.

"There's goes Vasudev's wife! Why is she staying at her brother's house? She must have done something to annoy her husband!' was the common gossip around the village.

Consequently, when Ramu, her uncle, wrote to her brother if he knew of anybody who could take his place for a month, she leapt at the opportunity to escape from the drudgery of the village and her brother had supported her in her wish that she would replace her uncle.

Chapter 28

"Amit, I only hope that are more women like Chaya who are brave to break away from the norm and be independent." Sumitra remarked as Chaya went back to the kitchen.

"Yes I hope so too and good for her", Amit remarked admiringly. "Mum, I will take Badal sightseeing again before his meeting at 2.30 p.m."

"Don't forget, Amit, we are going to Payal's wedding on Sunday, so don't make any plans. Badal, of course you will come with us?"

A gust of cool damp breeze blew across the room and Badal looked out of the window gratefully. The cool wind had blown a thin a thin spray of rain onto the veranda and Badal could hear the raindrops falling in a gentle patter as he nodded his head.

"Gosh, I had forgotten", Amit left the room scratching his head.

Payal was his mother's sister's daughter who was engaged to a Sikh boy. Sumitra's sister Anju was not as orthodox as Sumitra, since Hindus and Sikhs readily inter-married without any objections from their parents.

The dividing line between Sikhs and Hindus had grown less defined since the last generation and Anju, like a lot of Hindus was also content to worship in a Sikh gurudwara (temple). Moreover, they liked Sukhdip, who was rich, travelled and successful in his profession.

The couple knew each other since childhood, when Sukhdip had gone abroad to study. When he returned, a qualified doctor, his English was fluent, indicating the resilience of being abroad. He cut a dashing figure with his tight black turban - and his black shirt with belted trousers gave him the appearance of a pirate.

Sukdip too was pleasantly delighted to find his childhood friend grown into a beautiful woman. When the question of marriage arose, she was naturally his choice, but the formalities of the union and question of the suitability were left to his parents, who also were pleased to confirm the alliance.

"Yes, I would like that very much for I have from my parents about Indian weddings and how elaborate they are, not only that, I have never attended a Sikh one.

"Yes it most certainly is, Badal." Devesh explained. "There are bands playing noisily by men wearing white uniforms, blue trousers, black boots and red caps, their trumpets blaring and drums thundering! There are gangs of boys earning few rupees for holding flaring oil lamps, grooms riding on white horses while around them their friends dance in the streets! The men of the bride/groom usually crown themselves with pink turbans, and girls pin sweet smelling flowers into their hair!"

"Sounds nice and come to think about it, I don't even have a Sikh friend, let alone know anything about them!" Badal reminisced.

"Well," Devesh replied "I will give you a little background to them. They are a proud, enterprising and assertive people, and even though they form only 2% of India's population and are represented in the Civil Service, Medicine and Sport. They are also forefront in Commerce and Farming and play a dominant part in the transport industry by providing Sikh crews for Lorries."

"Yes, I noticed that." Badal remarked for he had frequently seen a turbaned Sikh with the light of battle in his eyes drive the taxis of India.

"Badal, you have not seen our garden" Devesh's voice interrupted his reverie. "Whilst you are waiting for Amit, let me take you on a tour of our gardens."

"I'd like that for I noticed your wife arranging some beautiful flowers. Are they from your garden?"

"Yes, they are", Devesh replied glancing at the colourful arrangement of flowers in the middle of the table. "Shall we go?"

They left leaving Sumitra giving orders for their breakfast to Chaya, who was still getting used to the new environment.

"Am I to presume that this is the last we have seen of the rain?" Badal asked.

"No, not at all", Devesh replied "no doubt we shall see the rain later on. It comes and goes as it pleases!"

The rain had decreased and they went into the front garden where there were individuals of droplets sparkled in the wintry sunshine.

The rain had left the garden with a fragrant smell rising from the earth. In some sections Badal could see clouds opening up, unfolding a blue sky beneath, and a shaft of sunlight slanted across. He looked with wonder and awe at a rainbow that had appeared, spanning the sky and encircling the town in a multicoloured arc.

****

Anisha had been listening intently with her chin cupped in her hands.

"I really admired my mother, Anisha, like Akram and Aijaz, my father too had many ways to control her, by his constant criticism, anger or ignoring her needs, yet she was always so cheerful. Even if she wanted to, I think she is not capable of any kind of decision making. Maybe because she never had to face a choice or any kind of responsibility in any important matter throughout her life, she had no training to make her decisions or to influence others."

"My mother was the same too, she was always responsible for others, a kind of nurturer, if you know what I mean, a quality that cements relationships." Anisha replied, then thought about what Badal had told her about his mother. "but Carma, this responsibility is dealt with differently by women - some married women become indifferent because of it."

"Maybe, but my mother wanted nothing other than to remain and make a success of her marriage! I think it was because of her that our home appeared happy, but underneath the comfortable air of domesticity was the tension between my parents and Amit's restlessness, and to top it all, I married Aijaz, who humiliated me at every given chance! And, Anisha, it was not only Aijaz who betrayed me, my second husband did too. But when I first met him, I thought he was so pleasant and caring!"

Carma's face looked white and exhausted from another sleepless night and her wet hair matted damply on her forehead, for in the brief time allowed, and no John to bully them, Carma had just about managed to shampoo her hair.

****

Chapter 29

"Dad, Badal, where are you?" they heard Amit's voice breezily as they walked back towards the house. "Badal, shall we leave?"

Amit joined them as they entered looking cool and refreshed in a pair of jeans with an open-necked shirt, for even though it was the monsoon season it was still hot and humid.

"You haven't had your breakfast as yet, Amit!" Devesh exclaimed. He looked exasperatedly at his wife. "Sumitra, hasn't Chaya got breakfast ready as yet?"

"Don't worry about it dad, if you don't mind, Badal, we will skip breakfast as we are running late", Amit looked sheepish. "We'll leave and just stick to an early lunch. Is that alright with you? In fact I think we will have an early lunch first!"

"That's fine", replied Badal. 'm ready, but I just have to collect some papers for the meeting with Mr Varma. Will you drop me off there directly after lunch?"

"Of course", Amit answered. "That will be no problem at all"

Badal hurriedly collected his documents and as he went downstairs, saw Sumitra bustling about, giving orders for the day, and admired her hospitality and warmth.

He hoped Sunetra would be like her, for he realised he liked being spoilt and pampered! Although he considered himself to have a liberated outlook, he expected his wife to be old-fashioned and subordinate, as social traditions and norms had helped to stereotype him.

"I'm going to the office, Sumitra", Devesh shouted to his wife as Amit and Badal were getting into the car.

"Why are you going to office so early?" Amit asked.

"I have a problem at work, one of my married employees is living in the company's accommodation but has recently separated from his wife and was forced to leave home. He, in retaliation surrendered the lease for the company accommodation and said he is in no way to be held viable for the rent to be taken from his salary. When the company asked his wife to vacate the home, she filed suit, claiming that it was her matrimonial home! What am I supposed to do? Anyway, l will see you all in the evening."

"Best of luck with it!" Amit said getting into the car followed by Badal.

There was another crash of lightening and thunder and the wind blew a thin spray of rain into the windscreen of their car. The streets were still soaked in rain after the thunderstorm the previous night, and shallow pools of water were on the roadway and a big tree had fallen down in the night, crushing a few roadside stalls.

Badal glanced out of the window as the driver weaved his car in an out of the traffic.

Devesh was right about the weather, for the breeze that had blown the clouds away, had swept them back again. There was a sudden flash of lightening which outshone the strip of sunshine that had tried to appear followed by a clap of thunder.

He saw crowds of people splashing to work, under black umbrellas, stomping diligently against the monsoon storm.

"I see that a lot of women go to work here," Badal remarked, glancwing out of the window. "I don't think I would like Sunetra to work, for according to me either a woman is cold and career minded or family minded and warm!"

"I don't think that is necessarily true, Badal, but yes the women here do work hard."

Working women were holding their wet, brightly coloured synthetic saris with one hand and their dripping umbrellas in the other. Amit imagined they would arrive at work with their matching bangles jangling, mascara running down their cheeks and hair all wet.

"Oh yes, even though they are always depicted as living traditional housebound lives, Delhi, is a city of working women, middle class women and girls – office workers, bank employees, clerical staff, teachers, nurses etc."

There was another crash of lightening and thunder, which emphasised the tempo of the rain, and there were pools of water on the roads and on the pavements.

"I don't understand how the weather can change so drastically", exclaimed Badal "
"Yesterday it was so hot - actually, it's still hot and humid!"

Amit glanced at Badal who was perspiring and felt sorry for him. It was difficult enough for people who lived in India, it must be doubly so for him.

The driver was contriving the car in and out of the traffic in an expert manner with one hand whilst he had his other hand on the hooter all the time, honking needlessly, warning others. All the other drivers did the same, and the traffic was noisy, to say the least. There were so many cars going both ways that it was difficult to know who was on the right side of the road!

"It's a surprise to me that they did not have an accident!" Badal exclaimed.

Suddenly, Amit bent forward and whispered in the driver's ear.

Badal wiped his face with his handkerchief then tucked it back into his pocket and saw that the street was thronging with people and traffic. They passed people sitting on the roadside vendors of all sorts, and Badal saw could see a little thin girl, undernourished and exhausted sweeping the pavement in the drizzle. Nearby her father/husband was sleeping under a shelter of cloth.

Badal was hungry and he opened his mouth to ask how far the restaurant was when they turned into a lane and parked outside a house.

"I'm starving", remarked Badal, preparing to get out of the car. "Is this where your famous restaurant is?

"No, don't get out of the car as yet!" Amit put a hand on Badal's arm. "I have brought you to Carma's house. I don't think you know but she is married."

****

"Anisha, I don't what was worse, staying with Aijaz or meeting my husband, coming to London or….here!"

"That bad huh?" Anisha remarked sympathically

"And more, believe you me!" Carma wrung her hands and started pacing the cell in an agitated manner, then as if to forget her past decided to concentrate on the present. "tell me, Anisha, is it my imagination, or do some of the prisoner's look as if they are on drugs?'

"You are right; they are."

"Really? But what I don't understand is how they get away with it. Don't the prison officer's don't know who supplies them?"

"No, they don't for usually dope dealers are very cunning and will find a way to get the drugs to the inmates."

"I find that hard to believe, with all the strip searches and all."

"They do not make difference, anyway, was Caste the only reason your parent objected?" Anisha asked.

"Huh? Oh yes, well, yes, I think it was compounded by the fact that he was a horrible man also. My father was correct in his judgement. But having made one error of judgement in assessing Aijaz's character and learning from it, I made another when I married my husband…the present one I mean. When Amit came to see me with him I was so excited for in my dreary life with Aijaz I did not have many things to look forward to! But of course, Aijaz managed to ruin the day, as usual!"

****

Chapter 30

"No, I didn't know Carma was married, Sunetra told me a lot about her and I presumed…What?" He looked impatiently at Amit for clarification.

"It's a long story", Amit replied looking down at his hands. "and one that we don't have time for now. But the gist of the matter is that she married against my parents wishes, and nowadays my father will not even hear her name mentioned in the house."

"I thought your parents seemed sensible and reasonable folks!" remarked Badal, in astonishment

"Not so", Amit replied with a grimace and clenching his fists in frustration. "I knew my father would be difficult, but did not anticipate my father's reaction would be so severe– he has disowned her and so have our relations. They are afraid that society, which does not given its permission for inter-caste marriages, although views re changing now, would unleashe its so-called righteous claws, and they like to think that by not speaking to Carma they are preserving and strengthening the basic family structure. Though I don't know how," he muttered

Badal looked bewildered as Amit continued.

"My father can be stubborn like hell. India is a society of 'position' in one form or another. For some people position or status enable them to have influence so they can exercise power and maintain their place in society. For others, it is looked on as a bargain for making money in selfish ways. For my parents, it means the preservation of family culture!"

"I am amazed at how strongly the caste system is wound in India's society"."

"Badal, believe me, I too am confused by its influence on Indian life, for I have seen how it imprisons a man in his day-to-day function, though I believe it originally started as a useful division of labour in rural society."

"You mean the caste system has a positive side to it?" Amit remarked incredulously."As far as I can see, it only manages to overturn reason and justice. Not only is it ruthless but also immune to compassion!"

"Not only that but it instills prejudices and produce a maze of rules. The only positive thing about it is that it is a complete community offering a firm identity and stability for some people."

"But is it positive? Nobody deserves to be ostracised for their love, but it is nice to know that at least you are in contact with her."

"Yes, unbeknown to my parents, that is. She is my younger sister and I have been close to her and have always protected her. She is a warm and affectionate person, as you shall see. I'll explain later for Carma will be waiting for us. But I do think that in this instance my parents are right...I don't like the man she married anymore than they do. Do you know he beats her?"

"So why doesn't she leave him?" asked a horrified Badal.

"I tried to persuade her, but like my father she is stubborn!"

"She knows we are coming?" Badal was sweating profusely.

"Yes," replied Amit "I phoned her whilst I was getting dressed".

He opened the door of the car, and at the same time the door of the house was flung open and a girl with long brown hair billowing around flung herself at Amit.

Badal judged her to be no more than twenty-one years of age with porcelain white skin. She looked fragile and beautiful and her face lit up with joy when she saw Amit.

<u>Chapter 31</u>

"Amit!" she smiled excitedly and there was an expression of shy pleasure of her face. "It is good to see you. It's been such a long time" she sighed as her eyes narrowed and her face became pensive.

"Carma, how are you? Oh, this is Badal, and Badal, my younger sister, Carma." Amit affectionately pulled his sister's hair.

"Hello," Carma's voice was gentle as she greeted him."Amit has told me a lot about you."

Badal could not pin point what her brown gentle eyes conveyed, what was it – distress, grief or just plain hopelessness? There was stubbornness in her well-defined face, which was reflected in the determined set of chin

"Come in", said Carma "you must be hot, for even though it is the monsoon season, it is just the beginning and one can still feel the heat. I've got some cold drinks waiting". She took Amit's hand and grinned cheekily at her elder brother. "With lots of ice, without the iceberg!"

She had, what seemed to Badal, the most essential and desirable of human ingredients – the quality of natural charm.

However Badal noticed that even though she was laughing and talking, Carma's laughter had a desperate sort of gaiety.

Amit laughed heartily. "Not you too!" he exclaimed, but stopped suddenly.

Carma's eyes, which had for a moment been lively with merriment, hooded and moistened with unshed tears. She wiped them with her scarf and tried to change the subject.

Badal was touched and dismayed by the clear unhidden loneliness of her attitude.

"Bhaiya, can you take Badal into the sitting room? I will just bring the drinks." Carma said her face white and strained. She vanished into what Badal thought would be the kitchen.

Amit took him into a room that had a divan and two chairs, one of which was broken. The paint of the room was fading and the plaster was peeling. There was one small fan in the room, which was whirring with jerks. Badal was surprised at the roms condition after having stayed in Devesh's house, for there was splendour and here was poverty.

It confirmed his belief that India was a land of contrasts and consisted of two worlds in one city – the rich and the poor, the past and the present.

Carma came back into the room carrying a tray with cool iced drinks on it still mortified at the mention of her father. Although she had realised soon after her marriage that her father was right about Aijaz, she was reluctant to make a humble approach to him. For although all her life she she had meekly loved and obeyed her father, her love had been more from duty, and at at present she could only love him with guilt and resentment.

She could never rid herself of the shadows of the men in her life, wishing she could be liberated from all sentiment of being a woman - of being her father's daughter and now her husband's phantom.

Amit noticed the unhappy expression on Carma's face. "Carma, are you worried about something? You look pale".

"It is nothing; I think I might be coming down with the flu or something".

Carma spoke in a husky whisper, but even though Badal could detect a tremulous note in her voice, he was touched by the maturity and poise of the young girl with a withdrawn expression, which asked nothing and expressed nothing of what she felt.

The thunder rattled behind the blackening clouds, but she was so immersed in an inner conflict that she did not hear them till Amit broke into her reverie.

"Sis, are you sure you are all right?" Amit asked again, frowning.

"Of course I am fine," Carma smiled.

She offered the tray with sweetmeats on it to them. She had regained her composure and managed a cheerful expression on her face that did nothing to betray her unhappiness.

"How is Aijaz?" asked Amit, though he did not really care how he was.

"He is fine," Carma replied. "He's just gone out and...".

"How come?" asked Amit in surprise, for he had particularly chosen this particular time of day so he would not have to meet Aijaz. "Didn't he go to work?"

"Uh, no", replied Carma uncertainly.

She did not want to reveal to her brother that Aijaz had no job and they had nearly run out of the meagre saving that Carma had accumulated. She tried to disguise their dilemma in her tactful way.

"One of his uncles is not well, so he had to take a couple of days to see to him". She hoped that Aijaz, in case he came, would support the story that she had made up at the spur of the moment.

Chapter 32

At that moment Aijaz walked in the room, surprised to see Amit, yet pleased, for he was hoping that once Carma's family realised the financial condition they were in, they would be able to give Aijaz a job in the family business, and eventually a share in it.

The only reason he was without a job was to corner her family into helping, a ploy which till now had not worked – he hoped with the arrival of Amit would change matters as he saw the circumstances Carma had to live in.

"Amit, I am glad to see you", Aijaz smiled at him, turning on his charm, but eyed Badal with suspicion.

Badal could understand why Carma had fallen in love and married him, for he was a handsome man with gleaming black hair, finely arched black brows, and small beady eyes tinged with thick black lashes. But like Amit, he did not like him for his beady eyes were constantly shifting ,reflecting a sly,cunning man and selfish man.

"Carma, where are your manners?" Aijaz demanded abruptly and rudely as he sprawled indolently on a chair. "Amit, you will stay for lunch, won't you?"

Carma drew in her breath in dismay. She looked at Aijaz in amazement as her hands that were on her lap clenched and unclenched. She was surprised at Aijaz – he knew there was nothing to eat in the house, how could she offer lunch to her brother and his friend? Why did he always have to humiliate her?

"Yes, we'd love to", Amit replied, as he wanted to spend time with Carma to see what was troubling her.

Carma disappeared into the kitchen, wondering how and what she was going to do. Aijaz had seen the worried look on his wife's face and followed her.

"Aijaz, why did you have to invite them to stay for lunch?" Carma asked exasperatedly "you know there isn't any food, even for us!" She lifted her hands, and then let them fall to her side.

"Why, what have you done with the money I gave you last week?" Aijaz's voice lashed at her as his eyes narrowed.

"That was a week ago, and we have been eating since then, you know. What you had given was not enough anyway and things are so expensive these days…!" Carma's face was distraught and her hands were clasped tightly together.

"It's up to you to figure out how to make ends meet. You know I am not working and… Why don't you ask your parents for help if you can't manage? I have been asking you to give me an account of how and where the money goes!"

"How can you say that?" cried Carma in a forlorn voice. "You spend money on whatever you want, whenever you want, but you get angry and blame me when there is none!"

As usual Aijaz ignored her. "However it is to our benefit that Amit undergoes what we do. Maybe he will understand then that we have no money. I feel it is essential we have Amit on our side – hopefully he will be able to convince your father of our grim situation so they will be able to help us". Aijaz waved his hands excitedly at the prospectus of being finally accepted by his father-in-law.

"Aijaz, you are a hoaxer and deceitful! Carma said with disgust, an insulted look in her eyes. "Moreover, father is very stubborn and won't help under any circumstances."

"What about your mother? Does she not want to see her only daughter comfortable?" Aijaz asked with irony.

"Even if my parents wanted to help me I wouldn't let them. I made the decision to be with you, for better or worse!" Carma's voice quivered, but she stood superbly straight and arrogant.

She felt tears of anger sting her eyes, but was too ashamed to cry. Although she was raging with anger and frusteration, the only outward sign were her tightly compressed lips. Suddenly Carma heard a cracking sound and felt a sting on her cheek.

"You will do as I say!" Aijaz hissed, digging his fingers into her arms. "And I want you to serve food, whatever it is, and whatever the quantity!

Carma whimpered as the pressure of his fingers dug into the soft flesh of her arms, then ruthlessly shove her aside and leave the kitchen, slamming the door after him.

Carma wiped the tears that had started trickling down her cheeks as she heard the roll of thunder accompanied by silver shafts of silver streaks of lightening flash across the skies.

The sadness she had been carrying around spiralled into a sudden hysteria and her hands started shaking. Standing still in the kitchen she tried to take control and be calm, reminding herself again that panic never really accomplished anything. The blood rushed to her face as her head started spinning with the impact of Aijaz's slap.

She rinsed her cheek with cold water and felt the sting subsiding. She tried to think of a method to serve a proper meal without arousing Amit's suspicion, for she could cope with Aijaz later.

Her anger and humiliation gave her courage and her head jerked up as a thought occurred to her – her friend owned a restaurant around the corner, so she quickly slipped out of the kitchen past the sitting room, where she could hear loud of voices.

As usual, Mr Khurrana was helpful when she explained the situation, she returned with snacks that Amit had not as yet introduced Badal to. She knew that Aijaz would be livid with her – they had no money and nor were they likely to have any tomorrow, but at least for today Amit would go home knowing Carma was well settled.

She ran back to the house and was laying out the dishes when Aijaz began shouting.

Chapter 33

"Carma, where are you? Haven't you prepared lunch as yet? Isn't there anything in the house?"

Aijaz smiled for taunting and hurting Carma, in private or public, and seeing her vexed gave him a feeling of satisfaction.

"Everything is ready, Aijaz."

Carma placed the savouries on the table, noting with satisfaction the look on Aijaz's face when he saw the variety of dishes she placed on the table.

"Carma", Aijaz raised his voice and gesticulated at the food. "Is this what you serve your brother? I'm sure they are hungry and would like a substantial meal". His eyes were like steel and his voice, which was rising higher, shook with anger.

"Don't worry, Aijaz", Amit hastily intervened. "I had promised Badal anyway that he should sample the food we are so famous for. I mentioned it to Carma this morning, who kindly remembered. Thanks sis." he said turning towards his sister reassuringly.

"I'll get some plates," Carma said in a quivering high-pitched voice and hurried from the room into the kitchen.

The expression on Aijaz's face was harsh and a nerve flickered at the side of his mouth.

"Thank you, Carma", said Badal, clearing his throat. "It was really very kind of you to remember that I wanted to taste the specialities of India."

He sat quietly watching Aijaz who appeared, amongst other things, an egotistical and conceited man, and his dislike for him developed ten-fold when he saw the way he humiliated Carma. However, even though his aversion to Aijaz increased, so had his admiration and respect for Carma. She was so affectionate and gentle, and yet so proud. It appeared to him that Carma had a great capacity for suffering and would not minimise it, like some women, with self-pity. Even with Carma's genteel upbringing, her home, simple and ordinary though it was, compared to what she had been accustomed to, was like a palace to her for the four walls held her dreams and expectations of a happy future.

Badal was reminded of Anisha; both had smiles of such genuine sweetness with their eyes reflecting innocence. But there the semblance ended, for their temperament seemed to be made up of contradictions- Anisha had been more of an extrovert, Carma seemed so quiet. Carma had sacrificed so much for the man she loved; Badal wondered if Anisha would have done the same? His eyes darkened with an inner anger which was not so much out of jealousy than that of a spoilt child whose toy has been taken away.

"These little balls of chapatti have to be eaten with the spiced water – I will start first to show you how they are eaten, it's an art!" Amit chuckled trying to lessen the tension he could sense between Aijaz and Carma.

He followed Amit's cue and dipped the round ball in the water ant then into his mouth where it melted. He could taste the cold yet spicy water and whatever he had been expecting, it was certainly not this, for it was really delicious.

Aijaz saw them eating with relish and the expression on his face as he looked at Carma was almost a hideous mixture of grief and anger which distorted his features. His hands clutched the arms of his chair so hard that the veins began popping below his knuckles. His mouth twisted and his eyes became cold.

This was the second time Carma had ruined his plans – he was beginning to regret the day the day he married her. He thought she would be timid and meek, but had not reckoned with her fierce pride and determination

Carma saw Aijaz glowering at her and went into the kitchen againand took several breadths, large sounds that echoed in the kitchen. However, it was more to avoid having to eat as there was barely enough food for two. She had barely been in the kitchen for ten minutes when she heard her brother's voice saying that they were leaving.

****

"Amit knew that Aijaz was violent towards me for I had phoned him at one time. He had persuaded me to leave him, but how could I go back home knowing how my father felt? Anisha, happiness came to me like a magician's artifice, show me a glimpse of might have been and then vanish!" Carma disclosed sadly.

Anisha stopped her pacing and stared into the bedlam in Carma's eyes.

"Maybe father would have agreed to forget the whole situation if I admitted my mistake and left Aijaz, but I was stubborn. I continued to cover up Aijaz's failings for a long time till I finally broke."

"Carma, I am so sorry…." Anisha massaged her temples, a habit, Carma noticed, was occurring often. She often felt that Anisha was

Sometimes Carma noticed that Anisha seemed depressed and she had lost weight for her clothes hung loosely on her.

Carma could understand her despair and heaved a deep sigh. She felt a knot in her stomach as she thought that maybe she too was destined never to have the strength that came from freedom?

****

<u>Chapter 34</u>

"Carma", Amit called. "we are leaving.Thank you very much for a delicious meal and…" he stopped as Carma ran in from the kitchen and flung herself at him.

"Amit, don't go as yet!" she cried, "We have not had a chance to talk". Carma's eyes were bright and beseeching as she took told of his hand and held it tightly in her own.

She looked nervously at Aijaz, whose his face had assumed a look of frigidity that Carma knew would be followed by violence.

"Carma", Amit said gently, returning the grip of her hand and seeing the fear in her eyes. "we have to go but I promise I will talk to you soon. Oh, by the way, I forgot to mention that Payal is getting married…to Sukhidip and they wanted you to be there. The wedding is to be on Sunday; shall I come and pick you up?"

"Who's Payal?" Aijaz asked, as his eyes narrowed suspiciously.

"A cousin…." Amit replied tersely.

Although he doubted Carma would only be welcome at the wedding by Payal and not her relations, at least it would give him a chance to get Carma away from Aijaz.

"Is it going to be a quite affair?" Carma asked.

"Oh no….! It is going to be held on a big scale, being an only daughter and all that. After the wedding at the temple they are going to have a reception in one of the five star hotels."

"Of course, I have always been very fond of them, I'd love to come." Carma replied.

"Amit, why don't you come again next week for lunch", interrupted Aijaz, his eyes glittering.

His words sounded insincere and mocking and in his eyes there lurked something dark and unfathomable. He did not want Carma to meet anybody or go anywhere, and always managed to start a fight if ever she did venture out.

Carma shook her head slightly and glanced fearfully at Amit. Aijaz intercepted the look and Carma drew in her breath and frowned as she kneaded her arm with her hand. She found that she was caught in a web of hurt, and could no longer predict when the next violence would erupt, with the result she was constantly on edge.

She did not have to sustain any physical wounds or be subject to any physical assault – because just the depth and severity of Carma's emotional reaction to Aijaz's continued violence was dependant on how serious the perceived threat was going to be. And sometimes Carma built up these defences for nothing, fending off an attack that never materliased.

"Amit", Badal said getting into the car, "you are very lucky to have a sister like Carma" Badal clutched the door as the drive turned sharply to avoid the scooter that had suddenly decided to overtake the car in the opposite lane.

"Yes, I know", Amit replied."Unfortunately that B....Aijaz does not and is violent towards my sister! And the worse thing is that I cannot do anything about it!"

"Why doesn't' she leave?" Badal asked, his anger towards Aijaz spiralling.

"Well, I think I have started the ball rolling…"

Badal clutched the door and wished for the comparatively smooth driving of London. He shuddered as he looked around him at the three wheeled ugly contraptions called auto-rickshaws, for they spluttered pollution from their exhaust and were making rattling noises as if they would fall apart!

There was a man lagging near a bus stop, who, as soon as an overcrowded bus arrived, ran in an effort to heave himself on it, and as soon as it accelerated, was left hanging desperately half hanging and dangling. To Badal's amazement, this dangerous feat was accomplished to the encouragement and cheers of bystanders.

Amit asked the driver to slow the car. "I think this is the road you are looking for. What did you say the number was?"

"Thirty-four", replied Badal looking at the business card "and this is it". He opened the car door and stepped out as the car stopped.

"Wait, shall I send the car for you?"

"No thanks," Badal said confirming the address "Mr Varma said he would drop me afterwards. Thanks all the same"

****

Carma and Anisha were walking down with the others to the excerise yard. Carma was glad to see the patch of green grass and the few shrubs in the yard. They walked around a few times, stretching their legs, then went to the bench. However, as they neared it Carma saw that it had been spat on.

"Yukkk….." Carma shuddered in disgust.

"That is done in spite, you know, sometimes prisoners from other wing…."

"No, Anisha, I don't believe that!" She saw some women from their wing look their way then snigger amongst themselves. "Maybe it is somebody from this wing. You know, I used to think that it is only the prison officers who bully us, it seems that prisoners do it too!"

Suddenly Diana rushed past, tears streaming down her cheeks, and taunts and jeers followed her.

"'ey, Diana, where yu goin? 'R' yu goin to yer friends to tell of me? Fuckin 'ell, I don't care!"

"'ey Diana, if yer 'usband comes, give 'im my 'ove!"

"'e won't come 'ere, 'is other woman is pretty!"

"There's prison justice for you, Carma, it seems we are not the only ones who are harassed." Anisha remarked.

"Poor thing! She does not deserve this kind of…" Carma choked angrily.

She had thought that by exploring the debris of her past, she could become calm and rational to face her present, but on the contrary she was becoming disoriented and regressive. Exploring and replaying the early hurts and betrayals had drawn out the stubborn and angry part of her. Carma was beginning to find it difficult to handle first her past, then her present, and the thought that her present was going to be her future filled her with horror.

"There is so much negative energy in the prison, Carma, that I don't really blame the other women. They just get bored so…..!."

"Anisha, you are justifying the women, as usual. It is not them that I blame but the prison service, for doesn't it know the consequences of this negative energy? Maybe somebody should tell the authorities."

Carma, like so many other people, had been reluctant to shatter her fragile illusion of a fair and honest and legal system, and had been trying to search deep for allies and help in the system. However, so far, at least in this prison, she had only been confronted with shallowness and hypocrisy, whilst others, sometimes even the guilty, walked freely.

"Being labelled a 'grass' is worse than anything a prison officer can do." Anisha remarked as they walked back to their cell.

"I still don't think she should be harassed so..."

"What yer sayin? That I'm fuckin wrong? Maybe yer two 'r' also like 'er.! 'ey, Mandy…!"

"Oh no! She was just looking for chance to bully us! Come at this point, the cell is the safest place to be in!"

As they entered their cell, Anisha turned to Carma."Did your mother speak to your dad"

"Yes……she did." However, Anisha could detect a gentle reproach in her voice. " She tried, but she never could persuade Father."

"At least your mother tried and you got some kind of support from your brother, but Azaria…" There were tears in Anisha's eyes. "She is my sister …!"

"I agree, Anisha, her attitude towards you was and is unforgivable, but I have come to realise that it is only by internall forgiveness can one be truly free. I notices Mandy was looking subdued, not her usual boisterous self, picking fights with all?"

"She has found out that her mother has cancer and was hoping to visit her but….."

"I thought prisoners were allowed compassionate leave?"

"They are, but the prison officers are putting obstacles in her way. Not only has she annoyed them but this is the time they can wield

"I cannot but help think they might be right, you know for I feel that Mandy has deliberately pursued her own selfish interests regardless of others, not only in prison, but outside too."

"I agree that she seems to be one of the people who cannot be reformed, for her problem lies deep in her personality, and most probably in her environment that could not be changed or influenced."

"Bad as things are with us, I cannot help feeling that our circumstances are better than some woman. Take Chaya, Ramu's niece.and others of her class." Carma said, wiping her brow.

****

Chapter 35

Chaya was hovering near the door, sensing, by the sober looks on everybody's faces and the tension in the house that something important was being discussed.

Her uncle Ramu had told her about Carma, Sajata and Sumitra and how each one of them, in their own way was unhappy. She had been surprised, for she always believed the wealthy were happy and it was only the poor who had to endure the violence and injustices.

Chaya especially felt sorry for Sajata, who she liked, as she was aware of the work that she was trying to accomplish. She wished she had known about her group a couple of months back, for maybe they could have helped her cousin.

Champa had been arrested and put in jail, her only crime being she was from a poor family who had dared to object to her land being taken over by a man of higher caste. As the police were slaves of the higher caste, Champa was arrested, put in a lorry with other prisoners, taken to a prison and locked in a cell.

Chaya went to the jail a few days later and was made to sit on the floor in a big waiting room. Alongwith the others, she sat for a long time, as the guards wanted a bribe before allowing any of them to meet their relatives.

"How much money will you give us if we let you visit your cousin?" They sneered at her at her.

"I don't have any money and anyway, she is innocent!" Chaya tried to reason with the police officers.

"Get out!"You can visit you're her tomorrow!"

She went the following day to the prison, and its concrete walls, locks on doors and men in uniform frightened her.

She waited impatiently for what seemed like hours in a roomful of prisoners and policemen. Everybody was swearing and using bad language and she could see that relatives, mostly village people, clasping parcels of home cooked food hanging around in the veranda. There was a prisoner in leg irons and chains being protected by listless looking guards in Khakhi who had rifles slung over their shoulders.

After a long wait, she was finally allowed to meet Champa, who looked thin and scared.

"Why are you looking frightened, Champa, you will be out of here soon."Chaya tried to reassure Champa.

"I am afraid, Chaya, very scared. The policemen tortured me as soon as they got me in the police station. To top it all, the smell in the prison is disgusting and there is no water either!"

Chaya was shocked. "You should complain!"

"To whom?" Champa replied resignedly. "When I was locked in a cell, I told the other women what I was going to do, and do you know what they said? They all shook their heads, and said that I was lucky as some policemen raped a woman when they arrested her, whether she was a criminal or not!"

"But can't you complain to the judge when you go for your trial?"

"They have threatened that they would beat me and my family if I ever said a word to the authorities."

Chaya had not known how to help Champa, for she had had no money, and even if she had, the poor people were not granted bail. Chaya was staying with her brother, and she left Champa frightened and scared.

Chaya spoke to her brother about her cousin.

"What can I do? The police will not hesitate to arrest me too and then who will look after my family?" He helplessly spread is hands in a gesture of defeat.

And when Chaya went to prison the next day, she was told that Champa had been transferred to another prison and with her limited resources she had tried to find her, and till today, Chaya did not know what had happened to her.

Chapter 36

"Chaya! I'd like a cup of tea please." Chaya was brought out of her reverie by the voice of Sumitra. "And I want to discuss tonight's menu with you", she added as Chaya hastened to the kitchen.

Amit, meanwhile, kept hearing Carma's voice crying and Megan's face appearing in front of him. Maybe if there had been someone to hear Megan's silent cries, she would have been alive?

Whenever he saw the unhappy countenance of Chaya he was reminded of his sister. What if Carma did something drastic like Megan? Amit was even more impatient because he would have liked to help her on his own, but he was dependent on his father, for being a member of a joint household, their income was pooled. Any expenditure was made from the common purse, and all decisions in relation to finance were taken jointly, with his father's approval.

"Oh, Payal said she might drop by later. I had phoned her.

He walked out of the room as Chaya walked in to discuss the day's menu.

Payal entered the room buoyantly, but the frown on her face showed her concern, for when she spoke to Amit, she had come at once after her shopping. She had met Aijaz once taken an instant dislike to him.

She was a girl of strong personality, who as soon as she entered a room, had everybody's attention. She was not a good-looking girl, but possessed a confidence and air that a pretty girl would envy. Her one asset, her magnificent hair, was swept back from her forehead into a large bun at the nape of neck and her complexion had a clearness and brilliance that owed nothing to make-up.

She kissed Sumitra on the cheek and flung herself on the chair, throwing her shopping on the floor with a grimace.

"God! I'll be glad when all this is over! I am tired of shopping and shopping and still more shopping! It never seems to end!" she exclaimed.

Her voice held a pleasant resonant timber but she looked guiltily at Amit and Sumitra, realising with a rare sensitivity that they were worried.

"Sorry, aunt!" she smiled and took the glass of water from Chaya and gulped the water in one go. "Whew! I needed that! Now, Amit, Aunt, both of you are so quiet, is everything alright?"

Amit explained as best as he could the existing situation between his father and Carma and recounted the visit to Carma's house.

Payal was in tears by the time Amit finished explaining.

"My God", she exclaimed in a subdued voice "I knew he was a bad 'un, but this is preposterous! Have you spoken to Sajata aunty?"

"What can she do?" Sumitra said, "She can't solve the sorrows of the world."

"So what can I do to help?" Payal cried. "You know I'll do anything."

It was Amit and Sumitra who looked guilty.

"We feel embarrassed in asking as we know you are busy preparing for your wedding, plus the reaction of all our relatives, but Carma has not confided in me as I am sure she would to you, so I was wondering if you would find time to talk to her. Amit has convinced her to come to your wedding."

"Of course I will, aunt. You know I am fond of Carma."

Just then Badal entered the room and Sumitra introduced him to Payal

"Congratulations!" Badal said, fanning himself. "I hear you're getting married on Sunday? Gosh, it's hot, even though it is supposed to be the Monsoon season!"

"Yes, I am, and thank you", replied Payal, accepting graciously Badal's felicitations and eyeing him critically. "I hope you will be coming?"

"I'd love to, thank you," replied Badal, "and now if you'll excuse me, I'll take a shower, again!"

He left the room fanning himself vigorously with a magazine, for although it was raining there was humidity in the atmosphere which Badal was finding claustrophobic.

"He appears to be a pleasant fellow," remarked Payal "He is engaged to Sunetra, is he not?"

"He is," affirmed Sumitra.

"I'll call Carma and confirm." Amit rose and left the room.

They were laughing when Amit re-entered the room 15 minutes later, his face pale and eyes bloodshot.

"That black guard scoundrel Aijaz…!"

"What's the matter, Amit, what has happened?" Sunetra asked.

Chapter 37

"What is the matter? Is Carma alright?" Payal inquired.

"That blackguard Aijaz...I will...!"

"Amit, what has happened? "

"I spoke to Carma, Aijaz's brother has suddenly come and is staying with them and she is terrible scared of him for he is a fanatic! She was crying, saying that Aijaz has been emotionally tormenting her by divorcing her every time he is in one of his rages! Not only that, she has not told him that she had been to the doctor."

"Is she alright? I do not know much about his religions, but I do know that the divorce is only complete if it is repeated in when in a calmer mood" Payal added when she saw the look on Sumitra's face.

"Yes, but apparently Carma says that he says it all the time and this has been going on for over three months. Her visit to the doctor puts a different complexion on the matter. We must help Carma escape from the house!" Amit was speaking to himself.

"Amit!" Sumitra was getting impatient. "What is the matter with Carma?"

"She is pregnant, Mum! She has not told Aijaz, but his brother knows and do you know what he has said?" Amit asked quietly. "That he will not have a niece/nephew who is not a Muslim! Both of them have got terrible tempers, and in her condition, with their temper, between them they will kill her!"

"Oh no! Poor Carma." whispered Payal. "Look, I have to go but…"

"Yes, of course." Amit replied vaguely.

"Thanks for coming and being here to help but I will have to speak to father," Amit walked Payal to her car, his face creased with worry.

"What the hell do you want me to do?" Devesh thundered his face white with anger, when Amit explained the situation to him.

Amit, by this time had realised that Devesh would not welcome Carma back home.

"Dad, will you hear me out? Aijaz has agreed that Carma can attend Payal's wedding on Sunday, and I was thinking that instead of her going back to Aijaz, we can bring her back home?" he looked pleadingly at his father, and cursed the joint family system, which made him dependant on his father.

"She should stay with her husband, whatever the consequences!" Devesh said maliciously. Sumitra and Amit both knew he had a ruthless streak but with his own daughter?

Badal entered the room, refreshed after his shower as Devesh stormed out of the room.

"Sorry! Have I entered a family discussion!

"No, come in, come in," Amit was glad to see Badal. "We're all worried about Carma."

Sumitra was sitting on the sofa, wringing her hands whilst Badal sat silently listening to the latest events that had befallen Carma."

"And every time he has been in one of his rages, which is often, he has been declaring divorce. So is she divorced or not? How much more complicated can her life become?" Amit put his head on his hands.

"I think she is." Badal replied. "I have a friend from the same religion., but I think it is not acceptable when in rage ut only when said calmly." He repeated Payal's statement.

"Well, he has said it in both ways…..Amit muttered

He suddenly looked up and stared at Badal, who had been a moral support for him throughout Carma's predicament. He was going to miss him when he went to London, he thought, when he had a sudden brainwave.

"Badal," he inquired "what would you think if I asked you if Carma could go with you to London? You know, start all over and all the rest of it?" he looked at him pleadingly for it seemed to him Carma's only hope. "I am planning to go to America and she can join me there later."

Before Badal could answer, Devesh entered the room after a short walk in the fresh air. He was feeling calmer, heard his son's suggestion regarding Carma and approved, although he was astonished that Amit was planning to go to America.

"And leave me to alone to run my business?" he thundered.

Badal meanwhile was surprised at Amit's suggestion, for however much he would have liked to help; it was different to have Carma as a responsibility, even for a short while. And what would Sunetra and his father have to say, even though she was their cousin. His indecision showed on his face.

"Did you say that Aijaz has divorced her'?" Devesh asked, temporarily forgetting Amit's announcement.

"Yes, that is what she told me."

"So that does mean that she is legally divorced and can marry again?"

Amit was exasperated with his father's line of questioning. "Yes, I am not sure, but that is what she told me!"

"In that case, Badal, I have another suggestion. You have met her; she is a young and beautiful girl, is she not? How did you like her?"

"Yes, of course, but why…?", replied Badal, looking bewildered.

"And is it difficult to get a visa?" Devesh enquired. "I hear they do not issue visas to young girls!"

"Yes, that's right, they are strict, but I think they do have exceptions – like compassionate cases or life threatening ones." Badal answered irritably.

"Badal, Yogindra was telling me that you have known Sunetra only for a short while."

Yogindra had told Devesh that Badal had also been involved with another girl at college, and judged him to be indecisive and impressionable.

"Badal, would you like to marry Carma?" Devesh asked bluntly. "And you know, being my only daughter, I would help with your business too."

Amit and Sumitra were shocked at Devesh's tactless proposition. Although both of them liked Badal, Devesh made it sound cold and businesslike and also as if he wanted to get rid of Carma.

Devesh could see the surprise and embarrassment on his son's and wife's faces, and decided to withdraw his suggestion having cleverly implanted the idea.

"I am sorry; my suggestion seems to have startled you. You are here for another week so… Meanwhile, Amit, you can go ahead and arrange for Carma to come here after the wedding." Devesh yawned as he looked at the surprised faces of Amit and Sunetra. "Good-night, everybody, I'll think you will all agree it has been a long day!"

"I'm sorry about that, Badal." Amit remarked after Devesh left the room. "I'm sure Father did not mean it."

"No, not at all," replied Badal, his mind racing. "After all he only has his daughter's welfare at heart,"

He liked Carma, and as Devesh's suggestion appealed to him and it was not as if he loved Sunetra! He decided he would ring his father to find out what he thought.

****

"So you finally left your husband with the support of your family?" Anisha looked out into the wet courtyard with tears in her eyes.

429

"If Payal was not married at time, I don't what excuse I would have given to Aijaz. He looked up to his brother and between them, I dread to think what they would have done to me and my baby!" Carma wiped her forehead with a trembling hand.

"They seem to no different than Kanan's family." Anisha commented as Jane started shouting.

"'er Mandy, did yer know tha Susan has been transferred to ….Wing…'

"Fucking 'ell, Jane, leave me alone! I don't care what 'appens to 'er."

"Thought yu would like to 'now anyway, I been told tht I've to share Sharon an' I don wannu a 'nonce' to be near me!"

"Tell the screw, 'wat yu telling me for?"

"Do something, Mandy, if yu don't I 'ill bloody kill 'er!"

"Heavens, Carma, should we tell Ruth or somebody?" Anisha looked worried as she looked at Carma.

"I am sure they will sort out their differences, Anisha, I don't know why you should worry about women like Sharon, Susan or Mandy. Now if you were that concerned about Sophie, Joanne, Radha or even Doris…"

"I don't know, Carma, I feel that most of these women have been frustrated in their lives because they have not been loved or cherished and have somehow lived keeping their bitter anger hidden."

"So they become emotionally unstable and violent? Anisha, are you justifying that?"

"Of course not, Carma, I am not justifying crime, but prisons were designed for men, you know, men who would band together in aggressive and defensive groups to survive. Women on the other hand, rely on home, children, family etc. For them being imprisoned in a single sex, childless, 'male' prison is what I consider to be not only punishment but also perversion! Anyway, you finally managed to go to Payal's wedding?"

Carma nodded her head, and brushed her silky brown hair from her forehead."It was every bit as lavish as I thought it would be."

****

Chapter 38

Badal and Amit had got up early to leave for Payal's wedding on Sunday to go to the Sikh temple, where it was due to take place.

"Badal, are you ready?" Amit had shouted as Badal came running into the room, out of breath. "Badal, you don't have to run, we won't leave you behind, here have a cup of tea first." Amit's eyes were twinkling.

Sipping his tea, Badal told Amit that as he wanted to help Carma, he would marry her. In reality, his father had informed him that Sunetra had run away from home with her ex boyfriend.

"That is wonderful, Badal. I am so glad, for I know she will be in good hands with you!"Amit asked as they got into the car.

"I have never attended a sikh wedding before so please tell me if....i have not attended many weddings at that.......!" Badal remarked as they entered the temple.

They had entered the porch where there was a counter with a man behind it took Badal's shoes, put it on a shelf behind him and gave him a metal disc with a number on it, along with a handkerchief to put on his head.

The temple was specially decorated for the occasion, and there were people already sitting cross-legged on the floor. The men wore bright turbans, and the women were in colourful clothes.

Badal joined Amit in the queue that went up to the Holy Book of the Sikhs, which was under a colourful canopy in middle of the room and had strangely written words on the front. Behind the Book, a man was sitting waving a stick which was made of silver and had hairs on one end, whilst men in black turbans squeezed black box organs, singing holy hymns.

They went to the Book, placed some money on the cloth in front of it, bowed respectfully, then went back and sat down with the congregation and guests on the carpeted floor.

Sukhdip, the bridegroom, was looking handsome, sitting erect and cross-legged in front of the Holy Book.

"He is waiting for Payal, who will join him there." Amit explained as he saw Badal's puzzled expression.

"I see, Amit, he is looking very handsome, I must say." Badal remarked.

Sukhdip was wearing a red turban decorated with gold thread woven around it and adorned with a feather plume.He was wearing a knee length ivory coat and clutched a curved sword.

"He is waiting for Payal, who will be joining him there."

"Why is he holding on to the sword?" Badal whispered.

"The sword is a symbol of his determination to protect his wife, and also a reminder of the fighting traditions of the Sikhs." Amit clarified.

After an hour of hymn singing, Payal entered, escorted by her relations and friends. She looked beautiful and tinkled and rustled like a Christmas tree for she was wearing a lot of jewellery. There were heavy necklaces of gold around her throat, and her wrists were laden with bangles.

On Payal's forehead was a gold disc, and her nose was pierced by a gold ring, as fine as hair, with a small jewel suspended from it. Her hands and feet were decorated with intricate designs of henna, and as she passed them, Badal saw that on her feet she wore gold anklets, and gold rings glittered on her toes.

She was wearing a crimson red silk tunic over red silk trousers gathered at the ankles, and her head was partially hidden by a heavy red and gold veil richly trimmed with gold that matched her ensemble.

She was taken to sit beside Sukhdip, and a saffron scarf was placed around the groom's shoulder by her parents, the other end of which was given to Payal. A Priest began to recite from the Holy Book, and after a while Badal craned his neck to see the couple had got up and were walking around the Holy Book. After the third round, some people had started showering them with petals of flowers at the third lap.

"Does that mean they are married?" Badal asked.

"No, they are officially married at the fourth lap."

After the four rounds were over, Payal and Sukhdip sat on the carpet of flowers as their parents' blessed and kissed them on the forehead, followed by other couples who came to garland the couple.

"Where is Carma?" Badal asked.

"She said she will meet us here somewhere," Amit whispered.

"Oh, I thought she might have changed her mind or something." Badal took the sweet halwa from a priest holding a large steel bowl, which signified the end of the ceremony.

Amit, Devesh and Badal went back to the porch to collect their shoes and then joined the other people who were going to the restaurant. There were a variety of dishes, including different varieties of curries, and it was finally evening before Payal was escorted to Sukdip's car.

She, along with her mother was crying and her father too had tears in his eyes. This was a cue to the guests that the festivities were over, and they repeated their congratulations before bidding the happy couple farewell.

****

"Where were you, Carma, I thought you said you were going to meet Amit at the temple?" Anisha asked her chin on her hands.

"I went, but did not have the nerve to face everybody. I just stood in the corner, and did not venture to meet Payal or any of the other relatives, for I knew that I would have been snubbed. I quietly got in the car with Amit, mother and Badal, but do you know my father declined to be in the same car, saying his friend would take him home?!"

****

<u>Chapter 39</u>

On the way home, everybody was silent, engrossed in their thoughts.

Carma felt cold and listless and she rested her head on the window of the car, wiping her eyes every five minutes. She thought of the earlier conversation with Amit on the mobile in which he outlined his suggestion that she leave India with Badal for her own safety.

Carma's desolate face tugged at Sumitra's heartstrings and she looked at her with pity in her eyes.

"Don't worry, everything will be allright." Sumitra said, putting her arms around Carma reassuringly, and as soon as they entered asked Chaya.

"Is Devesh Sahib home?"

"Yes, memsahib, but he has gone to his room. He said he a headache and did not want to be disturbed!"

Sumitra sighed and Carma eyes welled up with tears again for she knew that her father was avoiding her. She sat unblinking, without the little smiles and frowns and expressions she had usually shown, like an iceberg. She felt humiliated when suddenly her eyes flashed with anger.

"Mother, I won't stay here!" There was a catch in her throat as she lifted her chin. She felt confused, feeling angry, yet at the same time trapped.

"It has been a tiring day; I think I will go to bed." Badal tactfully withdrew.

Chaya entered with a tray of tea and placed it on the table in front of Sumitra. Amit had taken his tie off and was sitting with his legs stretched in front of him

"Have you thought anymore of what I suggested, I know it was only a couple of hours since but … You have to decide soon for Aijaz will be wondering as to your whereabouts. He is sure to presume you are here with us, and I have no doubt he will be here in the morning creating a scene!" Amit ran his fingers through his hair.

Chaya had been waiting for him to finish before she spoke "Amit Sahib, there is a telephone for you."

Amit looked distressed. "That must be Aijaz, what am I going to tell him, have you told him about the baby."

"No, I have not," Carma replied "He might accept the baby, even love it, but his family will never tolerate it. However, the only way to deal with him is not to let him know that I have left him permanently, but am only here trying to persuade my family. In fact tell him that my father is half convinced, he won't say anything then!"

Amit left the room muttering under his breadth and Sumitra looked worried.

"Carma," she inquired "tell me, I am confused. Amit has told us that you told him that Aijaz has been pronouncing Talaq every time he is one of his rages. Does that mean you are divorced?"

"I think I am," Carma replied. "For ever since he first said it, he has been repeating it, and has also stopped having relations with me for the last couple of months, and I think that sort of confirms it."

"Does that mean you are three months pregnant?" Sumitra asked."And why does he want you back?"

"Yes….and I did not even suspect! He wants me back just so that I can be under his control."

There was a dead remote quality in her voice that was disturbing and her eyes held a haunted look – full of loneliness, fear and sadness.

"That settles that," Amit said, entering the room. "He fell for it, hook line and sinker! He thinks that father is coming round to accepting him, Carma, what were you telling me about him divorcing you?"

"Oh good! That gives us some time! In answer to your question, Carma thinks she is divorced. That is good for that was the only reason obstructing in the way of…"

"And did you think about what I told you about Badal?"

"That seems to be the only way, but aren't there going to be Visa complications?" Carma asked nervously, her one thought to protect the baby, flee the country and Aijaz.

Her brow glistened with beads of perspiration. She shook with fear and her darkly shadowed eyes seemed to sink deeper as her pupils dilated with fear.

"We will to the British High Commission and explain the situation as it stands. Explain about Aijaz and his brother and how they threatened your life. I am sure they will understand!"

"Now go to sleep, and you'll see that everything will seem brighter in the morning after a good night's sleep!" Sumitra said tenderly and there was the softness of rich affection in her eyes and voice.

****

Carma turned and faced Anisha.

"Anisha, my whole life has been a series of dependencies but the weakness of my position never changed, –first I had to depend on a domineering father for supplying me with a roof and food, then on Aijaz for supplying the substance in believing in myself – even if had only been for a short period. Even my relationship with my present husband, I believed to be an attractive and nice dependency, but of course what I did not know was that it was only appeared so to hide its basic flaw!"

"I thought your parents were willing for you to stay with them?" Anisha asked.

"My mother would have loved it, not my father. And I would not have, not after his treatment on the evening of Payal's wedding! No, I would never have accepted handouts from my parents, because that is what it would have meant so by morning I was convinced that I was at the beginning of the end of yet another chapter in my life!"

"So that is how you came to be in London." Anisha got up to stretch her legs.

"I felt I had no choice, Anisha, for even though I was in the midst of my family yet I felt more alone than ever!"

"It must have been terrible to leave under those circumstances." Anisha whispered.

"It was, by the time I went down for breakfast, Amit had rung the British Embassy and explained the situation so they were ready to issue an emergency Visa. But you know, none of my family came to see me off, but, when in my mind, I said goodbye to everyone's faces of pity, and ventured into a new world I hardly knew, with a man I hardly knew, I nevertheless felt safe with him. Anisha, I felt like a tightly closed bud bursting yet again into blossom, but how wrong I had been again."

For Carma had not realised that the blue sky that she had seen was not the soft nurturing sky of spring, but the cold chilling sky of winter.

"Neither Amit nor your Aunt came to the airport?" Anisha asked incredulously

"Not even then, for Amit had to go to the American Embassy for an interview, and apparently there was some news about Nitin uncle, so Sajata aunt had to go to a prison where he was supposed to be held"

"Well, that is good news in a way, I suppose. Amit knew though that you were with a man he trusted."

"And how wrong he was! I remember the flight vividly; when I fastened the seat belt with trembling fingers, and a few seconds later the plane begin to move slowly along the ground, taking me away to a new place, and actually I could not wait to leave."

"Was it the first time you flew?" Anisha asked, her chin in her hand.

"Yes, it was and after what seemed to me a long time, the plane began to move along the ground and the plane taxied past the airport and to the runaway, where it slowly turned and stopped. As soon as it engines rose to a ferocious roar my ears were ready to burst. That is when barley sugar, sweets and cotton wool were handed around by the stewardess."

"You seem to remember everything in detail…." Anisha remarked in surprise.

"It is surprising, isn't it? Maybe because it was my first time…anyway…the engines roared so fiercely that I had to put my hands over my ears to try and shut out the deafening noise! The plane moved forward, first slowly then faster and faster till we were rushing along the ground. The plane became faster, till it ran more smoothly, with no jars or bumps. At last we were off the ground, skimming along up, round back over the road.

"It was fascinating, Anisha, as I looked from my window and saw a little toy train puffing below, dolls houses and toy cars on the roads. The plane climbed higher and higher till suddenly the earth below lost my interest for there was nothing human or alive I could see and everything had became a large map.As the plane flew on a fluffy pavement of clouds, I said a silent goodbye to everything I had loved, the happy times, the family I loved!"

"That must have been very painful for you."

"Oh, it was, but after a while I began to recall the past.. I remembered laughing hysterically with Payal over some irrelevant episode, laughing with Ramu, whom I considered one of the family, helping mother decide the menu for the day without father's knowledge. I even thought of the happy times with Aijaz! But when I thought of miserable times with him my sense of security with my husband became just the more precious. I thought I was lucky to be given a second chance, and was placing and framing my future dreams under his feet, so to speak. I did not realise that he would so cruelly step on them!"

"Did your husband know how big a step you were taking in severing all ties and how emotional it must have been for you?"

"No, that should have triggered an alarm bell for he just yawned and started reading a magazine! But I arrived at London airport with high hopes of a new beginning. How wrong I was! Anyway, here I am...."Carma looked around her bitterly,"it seems my life has always been a prison of sorts!'

For once again she had been wrong in her judgement for she had liked Badal, found his eyes bright with intelligence and conviction, weighed the sincerity in his words and had found no sham in them.

"Was he a violent man like Akram?"

"Yes but not in the same way, whereas Aijaz' was physically abusive, my husband kept the dark side of his nature buried, whilst he mentally tortured me by playing mind games, manipulating, deceiving and bullying me! His attitude, together with being in a new place really terrified me."

"And being pregnant did not help, I suppose." Anisha exclaimed. "Does he take care of the baby considering it is not his?"

"Abhay is his son, Anisha, for I had a miscarriage immediately on arrival in London, which affected me badly as the pregnancy was quiet advanced. That depressed me and he used to pass snide remarks on my appearance, which I had begun to neglect! But when I became pregnant with Abhay, I was over the moon!"

"In short, not a very understanding and compassionate man, huh?"

"Not at all, Anisha, for when I turned to him for some sign of compassion, he turned from me with a sneer. He told me with a cold voice and eyes that glinted like steel that the only reason he had married me was because my father had promised to further his business! I thought my heart would break for after my long standing fear of being beaten, crowded and impaired upon by Aijaz, I could not bear the thought that it was going to happen all over again! The only nice thing that happened out of all this was Abhay and he has been the light of my life. I have been a victim, Carma, we both have and are".

But your uncle, your dad's brother was here? Could you not gone to him for help?"

"Not really for he was engaged to my cousin and although my father though he would understand this was the only way out, they didn't!
"Carma, do you know the meaning of vitim?"
"I do not, and I don't think I want to know!" Carma jerked her head up. "To me the word evokes a sense of unease and pity which is often tinged with contempt. A response that always leads to the isolation of the so-called 'victim' as is if she was in some way wearing a stigma! You know what I am talking about, Anisha; you were treated in the same way. I thought I had left Aijaz for good till the day he phoned and my life, such as it was, had come crumbling down like a pack of cards!"

The memory of that day she had suppressed, but it now backed up like water behind a dam, rising higher and higher, till it reached the brim of her consciousness. A pebble of thought, dropped so innocently by Anisha, had pierced her surface tension, and she was filled with a memory that brimmed with betrayal.

****

<u>Chapter 40</u>

"Carma, you cannot hide from me!" Aijaz had shouted over the telephone. "I know where you are, and that you've got my son!"

"Aijaz! How did you know where I was!"

Carma started crying, and seeing his mother crying, her son, who was playing happily, started tugging her sari and yelling. Carma picked him up and pressed him protectively against her, but Abhay stiffened, freed himself and watched her solemnly. He rotated his dummy as he sucked it and started twisting his mother's ears till she winced.

"You are mistaken, Aijaz, he is not your son."

"Don't lie to me", Aijaz shouted, "I found out from the doctor. You were pregnant when you left me." He started yelling and shouting.

Although he was on the phone Carma instinctively cowered against the wall.

"I know where you live. I can come and get him anytime, you bitch". He snarled and slammed the receiver.

Carma with trembling hands put the receiver down. She sat on the chair and wiped her eye with her sari and tried to soothe her son.

"It's alright, baby", she murmured gently.

She had tried to tell Aijaz that Abhay was Badal's son as she had had a miscarriage soon after arriving in London, but Aijaz's psychological manipulation and emotional abuse had,s as usual, robbed her of clarity of thought and judgement.

It had been a grey afternoon and the wind had drifted into a clammy fog. Trees were slouching in the wind and the mist and damp weather were making home a warm and comfortable and dear.

She was still crying and her eyes were red and swollen when Badal came home.

"Whatever is the matter?" he asked seeing Carma sitting on a chair with Abhay on her lap.

Carma's eyes revealed her pain before she expressed what had happened – then she told him about Aijaz's phone call and the threat he had made.

Badal was angry and he roared and fumed but camouflaged his innermost feelings..

"Carma, there is no need for you to be afraid, you are with me now." His charming tactic was a façade that hid his ruthlessness

"But Aijaz will take Abbhay from me, he thinks he is his son, I know he will, you don't know what he is capable of. He will take Abbhay just so that his brother can kill him in the name of religion, thereby becoming a martyr"!

Abhay started crying again for he had never seen his mother so upset. He lifted up his head and stared at his mother, thrusting his dummy that was hanging around his neck into his mouth and tucking his little brown head under Carma's chin. Carma kissed him tenderly as Abhay laid his cheek against his mothers.

Badal took Abhay from Carma and put him on his knee. Abhay gave a gurgle of delight and sat on his knee, wide eyes fixed on Badal, brown wisps of hair that were so much like Carma's glinting like dust over his ears. Badal smiled proudly as Abhay put his fat arms, the sleeves of which were tight on his arms, around his father's neck and tried to stand on his father's lap. He fell with a thump and pushed one of his fat little fists into his brown curls and began to twist his fingers around his shell like ears. After some time he started whimpering so Badal put him on the floor.

Carma tarted crying again, and suddenly bent down and scooped up Abhay in her arms. She clung to him tightly, afraid to leave him.

"Of course he won't", Badal snapped. "Abhay is my son; all you have to do is to tell him so I don't know how he found out about him in the first place."

"He went to our doctor in India", replied Carma, gently rocking Abhay, who was dropping off to sleep in his mothers arms. "Our family doctor and he confirmed my pregnancy at the time when I was married to Aijaz. I think Abhay is finally asleep," she remarked as Abhay's eyelids fluttered and his head drooped on her shoulder.

As she got up Abhay's eyes flew open, but when Carma had put her mouth close to his forehead murmuring soothing inarticulate sounds he slept again soundly.

"Anyway, you will be home all day as you do not work, so he will be safe." Badal's gentle voice changed into a taunt. "Carma", he asked sharply, "have you heard what I just said?"

Carma smiled wanly "I did hear what you said. That you will be home to look after Abhay."

"I'll put Abhay to bed.." She left the room and left Badal reluctantly marvelling at her strength and determination.

He rose and went into the kitchen – it had been a long day and he was hungry.

The kitchen was a fine spacious room, looking out into pleasant gardens and was a room that reflected homeliness and warmth. The room was usually fragrant with smell of freshly baked breads or the sharp aroma of Indian spices, for Carma was fond of cooking and baking.

She would move with agility between the table and sink, placing dirty bowls and spoons and/or cleaning up after Abbhay had made a mess on the floor.

However, today, Badal found with irritation that it was cold and empty.

Chapter 41

He went back into the lounge and ordered a pizza, even though they somehow reminded him of Anisha, then pulled himself together and thought he must never regret what might have been.

For the past that had not happened was as hidden from him as the future he could not see, and Badal felt no loss at her absence. They had been young and carefree, with the sweet enthusiasm of young years – years of dreaming, living in a world of shaping their illusions, where realities like health and wealth had been taken for granted. Harsh realities like unhappiness and separation had not existed for them.

However, Badal reluctantly acknowledged that Anisha had been a good and decent girl, open and honest, and the brief time he had spent with her had given him a strength that would not diminish. He was confused about his feelings for her, the word love had occurred to him, but it did not touch his emotions at present.

Carma entered the room and saw Badal sitting quietly. She looked affectionately at him, and then blushed in embarrassment for she had oame to love Badal with all his faults but also knew he did not reciprocate her feelings.

Badal had been startled and shocked when she had impulsively revealed the extent of her affection for him. After that day, Badal started regarding her with neither bitterness nor dislike – he simply became indifferent and distant.

Badal looked at her with a faint smile. Carma did not know about Anisha, though she had been aware of his short relationship with Sunetra, a relationship which he had recently revived as Sunetra had left her boyfriend (again)and was living with her parents.

"I have ordered a Pizza"

Carma nodded her head silently, reflecting that time and change of season had only deepened the doubts and paradoxes which had beset her earlier. She restlessly got up and walked to the window.

A heavy anvil shaped cloud with a livid base had forced its say across the eastern and southern skies, blotting out the setting sun and seeming to load the air with moisture. She heard a faint rumble and saw a bolt of lightening across the heavens. There were rolls and bulges of dark clouds covering the skies, and the light drizzle formed a thin dirty curtain of mist before the landscape.

As Carma stood near the windowsill, she bit her teeth into her handkerchief, afraid of Aijaz and what he was capable of. She pulled the thick curtains across the window and stood with her face nestling in them, resting her cheek against the edge and protecting her from the cold windowpane. She stood motionless and still and there was something ethereal and illusionary about her.

Carma was startled when suddenly the doorbell rang .

"Carma, can you take that? I'll lay out the plates in the kitchen." Badal went into the kitchen and opened the fridge to obtain the cans of cocoa-cola and sat on the dining table waiting impatiently for Carma.

"Come on, hurry up Carma, you know I am starving!' There was no reply so he hurried out into the landing.

He noticed with surprise that even though the front door was wide open, there was no one at the door.

"Carma," he yelled, "I have got cash on me, come on down, hurry up, I think the delivery man has gone....." There was still no answer, so he hurried upstairs, and when he did not find Carma, went out into the garden

"Carma, where are you?" he yelled.

First, he went around the opening and closing doors, satisfying himself that Carma was not in the house, then quickly toured the garden and went back into the house. To wait for Aijaz's phone and sure enough, after 15 minutes the phone rang.

"Aijaz here, this is to let you know that I have got Carma with me."

Badal was angry because he had not aimed for Aijaz to take action so swiftly for it was Badal who had masterminded the kidnapping. It unnerved him to think that Aijaz had taken control, for he was far too headstrong to think clearly.

"What do you want, how is she?" Badal queried, hoping Carma would be near to overhear the distress in his voice.

"Would you like to speak to her, maybe she will tell you what I want." Badal heard the traffic in the background and assumed that Aijaz was phoning from his mobile.

"Yes, yes, you creep, put her on the line." Badal said impatiently.

"Hello, Badal." Carma spoke faintly.

"Carma, I cannot hear you! Speak loudly, where are you, he hasn't hurt you, has he?"

"I am fine, Badal, but look after Abhay and…"

"That's enough!" Badal's brusque voice came on the line.

"What do you want? Is it money, I will…."Badal yelled.

"I want my son! You did not tell me that Carma had my son!" yelled Aijaz. "For two years you kept me apart from my son. I do not want Carma; she can come to you as soon as you have given me back my son!"

Badal heard the crack of a slap, struggling and then Aijaz was back on the line."I have put her to sleep for the moment, but why didn't you tell me about my son?"

"Listen, Aijaz, Abhay is not…."

"I will wait to hear from you before…." Badal heard the threat in Aijaz's voice before the phone went dead in his hands.

.

****

The thought of Abhay had brought tears to Carma's eyes.

"It is not my kidnapping that was so painful, but what Aijaz told me!"

Before she could explain, the cell door opened and Ruth walked in with some papers.

"Ruth, I have not seen John for some time? Has he been suspended again? I heard he assaulted Susan?" Anisha asked.

"Er, I don't know, Anisha, but you know the gossip around here, half of it is not true anyway."

However, Ruth looked uneasy, and Anisha knew she was trying to be loyal to the prison system.

"Carma, you did not tell me that you were an Indian citizen." She took out a form and Carma recognised it to be one of the forms she had filled.

"I am not, I mean, I was, but am a British citizen now." Carma replied in surprise."Why?

"Apparently you are not, we checked. It might mean that you might have to go to India to stand trial."

"Oh, no I do not want to back to India. I don't know where my parents have moved to and my brother has gone to America!" Carma gasped putting her hand over her mouth. "There must be some mistake, for my husband assured me that he had taken care of all the legalities."

"There is no mistake, Carma, you are not a British Citizen." Ruth left Carma looking at her in amazement.

"Anisha, I do not understand what is happening?" There were tears in Carma's eyes.

"Carma, don't worry, I am sure there must be a mistake, you'll feel better after a cup of tea!"

They had been waiting in their cells for their breakfast call, which was as usual late, and the women first started shouting, and then became abusive. As was usual, tempers snapped and Carma could hear fists against the cell doors. They heard shouting and creaming from the cell next to theirs

"F..k off, you…!"

"Wait till I get my hands on you!" was the reply.

A burly prison officer came waddling down the corridor.

"Shut your mouths, you feline creatures you….!" She removed a key from a large iron ring on her belt and unlocked the door and dragged Catherine out.

Catherine was screaming. "We want our breakfast!"

"Who do you think you are? You will eat when we tell you, or not at all!" the prison officer barked as she tried to take her arm, but her arm was slapped away.

"Leave me alone!" Catherine's eyes challenged the prison officer and her face was ablaze as she looked around her wildly.

"She is finding it hard to cope, that one." Anisha remarked. "What is it that Aijaz said that was so painful?"

Carma's face became white with fear and perplexity as she recalled the conversation she had with Aijaz, and suddenly looked like a child that cannot understand, was afraid and wanted to cry. And slowly the tears gathered in her eyes again and trickled down her cheeks.

Carma felt a chill in the cell and shuddered. After a while got up and walked toward the barred window passing Anisha staring out of the small window.

"Anisha, when Aijaz told me the truth about my husband and what he had done, I was surprised and shocked!"

"You are not telling me everything, Carma, was he behind the kidnapping?"

Carma nodded her head slowly.

"Yes, but although I knew he could be selfish, indifferent, bad mannered, I never thought him capable of treachery or any kind or cause deliberate harm. "

"Carma, I only had one family member betray me, you have been betrayed so many times by your nearest." Her eyes were brimming with affection and pity.

"True, but being betrayed by Badal M was the last straw!" Carma said absent-mindedly.

Carma looked around her in the prison then returned to her thoughts, of the lesson she had learnt, and savoured the new insight of wisdom as if it were the juice of a ripe fruit.

"Badal? You don't mean Badal Mittle do you?" Anisha turned her head in surprise.

"Yes, yes, but how do you…..?? She stopped as she saw Anisha's face, which had paled.

"Yes, yes," Carma replied, astonished at Anisha's reaction. "that is my husband's name. Badal Mittle. I not mention it?"

"No…..do you know which college he went to and what year?"

"He never did tell me much about himself, but I think he went to King's College in 1983…Anisha, are you alright?" Carma asked.

Anisha had started trembling and her pale face reflected the fright and resentment of an insecure child.

So it was the same Badal – her Badal who was Carma's husband! Something inside her trembled as she tried to clutch at the familiar branch of hope. However, she felt there was now another dilemma facing her. Should she let Carma know that she and Badal were once engaged? She cast her eyes downward and bit her under lip.

'This is infuriating', she thought 'I had hoped that at least he would be the light at the end of the darkness of my adversities. But it appears that he has always been out of my reach like a firefly glowing in the darkness, so close yet so elusive!' She sat trembling with tears stinging her eyelids.

Chapter 42

Suddenly, the remote parts of her life started to parade before her eyes again – this time each labelled with a tag "past and cannot return". It seemed to Anisha that Fate had not tired of the plot it had woven around her, for it seemed that it laughed whilst showing her the person she thought she left behind, but could not have.

Kismet had not torn up the script of the plot, not as yet undone the existence it had created for her. Anisha creased her forehead in perplexity as she thought how cruel fate had made her forfeit her love for an adulthood over which she had no control. Fate had snatched hope from her as easily as a child smoothes away a message on the sand.

However, in retrospect she realised that maybe her love for Badal had not been love but an infatuation with romance, a fantasy notion of what how love should be.

So far she had managed to suppress and control her feelings of hopelessness, claustrophobia, self-doubt and frustration, but Carma's disclosure had become a symbol of all these emotions.

Anisha wanted to share her newfound knowledge with Carma, but did not know where to begin. She considered Carma her only friend, and rejection from this newfound source would devastate her. On the other hand she knew it was important to share and offer this kind of trust if their friendship was to continue.

"Carma, there is something I ...", her voice was a husky whisper, yet every nerve in her body was frightened with the wish to be silent - and her well-toned instinct that shut her off protectively from everyone came up and she was silent.

Although the discovery shocked her, Anisha could not understand why she felt so deeply about Badal's marriage. Anisha presumed it must be because it had turned out to somebody as close to Carma, for she would never now willingly ruin her life by including Badal in hers.

Anisha breathed deeply, wanted to do something, anything to occupy herself constructively, but the long periods of idleness had weakened her ability to act and she was alienated to the role. She sat looking down, her head shaking and her lower lip pouted.

"You were going to say...? Is anything the matter, Anisha?"

"No, nothing is the matter, Carma; I am alright – just my usual headache, that's all."

Although she was disappointed, Anisha could not switch off her emotions easily and she neither had the practice not the inclination. She had heard too many false promises in her life to give herself with ease or withdraw from a friendship without truly meaning it. She felt remote, aware of her inability to take people casually enough to be safe from emotional harm. But anyway, she had been planning far ahead of times with Badal – God – she was not even sentenced as yet. Everybody she loved had been taken from her. Her mother, father, Azaria's betrayal, Akram and Badal had too so why had she been expecting anything from him? Nevertheless, Anisha had needed that glimmer of hope to get her through, what she knew, would be miserable years.

Anisha could feel her head aching and an odd kind of ringing, like out of tune guitar strings drumming in her ears. Her hands were sticky with clammy perspiration from her fingers. She was looking wordlessly at Carma; eyes round and like glass, opaque and shiny and their unblinking and unfocused stillness increased Carma's fear.

"Anisha, are you okay?" she asked again.

"I am fine, I think I will go to sleep now." replied Anisha, moistening her lips with her tongue.

She tried to think of some remark but some intangible force in the room sapped her remaining will and vitality. The spring of wit and humour that she thought was limitless dried up, leaving her with a discouraging hollowness.

"It seems that higher powers than we humans can understand are channelling the course of my life", she muttered inaudibly. "I do not know where, but I presume it is towards the fulfilment of my destiny, whatever it may be," she looked around her cell.   "Everything is ordained, written in the stars – whatever transpires now and whatever transpired before must have had some meaning,"

"Anisha, are you feeling all right, what are you saying?"

Carma looked worried as she saw Anisha's face twitch nervously; her trembling hands that had started to clench and unclench into fists, nails biting into the palm of her other hand, leaving them red.

Anisha did not answer her but sat looking vacantly ahead. Her dark hair stuck damply on her forehead with sweat and her forehead and skin looked pasty with the kind of sheen that comes from a fever or chill. Looking out of the little window of the cell, she thought she saw a million stars, all shining faintly.

"Just enough light so I can see in the darkness!" She thought ironically.

"Anisha, say something! Have you got another one of your headaches? Shall I call the Ruth?"

"I'm fine," muttered Anisha.

"As I was saying about Badal…"

"I don't want to talk, please, I am very tired,"" Anisha replied sharply, twining and entwining her fingers nervously.

She shuddered and got into bed, lay down, then pulled the blanket closer around her, trying to sort out the confusion she was feeling and trying to untangle her emotions. Just as she began to feel that she was to remain an imprisoned bird whose singing was destined to be hushed, she heard the voice of destiny whispering and calling.

Chapter 43

In the morning the prison officer's shouting and the bell awakened Carma, who had finally managed to dose off.

"You lazy sods! Get up!" There was a jangle of keys as Ruth unlocked the prison cells.

"Good-morning Anisha." Carma said climbing out of the bunk bed and rubbing her eyes.

Anisha did not answer, and when Carma saw that she was fast asleep, her black lashes resting against the softness of her skin, she left her sleeping and went for a quick wash.

However, when she came back she was surprised that even though the breakfast had been called, Anisha was still asleep.

It's breakfast time, Anisha, time to get up! Anisha, get up! You know how furious the prison officer gets if we…" she quickly braided her hair whilst talking.

Finally Carma shook Anisha, but she was lying so still and white that Carma was frightened and rang the bell for the Prison Officer.

Ruth hurriedly opened the cell door and found Carma wildly gesticulating at Anisha.

"She's not opening her eyes! I have tried to wake her but…"

Ruth quickly went to Anisha's side and lifted her white lifeless wrist, stunned that she could not detect Anisha's pulse. A white tablet fell from Anisha's listless hand and Ruth shook her head in bewilderment.

"Where did she get those from?" Ruth whispered "My God, what has she done? I'll get the ambulance".

Anisha face looked peaceful and soft in repose as the lines of sorrow were wiped away.

As her body was taken from the cell she left behind her a deep deadly silence, like a silence that comes after a storm. Carma was bewildered and stunned, not believing Anisha had taken her own life, for she had thought her to be the stronger of the two, although in the last couple of days she had noticed she was not her usual self.

"Is that what she was planning all along? She must have been to have saved all those tablets. Perhaps Anisha was like a delicate exotic flower that needed the shelter of a greenhouse, a flower that could not have survived the cold winds for long.'

Carma's friendship with Anisha was cultivated, grown and flourished in the shade of the prison walls, and her death hit Carma hard, and wave after wave of conflicting emotions stormed over her. In life Anisha had not only tried to maintain her illusions, but helped Carma to maintain hers.

Anisha had a desperate desire to believe in justice prevailing, and her good nature had not believed in a bitter and cruel reality that could and did destroy lives leaving behind shattered dreams. Although Anisha had been abused emotionally and physically, she had harboured cheerfully broken bones and a broken spirit. But for all her endurance and determination, ultimately Anisha had neither walked away nor run from her troubles, she had just snapped.

Resentment too engulfed Carma, resentment that her only friend had left her. The grief that affected her was like a pebble tossed in a pond – each thought generated another thought in an ever-widening circle of anger and anguish, guilt and resentment, until Carma felt nothing but the reality of her desolation and extradition, for Ruth had confirmed that she was to be sent to India to face trial.

Carma had had faith in Kismet, but was beginning to doubt it's so called infinite wisdom when it came to deciding whom to punish and whom to help.

Epilogue

Azaria quickly hid the letter behind her as Saleem entered the room.

"Is there a letter for me, Azaria?"

"No, there is no letter for you." Azaria replied quickly, and then ran outside to read the letter again.

The letter was from the prison service, informing her about Anisha's death. For a moment Azaria was filled with guilt, for she was the one who had killed Anisha's husband and allowed her sister take the blame, but when she weighed it against her happiness, her guilt gradually faded away.

"Azaria, what are you doing outside? Is anything the matter?" Saleem asked.

"No nothing is the matter, everything is just fine." Azaria crumpled the letter and threw it into the bin as she smiled and entered the room.

****

Badal was having breakfast and reading the local newspaper when Carma's photo stared at him from the page. He read with satisfaction that she was being deported to India to stand trial for murdering her ex-husband.

His lips curled in amusement as he placed the paper on the table and sipped his tea. Now no-one in London would know the truth about her innocence, and Carma's family had all moved from Delhi, so there was no-one there she could turn to for help. Now no-one would know that it was Badal who had engineered Carma's kidnapping.

He recalled the day he had gone to see Aijaz, however, he had been surprised to find him alone and lying in a pool of blood. He had quickly felt his pulse and found it to be beating strongly.

He had put two and two together and realised that Carma must have struck Aijaz; panicked at the sight of blood and run, presuming she had killed Aijaz.

He had sat with his head in his hands, stunned at the obstacle that had arisen, quickly trying to think of a way he could turn the disaster into his favour.

Everything had, so far been going smoothly and he hoped to marry Sunetra after Carma was out of the way.

To Badal, life was a passion, intoxication, and a game to be played and as for women, his scorn could hardly be hidden. Fools of women! It was so easy to make them think you loved them when you wanted– that was all they cared about- they were slaves to be treated as such to further one's ends.

And as he was not going to have his plan ruined he had taken the vase in his gloved hands and struck Aijaz hard, making sure he was dead.

As a back up plan, he had not changed Carma's passport into a British one, and she being the naïve girl that she was, had trusted him completely thought he had! That, he thought, had been a stroke of genius on his part!

****

Carma's extradition orders came soon after and she arrived at Delhi airport in the heat of the afternoon. The day was hot with the glare of the sun and the dust although the afternoon breeze had the occasional whiff of hot air.

As she was driven down one of the many tree-lined avenues to a police station, Carma looked around her in surprise. She had forgotten India's pageant like street life that not only brimmed with endlessly moving crowds but also shimmered with light dust laden light. - Its vivid flashes of colour and spicy scents, landscapes layered with majestic relics that were exotic and elusive.

She breathed in the hot choking dust, her ears assailed by incessant and continuous noise. As she looked around her she felt that its people had for centuries lived under justice in an imperfect form. So how could she expect justice when it had a tendency to be either overlooked or distorted, or both?

Carma entered the police station, and whilst a lot of people were clamouring to talk to the chief Inspector, she was escorted to a man sitting at the desk in the middle of the room wearing horn-rimmed glasses. His manner was curt and he barely looked at her. He wrote her name in a ledger and with a rubber circle printed a circle around her wrist. He finally looked up at her and as she looked at him with her head held high, her proud and aloof manner infuriated him.

"Wait outside with the others for the car to take you to prison where you belong!" he barked.

"But I don't know….I haven't… "Carma's voice faltered. She stood with her arms clenched at sides.

"You think you can do whatever you like and get away with it! Hey, you lazy chaprasi boy, what are you doing? Take this 'memsahib' to the others!"

Carma watched with fear the sudden flare of temper, for Amit and Sajata had often told her about the bloodthirsty police, of the lack of control that made the existence of honest police officers impossible.

Carma's mind was barren and bereft of hope as she was lead outside where she sat with the other prisoners to wait for the life they knew to end, and to start afresh to lead their lives as caged animals.

Some wore defiant expressions, some filled with hate and some filled with despair. Some were hardened criminals, some, like her must have committed a crime of passion, of self-defence. However, Carma was aware that whatever the case, the inmates would be in prison for a much longer time than the maximum sentence..

When the woman prisoner sitting next to her saw that Carma was looking at her she looked away and Carma was reminded of Mandy, Susan and Radha. She missed Anisha, and knew she was going to find it difficult to get along with the other inmates, for she disliked running down others and had no interest in flippant crudities. Two policemen sitting opposite stared at her, winked and made obscene gestures.

Kismet

Carma was frightened and wished again she that had not married Badal. She wiped the tears coursing down her cheeks with her hand.

However it seemed as if Fate had been beckoning to her – it had displayed something pleasant and at the same time arranged an appalling calamity for Carma – just like a cloud, after promising relief from the excessive heat of a long summer, destroys a tree by lightening.

Carma would have been happy to serve her term in prison in London; content with the knowledge that at least she would be in the same country as her son. However, it seemed that her life was like an airship – it inflated and deflated – it changed form and as soon as Carma had made out what shape it was, it became something else. It always had a string attached to it, and it seemed to Carma that she was forever running, pursuing it but never able to grasp it.

Carma swatted a fly that was buzzing near her head and wiped the sweat, which had mingled with the tears from her brow and face. Nearby she could see a dozen constables lying sprawled on a chirpoy bed under a tree.

By the time the van came to take them to the prison, it was night and a pale moon had become visible. First the clouds started to come in strands of white, but the moon wiped them off its face. Then they came in large billows, blotted out the moonlight and turned the sky a dull grey. However, the moon fought its way through occasional patches of rain and sparkled like silver.

Carma shuddered when she saw the bolts on the iron gates of the prison. As they opened to let them in, she knew that freedom would yet again be an abstract word for her, and never again would it be a physical tangible condition to be savoured and enjoyed. No more for her the breathing either of fresh air or hope for any privacy. Ahead of her was a life of suffering, not only by fighting losing battles against fleas and sleeplessness, but also from repeated bouts of dysentery, malaria and cholera.

She was taken through a door into a courtyard, then through an enormous metal door with a heavy handle. As the enormous metal doors shut behind her, Carma felt like a flower that has first been dried then pressed into the leaf of a book.

Carma had always believed that the enforceable rules of justice granted her certain rights, however, they had not provided a safety net either for herself, or for Anisha at a time when they needed it the most.

****